WHEN SHE WAS BAD

WHEN SHE WAS BAD

Kate O'Mara

SMITH GRYPHON
PUBLISHERS

First published in Great Britain in 1991 by
SMITH GRYPHON LIMITED
Swallow House, 11–21 Northdown Street
London N1 9BN

A CIP catalogue record for this book is available
from the British Library.

ISBN 1 85685 002 1

Keyboarded by Wilcom Services, London
Printed in Great Britain by
Butler and Tanner Limited, Frome, Somerset

To Patricia
in gratitude for Leonie and Elizabeth

Prologue

Leonie crouched on all fours amid a rumple of satin sheets, gazing intently at her reflection in the huge gilt mirror. The bedroom was almost dark, lit only by a dusty glow from the late-morning sunlight filtering through the heavy shutters. But even in this dim light she could make out the curved firmness of her thighs and stomach as she rocked back and forth.

She gasped as Rob's hands gripped her buttocks and he thrust himself into her with mounting intensity. Her lips were parted now and her hair swung to her shoulders in an auburn tangle, damp strands clinging to her forehead with the sweat of passion. Soon she was watching, fascinated as her lover's hands slid along her body and reached for her nipples. He caressed them lightly, making her gasp with pleasure.

Moments later Leonie squirmed out from underneath Rob and gently pushed him over on to his back. Looking down at the handsome, tanned face of her lover, his cat-like grey eyes dark with passion, she felt a fresh surge of lust. Slowly she lowered herself on to him, pushing his arms back into the pillows and holding them there. As she leant over him, her breasts brushed against his mouth. He responded hungrily.

This love-making was the best Leonie had ever known; physically she and Rob were perfectly matched. In her heart she sometimes feared it was too good to last but, as before, she put all such thoughts out of her head and abandoned herself to the voluptuous joy of the moment. It was another half-hour before, cradled in Rob's arms, she fell into a deep and satisfied sleep.

All too soon she became dimly aware that Rob was stirring restlessly. She felt his careful movements as he eased himself gently away from her, then heard the click of the bathroom door followed by the rush of running water. By the time he returned from the shower a few minutes later she was propped up on one elbow, wide awake.

'I'd say,' observed Rob, looking at her with a trace of smugness, 'that you've been well and truly fucked.'

'I've known worse,' she said, smiling at him. 'Don't think I didn't appreciate your efforts.'

'Believe me, it was a pleasure.'

'It certainly was.' As she spoke she rolled off the bed and sauntered towards the bathroom, brushing a teasing hand over his groin as she passed him. Then, before Rob could move, she was gone, shutting the door firmly behind her.

His roar of frustration echoed through the apartment, but Leonie only grinned to herself as she stepped into the shower. She knew perfectly well that as soon as he had calmed down he would grab his script and immerse himself in preparation for the day's work. He was enjoying his star role in the film, working hard at it and doing a damn good job too. She had made the right choice: if she hadn't known it already the reactions of technicians and crew would have told her by now.

Perhaps it had been foolhardy of her to cast Rob in the lead, especially at a time when the initial fuss about them had finally died down. But as co-producer she wanted the best, and she knew that Rob was perfect for the part. Besides, it was an ideal opportunity for him to prove himself to the wider public that his talent and good looks deserved.

They had been together for over a year now. The gossip columnists had had a field day when the news of their relationship had first leaked out. After all, Leonie O'Brien was a big star on both sides of the Atlantic, while Rob Fenton might be a fine actor but he was in no sense a name. A fact which at the beginning had seemed totally unimportant to them, but now . . . sometimes she wondered.

Leonie soaped herself thoughtfully. The scene to be shot that afternoon was set in a bordello, swarming with beautiful girls. Rob and women . . . she had soon heard, when she had joined the cast of *Much Ado About Nothing* at one of London's West End theatres on Shaftesbury avenue, about his reputation as a womanizer. It was hardly surprising. Those dark, lithe, good looks – the astonishing grey eyes fringed with sooty black lashes, combined with an almost unfair amount of charm – made a devastating combination. His sexual magnetism had for Leonie put the respected middle-aged actor who was playing Benedick opposite her Beatrice completely in the shade.

Rob had sworn to her time and time again that he was no longer interested in any woman but her. Well, she wanted to believe him and so far there had been no real evidence to prove otherwise. But, though they tried to make it into a joke, he was still incapable of ignoring a really pretty girl and, God knows, there were plenty in this film. And it made him feel good to see that soft look come into a woman's eyes when he smiled or cracked a joke – Leonie was far too observant not to be aware of that.

She sighed, and smiled wryly to herself. This was the price you paid for the pleasure that a man like Rob could give you. If, in a moment of weakness, he was tempted – and she knew it would happen one day if it hadn't already – she hoped she would have the strength of mind not to let her disappointment outweigh all the good things about their relationship.

Had she, she wondered, been a fool not to give herself a part in the film? If she and Rob were acting together, wouldn't that bring them even closer? No, she wanted Rob to have the limelight on this occasion, and he himself was insistent that they shouldn't act together again until he had, as he put it, 'proved himself'. Probably he was right – though it didn't seem to occur to him that by giving him his starring role she was using her position to help him every bit as much as if they had appeared on screen together. Not that she minded – it was just that sometimes the sheer bloody frustration of not being out there with him in front of the cameras, where she belonged, was almost too much to bear.

Suddenly Leonie realized that she was shivering. Damn, the water had run cold. Even in this luxurious *palazzo*, Roman plumbing had its shortcomings. Leonie stepped out of the shower on to the cool white marble floor. She snatched a fluffy peach towel from the rail, and vigorously rubbed herself dry, revelling in its friction against her skin. Then, wrapping the towel around her like a sarong, she walked through to the kitchen, cool and dimly lit like the rest of the apartment.

Rob had got there ahead of her and was raiding the fridge, dressed only in underpants and dark shirt, open to the waist. Leaning against the door-frame, she looked him up and down.

'I want you all over again,' she said, moving towards him and running a thoughtful finger down his chest.

'No time,' he replied briefly, stepping aside with a smile. He took a carton of orange juice from the fridge and emptied it into two glasses.

'What's your call?'

'Two forty-five in make-up.' He plopped ice-cubes into both glasses and handing one to her, drank deeply from the other. Then he put the glass carefully down on the tiled counter, pulled her towards him and kissed her. His mouth was cold from the iced juice and he smelt musky, in spite of his shower.

'It's no good. I've got to go,' he said, breaking away with reluctance. Then he grinned. 'I like working for you, you know.'

Leonie smiled, 'I like it too. There's just one thing that would make it perfect . . .' She hesitated.

'Which is?'

'I wish we were acting together. I wish I was playing opposite you. It would be fun, wouldn't it?' Her voice was almost, but not quite, pleading.

Rob's expression changed. 'You know what I think about that. Yes, it would be great – but I have to prove myself first.' When Leonie didn't react he went on, frowning slightly, 'I want everyone to know I'm in your league, that's all.'

'What do you mean? We are in the same league. You're a very fine actor.'

'You and I know that – I want the world to know it. I don't want it to look as if I'm just riding on your career.' He turned away and started searching in a cupboard.

'You're a good actor, that's all that matters. We work well together – why shouldn't we act opposite each other?'

He did not reply, but went on rifling through the shelves.

'What are you looking for?' demanded Leonie.

'There must be something to eat in this bloody flat,' he said irritably.

'There's masses of stuff,' she replied, determinedly amiable. 'What is it you want?' She spoke as though to a truculent child.

'I want a biscuit.'

'Biscuit! You've just had your breakfast!'

'Is there some house rule that says I can't have a bloody biscuit when I want?' He was petulant now.

She looked at him with a hurt expression. 'Rob – don't.'

'Don't what?'

'Don't let's quarrel. We were so happy a moment ago.'

'I'm still happy – aren't you?' he demanded aggressively.

'Not when you shout at me like that. It never occurred to me you'd want biscuits. You're always going on about your weight, so naturally I don't buy them.' Leonie's voice rose. 'I don't think it's fair of you to criticize. I'm sweating blood for you – and the production team, and the money boys, and the unit. Do you think it's easy, trying to keep everyone happy? Well it isn't, I can tell you.'

Rob stopped searching and stood watching her as she spoke. 'Have you quite finished?' he asked.

'No,' she snapped. 'You're a wonderful actor, I love you to distraction – and from now on you can buy your own bloody biscuits.'

Rob's face cleared and he began to laugh. 'Leo, you're priceless. That fucking temper of yours – it finishes me every time.'

He gathered her into his arms. 'Don't let's argue. You know how much I love you.'

The change in his mood was lightning quick, as so often before. In a way it was part of his charm, this unpredictability. Deep down he was still so much of a boy in many ways, thought Leonie, nestling happily against his broad chest. Now he would be doubly tender and loving. He always was when they had quarrelled. Sometimes Leonie wondered if he was frightened of pushing her too far – they both knew how implacable she could be in one of her rages – and yet at the same time he couldn't seem to help testing his own strength against hers. Perhaps, consciously or not, he was trying to make up for her success by asserting his own masculinity.

For now, Leonie was content to bask in the sunny calm that came after the storm. She snuggled closer to him, enjoying the strength of his arms around her.

'Do you really love me?'

'I adore you. You're the best thing that's ever happened to me. Of course I want us to play together – I just want it to be right for us, that's all.'

Leonie looked up at him, eyes wide and innocent.

'Nigel mentioned the other day that we had been offered a play – for the two of us,' she said in honey-sweet tones.

'Let's do it, then.'

She smiled. 'But you don't even know what it is yet.'

'Doesn't matter, so long as I am with you.'

'Oh, darling,' utterly disarmed, she nestled closer, planting feather kisses just below his ear.

'And I am playing the lead, and have top billing,' he added.

Laughing, Leonie thumped him playfully on the shoulder. 'Oh you're impossible.'

'I know, that's why you love me.' His tone was infuriatingly complacent. 'Anyway, what are you up to today?'

'Lunch with Justin Hamilton-Brown from the *Sunday Chronicle*. How could you forget.'

Rob looked scornful. 'A bloody journalist. Well that's nothing to get excited about.'

'A *writer*, not a journalist,' corrected Leonie. 'And he's doing an in-depth profile, so there.'

'Don't kid yourself, they all ask the same crappy questions. So tell me, Miss O'Brien,' he went on in a flat, whining tone, 'do you feel ready to tackle Lady Macbeth yet? Or Gertrude? Perhaps you might consider asking Mr Fenton to play Hamlet.'

He ducked as Leonie hurled the empty orange-juice carton at him, and caught it deftly. 'Now, Miss O'Brien, let's talk about you and Mr Fenton. You don't want to? Oh dear, our readers will be so disappointed. Can I make something up, then?'

Leonie laughed. 'You are ridiculous, Rob.'

'Not half as ridiculous as you'll look when you find out I'm right,' he said, strolling away towards the bedroom.

Leonie followed him, smiling to herself. She watched as he pulled on a pair of beautifully cut, pale linen trousers and buckled the leather belt at his waist.

'I'm sure I've lost weight. I can't be eating properly.' He looked at her mischievously.

'You look wonderful,' she said in a firm voice.

'I know.' He picked up wallet and keys from the dressing table and shoved them into his back pocket, at the same time slipping his free hand surreptitiously inside her towel to stroke her breasts.

'Bastard.' She pushed him away, laughing. 'Better get a move on or you'll be late.'

He slipped on his shoes and ran for the front door, fastening on his gold Rolex watch as he went.

'I may see you later,' he called over his shoulder.

'You'd better,' she yelled, but her voice was drowned by the slam of the door.

With the clatter of Rob's feet still receding down the stone stairs, Leonie flung off the damp towel and grabbed an ivory silk robe that lay crumpled by the bed. She slipped it on and hurried through the drawing-room and out on to the balcony, in time to watch Rob sprint to the silver Mercedes convertible parked illegally in the side street below. She saw him pause for a moment in the act of getting in, obviously distracted by the sight of an attractive young girl with waist-length auburn hair, whizzing past on a Vespa.

As if aware of Leonie's scrutiny, Rob glanced sheepishly up at the balcony. He shrugged his shoulders then got into the car, throwing her a dazzling smile. From the glove compartment he took a pair of Ray-Bans. He put them on, glanced at himself in the driving mirror, switched on the engine and roared away into the noonday heat of Rome.

As Leonie wandered back into the cool of the big *salotto*, she saw again in her mind's eye the red-headed girl on the Vespa. Once upon a time, she had had hair like that herself: a glorious copper mane right down to her waist. Now . . . she gazed at herself in one of the huge gilt-framed mirrors that lined the walls of the apartment. Now the tumbled red waves were still there . . . a little darker, a lot shorter . . . but the face they framed, though lovely, was undeniably that of a woman in her forties. She was old enough to be that girl's mother, and – the thought she had tried so often to suppress shot through her with a stab of anguish – she was very nearly old enough to be Rob's mother, too.

1

Outside, Rome was burning. The tourists emerging from the Sistine Chapel were blinded by the dazzling sunshine, and struck by the overpowering heat. They stood blinking in the dazzling light. Like prisoners in the last act of *Fidelio*, thought Beryl Willoughby as she paused in the entrance, waiting for them to move on.

She knew about opera. Her love of music was one of the things that had brought her to Italy on this holiday. It was the first time she had ever been abroad on her own. The first time, at fifty-two. Not that she had been abroad much while Arnold was alive – just a couple of holidays in a small hotel in Brittany, their honeymoon in Paris, a disastrous package tour to Tenerife.

Arnold hadn't like abroad very much – he had hated hot sun and what he called 'mucked about' food, and had resented not being able to understand the language. He preferred the Lake District, so that was where they had spent most of their holidays during their twenty-two years of married life.

Arnold would have loathed Italy, thought Beryl. She, on the other hand, was having a wonderful time. She adored the light, the warmth, the wonderful architecture, the herby, oily unfamiliar food and the potent red wine. They had visited several European cities on this music-lovers' tour, but Rome was certainly her favourite so far and Italy her favourite country.

The one thing that Arnold would have enjoyed was the music. That evening at La Scala two days earlier, for example – even he would have agreed that hearing Verdi's *Rigoletto* sung in that incomparable theatre was an experience worth crossing Europe for. After all, a love of music was the one important thing she and Arnold had had in common. It was what had brought them together in the first place all those years ago.

At nearly thirty, Beryl's looks were no more than passable. She had straight, mouse-brown hair, a trim figure, and a pleasant, unremarkable face redeemed only by a pair of expressive grey-green eyes. Her soprano voice, however, was truly beautiful. The only child of elderly parents, and with a dull job as secretary to a firm of solicitors, she was unused to mixing with people of her own age and painfully shy. The year before, both her mother and father had died within months of each other, leaving her alone in their small semi-detached house on the outskirts of the little Sussex town of Ashebourn.

In her late teens and early twenties, Beryl had had one or two boyfriends, but the relationships had fizzled out almost before they had started. More recently, all her time had been taken up with work and with looking after her increasingly frail parents. There had been no men in her life for years. Now she realized that if she did not act soon she faced a lifetime of loneliness. That was the moment when she spotted the notice in Ashebourn library. 'Ashebourn Choral Society needs new members,' it read. 'Can you sing like a bird? If so, come and join our flock.' Plucking up her courage, Beryl attended an audition and was eagerly accepted. It changed her life.

The Society met on Friday evenings at 7.30 in the town hall. Beryl loved it. And she soon came to love Arnold Willoughby, a dark and quietly attractive middle-aged man who sang in the tenor section. When their eyes had met over the tops of their sheet music during a rousing chorus of *The Dream of Gerontius*, Beryl had hardly dared believe the obvious interest she saw in his eyes. She was thrilled when he offered to escort her home after choir practice and even more excited when he shyly repeated the offer the following week.

Soon Beryl plucked up the courage to invite Arnold in for supper. Her looks may have been no more than average, but the years of looking after her parents had made her an excellent cook and a first-class housekeeper. Arnold, who lived alone, was most appreciative of Beryl's delicious food. His visits became more frequent and their friendship grew.

By no means unattractive, Arnold also seemed kind, gentle and considerate. Perhaps he was not terribly exciting, but at her age Beryl felt that she could not expect excitement in a man. At forty-two, he had never been married, and at first Beryl could not understand why this prize had not been snapped up years before by some other discerning woman. She soon learned, however, that Arnold had lived with his adored but very demanding widowed mother until her recent death from a stroke.

A year after Beryl joined the Ashebourn Choral Society, she and Arnold were married. The music at the wedding service was, naturally, superb.

Arnold worked as a chemist for a big pharmaceutical company. He earned a good salary and had always been careful with his money. He and Beryl were able to buy a comfortable four-bedroomed detached house in one of the town's best residential areas. Beryl left her dull job and devoted herself to making Arnold comfortable, a task at which she succeeded very well.

The marriage was on the whole a happy one, their relationship placid and generally harmonious. Somewhat to Beryl's disappointment they slept in twin beds and Arnold's love-making was infrequent and very restrained. She said nothing to him about this – after all, he was such a good husband in other ways and as far as she could tell sex was probably overrated anyway. They remained members of the Ashebourn Choral Society and occasionally went to the opera in London at the Coliseum or, on one memorable occasion, Covent Garden.

As the first year of marriage slipped uneventfully by, Beryl began to realize that she wanted more. She yearned for love and affection. Or rather she yearned to give love and affection, but it became quite obvious that, fond as he was of her, Arnold wanted no more than comfort and companionship. She started to watch other women as they wheeled their babies round the local supermarkets or played with their toddlers in the park. She realized that she too wanted a child.

Beryl's desire for a child intensified until at last she told Arnold, who had never showed any interest in children, how she felt. He seemed surprised and at first reluctant but, realizing she was serious, he eventually agreed that they would try for a baby. Two years later, however, they were still childless. Beryl, becoming desperate, attended a fertility clinic and discovered that physically she seemed to be perfectly capable of having a child. The problem had to be Arnold; but he refused with horror when she tentatively suggested that he should undergo some tests. There was, he assured her, absolutely nothing wrong with him and, as if to prove it, his tepid love-making became almost passionate for a few weeks. But still Beryl did not conceive and she began to despair of ever being a mother.

She was on the verge of becoming seriously depressed when a stroke of good fortune changed their lives for ever. Winifred Miles was a friend of Beryl's and a fellow member of the Choral Society. She was also a foster-mother, a kind, homely woman to whom Beryl had long since confided her desire for a baby. One day Winifred telephoned Beryl in great excitement. She had in her care a beautiful baby girl who was to be offered for adoption. If they chose, with Winifred's help Beryl and Arnold could soon find themselves the happy and legal parents of a lovely daughter. Winifred confided to Beryl that the mother was a struggling actress who had been deserted by the father, a university boy. So the child would undoubtedly be both bright and beautiful.

Beryl was enchanted by the idea and set to work to persuade Arnold. He agreed, a little reluctantly, at least to see the baby, but his resistance crumbled as soon as he set eyes on her – she was adorable. After the initial adoption papers were signed, a fee was handed over to Mrs Miles and one Sunday Beryl came home clutching her precious bundle; life at Milton Gardens was never to be the same again.

Beryl found parenthood very rewarding and she and Arnold were the perfect mother and father to the little girl, whom they called Amanda. They were firm, loving, and kind: neither too strict with her nor over-indulgent. Amanda was an attractive and intelligent child, though it soon became apparent that she had a mind of her own and a temper too. She and Beryl had more than one battle during her childhood, especially over bedtimes and the rationing of television viewing, but Beryl's loving firmness almost invariably won the day. So Amanda's childhood slipped uneventfully by into her teens, with school and friends, girl guides, good music and domestic harmony filling her life – or at least, so Beryl and Arnold thought.

It was break-time on a sunny autumn morning at St Monica's, the smart and expensive girls' private school that Beryl and Arnold Willoughby thought only just good enough for their cherished daughter. Amanda, aged fifteen, would be doing her GCSEs the following year and, as a bright girl, both her parents and teachers hoped that she would do well. The one small cloud on their horizon was that Amanda was becoming just a tiny bit awkward as her teens progressed. A little sloppier in her dress, untidier in her ways at home and school, a touch withdrawn and sometimes almost sullen – she was no longer the polite, eager child of whom Beryl and Arnold had always been so proud.

Anxiously, they had questioned her teachers about her progress at the last parents' evening, but the St Monica's staff had been reassuring. It was a common phase among adolescent girls, they told the Willoughbys. Amanda was basically a sensible, level-headed child; she would soon settle down and take her work seriously again.

As the crowd of green-clad girls streamed out into the playground, a small, slim red-head stood a little to one side watching them, a cross expression on her very pretty face. Amanda was waiting for Melanie, her best friend. She had something very important to tell her.

Her frown had deepened still further by the time Melanie appeared, dawdling along amid a group of their classmates. Without a word of greeting Amanda pounced, gripping Melanie's painfully as she dragged her away into the cloakroom.

'Ow,' squeaked Melanie, a plump, pink-faced blonde, 'whatever's the matter?'

Amanda thrust her down on to the bench in a dark and dusty corner that was their favourite hiding place. Here they had shared many secrets during their friendship, but Melanie was totally unprepared for the bombshell that Amanda was about to explode.

Amanda glanced round to check that they were not going to be overheard. 'I think I'm pregnant,' she said quietly. Melanie gasped in horror. Amanda already had something of a reputation among her friends for her exploits with the opposite sex, but this was a major disaster.

'How do you know?' she asked, in a shocked whisper.

'How do you think, stupid? I've missed my period, of course.' Amanda tossed her head defiantly, swinging her glossy ponytail from side to side.

'What are you going to do?'

'Get rid of it, naturally.' Again Melanie gasped. 'Well, you surely don't imagine that I'm going to have a dear little baby stuck in a bloody pram by my desk next summer when I take my exams, do you?'

'What does your mother say?' demanded Melanie, all agog.

'I haven't told her, thickhead, that's why I'm telling you. I had to tell someone, it's driving me crazy. Now, listen, your brother's a doctor, isn't he?'

'Not exactly. He's only a first-year medical student.'

'Well, whatever year he's in, he must know where I can get an abortion. You'd better ask him, or you can just forget about being my friend.' Amanda's voice, for Melanie, held real menace.

Melanie was too much in awe of her strong-willed friend to disregard her orders. Two weeks later she tackled her brother when he came home for the weekend, but he was shocked by her questions and, once he had established that it was not Melanie herself who was pregnant, told her to tell her friend to see her GP. Meanwhile Amanda had had grown more and more panic-stricken as the days passed. When Melanie finally reported her lack of success, she was furious.

'What the hell am I going to do?' she asked angrily.

Melanie quaked. 'You'll have to tell your parents.'

'Don't be stupid, I can't possibly. You don't know what they're like.'

'I've met your mother, she seemed very nice.'

'Exactly, she's very nice. It's never occurred to her that I've even held hands with a boy, never mind gone the whole way. She'll go mad; they both will.' Pale with rage and misery, Amanda stalked away.

Two days later, however, Melanie arrived at school in the morning to meet her emerging from the loos with a broad smile on her face. 'It's all right. It's come, it's come!' she exclaimed jubilantly.

'You mean you're not pregnant after all?'

'No! Isn't it wonderful?'

'Oh, Amanda, what a relief!'

'I should say. Listen are you coming to the party at Don's place this Saturday?'

'Mummy won't let me. Anyway, you know what he's like. He'll spend the whole evening trying to get you into bed.'

'He won't have to try very hard, I think he's really sexy.'

'Mandy, how can you!'

If Melanie had thought that Amanda's narrow escape from pregnancy would put an end to her reckless behaviour, she was quite wrong. Up to this moment the full knowledge of Amanda's wild ways had been confined to a handful of deliciously shocked schoolfriends. Now it was as if she could no longer be bothered to hide her rebellion.

At home she became rude, sulky and disobedient. In class she was alternately sullen and cheeky, using her quick wits to score off the teachers and keep her friends in fits of horrified giggles. Her school-work went rapidly downhill; her reports became worse and worse. Beryl and Arnold were plunged into despair by her behaviour. They had brought her up so carefully, and yet they seemed to have raised a monster. Surely they deserved better than this after all their trouble?

Beryl, sitting up late one night waiting for Amanda to return from one of the parties she seemed to attend every weekend, stared into the flickering embers of the living-room fire and wondered ruefully if Arnold hadn't been right to be so unenthusiastic about the prospect of children. She knew that many of her friends and acquaintances were having similar problems with their teenagers, but Amanda seemed so determinedly ruthless in her behaviour. Was it something about being adoptive parents that caused such problems? They had never told Amanda about her real parentage, but did she somehow sense that she was not really theirs?

At least in her absence the house was quiet. When she was at home she insisted on playing that ghastly rock music at full blast, driving poor Arnold nearly demented. Beryl sipped at the brandy which she had found herself drinking more and more often last thing at night to help her sleep. She had said nothing to Arnold, but she was convinced that Amanda too was steadily raiding the drinks cabinet.

And her clothes! Apart from her school uniform, in which she looked at least passably tidy, Amanda spent her whole time in ripped and filthy jeans covered by an oversized sweatshirt, itself none too clean. Her hair hung in lank, greasy strands and her complexion was pallid and spotty. Oh my once beautiful daughter, thought Beryl, hearing with relief the slam of the front door and bracing herself for the inevitable confrontation when Amanda discovered she had waited up – if your real mother could see you now she'd probably be only too glad she gave you away.

On Amanda's sixteenth birthday, Arnold and Beryl decided to make a special effort to overlook her behaviour and arranged to take her out for a special birthday dinner. But that evening, Amanda did not come home from school. This was not altogether unusual. Sometimes she stayed the night with a friend without warning them beforehand. But the following morning the school secretary rang to ask why she had not appeared in class, and when, by the evening, there was still no sign of her, her panic-stricken parents telephoned the police.

Amanda had been missing for a week before she was discovered on the outskirts of the town, squatting with a group of unemployed youngsters in a big old Victorian house boarded up with corrugated iron and due for demolition. She would say nothing about why she had left home, or what she had been doing.

Once back home, Amanda mooned around the house, pale and listless. She started refusing to go to school; there were even days when she refused to get out of bed. She seemed to have lost all interest in life.

During the next two years Beryl and Arnold felt as if they were plunging deeper and deeper into some horrible nightmare. They tried every means open to them of returning Amanda to some kind of normality, consulting doctors, social workers, even a psychiatrist. All their efforts were in vain. Amanda remained listless, apathetic, sullen, only showing some spark of animation when she went out with her appalling friends – a group whom her parents regarded as certainly layabouts and probably drug addicts too.

Beryl was not a demonstrative woman by nature, but once, desperate for some response from Amanda, she attempted to take the girl in her arms, only to be threatened by a pair of scissors and a shower of verbal abuse. Another time, driven by anger and frustration, she suddenly hit out at her daughter as she lay fully dressed on her bed, refusing to get up, clad in the filthy clothes she had worn for days without changing. But Amanda endured the attack with terrifying calmness, her impassivity more frightening than any aggressive response would have been.

So Arnold and Beryl endured their ordeal, coping with each stage in Amanda's deterioration with a kind of grim, quiet acceptance. One shaming milestone was the day Amanda's headmistress called them in for a meeting. In view of Amanda's continuing unexplained absences from school and her overwhelming lack of enthusiasm on the odd occasion she did attend, she suggested gently but firmly that the resources currently allocated to her school fees could be better utilized elsewhere. Amanda left St Monica's at the end of the summer term, without sitting her GCSEs, and embarked on a series of increasingly short-lived clerical jobs.

The enormous tension and strain the Willoughbys were both under took its toll. Arnold's health began to suffer; he lost his appetite and looked grey and old. He resigned from the Choral Society in a fit of depressive indifference and increasingly often he would disappear to his study after supper and lock the door, remaining there all evening. Beryl continued her choir attendance and tried to forget her troubles by singing. When she returned she would raid the drinks cabinet and find more and more that alcohol seemed to help, at least temporarily.

The end came suddenly and unexpectedly when the doorbell rang at four in the morning. Arnold opened the front door to two police officers who informed him that Amanda had been arrested with a group of youngsters for being in possession of drugs. Her case would be heard in the magistrates' court in a couple of months time. Would they please make sure that she turned up for the hearing. Amanda herself was sitting in the patrol car outside with a woman police constable.

Back in her parents' custody, Amanda slumped on the living-room sofa, saying nothing. Arnold sat by the fire, gazing into its dying flames with an expression of despair on his face. He was only sixty-five, but Beryl thought he already looked like an old man. Throughout all their time of torment the three of them had never managed to have a real talk about Amanda's behaviour. Now, finally, Arnold broke the silence, and the Willoughby household erupted as after years of mute endurance, he at last demanded an explanation.

It seemed that Amanda herself, shaken by her arrest, was for once prepared to talk. At first she was reluctant and monosyllabic but suddenly she flared up, defiantly explaining that she had been invited to spend the night with her friend James after a party.

'You can't stand him because he's black, can you?' demanded Amanda in an aggressive voice.

'Of course that's not true, dear,' Beryl replied placatingly, only too pleased that Amanda was actually telling them where she had been.

'Yes it is. Go on, admit it, you can't bear the idea of your darling little girl sleeping with a black man.' There was a shocked silence.

'You mean you've been to bed with this boy?' asked Beryl at last.

'There you are, you see, I knew it. You don't like it.'

'It's nothing to do with his colour.' Beryl hesitated. 'You mean, he's your – lover?'

Amanda threw back her head and crowed with laughter. 'He's one of them.'

Beryl stood gazing at Amanda in horror. 'Arnold, for God's sake, say something,' she implored, looking round desperately at her husband. 'Arnold?' she persisted. But Arnold only stared impassively at the fire. Beryl turned back to Amanda. 'It has nothing to do with his race. We don't mind who your friends are, but you must remember, you're still very young. Why, why . . . I, had no idea . . .' Beryl stammered, not able to find the words to express her emotions. 'I mean we naturally assumed, that you were still – still a virgin,' she blurted out.

Amanda exploded with laughter again. 'A virgin!' she exclaimed derisively. 'What century are you living in?' Beryl looked helplessly to Arnold for support, but he remained stony faced.

'But think of the other risks you're taking,' protested Beryl. 'I mean, you could get pregnant, and what about Aids?'

'Oh, don't worry about that. I always make sure they stick a condom on. Usually I put it on myself – with my mouth.'

Arnold suddenly leapt to his feet. 'Shut up! Stop it! Shut up, you dirty little whore. Shut up and get out!' His face was livid and he was shouting at the top of his voice. Beryl stared at him in amazement. She had never seen him like this before; he was completely out of control. Even Amanda looked shaken.

Arnold was incensed, he was almost foaming at the mouth. 'Get out! Get out of my house!' he thundered. 'Get back to your black bastard, you filthy bitch!'

Amanda suddenly lowered her head and narrowed her eyes. 'You watch who you're calling filthy,' she threatened. 'I know about you, you dirty old man!'

Arnold, beside himself with rage, lunged at Amanda and started to shake her. Beryl screamed in terror and threw herself at him, trying to separate them, as Amanda kicked, bit and scratched furiously. Finally, winded, Arnold staggered backwards and sank into an armchair, while Amanda lay sprawled out on the floor. She glared at him balefully.

'You bastard!' she gasped. 'You dare tell me I've behaved badly. You're not fit to call yourself my father.'

'I'm not your father,' he said. Beryl went limp and leant against the door, heart thudding uncontrollably.

'Arnold. . .' she began, in a pleading tone. Amanda looked from one to the other in amazement.

'Oh, I see,' her voice sounded gleeful. 'So mummy was a naughty girl, was she? Beryl got herself pregnant, did she? And had to get married?'

'No, no,' Beryl protested, making a feeble gesture with her hand as though trying to push everything away. 'It wasn't like that.' But Amanda wasn't listening. 'I don't believe it,' she went on, wonderingly. 'My own mother.'

'She's not your mother,' said Arnold, his triumph complete.

There was silence. Amanda sat very still, staring at them both in amazed disbelief. Beryl sank to her knees, and started to sob quietly. Finally Arnold got up. There was a strange look on his face and his hands seemed to be twitching uncontrollably. 'I'm going to bed,' he said. Blindly he pushed past Beryl, his face white as a sheet. An uncomfortable silence descended. Beryl half-sat, half-lay on the floor drained and lost for words.

'Is it true?' Amanda asked eventually. Beryl nodded miserably.

'I don't believe you.'

Beryl turned a tearful face towards her. 'It's true,' she said simply.

'You'd better tell me,' Amanda said, now completely subdued. Beryl slowly got to her feet, and approached Amanda, extending her hand in conciliation.

'I just want to know the truth.' Amanda brushed Beryl's hand away as she spoke.

Beryl ignored the rejection. 'I'll go and make some cocoa, and then we can talk,' was all she said. They sat up for what was left of the night, sipping mugs of hot chocolate, while Beryl told Amanda the story of her adoption, simply and undramatically.

The next morning when Amanda and Beryl met in the kitchen there was an uncomfortable silence. Beryl busied herself filling the kettle. Finally she said, 'Your father's late.' As soon as she spoke she realized her mistake.

'You mean Arnold presumably,' said Amanda coldly.

'Yes, of course I do. How silly of me.' Flustered, Beryl started methodically cleaning the worktops, which were already spotless.

After a few moments she asked 'Would you like some breakfast?' in a neutral voice.

Amanda looked at her in amazement. 'You're acting as though

nothing had happened,' she said.

Beryl continued cleaning, scrubbing more obsessively than ever, but she did not look up. 'It's a bit late for porridge, but we've got plenty of eggs,' she added.

'Did you hear what I said?' demanded Amanda.

Beryl refused to be drawn. 'Go and see if Arnold wants some tea, there's a good girl.'

'I don't believe this. You're not going to talk about it are you?'

Beryl poured the boiling water into the teapot.

'Listen to me, you bloody bitch,' said Amanda fiercely. 'I'm talking to you. You can't go through a scene like last night and then pretend it never happened.'

Beryl's lower lip began to tremble, but still she did not speak.

'I want to know who my real parents are!'

Beryl leaned against the sink, her head bowed.

'Well?' asked Amanda. 'I think I'm entitled to know, don't you?'

'I don't know who they are,' Beryl said finally in a small voice.

'You don't know!' jeered Amanda. 'You must know.'

'No,' insisted Beryl.

Amanda looked nonplussed. She thought for a moment. 'Well, presumably all you have to do is look on my birth certificate – don't you?' she added as she saw Beryl's face.

'We don't have your birth certificate.'

Amanda stared at her in disbelief. 'Then who does?'

'The adoption society. They hold the records.'

'But – but, supposing I needed a passport or something?'

'Then we would have to apply to the adoption society for a copy.'

'All right then,' said Amanda patiently. 'Let's apply for a copy.'

'It wouldn't make any difference. The names of your r-real parents wouldn't be on there – they would only give us a shortened version because the information is confidential.'

'You mean, you really don't know who my natural parents are?' Amanda's voice was genuinely astonished. 'You didn't know what you were adopting? I mean, I might be the daughter of a mass murderer for all you know.'

'We were assured that both your parents were well-educated people, with no record of any criminal activity – we did ask,' Beryl added self-righteously.

'Oh, well that's a comfort, I suppose. You mean I'm not likely to turn into a Lizzy Borden and chop you up in your beds?'

Beryl tried to smile but failed. 'Why don't you have a cup of tea?' she asked, starting to pour one out.

'Of course, that would solve everything, wouldn't it?' remarked Amanda sarcastically. 'So how do we find out?' she persisted.

'Why not leave well alone, dear?' Beryl said faintly. 'We're your parents now – we've brought you up – we've always tried to do our best for you.' She choked back her tears. Exhausted from lack of sleep, she was at a complete loss as to how to deal with the situation. Why didn't Arnold come down and help her? At least he could do something to make amends for last night, she thought. It was all his fault; if only he hadn't allowed Amanda to goad him into blurting it all out.

'No, I bloody well won't leave it alone,' shouted Amanda. 'I must know. It doesn't surprise me that you're not my parents. I'm nothing like you. Oh, I'm not just talking about looks – we've nothing in common, nothing at all.' Then she added contemptuously, 'Anyway, I want to know, I'm going to find out whether you like it or not.'

Beryl sighed in resignation. She knew Amanda well enough to realize that she would do as she pleased. The girl had been hard enough to control when she was a child and for the last few years she had been simply impossible. Perhaps, thought Beryl hopelessly, it was all due to some hereditary flaw. Perhaps it was not her fault at all, but that of her natural parents.

'So, how do I find out?' Amanda demanded again.

'You'll have to go to the adoption society and ask them,' said Beryl reluctantly.

'Will they tell me?'

'I imagine so. A law was passed not so long ago that made it possible for adopted children to find out the identity of their natural parents.' Beryl was only too aware of this fact, and her heart had sunk when she had heard the news. It was as though she had had some premonition of just this situation. 'But not until they're eighteen,' she added.

'Well, we've timed it just right, haven't we?' said Amanda coldly.

'Take a cup of tea up to your father, there's a good girl.' No, not her father, thought Beryl. But it was hard to break the habit of eighteen years overnight. She was unequal to this conversation; it was wearing her down.

'He's *not* my father, as he pointed out so dramatically last night.' Amanda echoed her thoughts. 'I think he could have been a little more tactful, don't you? Perhaps broken the news a little more gently?'

Beryl ignored her. She decided to take the tea up to Arnold herself. It was high time he was out of bed. Amanda preceded her into the hall and went straight to the telephone directory beside the phone. Beryl paused at the bottom of the stairs. 'What are you doing? Who are you going to ring?' she asked in an anxious whisper.

'The adoption society, of course,' replied Amanda airily.

Beryl glanced apprehensively up the stairs. 'Amanda, please, not now. It'll only upset your – it'll only upset Arnold – I don't think he was too well last night.'

'Well he made me feel bloody sick, I can tell you.'

Beryl abandoned the fruitless conversation and went upstairs. Amanda flicked through the telephone directory for a few moments, paused, then began to dial a number. Suddenly Beryl appeared at the top of the stairs, her face distraught.

'Amanda, quickly, phone for an ambulance. Never mind what you're doing, dial 999 now!' She spoke sharply and urgently and for once Amanda obeyed her.

'What's the matter?' She too had gone pale as she looked at Beryl.

'It's your father. I think he's had a stroke.'

'What can I do for you?' The speaker was a pleasant-faced woman of about thirty, who was obviously keen to help. She reminded Amanda of social workers she had met in the past. Their offers of help had always been rejected, but this was different.

'I want to find out who my real parents are,' she said abruptly.

'I see.' The woman took out pen and paper. 'Could I please have your name and date and place of birth, as well as the names of your adoptive parents?' Amanda supplied the details. The woman wrote them down.

'Are you familiar with our procedure?' she asked when she had finished.

'What do you mean?' said Amanda blankly.

'If anyone wishes to trace their natural parents, we first take their details, then we consult our records, and then we inform the natural mother that their offspring is trying to contact them. I assume you do wish to contact your mother?'

'Yes, I do. Are you saying that you're not going to tell me who my parents are?'

The woman looked at Amanda sympathetically. She knew how frustrating people found their procedure. 'We have to contact the mother first to see if she wishes her identity to be known.'

'And if she doesn't?'

'Then I'm afraid there's nothing you can do.'

Amanda gazed at her for some time, hostility in her eyes. 'What about the father?'

'The identity of the father is seldom known in cases such as these and is therefore not on the birth certificate.'

'Why would the mother not wish to renew contact?'

'For her, the experience will almost certainly be a traumatic one, and in ninety per cent of the cases where contact is made the outcome is not happy.'

'Why on earth not?'

'Guilt, in the case of the mother, and a feeling of rejection on the part of the child. These are just two major factors.'

'Well I shall have to take that risk, won't I?' Amanda's tone was brusque. She had not come here to be fobbed off.

'Very well,' sighed the woman. 'We have your details. We shall try to contact your mother for you. But if, for example, your parent has moved abroad, it could take a long time to track her down.'

Amanda was beginning to feel that this visit was a waste of time.

'Well, thank you for your help.' She made an attempt at politeness, unconsciously proving that at least some of Beryl's early training had not been without effect. 'I'll hope to hear from you soon.'

'We'll do our very best for you.'

The interview was over and Amanda left the offices of the adoption society feeling thoroughly dissatisfied. How could she bear to wait months, even years, to find out who her real mother was? She would tackle Beryl again. She was quite certain that she knew more than she had already revealed.

When she returned to Milton Gardens, she found Beryl curled up on the sofa in the living-room, deep in one of the historical novels that she borrowed in quantities from the local library. Reading these was one way in which, in recent years, Beryl had found a much needed escape from reality. 'How did you get on?' Beryl asked apprehensively, putting down her book. In the month since Arnold's stroke, Amanda had become almost approachable again, but there was no telling what mood she might be in now. Beryl was also feeling guilty. She had lied to Amanda when she told her that she did not know the identities of her parents. Winifred Miles had given her both their names before she handed Amanda over. It was strictly against all the rules and Winifred had sworn her to secrecy. She would probably lose her job as a foster-mother if what she had done ever leaked out.

Amanda slammed her bag down on to the teak coffee table, her face tragic. 'It was a complete waste of time . . . she wouldn't tell me a thing.'

'Oh,' said Beryl blankly. 'What, nothing at all?' She hadn't anticipated this.

'They said they'd try and contact her . . . and then see if she will let them tell me who she is. It could be months, and even then I might never know . . . if she doesn't want me . . .' Amanda's voice trailed off into a flood of tears.

Guilt pricked at Beryl more sharply. The girl seemed distraught.

'I feel so awful,' Amanda sobbed. 'I'm sure the reason I've been so mixed up is . . . is because my m-mother is really a bad person.' Weeping, she sank into the nearest chair.

'Oh no, she's not.' Beryl was torn between concern for Amanda and the desire to protect her friend. 'Come on, my pet, there's no need to cry.'

Amanda turned to her, eyes brimming with moisture. 'She must be,' she said in a choked voice. 'You've been so kind and good to me . . . and I've behaved so badly. I've known all along I must be adopted because there are really bad things inside me.'

Beryl was horrified. She could hold back no longer. 'That's simply not true, Amanda. Your mother is a lovely person. She's not bad at all.'

Amanda gazed at her, tears streaming down her face. 'I thought you said you didn't know her,' she said accusingly. 'You lied to me – I can't believe it – I never thought you would lie to me.' Her shoulders heaved as fresh sobs began to wrack her body.

Beryl sat down beside Amanda and took the girl's hand in hers. 'I'm sorry, Amanda. I only did it for the best. You see we weren't supposed to know who your parents were. Your foster-mother told me, but she made me promise never to tell another soul, not even you. I thought if the adoption society would tell you then I wouldn't have to involve her – you see, she could lose her job if they found out.'

'But – but, you said you didn't know my mother. How do you know what she's like? She was a friend of yours, wasn't she? That's why you took me in – she was your friend and she got into trouble, she couldn't keep me, she wasn't married and . . .' Amanda was frantically trying to piece it all together, 'and you were married, so you took me for her sake.'

'Amanda, this is all nonsense. She wasn't a friend of mine, but your foster-mother was. She was a member of the Choral Society and she knew how much I wanted a child. It was because both your real mother and father were artistic and talented that she thought Arnold and I would be suitable parents.' Here she paused in confusion.

'What is it?' asked Amanda, sensing she was on to something.

'Arnold wasn't sure. I had to be able to tell him who your parents were before he would agree to have you. I made Winifred tell me. She didn't want to, but I was so desperate, I didn't care, and you were such a beautiful baby.' Remembering, Beryl was starting to feel near to tears herself. 'You had your mother's colouring. She was a lovely looking girl – she still is.'

Amanda stared at Beryl. 'But I still don't understand how you know what my mother's like now. Who is she?' she asked in a whisper.

'If I tell you, you must promise not to try and contact her yourself. You must wait and let the adoption society do it for you.'

'I promise,' said Amanda. 'I just want to know her name, truly I do. That's all that matters.'

'All right,' said Beryl. 'If you're sure.' She paused for a moment. 'She's Leonie O'Brien, the actress. So you see, Amanda, there was nothing for you to worry about. You can be proud of her and I'm sure she would be proud to know that she had a daughter like you.'

'And my father, is he an actor too?' asked Amanda eagerly, pressing her advantage. She could hardly believe what she was hearing. She had always admired Leonie O'Brien: there was something about the looks and style of the beautiful red-headed star that she had always found powerfully attractive. Now she knew why.

'No, he's not an actor.' Beryl looked serious. 'I suppose you may as well know. He's a Conservative politician. I'm afraid he treated your mother very badly – he let her down dreadfully, poor girl.'

'What's his name?' Amanda breathed.

Beryl looked at the young face, alive with curiosity and a hint of trepidation. 'Simon Brentford. He's a minister in the Department of the Environment now, I think,' she said, with some reluctance. She went on with her story. Having started, she might as well make a good job of it. It would be a shame if Amanda felt that she had been equally rejected by both her parents. 'Of course, he was very naughty. He said he would pay to support the baby – you, dear – and then refused. Poor Leonie had no option but to have you adopted. She was right at the start of her career then. She couldn't have kept you, much as she wanted to.'

She suddenly looked at Amanda. 'You won't breathe a word of any of this, will you? You know I shouldn't have told you?' she said guiltily.

'Oh, but I'm so pleased you have – you're a darling.' Amanda hugged her spontaneously. 'I shall be really good from now on – I promise. I'll get a proper job, I'll even help you look after dad.' She gave a small laugh. 'I mean Arnold.'

Over the next few weeks Beryl became a much happier woman. True, Arnold was seriously ill, but they had grown so far apart in the last few ghastly years that his illness made little difference to her life. She had always waited on him hand and foot, so she simply continued to do so. Admittedly, there was the added unpleasantness of bedpans and strip-washes, but she had help from a day nurse who came in from time to time. It could have been worse, she thought philosophically.

Amanda continued to improve. Her hair, washed and brushed once more, was again a glorious chestnut mane, her skin cleared and her hazel eyes gained a new sparkle. She started dressing like the very pretty girl she really was and got a job in the local library which she actually seemed to enjoy. Her drugs charges proved less serious than Beryl had feared, and she was let off by the magistrates with a small fine and a stern warning about repeating her irresponsible behaviour. Her relationship with Beryl settled down to something that felt almost like a real mother-daughter friendship.

Then, within a year, two things happened within a month of each other that would change their lives irrevocably. First of all Amanda received a letter from the adoption society. It informed her that her mother had been traced, but that no direct contact had been possible. They understood through an intermediary that a meeting would not be feasible immediately as she was out of the country, but they would try to arrange contact as soon as she was back in England.

Then Arnold died.

Amanda was stunned by the news from the adoption society. It had never occurred to her that once they traced her mother they would not be able to arrange an immediate meeting with her. She had imagined a tearful reunion, preferably at an airport, in full view of the world's press and eagerly recorded by television camera crews. She would be whisked off to Hollywood, where her days would be spent lolling by a swimming pool in the sun and going to acting classes. Finally she would make her film début opposite her mother, receive rave notices and become an even bigger star than her parent.

While she had thought that the adoption society were working to arrange all this she had been prepared to wait, but now she was impatient. After all, she knew who her mother was. All she lacked were the money and resources to go and find her, and make her face up to her responsibilities. She had promised Beryl not to try and contact Leonie herself, but Beryl need not know what she was planning. Besides, what was a promise? Her father had broken all his promises to her mother, it seemed, and yet he was now a powerful and respected man. Her father . . . an idea began to dawn as she thought about him: a very good idea it seemed to her. She wouldn't write to her father, Simon Brentford. She would write to his wife. Amanda felt certain that *she* would want to help.

2

Elizabeth Brentford's first reaction to Amanda's letter was that it must be a hoax. Then she thought again. She hardly ever went to the cinema and seldom watched television but even she knew of Leonie O'Brien. Years ago, before she and Simon had become engaged, she had heard rumours that he had been seeing an actress. At the time she had thought little about it; she had had other boyfriends too, it was really none of her business. But if that actress had been Leonie O'Brien – and her age would make it quite plausible – then maybe, just maybe, this preposterous story could be true.

Alone in her pretty upstairs sitting-room she considered the possibility. This light, airy room decorated in cool blues and greens had become her sanctuary. It faced south over sweeping lawns towards the lake – the tranquil view breathed a calm which she needed more and more as she grew older. This was the one place where the family respected her privacy; none of them would enter uninvited, not even Simon himself.

Elizabeth like to read her letters alone and without interruption, especially when, as today, she had received one of the long and invariably entertaining bulletins from her friend Caroline in Somerset. Sorting through her less interesting correspondence first she had dismissed the envelope addressed to her in an unknown feminine hand as something to do with her charity work. When she tore it open and studied the astonishing contents she was profoundly grateful for her privacy. Once the first shock had died away she realized that, if this girl's claim *was* by any chance true, she needed plenty of time to consider the options.

Elizabeth Brentford, née Cavendish, was a survivor. She knew it herself, and she knew too that the basic toughness underlying her pretty, feminine looks and manners was one of the reasons Simon had married her. There were a number of others, of course. She cast her mind back seventeen years to their wedding. It had been a glorious day in June and the big yellow and white striped marquee in the grounds of Hambury Manor, her family's Gloucestershire home, was filled to bursting with over three hundred friends and relatives.

Elizabeth's parents, the Rt Hon. Desmond Cavendish and his wife, Lady Lavinia, herself the daughter of a baronet, had connections throughout the English upper classes and it seemed as if most of them were here today. Simon's family, though 'perfectly respectable' as her mother would say, were less in evidence. His father, a country GP, and his mother were hovering somewhere, looking thrilled but a little over-awed by the dazzling collection of relatives which their clever son had just acquired. The sacrifices which they had made in sending him to public school and then to Oxford were now bearing fruit in this brilliant marriage and the beginnings of what looked like a very promising politi-cal career.

Waiters whisked about with trays of champagne, waitresses with canapés and bowls of strawberries. It was getting hot in the tent, and the occasional breeze was welcome. Elizabeth, dazed with all the con-gratulations, had moved to the edge of the tent for a breath of fresh air when an especially strong gust caught her white lace veil and sent it streaming out sideways. Turning to snatch at it, laughing, she caught sight of Simon, under one of the big cedars across the lawn, engrossed in conversation with an extremely lovely girl.

A small tingle of jealousy shot through her, which she quickly brushed aside. How ungenerous of me, she thought. This is my day – the most perfect wedding any girl could wish for – and surely I don't begrudge another girl a few moments with my handsome husband. But she could not avoid the nagging feeling that it would have been still more perfect if her bridegroom had only had eyes for her.

Almost against her will, she found herself moving towards them. As she approached she saw Simon run his fingers lightly across the girl's breasts, making her giggle. The moment she noticed Elizabeth, the girl began to move away with a guilty expression on her face. Simon turned to look at the intruder with annoyance and to Elizabeth's dismay his expression did not change as he recognized his wife of a few hours.

'Spying on me already, Liz?' he asked truculently. Elizabeth realized with surprise that he was rather drunk. This was not like Simon; she could only put it down to the stresses his wedding day always placed on a man.

'Of course not, darling,' she replied gaily. 'I just wanted to make sure you were all right. It's ages since I set eyes on you.'

Simon surveyed her unsmilingly. 'Don't start checking up on me, I won't have it.' Then he turned and, taking the girl by the arm, led her away leaving his bride standing alone, hurt and humiliated. It was the first of many times when Elizabeth was to ask herself if she had not made the most horrendous mistake in marrying this cold, handsome, arrogant man.

Later that afternoon they set off on their honeymoon. Elizabeth chatted lightly about the incidents of the wedding day, trying hard to suppress any misgivings. Simon was reserved and monosyllabic, unresponsive to her coaxing. That night in the big four-poster bed at the Bear in Woodstock he was almost violent with her, rough and abusive. It was not at all the gentlemanly seduction that she had expected from a man who had courted her with such style and charm.

The following morning they flew from Heathrow to Barbados, sitting silently side by side in the Club Class section of the British Airways TriStar. Simon buried himself in a book, emerging only to accept every free drink that was offered. Elizabeth stared out of the window at the perfect blue sky, sipping orange juice and wondering again what on earth she had let herself in for with this marriage.

During their two weeks in Barbados, however, things improved a little. Simon's love-making became gentler – Elizabeth even learned to enjoy it – and though they rarely talked about more than the day-to-day trivia of their holiday he was kinder and more considerate. She began to relax and concentrate on acquiring a perfect golden tan, which gave a new lustre to her fragile blonde beauty.

By the time they returned to their new home in England – Wortham Manor, a perfect small Queen Anne house in ten acres of Berkshire, given to them by Elizabeth's parents – the newly married couple were far more at ease with each other. But they never achieved that automatic freedom of communication that Elizabeth had always thought should be at the heart of a good marriage. And as the weeks and months went by, Simon gradually began to withdraw into his work until Elizabeth began to wonder if she had ever really known him.

In the early days they made love frequently, but gradually the times when they came together became fewer and fewer. Elizabeth was not altogether sorry. She had never been sure whether a session in bed would be slow and gentle, or whether she would end up the next day having to dab her weals and bruises with iodine. She too started to withdraw, and the charming, outward-going girl was gradually replaced by a serene, reserved woman. When Kit, their eldest boy, was born eighteen months after they were married she poured a wealth of thwarted affection into her baby, as she did again when James arrived two years later.

It was around the time of her first pregnancy that Elizabeth first began to suspect Simon of infidelity. Unwilling to believe it so early in their marriage she dismissed the idea, and was soon distracted by the arrival of the baby. Her suspicions were aroused again during her second pregnancy. She noticed that Simon stayed up in town more and more but, when she tackled him about it, he argued that pressure of work was making his absences imperative. Then, James was born, and with two small children Elizabeth was far too busy to worry.

Anyway, Simon was working hard. As one of the youngest MPs in the House of Commons he had attracted attention from the moment he gained his seat, and he was soon climbing relentlessly up the political ladder. His first government post was a very junior one, but it came early in his career. Thereafter his rise was assured. Elizabeth saw less and less of him, content to stay in Berkshire with the children while Simon spent week nights, while Parliament was sitting, in their small two-roomed flat in Dolphin Square. As the boys grew older and were sent away to school she started to devote her time to raising money for charity and to local good works like Riding for the Disabled. In public she remained the loyal Tory wife, staunch in support of her husband. She did indeed respect Simon's ability and political commitment and was prepared, whatever the shortcomings of their relationship, to do her best to help him achieve his ambition of a Cabinet post.

By the time Elizabeth realized that there was no doubt about her husband's infidelity – a laughably predictable matter of a compromising note found carelessly stuffed in the pocket of a suit to be sent to the cleaners – she was able to treat it with the same stoic indifference as she did the many public and private slights that she received at his hands. As his career progressed these became fewer and fewer. After all, Simon was no fool and he seemed to recognize that, apart from his looks, Elizabeth, with her money, charm and connections, was one of his greatest assets. Elizabeth, for her part, clung to her marriage with a steely determination to see it through. To leave Simon would be unthinkable – it would not be a question of letting him down but of letting herself down, of not seeing the job through. One ploughed on in adversity. One did the right and decent thing. This was what she had learned at home and at school, and nothing and no one would deter her from her duty.

On the morning that Elizabeth received Amanda's letter Simon was, for once, at home. He was in his study working on an important speech and would probably stay there most of the day. Simon hated to be disturbed when he was working and was always furious if anyone interrupted him. On the other hand, thought Elizabeth, if this letter were genuine it should be dealt with as quickly as possible. One whiff of a scandal like this and Simon's career would be in jeopardy. Once the gutter press got hold of it there would be no stopping them.

Elizabeth reread the letter carefully. The girl meant business, there was no doubt about that. There was something implacable in her tone, as though she was determined not to be put off. She decided to wait until lunch before talking to Simon. A couple of hours could make little difference, after all, and he had been so irritable lately. She wondered vaguely if there was a new mistress on the scene. At least Leonie O'Brien, if indeed she had been a mistress, had been well before her time. But why had he never told her about the child?

She sighed heavily. Why did she stay with this man, who preached morality and the sanctity of the family in public while seeming to have no scruples at all about his personal life? There was her own pride, that part of her which felt it was cowardly and wrong to admit defeat. Then there were the boys, of course. She couldn't let the boys down, she had to be strong for their sakes. Now it seemed that if this girl's story were true Simon had a daughter as well. Strange, she had always longed for a little girl.

Elizabeth stayed in her sitting room all morning, working on a set of *gros point* seat covers that she was embroidering in her spare time. The work was soothing; Malkin, her big grey cat, kept her company, taking a deep interest every time the needle was pulled through the canvas followed by a tantalizingly long strand of wool. When the clock chimed one she folded her tapestry. Picking up Amanda's letter she left the room and went downstairs, followed closely by Malkin. She stopped outside the study door and knocked.

'Yes,' came Simon's abrupt voice. He looked up in annoyance as Elizabeth and the cat entered together.

When he was in a temper like this, thought Elizabeth objectively, you noticed the thin line of his mouth and the fact that his brown eyes were slightly hooded and sardonic. Otherwise he was still a remarkably good-looking man.

'Oh, I thought it was lunch. It's late.'

'It's only just one,' said Elizabeth soothingly. 'I expect Janet's on her way.' Right on cue their housekeeper, Janet, appeared at the door with a tray of cold meat and salad.

'Good, I'm starving. Just put it here, Janet.' He moved aside the papers on his desk.

'Very good, sir.' Janet put down the tray and, smiling warmly at

Elizabeth, left the room. As she went Elizabeth returned the smile which said plainly that Simon was not an easy man but they could cope. Malkin leapt on to the window-sill and stared out intently at the garden. Elizabeth hovered by the desk.

'What have I forgotten?' asked Simon in a resigned tone.

'What?'

'It must be something vital or you wouldn't be interrupting my lunch.'

Elizabeth looked at him coldly. She had the impression, sometimes, that he had forgotten that she was his wife. A serf. Yes, that's how he saw her, as a serf. Well this would make him take notice, for sure.

'I thought you ought to see this.' She handed him the letter.

Simon looked up in surprise at her tone of voice. 'It's addressed to you,' he said dismissively, glancing at the envelope.

'I think you should read it,' repeated Elizabeth firmly.

Simon shrugged, pulled out the letter and read it in silence. As he did so his expression changed. He threw it down on the desk and leant back in his chair, covering his face with his hands. 'Dear God,' he said in a low voice.

'Is there any truth in what she says?' asked Elizabeth.

'You don't make up a story like this,' he replied in muffled tones. 'Of course it's bloody true.'

Sensing the tension in the room, the cat turned its head to observe the scene with an unblinking stare.

'Why didn't you tell me?' asked Elizabeth.

'There was no need – it happened before I met you – it was unimportant.'

'I would hardly call an abandoned baby unimportant,' she said coldly.

'The baby was not abandoned.' Simon's tone was sharp. 'I arranged for a foster-mother to take care of the child.'

'But, if this girl is right, you failed to pay her.'

'She got in touch and told me about a couple who wanted to adopt the baby. It seemed the most satisfactory way out of the whole mess.'

'But,' persisted Elizabeth, 'it would appear that the girl wanted to keep the baby.'

Simon's face darkened. 'It was a ludicrous idea. She was supposed to have had an abortion, but she claimed it was too late. She was an actress, ambitious, she wanted a career. How could she possibly have coped, trailing a child around with her? No, it all worked out for the best.'

There was a pause. Malkin began to wash himself, his rasping tongue the only sound in the room.

'So what do you intend to do about this girl – Amanda?' asked Elizabeth eventually.

'Ignore her – she'll soon get the message.'

'I think that would be unwise. I believe she means business.'

Simon looked up, a hint of appeal in his eyes. 'What do you suggest, Liz?' He always called her Liz although he knew she preferred Elizabeth.

'You'd better see her. She may have it in mind to go to the press.'

Simon looked at her in alarm. 'We'd better be careful,' warned Elizabeth. 'We don't want to see this story in print.'

Simon groaned. 'God, no.'

'I don't like the tone of the letter. There's something calculating about it.'

Simon always trusted his wife's instincts in matters such as this. 'You're probably right. We'd better see her.'

'She wants to come this Saturday,' said Elizabeth.

'She can't possibly. It's the Commons squash tournament.'

'Pull out.' Elizabeth's tone was firm. 'This is important. Let's get it over with.' Without waiting for his reply she left the room. The cat jumped down from the window-sill and followed her, stalking off into the garden to chase away a sparrow that had no business to be there.

It was when Beryl was clearing out Arnold's study that she discovered the magazines. She had found to her surprise that the lower drawers of his desk were locked. Thinking they must contain important documents she forced them open, and found both drawers crammed with glossy magazines. She picked one up and flicked through it. Her incredulous disgust grew with every page.

The magazine was filled with photographs that were frankly beyond her wildest imaginings. Lurid and explicit, they showed men and women indulging in every possible, and impossible, variation of the sexual act. The captions, in German, were incomprehensible to her, but these photographs needed no explanation. 'Pornography,' she said aloud in revulsion, throwing down the magazine as if it had burnt her fingers. A tumult of nausea, jealousy and rage swept through her. She remembered their twin beds, Arnold's infrequent and indifferent love-making. Was this the real reason for Arnold's lack of interest in the physical side of their marriage?

After a while, Beryl realized that she was shaking uncontrollably. She poured herself a large brandy and then remembered that she had to ring the funeral parlour. Earlier that morning she had gone to choose a headstone for Arnold, and had found a beautiful white-marble angel playing a lute; the angel's mouth was open as though singing. 'In memory of my beloved husband and the love we shared through music' was the inscription she wanted. The angel was expensive – £1000 – and though Beryl had not begrudged the cost she had needed time to work out whether she could afford it before she made a final decision.

Well, now she had thought it over and reached the conclusion that a plain headstone would be quite sufficient, inscribed simply with the words, 'In memory of my beloved husband'. She poured herself another stiff brandy, and then another. No, on second thoughts, 'In memory of my husband' would be more appropriate, since he was no longer beloved. She drank some more. By the time she spoke to the under-taker she was drunker than she had ever been in her life. She ordered a headstone with the words 'In memoriam' and told him to forget the sodding angel.

Later, head throbbing and vision blurred, Beryl swept the entire contents of the desk into a black plastic rubbish bag. 'It's all got to go,' she said to herself. 'How many years was I married to that man – and I still didn't know him? I thought we were happy . . .' She felt a sob rising in her throat as she stood there surrounded by boxes of memorabilia: photograph albums, opera programmes, old Christmas cards, newspaper cuttings about the Ashebourn Choral Society accompanied by yellowing photographs. There was Arnold, just after she had met him – tall, dark and handsome, the answer to any maiden's prayer. She gazed at the photograph with its blurred newsprint, blurred still more by the tears that dropped unbidden on to the paper.

What on earth was she crying for? She didn't love him any more, hadn't loved him for some time. Long before he died the dream had faded. She wondered if Arnold had really wanted her to engage in perverted sexual acts like those in those disgusting magazines. He had never even hinted at it. Was it because he had lacked the courage to ask her, or did he simply not find her sexually stimulating enough?

Beryl screwed up the cutting and added it to the rubbish. 'I know I'm not sexy,' she murmured to herself. 'I'm not the sexy type.' She paused over an old copy of *Films and Filming* with a picture of Vivien Leigh on the cover. She was wearing a blonde wig as Blanche Dubois in *A Streetcar Named Desire*. Beryl wondered why she had kept the magazine then remembered that she had once longed to look like that. Someone had remarked that she bore a slight resemblance to the actress and she had nursed the idea over the years, harbouring a secret desire to have blonde hair cut in the same style, to make up her eyes in that exotic way. She had never worn more than a touch of mascara in her life – Arnold had hated her wearing make-up.

Beryl sat gazing at the picture, gradually making up her mind. There was nothing and no one to stop her now. She would make an appointment to have her hair cut and tinted; she would buy some really good make-up, lots of it; she would go to Cassandra's, the best and most expensive women's fashion shop in Ashebourn, and treat herself to a new wardrobe. Then she would be equipped to join the cultural trip that was being organized by the Choral Society: a musical tour of several European capitals including Paris, Vienna and Rome. It would be expensive of course. Very expensive. She would use the money she had saved on Arnold's memorial. He owed her that much.

Beryl entered the beauty salon in trepidation, feeling rather like a little girl going to her first party. *Beautiful People* was the salon's name, and Beryl hoped that it lived up to its promise. She approached the desk with timid step; a ravishingly pretty girl viewed her with a tolerant smile.

'Name?' the girl enquired.

'Willoughby,' she replied. 'Beryl Willoughby.' And found a wonderful sense of freedom in using her christian name rather than the usual Mrs. She had always called herself Mrs Willoughby or Mrs Arnold Willoughby when Arnold was alive. It was as though she had now found a part of herself again. She glanced around the salon: it was seething with activity. The music was loud and not to Beryl's taste, but she didn't care. This was a new and exciting world, part of the whole adventure. The pretty girl was writing a name in her appointments book. She looked up at Beryl briefly.

'You're having our all-inclusive treatment, madam? Is that right?'

'Yes, that's right.' Beryl clutched her handbag tightly. She suspected that this was going to be something of an ordeal. The girl behind the desk turned her head and called into the salon.

'Charlene!'

A small girl with straight dark hair, cut asymmetrically, stood expectantly with hairdryer poised above the head of her client.

'Yes?' she asked mildly.

'Your new customer.'

Charlene smiled at Beryl encouragingly. She looked kind and Beryl began to feel more cheerful. 'Dawn can start you off,' she said nodding at a ginger-haired youngster. 'I'll be with you in a moment.'

Dawn took Beryl's coat, then swathed her in a pink cotton overall. Beryl followed her obediently and sat in front of a basin. Before she leant back to surrender herself to her Dawn's ministrations, she gazed around her. The salon was decorated in art-deco style, pink and black with geometric mirrors and doorways. It was filled with women of all ages, most with that self-absorbed expression that comes from intense concentration on one's appearance. It was hard to tell if they liked what they saw as they gazed into the thirties-style mirrors. But to Beryl they all looked frighteningly stylish and sophisticated. If this place could have anything like the same effect on her, she knew her money would be well spent.

A creature from another planet emerged through one of the thirties doors. She had a horse's mane of spiky hair, the colour of red ink, fuchsia-pink eyelids and red false eyelashes. Her cheek-bones sparkled with glitter and her lips were black, as were her painted nails. She was chewing gum. All the girls wore regulation black pinafores over their everyday wear. This one had finished off the ensemble with high-heeled red lurex boots. She teetered towards Beryl, leaning over her to ask cheerily, 'Coffee, love?'

'Oh yes, please.'

'You can get me one as well, Adrienne,' Charlene chipped in. 'Then take a look at Mrs Parkin, I think she's nearly cooked.'

Charlene was now combing out what was left of her customer's crowning glory, which wasn't a lot, and showing her the results of her efforts in a back mirror. There was a brief silence as the music tape came to its conclusion. 'Tape, Karen,' Charlene called to the girl behind the desk. Then she left her post and came across to Beryl.

The salon doorbell dinged as another customer, an effervescent blonde in her forties, glinting with a mass of gold trinkets, bounced in. 'Oh, you're playing my favourite,' she enthused to Karen. 'I'm a bit late, dear, I'm afraid. Couldn't get away from the shop. This old bag came in, tried everything on, and then never bought a thing. Oh, I love this one,' and she joined in, singing tunelessly as she struggled out of her cream trench coat. 'It's pissing down out there.'

Beryl recognized the woman as the owner of Cassandra's, the very expensive clothes shop round the corner from the salon.

'You'll have to wait a moment, Mrs de Ville,' observed Charlene. 'Sandra's busy.'

'But where's Nikki? I always have Nikki.'

'Not today,' Charlene replied calmly.

'Why not?' challenged Mrs de Ville, appalled.

'Dunno, rang this morning to say she wasn't coming in; you'll have to wait,' said Charlene placidly, not the least bit fazed. She unwrapped

Beryl's towel and started to comb out the damp tangles. Mrs de Ville looked ready to explode.

'But I always have Nikki,' she insisted loudly.

'Another coffee, Adrienne,' instructed Charlene, without turning a hair. Adrienne disappeared at once, looking thankful to escape a potentially fraught situation.

Charlene flipped up a piece of Beryl's hair and looked at it, her expression non-committal. 'Did you have anything in mind?' she enquired pleasantly.

Beryl picked up her handbag and produced a page torn from a magazine. She handed it to the girl. Charlene regarded it thoughtfully for a moment. 'Jane Seymour, is it?' she asked eventually.

'It's Vivien Leigh,' said Beryl. 'In a film,' she added, idiotically.

'Oh,' said Charlene, handing her back the picture. 'It looks like Jane Seymour to me.'

'Can you make me look like that?' asked Beryl anxiously.

Charlene smiled. 'Of course, madam.' Dawn reappeared and Charlene issued her instructions. 'Mix up number 53A and number 16.'

Half an hour later, the shoulder-length locks which Beryl usually wore in a French pleat had been trimmed into a sleek bob which curved gently round her face, just brushing her jaw-bone. The shape transformed her appearance, making her eyes look larger and bringing the lines of her face into clearer emphasis. Now it was time for the colour, and some foaming cream was being painted on to her hair. It smelt horrible, but Beryl didn't care. She was beginning to enjoy herself.

Mrs de Ville, thankfully, was hidden under an infra-red machine and wearing what looked like an amazing head-dress of tissues and silver bits. It transpired she was having her highlights done. She had sulked for a while about her change of stylist, but had soon forgotten her bad humour and was chattering away loudly. Beryl would have liked to have asked her about her projected new wardrobe, but somehow the thought of actually interrupting the flow of energetic trivia was too daunting to contemplate. Somehow she would have to pluck up the courage to go to Cassandra's and look through the rails for herself, but for now it was her turn for the space-age machine, and she sat quietly and day-dreamed as its jets pumped hot steam on to her head.

'Mrs Willoughby?' Beryl was startled out of her reverie. 'Mrs Willoughby, are you all right?' Beryl looked up and saw Charlene's face peering down at her. 'I'm just going to take a look and see if you're done.' She removed the metallic dome under which Beryl had been isolated for the best part of forty minutes, then, carefully prising off a piece of silver foil, she pressed and prodded the hair to try and determine its progress. So far as Beryl could see, she appeared to have blue hair, but she didn't care. Everything was so new and exciting. The sounds of the salon gradually permeated her consciousness and she became aware of Chloe de Ville sitting reflected in the mirror opposite, flicking irritatedly through a magazine while her bleached blonde curls were brushed into submission. She certainly looked formidable enough, but Beryl determined on a visit to her shop later that day.

Soon, Beryl was looking at herself in a mirror as Charlene finished combing out her shining new hair. The dull mousy colour was gone, replaced by a gleaming shade of platinum-blonde that flattered her still-clear complexion. Beryl stared at herself in awe. 'You've done wonders, Charlene,' she said to the girl holding the mirror behind her. 'I wouldn't have believed it possible.'

Charlene laughed. 'I'm glad you like it. Now, madam, how about those eyelashes? If you like, we could dye them a few shades darker; you've no idea what a difference it could make to your eyes.'

Her eyes met Beryl's in the mirror and both women grinned conspiratorially. 'All right,' said Beryl, 'go on, do your worst.'

The electric bell sounded alarmingly loud as Beryl pushed open the door of Cassandra's. Some of the smarter members of the Choral Society shopped here, but she had always felt intimidated when she peered into the stylish cream and beige interior with its racks of designer clothes. The shop was empty, but Chloe de Ville appeared as if by magic, like the wicked fairy ready to welcome her latest victim into her lair. Her eyes narrowed in anticipation at the sight of Beryl and her heavily made up features creased into a smile. She knew Beryl slightly, of course, as everyone knew everyone else in the small community of Ashebourn, and she also knew that she was wealthy, especially since the death of her husband.

'Mrs Willoughby, what a delightful surprise,' she gushed. 'I've not seen you in here before, dear, have I?'

'No,' replied Beryl, realizing that her escape was now cut off. 'I've always been meaning to come, but my late husband wasn't too keen,' she added, untruthfully.

'Men!' agreed Chloe, philosophically shrugging her shoulders. 'Now, what can I show you? We've got a whole new range of lovely things in.'

Beryl gazed apprehensively around the room. All the clothes on the rails looked terribly brightly coloured to her. There were quantities of shiny fabrics, of splashy flower prints, of sequins and chiffon flounces. Where were the sober browns and navies that had always been her preferred colours?

'Well,' Beryl began uncertainly. 'Something to wear in the evening. To a concert.'

'This is just you,' pronounced Chloe, producing an electric-blue frock with an amazing cleavage which Beryl knew she would never wear in a million year.

'Well, yes, it's, it's lovely,' agreed Beryl. 'But I was thinking more of . . .'

'Now this, this is very special,' Chloe went on, pulling a heavily sequined scarlet dress from another rail.

Beryl looked at it in horror and took her courage in both hands. 'Do you have anything in lilac?'

Chloe looked astounded, as if such a question were quite unnecessary. 'Of course,' she said reprovingly. 'Perhaps you would like to follow me.'

In the other room, the colours of the clothes were more subdued, the fabrics softer-looking. Chloe cast an experienced eye over Beryl's figure. 'You look like a 10 to me,' she said, with the air of someone with many years experience of judging a customer's size, shape and weight at a single glance.

'Oh no, 12,' said Beryl, amazed at finding herself disagreeing.

'You don't do yourself justice,' said Chloe. It sounded like a repri-
mand. She was starting to pull something from the rail when the doorbell sounded sharply. 'Oh, excuse me a moment,' she said
apologetically. 'I'll have to leave you to have a browse round on your
own.'

As she disappeared, Beryl heaved a sigh of relief and began to look
through the rails. She paused at a beautiful deep violet dress in a silky
jersey material. Jean Muir, the label read. She looked at the price tag
and gasped. Oh well, she thought, in for a penny, in for a pound. In the
softly lit changing cubicle she surveyed herself in the mirror, wondering
again at the glorious swinging mane of platinum hair that fell just below
her cheek-bones. She took off her sensible navy skirt and cream blouse,
and, with trembling fingers eased the violet dress from its polythene
covering. The soft, creaseless material flowed through her fingers,
quite unlike anything she'd ever tried on before.

She put the dress on and surveyed the result. At that moment
there was a tap on the door and before she could speak it opened. Chloe
stood there with an armful of dresses, her attention totally riveted by
the sight in front of her.

'Well, I must say, you look absolutely lovely, dear,' she said almost
grudgingly. 'I rather fancied that one myself, but I think you look better
in it than I would have done.'

Beryl secretly agreed with her. She knew her figure was the better
of the two.

'I told you you'd be a 10,' said Chloe smugly. 'Now, I think you
might like to try some of these, too.' She held out the clothes with a
predatory smile.

Before she left the shop, Beryl had spent well over £2000 and had
a wardrobe which, she felt, would stand up to any scrutiny. But there
was also something much more important about her spending spree. It
had made her feel young, reckless and carefree – as if she were living
her own life for the first time in years. She dug in her handbag for her
credit card.

'Are you going somewhere special?' asked Chloe as, all smiles, she
took Beryl's Access card.

'On holiday. It's a sort of musical tour, you see. I'm going to visit some of the great musical centres of Europe. We'll be going to operas and concerts.'

'Oh yes, very nice,' agreed Chloe. 'I'm a Tom Jones fan myself,' she added. 'He's got such style, hasn't he?' Beryl smiled vaguely and murmured yes almost inaudibly. 'I quite fancy a bit of opera myself though, sometimes,' she continued expansively. 'Flamingo's good, isn't he?'

For a moment, Beryl was nonplussed.

'Domingo,' she corrected quietly.

'Yes, that's the one. Wouldn't turf him out of bed,' Chloe confided with a raucous laugh that made her gold charm bracelet shake and tinkle.

'Thank you, you've been very kind,' said Beryl as Chloe held open the door for her, completely oblivious to the fact that she had just been skilfully relieved of a huge sum of money. She gathered up the glossy black carrier bags with the silken ropes that formed the handles and went out into the light drizzle a happy woman.

Simon Brentford leant against the marble fireplace in the big drawing-room and gazed with apparently bored indifference at the attractive young woman who was claiming to be his daughter. She was sitting upright on the chintz-covered sofa immediately opposite him and there was a look in her eye he did not relish.

His pose was a well-practised front. He had discovered at an early age that a languid, impassive manner coupled with a contemptuous gaze from half-hooded eyes had a mesmerizing effect on his opponents. He had been one of the most feared of the prefects at his public school; his whiplash delivery of a highly sarcastic and painfully accurate remark was enough to bring about the demolition of almost any boy. His manner had also enabled him to play havoc with the opposition in Oxford Union debates and he had gone on to use it to great effect on the back-benches in the House of Commons. Now he attempted to use it to disarm the pretty, bright-eyed girl who, for all her youthful appearance, was the most dangerous opponent he had ever faced.

Elizabeth sat perched on the edge of an armchair. Her coolly beautiful looks belied the tension inside her. She gazed intently at Amanda, trying to read her face. Her only outward sign of emotion was a continuous twisting of her wedding-ring.

It was obvious that it would have a shattering effect on Simon's career if his unwanted love-child and his treatment of the mother, now a famous film star, became public knowledge. And it would be especially damaging just at this moment, when Simon was receiving unmistakable signals from the Prime Minister that a Cabinet post would soon be his. Elizabeth shuddered inwardly as she visualized the way the press would treat the news, and the reactions of Simon's political colleagues. In private, he might well be envied for his affair with a woman like Leonie O'Brien, but political expediency would certainly demand that his prospects be sacrificed on the altar of public morality. A disappointed, embittered Simon would quite certainly make her own life a misery. It was in both their interests to silence this girl in whatever way was most appropriate.

Simon spoke first. 'So what precisely do you want of me?' he asked. Elizabeth braced herself and Amanda looked from one to the other, apparently unsure of herself.

'I – I was hoping . . .' she faltered. Simon narrowed his eyes as if he sensed the enemy's unease and began to feel more confident of the outcome of this encounter. 'I was hoping to become one of the family. It's what I've always wanted.'

'Out of the question,' snapped Simon. 'How could we possibly explain you away? In any case, these Willoughbys are your family, so you tell us, and have brought you up in a perfectly acceptable manner.'

'But they weren't my real family. I didn't feel a part of them. They weren't like me,' Amanda blurted out. She had been prepared for an unwelcoming reception, but Simon's total lack of emotion was surprisingly hurtful. A spasm of pain shot through her as she understood that he was rejecting her unequivocally. For the second time in her life.

She decided on alternative tactics. 'Of course they looked after me as well as they were able, but I would love to have had the opportunity to go to university. But Arnold, my f-father,' her voice trembled as she spoke, 'is dead now. So I can't.'

Elizabeth's expression softened at her words, but Simon remained unmoved. 'Very regrettable, I'm sure, but we can't always have what we want in this life, can we?' he countered. The smooth glibness of his reply shocked Amanda again and she realized that straight talking was the only way to get through the icily impenetrable exterior of this man. Her father.

'I could always send myself to university,' she said brightly, but it's so expensive. Elizabeth was uneasy at the way the current conversation was going. She had no intention of letting it continue a moment longer, but it was Simon who created the necessary distraction.

Simon moved away from the mantlepiece and tugged at a bell rope. Ignoring Amanda's last remark he said, 'I am sure we could all do with some tea.'

'What a good idea, you must be gasping, Amanda,' said Elizabeth in a calm friendly tone, taking her cue.

The door opened and Janet, the housekeeper, entered. As Simon ordered tea for the three of them, Amanda studied her hosts, trying to assess them. Simon was very good-looking, she thought, but what a bastard he seemed to be. He couldn't even pretend that he was glad to see his long-lost daughter. Even Arnold, boring old fool that he had been, would have treated her better than this. Elizabeth, on the other hand, was quite nice. There was something about her that made you trust her. She decided that on the whole she preferred her father's wife to her father himself.

'Amanda,' said Elizabeth, breaking into her thoughts, 'I'm sure you'd like to wash your hands before we have tea. Janet will show you to the cloakroom.' Her tone was one that demanded obedience and Amanda found herself getting up and following the smiling housekeeper out of the room almost before she knew what she was doing.

The moment Amanda had left the room, Simon moved quickly to his wife's side. 'Liz, what the hell are we going to do?' Elizabeth now knew exactly what to do, which was what her husband expected of her. She had never let him down before.

'See her off, but for God's sake be nice to her, darling.'

'Do you think she will go to the press?' His manner was urgent. The matter had to be sorted out before Amanda returned.

'Not if you're nice to her,' Elizabeth insisted. 'Tell her you're sorry the way things have turned out, that you did what you thought was right at the time, and that you will try to make it up to her.'

'The whole thing could be a put-up job for all we know,' Simon said irritably.

'I hardly think so, darling,' said Elizabeth in a quiet voice. 'The facts can be checked, after all.'

Simon paced the room. 'We've got to nip this in the bud, Liz, or we'll be in big trouble.' He suddenly stopped in his tracks and swung round on his wife, smiling, as if a brilliant idea had occurred to him. 'I know, you talk to her,' he said coaxingly. 'You're far better at this sort of thing than I am.'

They looked at each other for a moment, before Elizabeth slowly replied, 'Yes . . . that's not a bad idea. I believe I might be able to get through to her.' She saw that, once again, she had become indispensable to him.

By the time Amanda returned to the drawing-room, there was no sign of Simon. Elizabeth came over to her, arms extended in welcome, and said warmly, 'I'm so sorry, my dear, this must be the most terrible ordeal for you, but you must understand it is for my husband too. It has all come as a terrible shock, you see. After you left the room, he was so distressed he broke down completely. I hope you will excuse him for a little while.'

The look of disbelief on Amanda's face as she spoke made her fear that she had gone too far. She sat down on one of the sofas and went on hurriedly, 'All his apparent lack of emotion – that's just an act. It's how he copes with his opponents in parliament. He's a man who never shows his real feelings. He simply doesn't know what to do in an emotional situation.'

'How difficult for you,' observed Amanda coldly.

'I've got used to it over the years. But please, Amanda, come and sit here next to me.' She patted the sofa. Amanda joined her reluctantly, sensing that the interview was not going as she had hoped and with a strong feeling that she was about to be fobbed off.

'I'm going to be completely honest with you,' Elizabeth said sincerely. 'You think you've missed out, don't you? But you haven't, you know. Simon is not a family man. He never spends any time with the children, he hardly ever sees them. He is simply not interested, you see. His career is everything to him. It's his whole life. We come very low down on the agenda, I'm afraid.' She laughed in a self-deprecating way.

Amanda felt tears pricking her eyes and Elizabeth took her hand comfortingly. 'Please try to forgive him. He was a very young man when you were born and he does so want to make it up to you. What do you say, can you forgive him?'

'I haven't much choice, have I?' said Amanda drearily. She felt baffled and disarmed by this poised, sophisticated woman who was being so unexpectedly nice to her. But, of course, Elizabeth would have been trained from an early age to handle awkward situations. After all, they were only trying to renege on their responsibilities, both of them. She stared at Elizabeth unflinchingly, and waited with some fascination for her next move.

'He would like to help you with your chosen career. You indicated that you would like to go to university? It is the kind of opportunity which shouldn't be denied to anyone of ability. Perhaps if you would allow us to help . . .'

Now Elizabeth stiffened imperceptibly before she rose and crossed to the walnut writing desk. She opened one of the drawers and took out a cheque book and pen. She judged the right amount to be £10,000. To Amanda, it would be a fortune: for them it was a small consideration, if it meant they could carry on with their lives as before. Money was one thing they were not short of in this household. Without hurrying, Elizabeth wrote out a cheque, and calmly and methodically filled in the stub. Then she handed it to Amanda with smile. 'I hope this will help, in every way,' she said softly. 'I know you'll want to be on your way now, so I'll see you out. I'm sure you'll understand if Simon doesn't say goodbye to you as well.' Then she walked to the door and held it open; the interview was at an end. As Amanda trudged down the long drive towards the bus stop she couldn't help wondering, in spite of the cheque stashed safely in her bag, if she had not just gained only a pyrrhic victory in their encounter.

The next day Amanda began to put her plans into action. Her first move was to pay the cheque into her bank. Then she handed in her notice at the library. Finally, she set about tracking down Leonie O'Brien. Ever since Beryl had told her that Leonie was her real mother, she had avidly collected any information that came her way about her life and career. She knew that Leonie was abroad – the letter from the adoption agency had confirmed it – and according to the gossip columns in the press she was in Rome producing her first movie, a costume drama called *Swords at Sunset* set in late-seventeenth-century France. It appeared that the film was being made in Italy rather than France because it was cheaper to make movies there. The problem was to make certain of her whereabouts. Amanda knew that stars like Leonie jetted about the world almost at a whim, and she did not want to set off to Italy on a wild-goose chase.

Her first step was to telephone the offices of Equity, the actors' union. A little careful questioning soon established that the best way to contact an actor or actress was through their agent, and that Leonie O'Brien's agent was Nigel Bechstein, of Nigel Bechstein Personal Management. Armed with this information, and with Nigel Bechstein's office telephone number, Amanda sat down to think. She had a good idea that if she revealed that she was Leonie O'Brien's long-lost daughter, her enquiries would be met with a deafening silence. On the other hand, she felt it likely that agents did not go giving out details of their clients' activities and whereabouts to just anyone, particularly if their client was as big a name as Leonie O'Brien. She had to find some way of getting Nigel Bechstein to answer her questions about Leonie without telling him who she really was.

At a loss, Amanda decided to make herself a coffee. Then, drink in hand, she wandered into the living-room and sat down, putting her mug on one of Beryl's magazines that was lying on the coffee table. As she did so, she noticed the shout line on its front cover, 'The Real Jeremy

Irons – Read Our Exclusive Story.' Of course – film stars always talked to journalists. Everyone talked to journalists. She jumped up in excitement and ran to the telephone. With shaking fingers, she dialled the number. 'Hello,' she said to the disembodied female voice which replied. 'This is Amanda Willoughby from *Woman's Dream* magazine. We're thinking of doing a feature on Leonie O'Brien and her new film. I wonder if I could talk to Nigel Bechstein about it, please.'

Exactly one week later, Amanda was on a flight to Rome.

Nigel Bechstein sat in his office just off London's St Martin's Lane and tapped his tooth with a pencil, his invariable habit when he was thinking hard. It was a warm afternoon and, though he had already taken off his jacket, he was sweating slightly in his sea-island cotton shirt. He loosened the knot of his Gucci tie; his collar was feeling uncomfortably tight. He was putting on weight, there was no doubt about it. Lunch at the Ivy had been delicious as usual, but he should have resisted having cheese *and* a pudding. Nigel looked down at his swelling paunch. Considering the way he worried about his clients, he should by rights have fretted it away years ago. Now, to make matters worse, he was worrying about one of the few who hardly ever gave him cause for concern – Leonie O'Brien.

It was the second phone call he had received from a young woman who called herself a journalist, asking if she could arrange an interview with Leonie. At first he had been perfectly happy to talk to her; after all, it was a common request and *Woman's Dream*, which the girl claimed to represent, was a popular and respected magazine. Then, as the conversation continued, he had begun to feel that the girl's questions lacked the coherence that he would expect from a professional writer. She seemed nervous, and she was oddly insistent in wanting information about Leonie's early career rather than, as he would have expected, her current activities.

He had finally got her off the phone by promising to talk to Leonie about arranging an interview when she returned to England. He had already confirmed that she was in Rome, before the girl's manner began to arouse his suspicions. Now he wondered if that had not been a mistake. The girl had rung back, saying that the magazine was prepared to send her to Rome and could she have Leonie's address there. Again, he had promised to call her back, but just now, he had asked his secretary to telephone *Woman's Dream* and find out if Amanda Willoughby was on their staff. Not much to his surprise, she had reported back that the magazine knew of no such person.

From now on, Amanda Willoughby would receive a polite but firm negative if she tried to contact him again, but he wondered if he should call Leonie, and tell her about the girl. The last thing he wanted to do was interrupt her in the middle of filming, and Amanda Willoughby was probably just another star-struck fan hoping to get close to her heroine; on the other hand there had been that recent business of the letter from the adoption society with its careful talk of a 'relative' hoping to contact Miss O'Brien. He had decided not to bother Leonie about it while she was so busy in Rome, but now he wondered if he had been wrong. If this girl and the adoption-society letter had some connection . . . well there had, now he came to think about it, been something rather odd about Leonie's early career. Nigel ran his hand over his receding dark curls in perplexity and thought back to his first meeting with Leonie O'Brien.

'What is it tonight?' asked Millicent James, the well-known casting director. She was a large middle-aged woman with cropped iron-grey curls, sharp black eyes and a bright-red lipsticked gash for a mouth. No one was more respected in the business than Millicent James and no one was tougher, as many an agent trying to get an audition for a hopeful client had discovered to their cost.

'*The Changeling*,' replied Nigel Bechstein, the most junior member of Hodge and Flowers, Personal Management. Millicent, who had not addressed the question to him directly, turned round and found herself looking at a smartly dressed young man with a fine head of unruly black curls. He was slightly too plump, but his melting brown eyes were soft and appealing. Millicent, who in spite of her formidable appearance was not unsusceptible to attractive young men, smiled slightly as she thanked him for the information.

Pressing his advantage, Nigel introduced himself. 'Nigel Bechstein, Hodge and Flowers,' he said, holding out a hand. Somewhat to his surprise, she took it. They were crammed together in the small bar at the London Drama Academy's Colley Cibber Theatre. It was first night of the end of year play and agents and casting directors, family and friends, directors and producers had gathered *en masse* to view the latest crop of hopeful young actors and actresses going through their paces.

Nigel was young and ambitious, he intended to have his own agency one day, and he wasn't about to throw up an opportunity of getting friendly with a highly influential casting lady. He was here on behalf of Peter Hodge and Donald Flowers, a well-established and much respected pair who had run a successful theatrical agency for many years. Both had been actors and with the instinct peculiar to that breed had a particular gift for spotting new young talent.

Nigel was determined that he too would prove himself a worthy member of the team. He was determined to find a star tonight or die in the attempt. Meanwhile, he would use every ounce of the charm he knew he possessed to chat up anyone who might help him in his present or future business. The noise, however, was deafening.

'Sorry, didn't quite catch that,' shouted Millicent, finally relinquishing his hand.

'Nigel Bechstein!' he bellowed. 'We spoke last week about Daniel Bourne.'

'Oh, did we?' She sounded as though she had not the remotest idea who Daniel Bourne was.

'He won the Anthea Gordon prize last year, you remember,' Nigel persisted. Millicent remembered only too well the rather pushy young man on the phone, who had tried to talk her into giving Daniel his big break. Prize winner or not, they both knew that Daniel was not star material. He was undoubtedly good-looking, and quite a good actor, but it was a mystery to Nigel how he'd managed to win the much coveted prize. He was almost too well spoken, too stolid, too reliable – staunch even – a thoroughly nice chap. Nigel suspected he'd won as much for his popularity as anything else and guessed he would make a good company member and perhaps a valuable character actor when he was older.

For the moment, he lacked the vital element so necessary to the star: danger. It was an indefinable quality which Nigel thought might have something to do with sexual energy. Charisma or presence many people called it, but though Daniel, a great bull of a man, certainly had a sort of presence, he would never set the stage alight. Millicent James was no fool and he hadn't succeeded in selling Daniel to her.

'How's it going?' he asked, making the most of the opportunity. She was at present casting a mammoth project, to be directed for the Old Vic by the great Sir Alex Taylor and ultimately filmed for television. Any actor's engagement in the project would last at least a year, and the artistic and financial rewards would be great; the competition correspondingly awesome. To get a client actually seen for a part was almost considered an accolade in itself.

'We're still seeing lots of people,' she replied airily. Lying cow, Nigel thought to himself, you're seeing an extremely select handful.

'Have you got a drink?' he asked, ignoring the snub.

'No, but I think someone's getting me one,' and she looked around, obviously becoming bored with the conversation.

'Allow me,' said Nigel. 'Let me guess,' he said winningly. 'G & T, am I right?'

'Yes,' she replied, looking mildly irritated. Before she could stop him, Nigel pushed his way to the bar and bought the drink. When he returned she was talking to Felix Lamont, entrepreneur extraordinary, whose next production Millicent was keen to cast. 'Oh, thanks,' she said in an off-hand way, sticking her hand out for the drink and returning to her conversation. Nigel hung around for a moment or two, looking at their backs, but it became clear that she had no intention of introducing him.

'What's the play tonight?' he heard her ask.

I just told you, it's *The Changeling*, you rude bitch, thought Nigel. So, quite obviously, Daniel didn't have a snowball's chance in hell, although she'd said at one point that he could be shortlisted. Keeping her options open, he supposed. Damn! And she'd turned down all their other suggestions as well. The encounter, which had seemed to start so well, had put him in a bad mood. He hated these dos. Always the same old faces. Everyone jockeying for position. And he had a lifetime of them ahead of him.

Nigel indulged himself for a moment in his favourite reverie. He was sitting behind an enormous desk, somewhere in the West End, and he was on the phone to Millicent James or someone like her. No. Millicent herself, he decided. Yes, he was talking to Millicent, and he was giving her a very hard time over one of his clients whom she wanted desperately. The money she was offering was going up and up, and he was still saying 'no'. He finally said yes at an outrageous figure, got the billing he wanted and a percentage of the box-office.

He sighed in ecstasy. His day would come, he'd have Millicent on her bloody knees to him. A shrill bell jolted him back to reality. People were starting to surge towards the auditorium doors. The money for the theatre had been raised by an appeal, launched by famous former pupils, and although small it was well equipped. For several years the Academy had joined forces with a major art school which specialized in theatre design, and whose pupils designed, made and painted both the scenery and the costumes for its student productions. As a result the standard was extremely high; the actors were spurred on by the knowledge that their costumes had been specially designed for them, and the art students by the knowledge that their work would be seen in performance and not merely in an exhibition or portfolio.

As was the fashion, the curtain was already up when the audience took their seats, so the set was visible, giving any interested director plenty of time to examine the designer's work. The set for *The Changeling* was impressive: highly stylized and very simple, with a sharply raked dull-pewter floor. Sinister looming arches brooded menacingly, setting the mood for the tragedy, while a single strategically placed chair, in an ornate rococo style, was draped with brilliant purple shot silk. The audience gradually seated themselves, and murmurs of approval could be heard amid the buzz of conversation that filled the auditorium. The level of chatter was high enough to put even more fear into the already thumping hearts of the nervous hopefuls backstage, who were waiting to go on and able to hear the babble from the audience over the Tannoy system.

Nigel Bechstein found his seat, sat down and began to study the cast list. He wondered if any among these unknown names would prove to have that elusive star quality that he sought. Then the house lights were lowered. Harpsichord music – violent and ominous – echoed over the empty stage. The play began. Two actors, not entirely at their ease, came onstage first to set the scene. They were followed by two servants, who were rather better. Then the girl playing the heroine, Beatrice Joanna, appeared with her waiting woman, and Nigel felt the first tingle of excitement. The actress who played Beatrice Joanna was small and slight with a pale intense face and abundant, dark-auburn hair drawn back into a snood that showed off her high cheek-bones. Even before she had spoken a line, she had a riveting presence that made Nigel sit up and take notice. He watched her eagerly, waiting to hear her first speech. Eventually it came.

BEATRICE: *You are a scholar, sir.*
ALSEMERO: *A weak one say.*
BEATRICE: *Which of the sciences is this love you speak of?*
ALSEMERO: *From your tongue, I take it to be music. . .*

Nigel agreed. Music indeed. She looked lovely and she had a lovely voice. As the play progressed he realized that she also had spirit, intelligence and vulnerability. By the interval Nigel knew that he had found his star. He had forgotten totally about Millicent James and it was only when he saw her in the bar that he thought to himself: You'll be on your knees sooner than you know, Millicent. I am going to represent – here he checked his programme – Miss Leonie O'Brien. She is definitely going to be a star and you are going to beg me for her services.

As the evening wore on he became more and more entranced by the young actress. She grew in confidence at each entrance and, although the lighting was dim, her incandescent presence shone through every scene. He was determined to get her – to represent her – and as soon as the show was over, he fought his way out of the auditorium.

The theatre had no stage door, so he was obliged to wait in the bar until she finally emerged through the pass door from the backstage area.

Nigel had consumed a fair amount of brandy by the time Leonie O'Brien appeared, looking pale and ethereal in a flowing garment of silvery crushed velvet. Her loveliness took his breath away and he thought, in a rare moment of fancy, that she resembled nothing less than some Celtic goddess. Nigel Bechstein never admitted it to himself, but the truth was that he fell in love with Leonie that night. It wasn't simply her looks, it was her air of vulnerability, as though she were in need of protection from a harsh world. Over the years he would keep a special place in his heart for her and, as he watched her standing wide-eyed, receiving with shy grace the fervent congratulations of her well-wishers, he felt he would do anything he could to help her.

Now he moved quickly to her side, pushing his way through the crowd. There was not a moment to be lost.

'Miss O'Brien, I thought your performance tonight was magnificent. I should like to represent you, but first may I buy you a drink?'

Leonie looked startled at his sudden approach. 'Good heavens!' she exclaimed, smiling enchantingly.

'Nigel Bechstein,' he said in a more abrupt manner than usual, giving her his hand. 'So, may I buy you a drink?'

'Certainly. I'm desperate for one!' She widened her eyes as she spoke and he realized that they were green, as deep and changeable as the sea.

Ignoring the people around her he took her arm and steered her towards the bar. She went with him, unresisting, and he sensed that she was drained by the emotional demands of her performance. A moment later, handing her the orange juice she requested, he sat her down in one of the few available seats. 'Now then, Miss O'Brien,' he said in his most persuasive tones. 'I am from Hodge and Flowers Personal Management, and I want you to join us.'

'You don't waste time, Mr Bechstein.'

'What's the point, Miss O'Brien? You're a very fine actress. I believe you can become a star. I'd like to help you to get there.'

Leonie gasped. 'Do you really think so?'

'I wouldn't stick my neck out if I didn't,' he replied.

Her eyes were shining. 'I don't care about being a star, Mr Bechstein, but I do want to be a very fine actress.' She spoke with a quiet intensity.

'So you'll consider joining us?'

'I can't.' She looked down at her drink.

'You already have an agent?' He was surprised. There had been no word on the grapevine of anyone having been picked up from the Academy as yet.

'No.' Her head drooped even further.

'Miss O'Brien. Is something wrong?' His voice was concerned. When Leonie finally looked up at him, her eyes were brimming over with tears.

'Mr Bechstein, you've been very kind. I appreciate your offer, more than I can say. But I can't join you now. If I came to you in six months' time, would you still be prepared to take me on?' She gazed at him beseechingly.

'Of course I would,' he said, puzzled.

'Thank you so much,' she said fervently. 'You don't know what this means to me.' The tears began to course down her cheeks. 'I'm sorry,' she gazed at him with a look of helpless appeal, 'I can't . . .' Abruptly, she stood up, thrusting back her chair, then before Nigel could speak she was gone, disappearing into the crowd. Nigel, astonished by her behaviour, sat staring at the half-empty glass she had left behind. In his limited experience, this was not the normal reaction of an unknown actress receiving an offer from one of the most prestigious theatrical agencies in London. It must have all been too much for her, he thought sagely. She seemed to be the sensitive type. No doubt she would contact him as soon as she had time to think things over. He had no idea then that it was to be nearly two years before he heard from her again.

Meanwhile Leonie had rushed to the nearest loo, where she was suddenly and violently sick. This proposal of Nigel's was the key to all her dreams, but there was one major obstacle in the way of accepting it. She was four months pregnant.

3

'Hey, Amanda! I wanna peanut and jello bagel and I wan' it now!'
'Me, too!'
Livingstone van der Velt, Jnr and his younger brother, Winthrop burst into the linen room where Amanda was ironing. They were both dressed in their new American football strip. The huge padded shoulders, helmets and guards looked grotesque on boys of five and eight and, thought Amanda wiping the drops of sweat from her forehead, were totally unsuitable for the heat of Rome in early summer.

After only a week as their temporary nanny, however, nothing surprised Amanda about the van der Velt household. She had found the job through an advertisement in the *Lady* before leaving England, having decided that she ought to try and hold on to as much of Simon's £10,000 as possible. It also made it easier to explain her hurried departure to Beryl, though she had seemed strangely preoccupied when Amanda announced her plan to go abroad for six months or so. She had murmured something about going on holiday herself soon, and perhaps meeting Amanda in Rome. It seemed so improbable that Amanda had not taken a great deal of notice. Beryl had been rather odd since Arnold's death and oddest of all was her extraordinary new hair-do – ridiculous for a woman of her age suddenly to go blonde like that, though Amanda had to admit it looked quite good.

She had been a bit surprised by the ease and speed with which she had got the van der Velt job – a quick telephone conversation had done the trick – but now she understood perfectly why the previous nanny had departed in such a hurry. There was nothing in particular wrong with the van der Velts themselves. Livingstone van der Velt, a plump, thirty-ish Californian, was the only son of extremely wealthy parents, with an enormous trust fund that enabled him to indulge in his love of fine art. He bought and sold paintings all over the world, and his current interest in Italian old masters had brought him to Rome for a year. As well as having a huge unearned income, he appeared to be both shrewd and knowledgeable on his subject and was making a great deal of money. His wife, Harmony, was a tall, fey brunette with a wealth of tangled curls, whom he had met while studying Art History at Berkeley. She had a tense, lean face and a serious manner – Amanda soon learned that she was a keen student of Eastern philosophy, forever finding a new religion to answer the big questions of life.

The problem was that neither parent appeared to have any control over their children, a pair of odious little tearaways, and Harmony in particular seemed utterly oblivious to their appalling behaviour. Amanda was feeling more and more sympathy for their previous nanny, and had begun to wonder how long she herself would last.

'Hey, come on, lady, I'm hungry,' said Livingstone Jnr, practising a line he'd heard on a new cop video and idly kicking the base of the ironing board with his new boots.

'Me too,' echoed Winthrop, who copied him relentlessly.

'You've only just had your breakfast, so shut up . . . and don't do that in the house,' said Amanda irritably, catching the football which Livingstone threw at her and slinging it back at him. He caught it and started to run around the room. Winthrop ran after him, screaming with delight. Livingstone tripped and the two tumbled into a basket piled high with clean clothes that Amanda had just ironed.

'Stop it! Stop it at once! You little beasts!' Amanda slammed down the iron, grabbed each one by the arm and yanked them away from the linen.

'You little bastards! I've just done those! Get out of here and play in the garden!' The children stared at her balefully but did not move.

'Go on, get out or I'll give you a smack!' As Amanda advanced on them menacingly, Harmony appeared in the open doorway.

'Mommy, mommy! Don't let Amanda hurt me!' Livingstone Jnr flew to his mother's side.

'Amanda, honey, what's going on?' Harmony asked mildly.

'I'm sorry Mrs van der Velt, but I've just done this ironing, and it's taken hours,' said Amanda. 'The boys have been very naughty.'

'I told you two to play outside until your pa gets home,' said Harmony gently.

'OK, mom,' said Livingstone Jnr, for once taking notice of his parent, much to Amanda's fury.

They disappeared into the adjoining kitchen and their screams and yells could be heard as they raced out into the garden. Soon there was the sound of a football being bounced back and forth, and Amanda heard a crash which sounded like one of the flower-filled stone urns which decorated the villa's terrace. Little sods, she thought, I hope they fall in the pool and drown. She started picking up the scattered laundry and Harmony bent to help her.

'They're not the easiest children, Mrs van der Velt,' said Amanda, by way of an explanation for her threat. She knew that Harmony strongly disapproved of corporal punishment, and she did not want to lose her job quite so soon. 'Thank you,' she added as Harmony neatly replaced some shorts in the basket.

'It's my pleasure,' replied Harmony ignoring, as she often did, Amanda's remark. Amanda sometimes thought that she went through life ignoring anything that she found potentially upsetting or distasteful. She resumed her chore. Harmony watched her for a moment, then said quietly, 'Why do I get such a strong sense of drama from you?' She gazed at Amanda intensely. 'Do you have some connection with the theatre?' She pronounced it the-ater.

Amanda hesitated, then said, 'Well, actually my mother is an actress.'

'Oh really? I guess I might have known.' Harmony sounded only mildly interested as if, her intuition confirmed, her mind was already drifting on to a new track.

Before she could float away entirely, Amanda grasped the opportunity. 'Yes, she is. By the way, you don't know anyone in the theatre here . . . or the film business, do you, Mrs van der Velt?'

The van der Velts had a constant stream of rich and well-travelled friends dropping in on them in Rome, and with their Californian connections it seemed to Amanda quite likely that someone connected with the movies would turn up sooner or later. In her limited free time she had not got very far in tracking down Leonie O'Brien; an introduction to somebody in the film world might make her task a lot easier. She did not hold out very much hope, however, so she could hardly believe her luck when Harmony replied, 'Sure, honey, why Julius and Mamie King are our guests at dinner tonight. Julius is Senior Vice-President of Global Pictures. They're great friends of Livingstone's parents.' Without waiting for a reply, she drifted out of the room, humming quietly to herself, leaving Amanda thinking furiously. A movie mogul in this very house – it was almost too good to be true. He would be sure know all about the film industry in Rome. Now all she had to do was work out a way of meeting him, and then ask a few pertinent questions.

Relieved to find herself on her own at last, Amanda finished the ironing and laid it neatly in a cupboard. Then she hurried to her room where something else that might lead her to her mother was waiting for her. Earlier in the week she had discovered an old copy of *Hello!* magazine at a local newsagent which sold foreign newspapers and magazines. Amanda enjoyed the magazine, and had asked the newsagent to keep a copy for her every week. She had stolen ten minutes to go out and collect the latest issue that very morning, and to her astonished delight the cover featured Leonie boasting, 'Leonie O'Brien invites us to look around her Rome apartment.' It was a heaven-sent opportunity, but she had been so busy with the boys until now that she not had a chance even to glance at it.

She ran up the stairs and flung herself on her bed, grabbing *Hello!* from the table. She opened it eagerly and turned immediately to the pictures of Leonie. They showed her on the set of *Swords at Sunset* in her new role of producer, and in her magnificent Rome apartment with her 'close friend', Rob Fenton, the star of the film. Amanda studied the photographs carefully, paying particular attention to the close-ups of Rob. She knew her mother had a boyfriend, but she had vaguely assumed him to be someone of the same age or older. Now she was amazed to see that Rob was young, and very handsome – she had never seen a more attractive man. What was he doing with a middle-aged woman like Leonie? Admittedly she was very beautiful, but she wasn't exactly young any more. Certainly not young enough for him.

It wasn't right, thought Amanda resentfully, that Leonie should be leading a life like this. If she'd been a proper mother, if she'd taken her responsibilities seriously and hadn't abandoned her daughter, it could have been Amanda herself living in a beautiful apartment with a sexy man like this Rob Fenton. Leonie didn't deserve all this, besides she was too old; whereas she, Amanda, had so much more to offer. She had all her mother's looks, but she was young as well. If Rob Fenton was to see her, surely he would prefer her to Leonie? Amanda had come to Rome with the intention of finding and confronting her mother. Now, as she studied the pictures of Leonie and Rob again, she began to wonder if it might not be very interesting to meet her boyfriend too.

As Amanda turned the magazine's pages, she spotted a small picture of the *palazzo* in which Leonie and Rob had their apartment. The article said that it was in the heart of Rome, close to the Piazza Barberini. That was only just across the Villa Borghese park from the fashionable Parioli district where the van der Velts' villa was situated. She decided to take a trip over there on her next free afternoon and see if she could find it. What with the Kings coming to dinner that evening, things were now going better than she could ever have dared to hope.

Thanks to horrible Livingstone Jnr, Amanda finally found the perfect excuse to be lurking in the vicinity of the front door when Julius T. King and his wife Mamie arrived. That afternoon the boys had been mercifully occupied for a couple of hours playing video games in the study, one of the rooms which opened off the villa's big, square, pillared hall. Later on, when Amanda had finally managed to drag them off to bed, Livingstone decided that under no circumstances was he going to sleep before playing one more video game on the television in their bedroom. The one he wanted was, naturally, downstairs in the study. Normally Amanda would have told him to shut up and stop being a pain in the neck, but as it was nearly seven-thirty, the time she knew the Kings were due to arrive, she decided to indulge him for once.

Without hurrying, she went downstairs to the study and began to search, rather slowly, through the pile of video games scattered on the floor, while listening intently for the clang of the bell that would announce the arrival of visitors. Sure enough, there it was, followed by the clicking heels of the maid, Patrizia. Then there was the sound of voices as Mr and Mrs van der Velt emerged from the drawing-room to meet their guests.

'Hi, Harmony. Oh my, don't you look adorable,' she heard a woman's voice say.

'Hey, Van, this place is really something else,' said a man. 'It's straight out of the Renaissance – or do I mean *Sunset Boulevard*?'

A burst of laughter followed his remark as Amanda, picking up the video she wanted, which she had in fact found five minutes earlier, strolled out of the study door. She found the two couples exchanging greetings in the centre of the hall. 'Oh, I'm so sorry,' she said in a confused way, making sure that everyone knew she was there. 'I didn't realize . . . I was just finding this video for Livingstone.'

She held out the cassette as evidence, knowing that the van der Velts' democratic principles would not allow them to ignore her once she had made her presence known. 'Ah, Amanda,' said Harmony, looking less than delighted to see her. 'Mamie, Julius, this is Amanda, the boys' new nanny. Amanda, I'd like you to meet our very dear friends Mr and Mrs King.'

She began to move away, obviously expecting Amanda to continue on upstairs, but Amanda had other ideas. 'I'm delighted to meet you,' she breathed, gazing at the Kings and especially Julius T., a stout, grey-haired man whose small shrewd eyes had lit up at the sight of such a pretty girl. 'Mrs van der Velt tells me you're something terribly important in the film business. That must be so exciting.'

It was blatant flattery, but it seemed to work. Julius King took her hand, a benevolent expression on his creased face. 'Don't tell me you'd like to be in the movies, little lady. I sure can't recommend it, not when it gives you ulcers like mine.' The others laughed.

'Oh no,' Amanda looked shy. 'I wouldn't dream of it. It's just that I love the cinema and I'm terribly interested in how films are made.'

'Well, sweetheart, if we were in LA right now, I'd love to arrange for you to take our studio tour, but . . .' Julius hesitated as he looked at his wife, a plump and pleasant-faced matron, who smiled warmly at Amanda and took over.

'Julius means, honey, that we're only here in Rome on money business. We won't be going anywhere near Cinecittà.'

'Oh, what a shame.' Amanda's face fell. She knew that Cinecittà was the name of the Rome film studios. An introduction there from someone like Julius T. King would have been ideal for her.

'Look here, if you're keen to meet people in the movie business, why don't you go somewhere where the youngsters hang out?' Julius turned to Mamie, 'What's the name of that restaurant Enrico told us about? The one the young crowd all eat at nowadays?'

'La Mosca,' said Mamie. 'It's a really cute place in Trastevere.'

'Amanda, honey' said Harmony, in a voice which had an unusual edge to its sweetness. 'Don't you think Livingstone will be wanting his video?'

'Oh, of course.' Amanda was only too happy to take the hint now she had some information she could use. She gave Julius a brilliant smile, Mamie a more restrained one. 'Thank you so much, Mr and Mrs King. I hope you enjoy your stay in Rome.' Then she bounded up the stairs, busily planning her next move.

La Mosca was in the basement of one of the beautiful but crumbling medieval buildings in Rome's Trastevere quarter, once the poorest part of Rome and now colourful and seedy in almost equal measure. In the evening meals were served outside in its pretty flower-filled courtyard, but during the day the intense heat drove diners inside to the cool of the interior. The décor was basic – the walls whitewashed and cracked, the floor-boards bare – but the food was excellent and cheap and the *trattoria* was never empty. It was a favourite haunt of actors, writers and artists, and had quickly been discovered by the cast and crew of *Swords at Sunset*.

As Amanda made her way down the slippery stone stairs to the basement, the unmistakable pungent aroma of Italian cooking, with its base notes of garlic, olive oil, and oregano, rose to meet her. The room was packed. The noise deafening. Amanda began to panic. There was no room at all; she was a fool not to have booked. She hovered on the bottom step, an uncertain expression on her face.

'Buongiorno, signorina,' exclaimed a cheerful middle-aged waiter as he whisked by her, bearing a trayful of food high above the heads of the customers. 'Un momento, per favore.' Amanda waited obediently, but as she looked around she couldn't possibly imagine how he was going to find room for her; the place was bursting at the seams.

She watched the waiter who had spoken to her stop at a long table where a crowd of good-looking youngsters of about her own age were sitting. He muttered something to one of them, a slim, dark boy who looked vaguely familiar. The boy glanced at her, smiled and nodded emphatically. When the waiter returned to Amanda he was grinning.

'Va bene, signorina?' he asked and, without waiting for a reply continued, 'Per una?'

'Si, grazie,' replied Amanda timidly. She followed him to the table where the dark young man was sitting. He rose gallantly as she approached and gestured her to an empty seat beside him. 'Ciao, signorina, come sta?' he asked, his brown eyes lively.

'Bene, grazie,' replied Amanda.

'Ah, Americana!' he exclaimed.

'Non, Inglesa,' corrected Amanda.

'I am Giovanni Frescaldi,' he said, settling down next to her.

'Amanda Willoughby,' she replied, holding out her hand. To her alarm and embarrassment he took it and kissed it.

'Allo Amanda. I am happy to meet you.' Then one of the girls on his other side asked him a question and he was off in a flood of Italian, of which with her limited vocabulary she could pick up only a few words. They seemed to be mentioning Cinecittà quite a lot. Could it be possible that she had managed to find some film actors, as Julius King had promised?

The waiter was at her side, asking for her order. Amanda looked helplessly at the menu, which she had not even begun to study, but Giovanni came to her aid. 'You must have the minestrone, signorina,' he said decidedly. 'It is the best.'

'You speak very good English, Giovanni,' said Amanda, smiling at him. There really was something very familiar about him. Who on earth was it that he looked like? 'Are you a student?'

Giovanni laughed. 'No no no, I am an actor. We all are. We work on an English film, so we must speak some English.'

'Oh, how exciting,' said Amanda, genuinely thrilled by this information. 'And what is this film?' She held her breath.

'It is called *Swords at Sunset*,' said Giovanni proudly, 'and I am stand-in for Rob Fenton.' Amanda took a gulp of wine, trying to hide her excitement. Of course, Rob Fenton. That was who Giovanni had reminded her of, though he was younger and darker than Rob had appeared in the photographs.

Giovanni clearly expected her to be impressed by his job, which of course she was, although not quite in the way he imagined. 'That's wonderful,' she said admiringly. 'You must be very good.' She was, she thought, playing the stage-struck fan to perfection.

'You are actress too?' broke in one of their companions at the table, a pretty girl with streaked blonde hair who had been listening to their conversation with interest.

Amanda shook her head regretfully.

'No, but I would love to be.'

'But you must visit us on the set!' said Giovanni with enthusiasm. 'Maybe you will be discovered.' There was general laughter at this remark. Amanda laughed too; yes, maybe she would be 'discovered'.

'Oh, really. I'd love that,' she breathed. 'When could I come?'

'When are you free?' asked Giovanni.

'I work for some Americans, looking after their children. I have some free time when the boys are at school.'

'Oh, Americanos. They pay well, yes?' he asked with keen interest.

'My sister Sophia is a cook. She want very much to work for Americanos.'

'Not bad,' replied Amanda. 'I could ask if any of their friends need a cook if you like.'

'That is kind, signorina Amanda,' Giovanni smiled at her winningly.

At that moment her soup arrived. It did not look like any minestrone she had seen before but it smelt wonderful. She took a spoonful. It was quite delicious. As she ate, the others started to talk among themselves again, chattering busily in Italian. Amanda began to follow a little of their conversation, and realized it was gossip from the film set. Leonie's name was mentioned but, frustratingly, she could not understand what they were saying about her.

After a while Giovanni spoke to her in English again. 'These Americanos you work for, where do they live?' he asked tentatively.

'Parioli,' said Amanda.

Giovanni whistled. 'Very expensive,' he said. 'Very rich people there.'

Amanda took the hint. 'I really will ask them if they know of any jobs for your sister,' she said earnestly.

Giovanni smiled brilliantly. 'And I really will make sure you come to the studio and see us,' he replied.

'When can I come?' asked Amanda.

'When is your next free day?'

Amanda thought quickly. 'Thursday.'

'Good. We see you Thursday at Cinecittà.'

'Where do I go?' asked Amanda nervously. Cinecittà could be a big place.

'Ask for me at reception at the main entrance,' said Giovanni confidently. 'Giovanni Frescaldi who is working on *Swords at Sunset*,' he added, with an arrogant lift of his head.

'Why aren't you working today?' asked Amanda, scraping up the last of her soup.

'They are shooting close-ups of the heroine and the villain,' said the blonde girl. 'No crowd artists required,' and she pulled a face.

Amanda had to try one more question. 'Do Miss O'Brien and

Mr Fenton eat here sometimes'

'Oh, yes, very much,' replied Giovanni.

'Why aren't they here today?' Looks were exchanged around the table followed by a few smothered giggles.

'When they have a day off, they usually spend it in bed,' Giovanni explained simply. Amanda had a fleeting memory of Arnold and Beryl, and thought again how different her natural mother's lifestyle was from that of her adoptive parents.

Rob Fenton knew his way around both the world and women. In his twenty-five years he had had considerable experience of both; his good looks and easy charm had seen to that. He was a good actor and a good lover and, with a career on the up and a beautiful woman at his disposal, the world was his oyster and he intended to make the most of it.

He wove skilfully through the frenetic Rome traffic in the silver Mercedes, his most prized possession, which he had bought with the proceeds of a television series he had made the previous year. The breeze ruffled his dark hair, and he smiled with pleasure as he thought about Leonie and their recent love-making. Leonie was good for him: good for his confidence, good for his image. She had class and being known as her lover was doing his career no harm at all. Before her, there had been a string of pretty girls, none of whom had lasted more than a few weeks. Rob had always shied away from involvement. He was young, there were so many beautiful women in the world, and they seemed to fall for him so easily. 'Why settle down,' he had always said, 'when you can have so much fun playing the field?' Sure, sometimes the girls themselves didn't see it that way. There had been one or two uncomfortable moments, some tearful accusations that he was a cold-hearted, self-centred bastard. But at the end of the day they always saw his point of view about not getting tied down, and if they didn't it really didn't matter too much. There was always another one waiting.

Leonie was different. She wouldn't stand for that sort of treatment – no way. He was well aware that to let her catch him even looking at another woman in any but the most casual way was to court disaster. It had been hard, but he had been faithful during their year together because she was worth it. Well, almost faithful. He'd flirted a bit, but that surely didn't count.

She was a powerful lady, Leonie, in more ways than one. Part of it was her age, part her personality and the effects of years of success. She never came the big star with him – he wouldn't have stood for it – but now and again the way she behaved couldn't help reminding him that she'd had her first big success in the theatre when he was only just out of nappies. It was at times like that he started to wonder how long their relationship could last. Terrific as she was, you couldn't ignore the fact that she had already passed her prime while his was yet to come.

Impatiently Rob sounded his horn as the car in front of him came to a halt. Bloody Rome traffic, it was always the same. However long you allowed yourself to get anywhere, the jams always got you in the end. Rob glanced in his wing mirror. There was a moped coming up just behind him, weaving its way through the stationary traffic. He watched it idly. That was the only way sensible way to travel in Rome, if you were brave enough. The driver was a pretty girl with long red hair. She looked vaguely familiar. Hadn't he already seen her, or another girl very like her, outside the apartment? Rob smiled to himself. Rome was full of pretty girls – it was one of the things he liked about the city – and quite a lot of them had red hair. The car in front of him began to move and he revved his engine, eager to get away. When he looked again, the girl had disappeared.

By the time he arrived at the studio twenty minutes later, he had forgotten all about her, but after two sightings he recognized her again immediately when he saw her with his stand-in, Giovanni. He had come on set to rehearse a scene when he noticed the two of them, standing to one side, talking earnestly. Intrigued, Rob strolled over to get a close look at her for the first time. She was a very attractive girl indeed. He wondered where Giovanni had picked her up.

'Are you going to keep all the pretty girls to yourself, John?' he said as he approached, smiling at the girl. Rob had addressed Giovanni by the English version of his name from the first day of the shoot and it had stuck. Quite a few members of the largely British crew had taken up the habit and Giovanni now responded easily to both names. He looked at

Rob and grinned. 'This is a new friend of mind,' he said carefully. 'Amanda is an au pair.'

Amanda bristled slightly at this reference to her lowly status. Not for long, she thought. One day soon she'd be up there alongside him in front of the cameras, a successful, sought-after actress.

Rob studied Amanda with interest as he held out his hand. 'Rob Fenton,' he said. She was certainly very pretty and, oddly, he couldn't help being reminded of Leonie. It was partly the colouring, of course, but Leonie must have looked not unlike this girl when she was the same age.

'Amanda is a great admirer of Miss O'Brien's, Rob,' explained Giovanni. 'She wanted so much to meet her . . .'

'I've seen all her films,' enthused Amanda, 'I think she's wonderful.'

'Funnily enough, so do I,' said Rob with a sly grin. 'You're a similar type, you know,' he added, candidly looking her up and down. Amanda pretended not to notice how his gaze lingered on her breasts, though the thin T-shirt she was wearing suddenly seemed a very flimsy covering indeed.

'Do you really think so. I'd love to meet her sometime,' she breathed.

'I said to Amanda that it will be all right if she comes to the studio, but of course today, Miss O'Brien is not here.' Giovanni sounded apologetic.

'Right, let's take a look at the next one,' called out Dave, the first Assistant Director.

'You must pay us another visit, Amanda.' Rob treated her to a smouldering look that he had perfected over the years.

'I'm sure Leonie would love to meet you.' Privately he doubted this. The girl was far too young and attractive.

'Mr Fenton, please!' bawled the Assistant Director, watching them from afar and disapproving. Dave Kelly was very fond of Leonie. They had worked together several times during her career, and she had asked specifically for him for this, her first picture as producer. He knew that when Leonie wasn't around Rob found it hard to resist chatting up a pretty girl and sometimes, he suspected, it went rather further than that. He didn't like to see it and besides he didn't want Rob distracted from his work. So far everything was going well, but with someone who had as little experience in films as Rob Fenton, you never knew.

'Sorry, got to go,' said Rob moving off. 'See you again, I hope.' He gave Amanda a quizzical smile and sauntered back to the set.

The rehearsal bell rang loudly. 'I think perhaps I'd better go now,' Amanda whispered to Giovanni. He too had noticed the way Rob had looked at her and thought it a good idea to get her out of the way. He liked Rob, but he had no illusions about him and women.

'It's all right, I can find my way out,' said Amanda to Giovanni as he escorted her off the set.

'Sure? You won't forget about Sophia, yes? Tell them she's very good girl,' Giovanni laughed as he waved goodbye.

Amanda hated being reminded of her current employment, but it was not for long, she told herself as she climbed on to her moped and sped away. Her plans were beginning to fall into place very neatly. It was going to be a particular pleasure to seduce Rob Fenton.

Tony Sneller was a journalist. The type of journalist Rob would have described as a scumbag. He made his living probing other people's wounds and prying into the personal tragedies which could be exploited, written up, and turned into saleable copy at a moment's notice. No sex scandal was too sordid, no disaster too horrific, but Sneller would mangle, embellish and sensationalize it until it fitted his sleazy requirements.

It was Sneller who was awaiting Leonie's arrival for lunch at La Callandra, one of Rome's smartest restaurants. Rome, on his first visit there, left him unmoved; its beauty and history meant nothing to him. The furnace-like heat did not suit his short, overweight build and he was sweating profusely, even in the air-conditioned restaurant.

His brief from his editor was simple. Dig the dirt on Leonie O'Brien and Rob Fenton.

'What's the angle?' he had asked.

'Don't be so fucking stupid. She's got big tits, and she's living with a good-looking guy, who's young enough to be her son. Can you imagine fucking your own mother?'

Sneller shuddered. It was bad enough fucking his own wife – a favour he seldom bestowed on her except when he returned from a week-long drinking binge, and then only to keep her quiet. She looked like the back of a number 93 bus, but he did not relish the thought of looking after himself again. He'd tried it once, when he first took up journalism as an apprentice on the *South London Bugle*, and had found it impossible to keep pace with the dirty plates and glasses and the ever-growing piles of filthy clothes. And the constant diet of baked beans and Indian take-aways had played havoc with his insides. He had looked around and found Mary working part-time in the local launderette, tied to an invalid mother whom she could only leave for a few hours in order to earn enough money to supplement a widow's pension and sick-benefit allowance.

Still, the interview with Leonie was worth the pain of a week in Rome. It was one he had long fancied. She had always turned him and his newspaper down in the past, but this time they had resorted to subterfuge. Miss O'Brien was asked if she would be interested in doing an in-depth interview on her new role as producer for one of the classier Sunday magazine colour supplements. The promised interviewer was Justin Hamilton-Brown, the supplement's top feature writer, who had recently returned from Hollywood where he had done a brilliant piece on Glenn Close. A photo session was also requested. The idea had worked brilliantly, but Tony was beginning to feel uncomfortable. It was one thing setting this meeting up, but what would Leonie's reaction be when she found him instead of Hamilton-Brown? He had heard that Leonie had a bit of a temper and he didn't relish being on the receiving end of it. He ordered another vodka to steady his nerves.

The vodka arrived at the same time as Leonie, looking cool and elegant in an ice-blue linen suit. He rose unsteadily to his feet to greet her and waited apprehensively as she was ushered over to the dark corner in which he was sitting. Heads turned as she walked towards him.

'Miss O'Brien,' he said in his most ingratiating manner.

The waiter bowed, pulled out a chair for her and waited for her to sit down. She stopped and stared accusingly.

'You're not Justin Hamilton-Brown. It's Sneller, isn't it? From the *Globe*?' she made the names sound like an insult.

'Temporarily attached to the *Chronicle*,' said Sneller quickly, 'you know we're part of the same group.' Leonie continued to look unimpressed.

'I'm sorry about this mix-up,' Sneller went on, 'I know you were expecting Justin, but he's been held up in India and the editor has sent me on ahead to do some groundwork.' His explanation was, he knew, clumsy. He was flustered by Leonie's abrupt manner.

'I see,' she said, sitting down reluctantly.

The waiter bowed again and Leonie ordered a mineral water.

'Why didn't someone contact me?' she demanded, staring hard at Sneller.

Tony Sneller clasped his vodka and prayed for inspiration.

'The *Chronicle* is very keen on this article. They know what a tight schedule you have, so the idea was that we do the photo-session immediately and, rather than mess you around, you tell me what subjects you want to discuss. Then if Justin is held up any more he can do the interview by phone once I've briefed him. Then we can wack it out on the first Sunday of next month.' He took a swig of vodka.

'I'm not interested in doing an interview on the telephone,' said Leonie. 'They never work. I don't mind doing the photographs some time this week, but I thought the whole point about the Hamilton-Brown profile was that it's always based on an in depth, one-to-one interview.'

'It is, normally.' Tony loosened his tie nervously. 'It's just that the timing of this one's a bit critical.'

'What's wrong with the following month?'

'He's already lined up the Prime Minister.' For once in his life, Tony was speaking the truth.

In spite of herself Leonie was impressed and Tony followed up his advantage. 'We alternate each month, you see: actor, politician, fashion designer, writer, philanthropist, whatever, you know the sort of thing.'

Leonie softened slightly. 'Yes, I do see your problem. Thank you,' she said to the waiter who had just brought her drink, and handed them both a menu. She glanced briefly at the list of dishes on the ornate cream card in front of her.

'I'm eating out tonight, so I'll have something very light.'

'With Mr Fenton?' asked Tony, his ferret instincts making him careless.

Leonie looked at him sharply, immediately on her guard. She ignored the question. 'I'll have a mozzarella salad. What about you?' she asked politely.

Tony cursed himself. He would have to be more subtle than this. 'Oh, lasagne, I think, and some of that garlic bread.'

Leonie could see why he was in such rotten shape.

'What will you have as a starter, Miss O'Brien? May I call you Leonie?' he asked.

Again she ignored him. 'The mozzarella will be fine, thank you.'

'That's how you keep your lovely figure, I expect,' Tony went on brightly, ignoring the snub.

'Probably,' said Leonie.

When the waiter had taken their order, Leonie studied the man opposite her. Why was he so unappealing? After all, he was clean enough, indeed the smell of aftershave was almost overpowering, and he was wearing an expensive suit even if it didn't quite fit properly. But there was still something basically shabby about him and, though he was probably only in his late thirties, he already had an unpleasantly blotched and puffy drinker's face.

'So, how can I help you, Mr Sneller.' Her use of his surname was intended to indicate that there was no possibility of putting the interview on a more intimate footing – if he was capable of taking such a hint, which Leonie doubted.

Tony Sneller braced himself, and took another swig of vodka. 'Trevor Grantley, my editor, would like to look at Leonie O'Brien, actress turned producer. So we need your thoughts on the difficulties you've encountered while making this transition.' He was stretching his exhausted powers of invention to the limit in a staunch effort to gain some credibility in her eyes.

'That shouldn't be a problem,' said Leonie coolly.

'So,' he continued, 'so, we would like some shots of you on set, chatting to the actors, the technicians, etcetera.'

'That's fine.'

'Then, er, some shots of you relaxing in your apartment, with Mr Fenton, of course.'

Leonie narrowed her eyes, smelling a rat. 'Why does he have to be involved?' she demanded.

Tony downed the last of his vodka. 'Well, he is the star of your picture, and obviously we hope to get shots of you together on the set as well.'

'I see,' Leonie considered his explanation. It did not seem unreasonable.

'How are you finding working with Mr Fenton?' He could not help himself.

'It's very enjoyable,' she replied carefully, 'although obviously I don't see that much of him. I spend most of my time in the production office.'

'Has it put any pressure on your personal relationship?'

'That's none of your business,' she said calmly.

Tony decided he might as well go for broke. 'Well, after all,' he said in an insinuating tone, 'you're the boss, on and off set, aren't you?'

 Leonie stood up abruptly. 'Cameriere,' she called.

The waiter immediately appeared at her side. 'Si, signora?'

'I'm afraid I am unwell. I'm going home. Mr Sneller will have my mozzarella salad. He appears to be eating for two anyway.'

'Very good, signora.' He pulled back her chair to let her out. 'I am very sorry.'

'So am I,' said Leonie.

'We will see you again, signora?'

'Most certainly,' she said. 'But in more pleasant company I trust,' she added, with a vicious glance at Sneller.

Safely outside in the Roman sunlight, she hailed a cab and sank down on to the back seat with a sigh of relief. God preserve me from the bloody press, she thought savagely, as it pulled away from the kerb.

Inside the restaurant, Tony Sneller was unperturbed by the turn of events. She had, he decided, been unnecessarily touchy; undoubtedly all was not well with her young boyfriend. Yes, there was definitely a story here. After lunch he would ring Trevor and request an extension of his Rome visit. He would then set about doing what he did best, seeking and spreading dirt. He pulled out his notebook and started to write: Leonie and Rob to split? He continued:

LEONIE O'BRIEN, 43, AND HER TOYBOY LOVER, ROB FENTON, 25, ARE READY TO GO THEIR SEPARATE WAYS. FRIENDS HINT THAT GORGEOUS HUNK ROB RESENTS LEONIE'S DOMINEERING WAYS AND INTERFERENCE IN HIS CAREER. LAST NIGHT, THE BUSTY BEAUTY PLEADED WITH HER LUSTY YOUNG STUD TO TRY TO PATCH UP THEIR ROMANCE.

Well satisfied with this beginning, Tony Sneller ordered a bottle of champagne and started on his enormous lunch. He finished with profiteroles smothered in chocolate sauce, washed down with a large brandy, and finally staggered out of the restaurant in the middle of the afternoon. On his return to his hotel he fell asleep on the bed, fully clothed, a happy man.

When Leonie returned to the apartment she kicked off her shoes, then removed her jacket and skirt. She noticed with dismay how crumpled her outfit had become. She loathed Tony Sneller and all his kind, but she hated even that little toad witnessing an exit that was anything less than perfect. She flung the garments down on to a chair, turned on the answering machine, and curled up in a corner of one of the huge cream sofas to listen to her messages. There was one from the studio reminding her of a costume fitting for the following day, another from her agent in London asking her to ring him and then a silence when someone, who obviously disliked speaking to answering machines, had not left a message. The silence continued for fractionally too long and Leonie glanced apprehensively at the machine, as though by watching it she would discover the identity of the caller. Silence. Then a click. Jesus, she thought, it's that bloody Sneller.

'I hate it when they do that, Boris,' she said out loud to a superb modern bronze sculpture of a rearing horse. Rob's cheerful voice, which came on next, was a welcome sound.

'Darling, I'll be finished by 9. I know you've had a wonderful lunch, so how about taking me out to dinner?' Leonie smiled wryly as she heard this. She was starving. 'Everything went OK today. The place is crawling with women – but none of them is a patch on you. I'll tell you all about it later. See you about 9.30, then. Love you.'

Leonie was surprised at the pleasure she felt in hearing his message. She was very much afraid that she might be falling in love with him, even though she had always sworn to herself that she would not let it happen. Early on in the relationship she had been able to convince herself that she would be able to keep a sense of proportion about the two of them. Now she was not so sure. She was beginning to find it hard to contemplate life without Rob; he was becoming necessary to her.

She sighed and rose from the sofa, picking up her skirt and jacket. She felt a little cooler now, and thought she would lie down for a while before making her phone calls. In the relative peace of late afternoon, the ever present din of Rome was surprisingly muted. Then the noise of a moped starting up sounded nearby and Leonie wandered over to the windows. Maybe a dispatch rider had delivered Rob's script amendments for the next day's shoot. She could see nothing, but she decided to go down and ask the concierge if anything had been delivered.

Slipping on her robe, she padded down to the lobby. The fat woman behind the desk smiled at the sight of her and pulled an envelope from a pigeon-hole. It was typewritten, bearing just her name. Obviously not a script. Mildly puzzled, Leonie carried it upstairs, tearing it open as she walked. Then she stopped dead in shock as she pulled out two blank sheets of paper, which sandwiched a single lock of bright auburn hair.

4

Elizabeth Brentford lay by her husband's side staring into the darkness. She could just make out the broad outline of Simon's back as he slept soundly, his breathing even and quiet. She gazed at him for a while. Why did he do it, why the hell did he need to do it? she thought savagely to herself. She had known the moment he had come home. She had been in the kitchen preparing their supper, chopping garlic for a salad dressing with one of her heavy Sabatier knives. He had come over to her and kissed her lightly on the cheek, touching her hair with his hand as he did so. The smell hit her at once, the smell of the other woman: musty, familiar and pungent. The shock of it made her want to lash out at him, but he did not see the look in her eyes. He had turned away quickly, asking her over his shoulder: 'Drink, darling?'

'Yes, please,' she replied, her voice calm, automatically continuing to mince the garlic smaller and smaller. 'Gin and tonic, a large one.'

She wanted to get him away from her. If he touched her again she thought she would scream. When he handed her the drink, she could not bear to take it from him. 'Put it on the side for me,' she said, controlling herself with an effort. 'My hands reek of garlic.' The smell was under his fingernails, partially disguised by soap and aftershave, but unmistakable. Those long, sensitive fingers of his had been dabbling in another woman's cunt . . . again.

After a couple of stiff gins, she found that by the time she sat down to dinner with Simon, she was able to talk to him quite normally. She listened as he droned on about some debate that had taken up most of the day. If he was telling the truth, she thought, when the hell had he had time to go to bed with anyone? Obviously, he was lying. Well next time, she would catch him out. She'd watch the bloody thing on television and see whether he was there or not. There was a cold empty feeling in the pit of her stomach as she watched him lying effortlessly while devouring his lamb cutlets. Yes, she thought, sex makes you hungry.

She kept up the front of wifely concern for the rest of the evening. When he said he was tired and wanted to go to bed early, she agreed with alacrity. Now, as she lay listening to his breathing, she had a sudden urge to put him to the test. She snuggled up closely to him and eased her hand around his body, stroking his chest. He stirred immediately.

'Ah, what is it?' he mumbled. 'What's the matter?'

'I want – I want you to make love to me,' she whispered, moving her hand gradually downwards.

'Oh, for Christ's sake, Liz, not now. It's been a long day.' He turned over and pulled the bedclothes more tightly around him, as though to keep her out. She lay on her back, tears pouring silently down her cheeks. She had tried to steel herself against rejections like this over the years, but sometimes it was very hard. She remembered how, when they were first married, he would make love at any time of the day or night regardless of the amount of work he had done. It hadn't lasted long, though. A sudden spasm of jealous pain shot through her as she thought of the other woman who had taken him away from her. What conscienceless slut was he seeing now, she wondered. She got out of bed abruptly and, putting on her silk négligé, went through to the adjoining bathroom. It seemed very cold as she stood there trembling in the darkness.

'Liz,' came Simon's voice after a few minutes, 'are you all right?'

'Yes. No, no, I'm not all right.' She tried not to sound pathetic but it came out that way.

'What is it? Aren't you well?' He sounded concerned.

'I'm just worried,' she said, playing for time, wondering whether she dared confront him. 'It's – it's that girl.'

'What girl?' Simon sounded wary.

It was easier to lie in the dark. 'You know, the Willoughby girl – your daughter.'

'There's no need to bang on about it. We all know who she is,' he said irritably.

'That's what worries me. Too many people might know.'

Simon sighed heavily.

'Well there's nothing we can do about it at the moment. Come back to bed, Liz, and let's get some sleep.'

She stood her ground. 'I can't sleep,' she said. Simon turned on the bedside lamp, got out of bed and put on his dressing gown.

'I'll go and make you a drink,' he said wearily, as he tied his belt.

Elizabeth was astonished. This was a rare occurrence in their marriage. It must be guilt, she thought, and almost laughed as she heard him crashing around downstairs. It was some time before he reappeared with two mugs. He handed her one. Cocoa, a bit lumpy but not too bad considering.

'I'm sorry. I didn't mean to disturb you,' she said.

He considered her for a moment. 'You're looking tired these days,' he said finally.

Oh God, she thought, it's a much younger woman. She was almost the same age as Simon, only a couple of years younger, but he seemed to be more attractive than ever now, whereas she had noticed a network of fine lines beginning to etch themselves into her once-perfect English rose complexion. She sipped her drink and said nothing, feeling helpless and humiliated.

'I've got Charles on to it,' he said eventually.

'Can he be trusted?' she asked.

'Charles? Good God, yes of course.' Then, as an afterthought, almost to himself. 'If I can't trust him who the hell can I trust?' Elizabeth said nothing but continued to sip her drink thoughtfully. After a moment

Simon muttered. 'We gave her money, for God's sake what more can she want?'

There was a small silence. 'Don't you have any feelings about her?' asked Elizabeth tentatively.

'None.' The way he spoke made it quite clear that the topic was closed. He gulped down the rest of his drink and turned off the bedside light. Elizabeth lay down, closed her eyes and tried to will sleep to come. Moments later he turned to her abruptly and, to her astonishment, started to caress her breasts. Soon they were making love. Elizabeth clasped her husband to her, feeling she had gained a personal victory. But even as he reached his all too rapid climax, she made a decision. As soon as possible, she would pay Charles Pendlebury, Simon's private secretary, a visit.

'How was it?' Leonie called out from the bedroom as the front door crashed open.

'Shattering,' yelled Rob. 'I'm knackered. Must have a drink – do you want one in there?' Leonie heard a thud as he slung his script on the drawing-room floor.

'No thanks, I'll be out in a minute.' She smiled at her reflection in the mirror. Rob was about to get a nice surprise. Very carefully, she began to outline her mouth with lipstick.

There was a clink of glass, then silence for a moment. Then Rob's voice, sounding faintly aggrieved, came through the door. 'What are you doing in there? Come out here, I want to talk to you.'

'Getting ready. We're going out to dinner tonight, or had you forgotten?'

He groaned. 'Oh God, yes, I'm sorry. Do we have to? I can't face getting dressed up again.'

'If you remember,' said Leonie patiently, 'it was your idea – you rang up and suggested it.'

'I know, but I'm starving now. Haven't we got anything in the fridge?'

'Yogurt . . . a bit of cheese . . . I didn't bother to shop.'

'What have you been doing all afternoon for Christ's sake?'

'Recovering from a bloody awful interview,' said Leonie tartly. 'About which you haven't even bothered to ask me. And when you do,' she added, 'I shall tell you that you were absolutely right. He was a shit.'

Rob laughed. 'Who? Hamilton-Brown? I told you so.'

'No, he wasn't even there. It was that fat slimeball Sneller from the *Globe*. I think they set me up; I must have been mad to agree in the first place.'

'Poor baby,' Rob's voice was sympathetic now. 'Come and tell me all about it. And then we'll go and cheer ourselves up with some lovely food.'

'Well I'm ready.' Leonie appeared in the bedroom doorway. She was wearing the simplest of dresses, a short black silk chemise from Jasper Conran that showed off her superb legs. There were diamond studs in her ears and her burnished hair was drawn off her face into the nape of her neck, Mexican style.

Rob, sprawled in an armchair with a Scotch in his hand, drew in a deep breath at the sight of her. 'Are you wearing stockings?' he said at last.

'Of course,' she replied.

'Suspenders?'

'Naturally.'

'Then come over here.'

Leonie sashayed over to him and stood looking down.

'Closer,' he said. She moved a little nearer. He stretched out his hand and reached under her skirt, sliding his fingers up her thigh until he had eased them under the rim of her lace pants.

'For God's sake, Rob. We'll never get out.' Leonie shivered with pleasure as he gently parted the lips of her vagina and began to touch her in the way that she liked best. Without removing his hand he pulled her down until she was kneeling in front of him. She undid his trousers, revealing the bulge in his shorts that never failed to turn her on. Cupping his balls gently in her free hand she pulled out his cock and took it in her mouth.

The phone rang.

'Leave it,' mumbled Leonie. He groaned as she began to work him with her tongue. The phone rang on.

'What's wrong with the fucking answering machine?' gasped Rob. The shrill noise persisted.

'Oh shit!' Moving with difficulty, Rob leaned over to the phone. 'Yes, who is it?' he asked in a strangled voice as Leonie continued her labour of love. 'It's your agent,' he breathed to her, closing his eyes in ecstasy and letting the receiver drop from his hand.

Leonie spat him out and snatched up the phone. 'Nigel, darling, I'm so sorry I haven't rung you back. It's been a hell of a day!'

Nigel's voice, sounding unusually concerned, came down the line. 'Leonie. Hi. Sorry to bother you, my love, but a rather odd girl got through to me a few days ago. She was asking a lot of funny questions about what you were doing nineteen years ago. Sounded a bit weird, so I thought I'd better have a word . . .'

Rob, an aggrieved expression on his face, got up and went into the bedroom. Leonie was still on the phone when he returned ten minutes later, washed and changed.

'Leo,' he mouthed crossly. 'Do you want to eat or not?'

'Must go, Nigel. I'll think about it and ring you back tomorrow.' She put down the phone, and turned to Rob, her face anxious.

'What was it?' he demanded.

'There's a girl who's been asking a lot of questions about me. She said she was a journalist, but . . .' Leonie's voice tailed off as she considered Nigel's news.

'So, what's the problem?' asked Rob impatiently.

'I don't know if there is a problem,' said Leonie slowly, a hideous suspicion beginning to form itself in her mind. No, no, it would be too preposterous. She thought of the peculiar blank letter with the lock of hair that had arrived that afternoon. She had put it out of her mind almost immediately – fans did the weirdest things and this had seemed relatively harmless. Now she wondered if it was meant to be some kind of message. And if it could possibly have any connection with Nigel's news.

'Leo, what on earth's the matter? You look as if you've seen a ghost.'

She shrugged. 'I'm sure it's nothing,' she said, forcing a smile.

Rob gazed at her for a moment, then said, 'Darling, if you're not going to tell me what's wrong and you've lost interest in my body, don't you think we should go out? Some of us have got to get up for work in the morning.'

Leonie pulled herself together. 'You're right. I'm sorry, I'm being selfish. Just give me five minutes to repair the damage.' She walked slowly back into the bedroom, sat down and began to reapply her make-up. As she gazed into the mirror her thoughts sped back in time nearly twenty years, reviving memories whose pain she had thought buried for ever.

In the beginning it had been perfect. Leonie was still at drama school when she first met Simon, at the beginning of her final year. As one of the most promising students of her generation, everyone predicted a brilliant future for her. In spite of her looks, Leonie's experience with men was limited. She had blossomed late, from a thin, plain teenager who was all eyes and mouth, with only her bone structure to hint of better things to come. The few boys she had met while at her all-girls' school had paid scant attention to her, preferring to chat up her better-developed friends. As compensation for her lack of social life she had worked hard at her studies and thrown herself heart and soul into the school's thriving drama group, where her outstanding ability was soon recognized and relied on.

No one was surprised when Leonie gained a scholarship to the prestigious London Drama Academy, but those friends who saw her at the end of her first term were amazed by the transformation in her appearance. At drama school she had learned how to move, how to dress and how to make the most of looks which, as she approached the end of her teens, were finally fulfilling their promise. But she had not yet learned how to cope with the interest this aroused in the men by whom she was now surrounded. The habit of believing herself unattractive was too deeply rooted and, confused and unsettled by all the attention she was receiving, Leonie again took refuge in her work.

By the beginning of her final year, Leonie was finally starting to gain some confidence. She knew now that she was a good actress, and she was becoming used to the idea that her looks were something out of the ordinary. She had even enjoyed one or two mild flirtations with fellow-students but on the whole, though she liked them as colleagues, she found most of them far too self-centred and competitive to be able to touch her more deeply. She was ripe for a serious affair and when Simon came along she didn't stand a chance.

Simon Brentford had come down from Oxford two years before, after a glittering undergraduate career which had culminated in his presidency of the Oxford Union. Charming, good-looking and ambitious, he had his sights set firmly on a career in politics and was already being talked of as a prospective candidate for at least one marginal Tory seat. Meanwhile, for as well as being ambitious he was also chronically short of money, he was working in a City bank, trying to pay off the huge overdraft he had run up as an undergraduate. Simon, to his chagrin, lacked the private income taken for granted by so many of his friends in his free-spending Oxford social circle.

They met at a party given by an Oxford acquaintance of Simon's, who been one of the stars of the undergraduate theatre and was now trying to make it as a professional actor. Leonie, who had been brought along by a gang of drama-school mates, was instantly attracted by the tall, well-dressed dark man lounging beside the drinks table. He looked confident, sophisticated, a real man – so different from the scruffy self-obsessed actors by whom she was surrounded. By the time they left the party together, Leonie knew that Simon was something special. When he took her back to his Islington flat and made love to her, tenderly and expertly, she knew that she was in love for the first time. As he whispered that he had never, ever, known a girl like her, she was sure that he felt the same.

For nearly a year they were inseparable. Though they rarely talked about the future, except in the vaguest terms, Leonie knew it was because they both had careers to carve out for themselves before they could think of settling down. Meanwhile it was enough that they were together, and so very happy. When the end came it was as sudden as it was inexplicable. One lunchtime, she telephoned Simon at his office to make arrangements for the coming weekend.

'Hello, darling. It's me.'

'Yes.' His voice sounded oddly distant.

'I thought I'd check to see what time you're coming to pick me up.'

'What do you mean?'

'I thought we were seeing each other this weekend.' Leonie was puzzled.

'Were we? I must have forgotten.'

'Simon, this is me, Leonie. You remember, your girlfriend.'

Silence. 'Si, are you still there?'

'Yes, I'm still here.'

'Then why don't you say something?'

'There's nothing to say.'

Leonie felt a cold sensation in the pit of her stomach. Surely this was not her Simon talking. He sounded so cool, so aloof.

'Si, if this is some sort of a joke, it's not very funny.'

'It's not a joke.'

'Are you trying to tell me that you don't want to see me?' She hardly dare form the words.

'Something like that.'

Her chest felt constricted, she could hardly breathe. The telephone box appeared to be revolving around her. 'Why not?' She felt the sobs starting to rise in her throat.

'I just don't want to, that's all. I'm sorry.'

'But . . . but . . . Simon.' Click. The line had gone dead. Leonie stood staring at the dialling instructions, too stunned to move. He'd said he didn't want to see her again. She could not, she simply could not believe it. Something must be dreadfully wrong with Simon. Soon he would come to his senses – he must do – and everything would be all right between them again.

But over the next two weeks there was no further word from Simon, and Leonie gradually came to believe that, inexplicable as it seemed, he really intended their relationship to be at an end. It was a time she lived through in a daze of misery. Her exams continued, but she went through them like an automaton, neither knowing nor caring how she was doing. At the end of two weeks there was a party at a big house in Holland Park, a twenty-first to which she and Simon had been invited as a couple. The boy for whom the party was being held was the younger brother of one of Simon's closest Oxford friends. Simon himself was almost certain to be there.

Leonie thought very hard before going. She was desperate to see Simon again, but if he was cruel to her she did not think she could bear it. Most of all she wanted to know why, why had he suddenly dropped her. What was he thinking about to behave so unreasonably, and what had she done to deserve this callous treatment?

When she entered the big cream Regency house on Holland Park Avenue she was pale and nervous but determined. She had lost weight in the past fortnight, but the long, fluid dress of dark green chiffon and lace that she had bought on the Portobello Road suited her still shapely figure. Her host greeted her with apparent pleasure but she sensed an undercurrent of surprise at her appearance. It seemed to her, as she walked through the crowded, high-ceilinged rooms in search of Simon, that people were looking at her and commenting.

Then she saw him, with a crowd of Oxford cronies. One of them noticed her and said something to him. He turned and stared at her, his face darkening. Leonie could see at once that this was not to be a happy reunion, but she forced herself to continue walking towards him. As if by magic, his friends seemed to melt away, leaving him alone.

'Simon', she said, as she reached him, 'I think I'm entitled to an explanation.'

Simon glanced around the room, a hunted expression on his face. There were several pairs of curious eyes upon them. 'Very well,' he said. He sounded bored and distant.

He led Leonie out into the garden. The trees were strung with fairylights and there was a steel band playing, but beyond the lights and the music was a small summerhouse, wreathed with honeysuckle. Simon pulled her into its scented darkness.

'Now, look,' he said, not unkindly. 'Don't be a fool, Leo. There's no point in making a fuss, you'll only upset yourself.'

'Simon,' said Leonie. 'Could you just tell me what's going on? I thought we were having a relationship. I was under the impression that I was your girlfriend? Or was I mistaken?' Chilled by his tone, her own voice was icy. Simon was silent.

'Well?' she demanded, temper rising. 'We've been together for nearly a year. Are you going to tell me it's over, just like that?'

'Leo,' said Simon calmly. 'It's over. Can't you just accept it?'

The words flew like barbed arrows into her chest, bringing hot tears to her eyes. 'Why?' she whispered.

'I've changed my mind.'

'But you said you loved me.' Leonie's tone was piteous. She could not believe that this cold, unfeeling man was the tender lover who had made her so happy.

'That was wrong of me.'

'You mean you never loved me?' she asked.

'I may have thought I did.'

'But not now?'

'No.' The word was final, but Leonie thought she detected a shade of hesitation in his voice. She pressed him, 'Have you met someone else?'

'No,' said Simon quickly. 'It's not that.'

'Well, why then?' She was sobbing openly now.

'I made a mistake,' said Simon awkwardly.

'A mistake!' cried Leonie, tears streaming down her cheeks. 'That's what I am is it? A mistake. Well, you've made a mistake all right, because I think I'm pregnant!'

'What!' Simon sounded genuinely shocked.

'I'm not absolutely sure,' she said, crying quietly, 'but it seems likely.'

'But you look so thin . . .' he began.

If she had not felt so dreadful, Leonie would have smiled at his bewildered voice. 'I know. I gather one does at first, but I haven't had my period for ages. I thought it was because of exams and everything, but I've been feeling sick in the morning as well.'

Simon was outraged. 'Why the hell didn't you mention this before?'

'I haven't had much chance, have I?' said Leonie wryly. 'Anyway I wanted to be sure first, in case it was a false alarm.'

'Jesus God,' he exclaimed and turned away, his head in his hands.

He sounded remorseful. Leonie moved towards him and put her arms round him. 'Oh, Si, please say you're pleased about it, please tell me it's all right again.'

'Don't touch me,' he hissed between his teeth. But she clung on desperately. 'Don't touch me!' He repeated, trying to pull himself from her embrace. She twined her arms even tighter around his neck.

'Si, please, I'm going to have a baby, our very own baby.'

He took hold of both her hands and pushed her away roughly. 'No, we're not. You're going to have an abortion!'

'No, no, no.' Leonie, stunned by his unkindness, was starting to lose control.

'For Christ's sake, shut up! Everyone can hear us.'

'I don't care,' wailed Leonie. 'I want them to know.'

'Shut up, Leo! Shut up!' He slapped her hard across the face. She stopped abruptly and gazed at him in horror. 'That's better,' he said. 'Now come on, be sensible. You're a talented actress, you've a great future ahead of you, and the last thing you need in your life at this moment is a baby. You must understand, it is over between us. It's nothing you've done or said. I haven't met anyone else. I made a mistake, that's all. Tomorrow you must see a doctor. If you really are pregnant, I will arrange an abortion for you. Now, I want you to go away quietly.' Before Leonie could speak he had pushed her firmly away and was gone.

In spite of Simon's insistence on an abortion, Leonie never really considered it as an option. When she had first suspected that she was pregnant, her first feeling was joy that there would be a child to bring her and Simon even closer together. Now, though Simon had abandoned her, she could not suddenly rearrange her feelings and reject the baby. In the beginning, she had wanted it. Abortion now, though it might be sensible, would feel like murder.

Young, naïve and optimistic, Leonie felt sure that she could cope with a child and a career. No matter what he had said, surely Simon would help her once the baby had arrived. Perhaps, when he saw it, he would even come back to her. She wrote and told him that she had decided to have the child and look after it herself. He replied, eventually, that she was a fool, but that he would make her a weekly allowance to help her care for it. She was not, however, to expect anything more than financial support.

Leonie left drama school in a blaze of glory, but those who predicted that she would next be seen on the West End stage, or with some prestigious national theatre company, were to be disappointed. For a while fellow-students and teachers wondered what had become of her but, as the slow months of her pregnancy dragged by, she began to be forgotten. Only a few close friends knew of her condition and she was determined to keep it that way. Like an animal nursing its wounds, she stayed close to the flat which she shared with Isobel and Tracy, two friends from drama school, emerging only to shop, take the exercise she knew she needed, and collect her social-security benefit.

The birth was a hard one. Leonie was young and fit, but her narrow hips and the baby's large head made for a long, pain-wracked struggle. At the end of twenty exhausting hours the child finally emerged, a little girl with a cross, creased red face and a fine down of auburn hair on the head that had caused so much trouble. Leonie, lying limp and shattered on the hard hospital bed, heard the child's first cry and stretched out her arms to receive her daughter. As the nurse gently handed her the child she looked down at this strange new entity and felt . . . nothing. Tears sprang into her eyes and she shook her head. 'I'm sorry . . . so very tired. Perhaps later.'

'Of course, dear.' Sympathetically the nurse took the child again and bore her away. Later, when Leonie was feeling stronger, they brought her back again and Leonie tried to feed her, but the milk would not come. As the baby tugged fruitlessly and painfully at her nipples, she felt a strange sense of disbelief. This little girl, who should have meant so much, seemed to have no connection with her at all. It was Simon she wanted – Simon who did not come even though she had sent a message to tell him about the baby – not this child.

Because of the difficult birth, Leonie was kept in hospital for nearly a week. During that time she learned to go through the motions of looking after the child, whom she decided to call Amanda, feeding her, changing her, cuddling her when she cried. But when she had time to think it became clear to her that caring for a small baby was a twenty-four-hour occupation, and that there was no way she could combine looking after Amanda properly with earning the money she needed to support her. With less regret than she had anticipated she decided that she would have to have Amanda fostered, at least temporarily. She telephoned Simon to tell him of her decision and he agreed that he would arrange to start paying a regular weekly sum to a foster-mother for Amanda's care.

Believing as she did that she had no strong maternal feelings for her baby, Leonie was unprepared for the sense of amputation as she handed Amanda over to Mrs Miles, the cheerful, middle-aged foster-mother. She watched in dismay as the woman seemed to make her child her own immediately; Amanda settled in her arms as she had never settled in Leonie's. She stood rooted to the spot as the woman left the room, carrying her child, knowing that she must go and yet suddenly finding it impossible to make her feet carry her out through the front door of the pleasant suburban house.

Isobel, who had an old and unreliable Mini, had been kind to bring her, but as they drove back to London Leonie could find no reply to her tentative attempts at conversation. Instead she sat, staring blindly out of the window, oblivious to everything except the gaping wound that seemed to have opened in her chest.

For the next month and a half Leonie took a Green Line bus to Ashebourn once a week to see her baby. Seeing her only at intervals, she became very aware of how dramatically the child was changing, developing with extraordinary speed from a helpless, dependent little animal into a sturdy, squalling personality. She thought Amanda recognized her, but she was not sure. It was almost more than she could bear to realize how much more pleasure and animation her daughter showed at the sight of her foster-mother.

On her sixth visit, Mrs Miles stopped Leonie as she was leaving and said awkwardly: 'I hate to mention this, Miss O'Brien, but I really can't manage any longer without being paid.'

'How many weeks are you owed?' gasped Leonie, completely dumbfounded. Simon had promised that he would make arrangements for the payments as soon as Amanda was handed over.

'All of them,' said Mrs Miles regretfully.

Leonie felt cold. 'Don't worry, I'll sort it out,' she promised, babbling. 'I am sure there's an explanation. He must be away or something.'

'Don't you know for sure, dear?'

Leonie realized her blunder. 'I'm staying with my parents. They don't really approve of him, so we haven't spoken to each other recently,' she lied desperately.

Mrs Miles looked at her shrewdly. 'How are you going to manage?' she asked. Her tone was not unkind. 'You've got no money and you're out of work, aren't you, love?'

Leonie nodded miserably. There were no auditions and no sign of work. She had tried for several temporary jobs, but so far had found nothing.

'What are you going to do if he doesn't pay up?' asked Mrs Miles. 'What about your parents? Will they help you?'

'They don't know about the baby,' Leonie confessed, her voice barely audible.

'Look, love,' Mrs Miles took Leonie's hand in hers, 'I know a couple, a really lovely couple who are just longing for a baby. They've been married a few years, but they can't have a child of their own. They've seen your baby and they love her.'

Leonie looked at her in outraged disbelief. 'What do you mean? You've shown them my baby?'

'They're friends of mine, dear.'

'She's my baby, MINE. I'm going to keep her and look after her and love her . . . always.' Leonie was shouting now. The baby started whimpering in the back room.

'Shush now, or you'll wake her,' said Mrs Miles soothingly. 'Look, love, I'm sure things will work out. You go home now and as long as I'm paid by the end of this week, we'll say no more about this little trouble.'

'You will be, I promise.' Leonie was unnerved now and longing to get away. She must ring Simon to ask him why he hadn't paid the money. He couldn't let her down. Once home, she ran to the phone box in the hall. Her heart was thumping as she waited for Simon to answer. The phone continued ringing until, just as she was about to give up, someone picked up the receiver.

'Yes?' The voice was female, elderly and unfamiliar. She had never met Simon's mother – it had sometimes puzzled her that Simon never introduced her to his family, but he had told her that they would only bore her as much as they bored him – but she knew that occasionally she stayed in his flat when she came up to London to do some shopping. This sounded as if it could be her.

'Could I speak to Simon Brentford, please?'

There was a long pause. 'Who is this?' The question was polite but wary.

'A friend of his.' Leonie's desperation made her brave.

Another pause. 'I'm afraid he's not here.'

'Oh no.' Leonie wildly wondered what to say next. The voice cut across her thoughts.

'He left for New York a month ago.'

Leonie nearly dropped the phone. 'When will he be back?' She was trembling now.

'Not for several months. He has been sent on an exchange by his firm. Can I tell him who is trying to contact him?'

'N-no. No, thank you.' Stunned, Leonie put the phone down. Her brain seemed to be exploding. Then cold logic took over. She knew what she had to do. She picked up the phone again and dialled Mrs Miles' number.

Five minutes later she walked into the flat, wearily took off her coat and went into her room. Then she sat down on the bed and stayed there for the rest of the day without moving, in total black despair. She was aware of her two flatmates holding whispered conferences about her in the tiny adjoining kitchenette. From time to time they brought her mugs of tea and once Isobel stroked her hair and murmured, 'It will be all right, darling.' Later Tracy squatted down beside her and urged her to eat something. She shook her head and sat on until dark, then mechanically prepared for bed and lay staring open-eyed into the night, praying that she might die, then perhaps the appalling pain would stop.

For three days this continued, then Isobel could bear it no longer. Handing Leonie a mug of tea which she accepted wordlessly, she suddenly rounded on her. 'For God's sake, Leonie, this is no good. You've got to pull yourself together.' She stopped as she saw the expression on Leonie's face. It was the look of a woman who had been subjected to some unspeakable torture. She sat on the bed beside Leonie and took the unresisting body into her arms. 'Oh, my darling, I'm sorry, I'm so sorry. I just can't bear to see you like this.' A dreadful rasping sound of anguish came from Leonie as slowly and painfully she began first to sob and then to weep uncontrollably. Tracy watched from the doorway without speaking as the two girls clung together, then she herself went back into the kitchen and cried silently into the washing-up.

The following afternoon Leonie went to see the baby for the last time. She talked for some time with Mrs Miles and finally agreed to hand over the baby to the couple who wanted to adopt her. 'Would you like to hold her?' asked Mrs Miles sympathetically.

'No, no I couldn't bear to.' And Leonie walked to the door of the back room where a wicker cradle stood by the window. Inside the cot, Amanda, her baby, her darling baby, was lying, dressed in primrose yellow; the sunshine was streaming through the window on to her, lighting everything with its golden glow. She turned away as Mrs Miles laid a hand on her arm.

'You're doing the right thing, love,' she said quietly. 'You're giving that child a real chance in life.' Leonie nodded and walked out of the house. She felt as if her heart had just been ripped from her body.

Some time later she found that she had kept one of the little socks the hospital had put on the baby when it was first born. She clung to the scrap of material as if it were a holy relic. For nineteen years she nursed her private grief and, though time dulled the pain, it was never entirely absent. Every time she heard a baby cry or a child call for its mother, she remembered what might have been if it were her baby, her child.

Later, when she was finally able to think clearly, Leonie knew that she never wanted to set eyes on Simon again. She also knew that she would never fully recover from the wound he had given her. The whole experience hardened her, even more than she realized at the time, and it was many years before she allowed herself to fall in love again. With no child to tie her she took up the broken threads of her career, applying for jobs in far-flung provincial reps which she would not even have considered when she thought she would have Amanda to look after. Less choosy now, she had no problem in finding work, and there were bleak winter months spent in cold, damp digs when she cried herself to sleep at night, remembering her little daughter and the impossibility of bringing her up in circumstances like these. For consolation and as a kind of twisted revenge she bedded a lot of men she did not care about and disliked herself for using them and discarding them.

In spite of herself, she could not avoid looking out for news of Simon. Light began to dawn about why he had left her so callously when, six months after they had parted, she heard from friends that he was engaged to Elizabeth Cavendish, a rich, beautiful blonde with an aristocratic background. What an appropriate wife for an aspiring politician, thought Leonie bitterly. Of course, a poor and unknown actress like herself was hardly in the same class as a wife for an ambitious MP. And the money would come in useful because Simon, as she now knew to her cost, had always been short of cash in spite of his well-paid job. In a way it was a comfort that he was making such a worldly marriage: it proved once more what a shit he was and how lucky she was to be free of him.

With a sense of inevitability, Leonie watched Simon enter politics and start to make a name for himself. Knowing him as she did, she was quite sure he would be content with nothing less than prime minister as his goal. Meanwhile her own career, after the period in the wilderness of the provinces, at last started to take off, and as she became more sought-after and successful she began to lose touch with his progress. Then the offer came from Hollywood, and she took off for LA and a career in films. For a long time, Simon was, mercifully, almost forgotten.

It was years later before she saw him again – just after her return from the States, where she had just completed a movie for which she was tipped heavily to receive an Oscar. Simon was now becoming a figure to be reckoned with in British politics and his name cropped up in the newspapers with increasing regularity. Leonie knew that he was still married to Elizabeth and had two sons though, she was strangely pleased to note, no daughter.

Nigel Bechstein, now and for many years Leonie's shrewd and faithful agent, had invited her to lunch at Rules to celebrate the signing of a new film contract. Leonie, sipping champagne and happy to be back in London, was gazing around her to see if any old friends were present while lending an ear to Nigel's stream of gossip about happenings in the London theatre. Suddenly the sight of a tall, dark man entering the restaurant, a pretty chestnut-haired woman by his side, caused her to freeze, champagne glass half-way to her lips. Nigel, his back to the room, turned to follow the direction of her stare. 'My, my, my,' he said, shaking his head in pained surprise 'he's taking a risk bringing her here.'

'Do you know him,' asked Leonie carefully. The once dark hair was greying slightly, but still thick, and the light marks of age only lent distinction to the handsome face.

'Who doesn't, these days,' replied Nigel. 'Simon Brentford, the Conservative's new golden boy. He'll have to be careful about where he takes his mistresses now he's been promoted. The PM doesn't like that sort of thing to get about, you know. Good-looking chap, isn't he? Have you met him, Leonie?'

The thudding of Leonie's heart gradually stilled and she took a sip of champagne. 'A long time ago,' she said eventually. 'Once was enough.' So long ago, and she had convinced itself it was all over, the pain buried deep within herself. And yet the sight of him, even now, had the power to move her in a way that both astonished and frightened her.

5

'What the hell is this crap?' Rob shouted, glaring at the tabloid newspaper he was holding. It was Sunday morning and he and Leonie were enjoying a precious few hours of relaxation together, something that was becoming increasingly rare as filming progressed. They had enjoyed a lazy breakfast in bed with fresh-ground coffee, freshly squeezed orange juice and delicious warm rolls called *panini*, and then Rob had gone out to see if he could lay his hands on any English newspapers. He had returned in triumph, his arms full. Now he looked as if he was regretting the enthusiasm for news from home that had led him to purchase the *Globe* among the others.

'What is it?' asked Leonie lazily. She was curled up in an armchair, still dressed in her towelling bathrobe.

'Listen to this!' He paused, and took a deep breath. ' "Leonie O'Brien and Rob Fenton to part" – what the hell do you make of that?'

Leonie sat up sharply. 'Let me see it.'

'Just a moment.' He went on, a frown on his handsome face, ' "Friends of the ill-assorted couple – " '

'Ill-assorted? What's that supposed to mean?' Leonie felt slightly sick. She had had enough of this sort of thing last year when the press had first got wind of her relationship with Rob. Her heart sank at the thought that it might be starting up again.

'God knows. Listen,' he insisted, ' "Friends of the ill-assorted couple, hinted last night, that all was not well with the ageing beauty . . ." ' Here he shot an unreadable sidelong glance at Leonie, who winced. ' ". . . and her young beau. Pressure of work is keeping the pair apart and both have been seen dining with others." What is all this? Where did they get it?'

'Let me see.' Leonie sprang up from her armchair and joined him on the sofa. Leaning against him, she scanned the front page. The lurid headlines leapt out at her. Though she knew there was not a shred of truth in them, they were an uncomfortable reminder of the fears about herself and Rob that crept into her mind when she was off her guard.

Ignoring her, Rob continued to turn the pages of the newspaper. 'Look, there's more inside. Bloody hell, what a ghastly picture of you, darling,' he said, insensitively, adding in a disgusted tone, 'and an even worse one of me.' The photo showed them in a restaurant. Both faces had the glazed expression of people caught unawares by a flash bulb. Leonie's eyes were narrowed, perhaps in laughter, perhaps in irritation, and Rob looked bored and petulant.

'When was this taken anyway?' demanded Rob. Leonie peered at the picture; the scene looked very familiar. 'I think it was the other night. When we went out to dinner at Pinciana. That's the Jasper Conran I was wearing.'

'I didn't see any photographers, did you?'

'Oh, I think I noticed a flash go off, but so what?'

'Well you might have known they'd be after us,' said Rob bitterly. 'Did you see who wrote this?'

Leonie read the byline, her heart sinking. 'Oh god, that prick Sneller. But he couldn't have got any of it from me. I was only with him for five minutes.'

'I told you you shouldn't have done that interview. The press is always bad news. You let yourself be conned, didn't you?' Rob's grey eyes were hard. Leonie wondered for a brief, chilling moment on whose behalf he was so angry. Did he mind for her or was it the effect on his own career he feared, the bad publicity of being branded, in effect, her toyboy? She forced the thought away. She didn't like this sort of press attention any more than he did, but she had had many more years of dealing with it. It was one of the penalties of fame. Rob was still a relative novice at handling these pressures. He would have to learn, but meanwhile she must be patient with him.

Gently, she took the paper out of his hands and laid it aside. She put her arms round him and pulled him towards her, kissing him on the lips. 'Ignore it,' she murmured, as Rob's rigid pose began to soften and she felt his body respond to hers. 'They must be short of news, that's all. Everyone knows they print rubbish. Don't let them get to you.'

'Mmm, suppose you're right.' Rob's voice was muffled as he lowered his head to her breasts, teasing her nipples with his tongue. Leonie sighed with pleasure as she let herself sink backwards on to the sofa, beginning to give herself up to the joyful familiarity of his love-making. For the moment, at least, her doubts and fears were forgotten.

It was only just light when Rob turned the Mercedes out of the side street and set off for the film studios. These early morning calls were a killer. Why the hell couldn't they stick to the continental custom of starting at two in the afternoon and going on into the evening? He knew time was money, and that they were trying to cram two days' shooting into one day in order to finish on schedule, but it was very tough if you were in as many scenes as he was. And especially tough when, like this morning, he was suffering from a thumping hangover.

The unit had been on location for the past three days, shooting the riding sequences. He was an adequate rider, but three days in the saddle had played hell with his thigh muscles and his rib-cage hurt from the continual twisting and turning in the saddle during the sword-fight yesterday. Even worse, he had had to swing down from the branch of a tree and pull the villain from his horse. Though his stunt double had done the actual drop, he had had to hang agonizingly from the branch for the close-ups and then spend what seemed like hours wrestling with on the sun-baked iron-hard ground with Carlo Fillippi, who played the villain. Well, he reflected with grim satisfaction, one thing was for certain, he'd be super-fit at the end of it all.

He would have felt a lot better if, when he finally got back to the apartment feeling like death, Leonie had been there to look after him. But for the past three evenings she had been out at the studios, locked in a series of late meetings trying to thrash out the problem of costings with the director, Colin Scott. There was a big ballroom scene coming up which was threatening to take them over budget and Leonie had been businesslike and preoccupied for days, scribbling reams of notes and making a series of lengthy phone calls to their US backers. Though Rob knew it was all part of her job, he still felt faintly aggrieved. Surely someone else could do at least some of it for her? Meanwhile he was having to come home to a dark, cheerless apartment with no Leo to pour him a stiff Scotch, run him a soothing foam-filled bath and listen with intelligent sympathy to his account of the day's trials and triumphs.

For the first couple of evenings he had stayed in and waited for her to come home, but last night, after an especially heavy day, the sight of the empty apartment had been too much for him. He knew Leonie wouldn't approve but he reckoned he deserved a break. Pausing only to dump his script he turned straight round and went out again, heading for the bar where he knew he would probably find Giovanni, his stand-in, and some of the rest of the cast. He only meant to unwind over a few beers and perhaps a plate of pasta, then go back and get an early night. But as the drink relaxed him and the cheerful young company of Giovanni and his friends, and their frank admiration of him, began to have its effect, the hour for leaving got later and later.

Rob groaned as he remembered. He had finally got in at two in the morning and Leonie, in bed but still awake, had not been best pleased. Her frosty reception still rankled. She had treated him like an irresponsible teenager when all evening he had been fêted as a star. When, three hours later, he had dragged himself reluctantly out of bed again to get ready for work there had still been a distinct coolness in her manner, which Rob resented. OK, so he had been a bit silly, but he had been working damn hard and he deserved a bit of fun. After all the fight was a piece of cake, he was a perfectly competent swordsman and it was simply a matter of concentration. He would take a couple of aspirin for his head and manage a twenty-minute catnap after make-up; that should do the trick. Or, better still, perhaps Giovanni would let him have some of those uppers he had been talking about getting hold of the other day. He saw the pink flush in the eastern sky as the sun rose over the Aventine Hill. The day promised well. Yes, he was going to be fine.

Carlo Fillippi, who was playing the villain of *Swords at Sunset* was a well-known Italian actor in his mid-forties. He had been labouring as much as Rob on the previous day's filming, but today he was in his element. He was a superb swordsman. Agile, and with a keen eye, he was a joy to watch, but not for Rob, who soon realized with dismay that he was having to work very hard to keep up with him. That morning they had tried unsuccessfully to get the master shot in the can, but it had required a whole series of retakes. Finally the despairing director had decided to abandon it and break the sequence up into small sections.

Carlo was unperturbed. He was accustomed to working with actors who were less competent swordsmen than he was and he looked forward to doing the master shot with Rob's stunt double. That would be worth watching. But when the decision was made, Rob's pride was badly hurt. He sat, trying to look unconcerned, while the make-up man hovered about him, mopping his brow with a chamois leather soaked in eau-de-Cologne. Fresh pan-stick make-up was applied and powdered down, and the hairdresser then redid his hair for the twentieth time that morning. Then, in the remaining time before lunch, they rehearsed the next sequence, a two-shot. This was easier for Rob. The blows and parries were very similar to those he had once learnt for a fight sequence in *Romeo and Juliet*. He felt at home and started to enjoy himself as they did the final rehearsal.

At the lunch break Rob returned to his caravan, his confidence restored. Although he usually ate with the unit he decided to eat alone, determined that nothing would disturb his concentration. He ordered a chicken sandwich, took a couple more of Giovanni's pills, and washed everything down with a coke. By two o'clock, he was ready to go and feeling supremely confident. He stepped out of the air-conditioned caravan into the glaring sunlight, determined to prove himself.

As the unit reassembled, the assistant director yelled. 'All right, everyone, final rehearsal!'

'Ripetizione finale,' echoed his Italian counterpart. The two leading actors took their places, the focus puller made a final check with his tape measure, the lighting cameraman gazed up at the cloudless sky and murmured his approval – no adjustments necessary there – and the two combatants lunged and parried. It was obvious that Rob was back on form and Carlo was smiling, happy to have a worthy opponent. Colin Scott muttered. 'Not bad, let's go for one.'

'Final checks, please,' yelled the assistant director. The make-up artist and hairdresser darted in to tidy up their victims yet again.

'OK,' shouted the assistant, 'stand by everyone, stand by for a take.'

There was a pause. The director allowed time for the two artists to brace themselves, then very quietly and deliberately, said, 'Action.'

Carlo lunged at Rob's throat, Rob's sword intervened to stop the blow and the two swords locked momentarily with a clash of metal. Then Rob pushed the other man off, taking advantage of the moment that Carlo took to regain his balance to lunge again. Carlo smiled disarmingly and parried the blow with ease. The sudden display of even white teeth irritated Rob irrationally, reminding him of his humiliation that morning. He set his teeth and started to fight in earnest.

The moves were rehearsed, but Rob was determined to show that his swordsmanship was as good as that of the older man. His lithe energy, combined with Carlo's brilliant technique, made for a breathtaking spectacle, and the members of the unit crowded round to watch. Then on his final triumphant thrust, Rob, beginning to tire in spite of his determination, was momentarily distracted by a movement in the crowd. He missed his footing and a stroke that was supposed to be aimed at Carlo's rib-cage went high and wide, catching him on the upper arm. The sword ripped through the fine material of Carlo's costume, cutting deeply into his flesh. Blood gushed out and Rob shouted in alarm as Carlo dropped his sword and pressed his free hand on to the wound. There was a moment of stunned silence.

'Cut,' thundered the director.

The make-up man rushed up with a wad of tissues to help staunch the flow of blood, followed by the unit nurse.

'Get an ambulance,' the director ordered curtly.

Twenty minutes later, a pale and shaken Carlo was being helped into the back of the ambulance. Rob was in his caravan, alone, drinking whisky and cursing himself for his stupidity. There was a tap on the caravan door. 'Yes?' snapped Rob, who wanted only to be left alone. The door opened and Colin Scott appeared. He looked at Rob, and then at the whisky. 'So what's the problem, mate?' he asked, in the cockney twang he had never lost despite years in Hollywood.

'Some bastard got in my eyeline,' muttered Rob angrily.

Colin watched him for a moment, then said quietly. 'No, what's the real problem? You were all over the shop this morning.'

Rob looked at him sharply. 'You don't have to tell me. I'm sorry, Colin, but I didn't sleep a bloody wink last night. I think I must have got a touch of sunstroke yesterday.'

'Sure,' said Colin. It was impossible to tell from his tone whether he believed Rob or not. 'These things happen.' There was a pause.

'Jesus, I feel terrible,' groaned Rob. 'How bad do you think it is?'

'He'll live,' said Colin. The incident was annoying, but he was philosophical about it. The scene would be rescheduled and the insurance would cover the extra days' filming required, which meant he could spend more time in the sunshine and there would be an extra week's salary. It could all have been a lot worse.

Rob was considerably less happy. He had never injured anyone before and the accident had shaken him badly. He was worried about Carlo and also worried about Leonie's reaction. He knew, and she would guess, that his hangover was at least partly to blame for Carlo's injury. Of course accidents could happen even on the best-regulated film set, but it was courting disaster to go into a fight scene like this in anything less than peak physical condition. His behaviour had been irresponsible and, worse, unprofessional. Leonie would not be pleased with him.

'OK, sunshine,' said Colin. 'I'd better go and pick up the pieces. You take it easy for a few minutes. Dave'll come and let you know what's happening.' He turned to go, then paused on the top of the steps and looked back over his shoulder at Rob. 'By the way,' he said, his eyes shrewd, 'I'd lay off the booze if I was you. It won't help any.'

A few minutes later there was another tap at the door. This time it was Dave Kelly, the assistant director. Dave, wiry, ginger-haired and middle-aged, had known Leonie a long time and Rob never felt that he approved of him very much. He looked at Rob unsmilingly. 'We've decided to pick up the scene with you and the Cardinal in his study. He's been called, and he's on his way over. We'll need you ready to rehearse in forty minutes.' His manner was brisk and cool. The unspoken message was that Rob was a pain in the arse, both for putting the shooting schedule up the creek and for damaging, perhaps seriously, a valuable and popular member of the cast. 'And,' Dave added with undisguised satisfaction, 'we've called Miss O'Brien. She's very upset and she's coming right over.' Without waiting for a reply, he left, slamming the door behind him. Hell, thought Rob.

There was a third knock on the door. 'Fuck off,' yelled Rob, feeling that he could not face anyone else. The door opened a crack and a worried-looking face appeared. It was Giovanni.

'John, I'm sorry,' said Rob wearily. 'I didn't know it was you.'

'All right,' said Giovanni. 'I have come to say how I am very sorry. I should not have kept you so late, last night.'

Rob smiled. 'Don't be silly. I should know when to stop. After all, I'm a big boy now.'

'I spoke with Carlo, as he was being put in the ambulance.' Rob looked at Giovanni expectantly as he said this. 'He said you are not to worry; it was not your fault. He say you are a very good swordsman.'

Rob laughed bitterly. 'Sure, Errol Flynn could certainly learn a thing or two from me.'

'I feel so bad,' said Giovanni, looking soulful.

'Don't worry. Now look, John, I appreciate you coming, but be a good lad and bugger off, will you. I've got some lines to learn in a hurry.'

'OK, fine. See you later, Rob.' Giovanni left the caravan looking considerably more cheerful than when he had arrived. Alone again, Rob took out the thick shooting script, and thumbed through until he found the new scene. He was annoyed to find that there was quite a bit of dialogue – it wouldn't be easy to learn it in just forty minutes. He wouldn't put it past that bastard Kelly to have suggested this scene, just to make things awkward for him. He laid out the script, propped his elbows on the dressing table and started to commit the lines to memory. They did not come easily – the image of a furious Leonie descending on the set was enough to ruin every ounce of concentration he had left.

Sheila Mackenzie had gone into the affair with her eyes open. At twenty-nine she'd been around a bit, she could handle it, or so she thought. She had had plenty of boyfriends, all her own age, all of whom bored her to tears. They were intelligent enough, well educated on the whole, but somehow never satisfactory. An independent girl, she was astounded to find that, even though they paid lip-service to the notion of female equality, most of the men she went out with seemed to be more interested in her body than in her very able brain.

Like most women who worked in and around Westminster she had eyed Simon Brentford from afar for years and found him extremely attractive. He was handsome – especially in contrast to the normal run of MPs – he had wit and charm but, more than that, he had ambition and the prospect before him of office in the highest levels of government. It was his drive, his hunger for power and his ability to satisfy it that gave him for Sheila an irresistible charisma.

As a senior personal secretary in the Department of the Environment, Sheila often caught a glimpse of Simon when, after he had been promoted to Minister for Urban Affairs, he visited the Department to confer with his civil-service advisers. She was also almost a neighbour. The tiny Berkshire cottage, left to her by her godmother, from which she commuted to London each day by rail was only fifteen miles from Wortham Manor, Simon's country house.

Even so, they would probably never have met if it had not been for a sudden, overnight attack of gastro-enteritis suffered by Frank, Simon's driver. By the time the message reached Simon that his car would not be collecting him as usual to drive him to Westminster it was too late to arrange a substitute. Reluctantly, for he disliked travelling on public transport, Simon decided that only way of making his important

9 a.m. committee meeting was to drive to Reading and catch an Inter-City 125.

So it was that Sheila, queuing for a cup of coffee in the crowded buffet car, found her heart missing a beat as she recognized the tall, well-groomed and almost unfairly attractive figure of the Minister for Urban Affairs making his way thought the milling commuters towards her. As he approached she could not resist a shy smile. To her amazement he stopped, looking down at her with a question in his heavy-lidded brown eyes.

'I know you, don't I?' asked Simon, who had noticed the attractive, long-legged red-head standing out like a good deed in a naughty world amid the pin-striped mass of male commuters.

'I don't think so,' replied Sheila, too shaken to be anything but honest. 'I mean, I know who you are of course, but we've never actually met.'

'Don't stand there dreaming, love. There's people waiting to be served if you don't want anything.' Sheila looked round and realized with a start that she was now at the head of the queue.

'Oh, I'm so sorry. Coffee, please.'

'Make that two. No, please let me.' As Sheila fumbled for her purse, Simon laid a restraining hand on her arm. The simple touch made her feel weak at the knees. He handed a buffet-car attendant a couple of pound coins with a lordly air, then picked up both plastic beakers of coffee. They edged away from the counter.

'Do you have to do this every day?' asked Simon, with a disdainful glance round the crowded, grimy carriage.

'Yes,' said Sheila shyly. 'I live in a village about ten miles from Reading. My godmother died and left me a tiny cottage there. I used to stay there as a child and loved it, so I couldn't bear to sell it.' She stopped, knowing that she was starting to babble, but Simon's proximity was having a quite devastating effect on her. To her immense relief, he smiled at her encouragingly.

'A fairy godmother, then,' he remarked, with what could either have been a gentle twinkle in his eye or a predatory gleam, depending on one's point of view.

Sheila saw the former. 'Yes,' she said, 'she had no children of her own and I was her favourite godchild.'

'Understandably.' Simon gave her another look, which brought a tide of red flooding over her fair skin. 'Shall we continue this balancing act,' he went on, apparently not noticing Sheila's confusion, 'or shall we find somewhere to sit down?' As he spoke, he was guiding her in the direction of the first-class seats.

'I don't have a first-class ticket, I'm afraid,' said Sheila sadly.

'That's all right,' said Simon. 'You're with me.' His tone expressed complete confidence in himself.

Once they were seated in first-class comfort, Sheila found herself, she did not quite know how, doing most of the talking. With a question, a wry comment, a look of rapt attention, Simon made her feel that she must be one of the most fascinating women he had ever met. When they parted at Paddington, she taking a tube to the office, he a taxi to his committee meeting, she felt that already he knew more about her than any of her boyfriends had cared to find out. During the day she went through her work on automatic pilot, unable to get him out of her mind. Those eyes, that laugh, that look of intense interest which somehow held such sexual promise – she shivered as she remembered, with a mixture of pleasurable anticipation and terror. This was the excitement, the spice of danger that had been lacking in her life until now. He had said nothing about seeing her again but she was sure that he was interested. The suspense of waiting for his next move was almost unbearable.

She did not have to wait long. At five o'clock an envelope was brought to her by messenger. Inside was a note: '7.30 p.m. The Albermarle. Ask for Charles Pendlebury.'

Sheila was trembling as she tried to take in the message. Charles Pendlebury was Simon's private secretary and a former colleague of hers. He was a quiet, attractive bachelor in his late thirties in whom she had once been mildly interested, but she had soon dismissed the idea. After throwing out one or two minor lures and getting no response she had reached the conclusion that he was simply not interested in women. She was convinced that Simon was merely using Charles's name as a front, but what had he in mind? She read the note again. The terseness of the message made her feel like a junior summoned to a prefect's room: 'My study. Six o'clock. Bring your Latin prep. Brentford major.' The tone irritated her. It was as if Simon Brentford thought she was a push-over. Well she wasn't and she simply wouldn't go, that was all.

Somehow, though, at 7.15 p.m., Sheila found herself sitting in a taxi which was taking her to the Albermarle Hotel. Impatiently watching the fare clicking up on the meter, she asked herself what the hell she was doing? As she walked into the hotel's green-carpeted lobby, trying to look like any other innocent guest, she asked herself again. There was no sensible answer.

'Mr Charles Pendlebury, please,' she said quietly to the hall porter.

'Yes, madam, he is expecting you.' His tone was bland. 'The Buckingham Suite, first floor, to your left.' Without looking up at her he continued to write in a large book behind the desk. Sheila was non-plussed. Somehow she had expected more of a reaction from him.

She made her way up the thickly carpeted stairs and stopped outside a set of panelled maple doors which bore the name 'Buckingham Suite' in raised gold letters. She hesitated for a moment, then tapped gently on the door. It opened instantly as Simon reached out and pulled her inside, slamming it shut behind her.

'Thank God you came,' he said. 'I thought you were going to let me down.' He moved away across the room, taking off his jacket and slinging it over a chair. 'What music do you like?' he asked in a peremptory tone, fiddling with the radio.

Sheila, still standing by the door, watched him in bewilderment. 'I really don't mind,' she replied timidly. Simon started to undo his tie. Then he looked across at her. 'Come on, for God's sake. I want you,' he said impatiently. Sheila stood her ground.

'Then you'll have to come and get me,' her voice was defiant. She was beginning to regret that she had ever agreed to meet this strange, abrupt man. This was certainly not how he had been on the train that morning.

Simon gave a short laugh. 'Don't play games with me. You know what you want.' He strode across the room and before Sheila could protest, began to drag her towards the bed. She tried to fight him off, resenting this arrogant appropriation of her body. As he struggled to remove her clothes, pinning her down with his muscular weight, she writhed beneath him. Soon, shamefully, she began to find the battle exciting. It was as if he was desperate to have her and his ardour inflamed her own. His hand found its way underneath her skirt and he pulled violently at her pants, ripping them off. Then, fumbling for his belt, he released his trousers and plunged himself into her. Their love-making was hectic, frantic, and cataclysmic. When it had reached its convulsive climax there was silence, broken only by their exhausted breathing.

After a few moments Sheila slipped off the bed and went into the bathroom. She felt hot, sticky and sore. The double-sized marble bath looked cool and inviting. 'OK if I have a bath?' she called back into the bedroom. Too bad if it's not, she thought, I bloody well deserve it. She turned on the taps, poured in a dollop of scented oil, then eased herself out of the few remaining bits of clothing she still had on.

There was a movement behind her, and she felt two cool firm hands clasp her breasts and a man's sinewy naked body pressed close to hers. 'Only if I can join you,' said Simon's voice in her ear. She leaned back, luxuriously, feeling his cock stiffen in response.

'I'll bet you were a tartar when you were a prefect,' she said eventually.

'How did you guess?' he replied, laughing quietly. 'Little boys are a perfect nuisance, didn't you know?'

Big boys can be pretty tiresome too, she thought, but when he made love to her again amid the scented foam he was as tender and considerate as he had earlier been violent and demanding. That night was the first of many they were to spend together.

Midday in the exclusive Roman suburb of Parioli: hot, dusty and still. Behind their tall, wrought-iron gates, its elegant villas slumbered under the hot June sun. The van der Velt villa slept too, its marble halls cool and silent – except for, somewhere in the very depths of the house, a dull roaring noise strangely reminiscent of feeding time at the zoo.

Amanda, in the kitchen, banged on the table yet again. 'Shut UP,' she screamed. 'If you don't shut up and eat up, you can forget all about any ice-cream. I'll eat it myself, I promise.' Livingstone Jnr and Winthrop stopped shouting for a moment and looked at her in pained surprise. Amanda looked at them. 'I mean it,' she said, with as much venom as she could muster. They shrugged and applied themselves to their spaghetti bolognese. It was almost more than Amanda could bear to watch them eating it, pasty strands writhing from their mouths, blobs of red sauce flying everywhere, but spaghetti was what they had demanded and she was deriving a perverse sort of satisfaction from making sure they got it down.

Usually she was spared the tiresome task of supervising the boys' lunch – the cook and maids were, in that soppy Italian way, only too happy to do it for her. But today was a half-day for the rest of the servants, so she was forced to take her turn. The noise level began to rise once more as the boys lost interest in their food yet again and began a fight using breadsticks as weapons, but before Amanda could intervene the jangle of the doorbell rang loudly through the kitchen. Automatically she waited for one of the servants to answer it, then remembered that there was no one in the house except her and the boys. The bell rang again, insistently. Wearily Amanda got to her feet and went to answer it, hissing 'eat, or else' to the boys as she left the kitchen.

A chauffeur was standing on the doorstep. He touched his cap as she opened the door. 'Buongiorno, signorina. Meeses King is here.'

Amanda looked beyond him at the sleek limousine with its tinted windows parked outside the gates.

'Mrs King? Mrs Julius T. King?'

'Si, signorina.'

'Ask her to come in, please.' He smiled, touching his cap again, and hurried down the path. Amanda watched as Mamie King was helped out of the car, then moved forward to greet her. 'Mrs King, how nice to see you again. Do come in.'

'Oh, hi, Amanda, isn't it?' said Mamie King with her sweet smile. Then she peered past her into the hall, an agitated expression on her face. 'I hate to trouble Mrs van der Velt, but I've been so upset about it that I just had to drop by and see if it was here,' she said rapidly, hurrying up the steps.

'I'm afraid Mrs van der Velt is out at the moment,' said Amanda, following her. 'She won't be back until later this afternoon.'

Mamie's face fell. 'Oh my God,' she wailed. 'I thought she'd help me find it. It's simply got to be here.' Amanda had never seen anyone actually wring their hands before. It was fascinating.

'Perhaps I can help, Mrs King,' she said sympathetically, ushering her into the cool of the hall.

'Well, my dear,' said Mamie, 'I surely hope you can. I have just the smallest problem, and if Julius T. should find me out, I guess I won't make it to Thanksgiving.'

'You've lost something,' said Amanda intelligently. Mamie King nodded sadly. 'What is it, Mrs King?'

'Just the most expensive piece of jewellery Julius T. ever bought me, that's all.' There was a note of pride in Mamie's voice. She went on, watching for Amanda's reaction, 'It came from the Duchess of Windsor's collection.'

'Wow!' said Amanda in spite of herself.

'I think I may have lost it out on the terrace, when we were having coffee after dinner. I know I had it before, because I checked it in the mirror when I went to powder my nose.'

'Perhaps we'd better go and look,' said Amanda. 'Could you describe it?'

'Oh, it's adorable. It's the cutest little frog.'

'Frog!' exclaimed Amanda.

'It's made of diamonds, with a huge emerald for its eye. Frankly, I'd have to say it was quite out of proportion to the rest of its body, but it was a very famous emerald,' Mamie continued as they made their way out on to the terrace.

'Goodness,' said Amanda, trying to imagine it. 'It must be worth a lot of money.'

'Just about $80,000,' said Mamie, getting down on her hands and knees to peer among the flagstones.

'How big is it?' asked Amanda, kneeling beside her.

'About one and a half inches long, I guess.'

After they had searched for a few minutes, Amanda straightened up. 'I'm terribly sorry,' she said, 'but I'll have to go and see how the boys are getting on with their lunch. I'll be back in a moment.'

'Sure, honey, I'll keep on looking.' Mamie's voice was weary and despondent.

Amanda hurried back to the kitchen. The boys had pushed their half-finished plates of spaghetti aside and were digging into a litre tub of ice-cream apiece. They looked up guiltily as she entered. 'Winthrop, Livingstone,' she snapped. 'Have you seen a little frog brooch, a sparkly one. It might have been out on the terrace the other morning.'

The boys gazed at her in silence, their faces blank.

'Well,' she demanded. 'I'll find out, you know.'

Continued silence, but a tell-tale flicker from Winthrop, the weaker of the two.

Amanda pounced. 'Tell me, Winthrop, I know you've seen it.' She grabbed his arm, digging her fingers in until he winced with pain.

'Ow,' he shrieked, 'I'll tell my pa on you, Amanda.'

'No you won't,' said Amanda cruelly, 'you'll tell me where that frog is, because it's very valuable,' she emphasized her point with a pinch, 'and your pa will be very angry if he knows you've taken it,' another pinch.

Winthrop started to snivel. 'OK, OK,' he whimpered, ignoring Livingstone's furious glare, 'I'll tell if you let me go.' Amanda dropped his arm. He rubbed it, watching her resentfully.

'Go on,' she said.

'Well we did sort of find it, on the patio like you said, and then . . . ' he began to weep, 'and then . . . we carried it to the pond so it could play with the other frogs, and then we lorst it.'

'Is this true, Livingstone?' asked Amanda sternly, looking at his brother.

'I guess so,' said Livingstone sullenly. 'Are you going to tell on us to pa? Will he be mad?'

'No,' said Amanda in a kindlier voice. 'I'm not going to tell on you –

provided you are very, very good boys from now on. Now, we won't mention it again, any of us, will we?'

Amanda left the kitchen and her chastened charges and made her way back to the terrace, where Mamie King was now sitting down, looking sad.

'I'm sorry I was so long, Mrs King,' she said, 'but I was asking the boys if they'd seen anything of your brooch. They play out here and you know what sharp eyes children have. But they haven't found it. It looks as if you must have lost it somewhere else, I'm afraid.'

'Well, honey,' said Mamie, 'I'm beginning to think you're right. I guess I might have lost it back at the hotel, after all. However, I can't spend any more time here, we're flying back to LA tonight. Thanks a million for your help, my dear, anyway.' She got to her feet looking tired and older. As Amanda accompanied her to the car, she turned to her with a final look of appeal. 'Look, sweetheart, you keep looking for that brooch, OK. It was just so adorable I really would hate to think I'll never see it again. If you do find it, get in touch with me in LA and you can be sure I'll be real grateful – *real* grateful.'

Amanda waved her off, then walked briskly back through the house and out into the garden. She made her way down the steps to the square lily pond, lined with statues, that was the focal point of the lower terrace. She walked around it for a while, gazing intently into the water, then with a grunt of satisfaction bent down and fished something out. Wrapping the object carefully in a handkerchief she stowed it in her pocket and strolled back towards the house, humming a little tune.

'Could I speak to Charles Pendlebury, please?'

'Speaking.'

'Oh Charles, it's Elizabeth Brentford.'

'Good morning, Mrs Brentford. I'm afraid that Mr Brentford is at the House.'

'Yes, I know. It's you I want to speak to.'

Charles Pendlebury concealed his surprise. 'Of course, how can I help?'

'I have to see you – in private.'

Charles glanced around him, as though eavesdroppers were everywhere. 'Certainly. When would suit you?'

'How soon could we meet?'

Charles Pendlebury had not held down his job in the civil service for fifteen years without learning how to deal with potentially fraught situations. He could hear the desperation in Elizabeth Brentford's voice. 'Lunch today?' he suggested calmly.

'That would be wonderful! Where?'

Charles hesitated fractionally. What could the problem be? The girl? The other woman? Either subject needed careful handling. He could take an extended lunch-hour today, with Simon safely occupied, but where? Any restaurant within shouting distance of Westminster was infested with politicians, journalists, or both, and they would be lucky to escape notice. He thought swiftly, then gave the address of his Albany apartment. 'We'll have some peace and quiet there. Shall we say twelve-thirty?'

'That would be perfect.'

When Charles replaced the receiver, he sat for a moment, lost in thought. He had admired Elizabeth Brentford for years. She was exactly his sort of woman – beautiful, serene, intelligent, a perfect wife and mother. It was beyond his comprehension why Simon should ever wish to stray. The women with whom he dallied were as different from Elizabeth as it was possible to imagine. Charles thought him a reckless fool, but he guessed that the same demon that drove Simon to scale the heights in his career also urged him onward to fresh sexual conquests. They were normally casual, unimportant affairs that posed no threat to the stability of his career or his marriage. His was simply an appetite, a need that had to be fulfilled.

Charles had often pondered idly on his own chances with Elizabeth. He knew that she liked his company and trusted him. They sought each other out and enjoyed each other's company when, as happened from time to time, they found themselves at the same functions. Now, it seemed, their relationship was about to take another step forward. She actually needed him, as a friend, an adviser, perhaps a shoulder to cry on.

From behind the heavy brocade curtains of his apartment, he saw a taxi cab draw up outside and Elizabeth emerge, looking around with an unusually anxious air as she paid the driver. Charles waited by the internal phone and answered it as soon as it rang.

'Charles?'

'Come on up, Mrs Brentford. I'm on the second floor.'

When he opened the door, her appearance all but took his breath away. He always forgot how lovely she was, with her blonde colouring, her fine complexion, her large slate-blue eyes. She was wearing an elegantly simple Chanel suit in a fine blue-grey tweed, the brass-buttoned jacket trimmed with dark grey braid. Beneath it, he glimpsed a silk blouse in a colour which matched her eyes. He smiled at her appreciatively as he welcomed her. She stood in the hallway and looked around her. 'What a lovely place, this is. I had no idea you lived here. It's one of Jack Worthing's addresses in *The Importance of Being Earnest*, isn't it – Albany?'

He smiled again. 'I believe so.' Of course, they had a shared interest in the theatre. 'I was very lucky to get the apartment when it came up.' He ushered her into the beautifully proportioned panelled living-room, simply but pleasantly furnished in a comfortable masculine style. At the far end of the room a small glass-topped dining-table was already set with two places.

'I've managed to knock up a bit of smoked salmon. Well, to be perfectly honest, Fortnums did. Can I give you a drink first?'

Elizabeth gave a small cry of delight. 'Charles, this is so thoughtful. I never expected it.'

Charles smiled happily. 'It's a pleasure.' He went on, 'I've some Chablis in the fridge. Will that do?'

'Lovely,' said Elizabeth. While he was gone, she wandered around looking at the room, taking in her surroundings with pleasure. Charles obviously had good taste: on the floor there were a couple of superb Shiraz rugs in glowing reds and blues, and his pictures included a beautiful little Paul Nash watercolour and a couple of admirable pencil drawings which looked very much like Sickert.

He soon returned bearing a tray of smoked salmon and lemon, a green salad and the bottle of white wine. Elizabeth was touched; it seemed a long time since a man had gone to so much trouble for her and even longer since she had been alone with one in his flat. It made her feel almost young again. Charles poured her a glass of wine and handed it to her. 'This is so nice of you,' she said sincerely. 'I can't remember the last time anyone did something like this for me.' She took a sip of wine and smiled at him gently.

'It's no trouble at all,' said Charles, looking a little confused, 'but I'm afraid I couldn't manage the brown bread and butter – the cupboard was bare.'

'But this is perfect,' she said going straight to the table and sitting down.

Soon, relaxed by the wine, they were laughing and exchanging parliamentary gossip as they demolished the delicious salmon. When they had finished it, Charles said apologetically, 'I'm afraid pudding is a rather ancient tin of gooseberries and the remains of some ice-cream that has been in the freezer since Jack Worthing's day.'

'What could be better,' said Elizabeth, starting to enjoy herself.

It was while they were tucking into this schoolboy treat that Charles suddenly said with a direct look, 'Now, what was it you wanted to talk to me about, Mrs Brentford?'

'Please, don't you think it's time you called me Elizabeth? After all I call you by your Christian name.'

'Your husband calls you Liz,' said Charles, as if to himself.

'I prefer Elizabeth,' she said quietly.

'Very well. Now why did you want to see me – Elizabeth?' He relished the sound of her name.

She looked down at her coffee and stirred it thoughtfully. Eventually she said, without looking up, 'Did you know that my husband is having an affair?'

'Yes,' said Charles curtly.

She gazed at him, her eyes pleading. 'Does everyone know?'

'No, of course not. He's very discreet.' He stopped short. Elizabeth looked as though someone had hit her in the face.

Charles realized he had blundered. He leant across the table and took one of her hands in his. 'I'm so sorry, please forgive me,' he said earnestly. But Elizabeth was not listening.

'What is she like?'

'Who?'

'This woman. Whoever she is.'

Charles thought it best to lie. 'I've no idea, I've never seen her.'

'But you are sure that there is someone?' she insisted.

Charles began to wish he had not been so honest. 'Yes, I'm afraid so.'

'Of course I've known it for some time,' said Elizabeth. Her face was composed now, but the underlying strain still showed in her shadowed eyes. 'I've known about the others too.'

For once in his life Charles did not have a ready answer. He looked at her in silence, admiring her more than ever for her gallantry. 'I think you're a remarkable woman, Elizabeth,' he said finally.

Elizabeth looked directly into his eyes. 'Do you?' she said. 'What's so remarkable about me, staying with a man who no longer loves me?'

Charles looked away and then said quietly, 'I'm quite sure that Simon loves you.'

'Are you?' The question was almost defiant. 'So why does he need other women?' Charles started to speak, but she interrupted him. 'Don't lie to me, Charles. It's kind of you to try to spare me, but I know that Simon has been unfaithful to me for years.'

Charles could only continue to hold her hand in mute sympathy.

'Why does he do it?' she asked, turning huge unhappy eyes on him.

He gazed at her troubled face, unable to answer. Suddenly she lowered her head. 'I don't think I can go on – I can't cope any more,' she said brokenly. He thought she might cry, but Elizabeth was made of sterner stuff.

There was a long silence and eventually Charles spoke. 'I want to help.'

'You are helping,' she said. 'I needed to tell someone.'

He took advantage of the moment. 'Elizabeth, I will do everything I can to make it easier for you. I – I've always had such a high regard for you.'

She smiled at him. 'You are a dear man, Charles. I like you more than I can say – and I trust you,' she added quietly.

'What can I do?'

'There's not much you can do. What is her name, by the way?'

But Charles was not about to reveal the identity of Simon's current mistress, even to Elizabeth. 'I don't know her,' he said.

This was not true. He had worked with Sheila before he joined Simon, and had liked her very much. She was an attractive girl, full of fun and energy, and he knew that Simon was making her deeply unhappy. Soon, when things became too serious, Simon would bring the affair to an abrupt end, as he had with all the others. They were all cast in the same mould: bright, intelligent, independent women who accepted the limitations of their position at first, but little by little became more deeply involved until they were desperately in love with Simon. Then, when the inevitable happened, Simon would drop them with cruel suddenness, and start looking for a replacement. Charles recognized that this was part of the power game that dominated Simon's life. He only wished he could take Elizabeth away from him and show her the appreciation and tender care that she deserved. He looked at her sitting opposite him and the thought made him dizzy with longing.

'I'll never leave him, you know,' she said, as though she had been able to read his thoughts.

The dream faded abruptly. As a boy he had been kicked on the leg by a bad-tempered horse. It had hurt a lot. Now he felt as he might have done if the animal had kicked him in the stomach instead. The shock gave him courage. 'You never know what might happen,' he said brusquely. 'You may change your mind.'

'I suppose anything's possible,' replied Elizabeth wearily, finally slipping her hand from his. She changed the subject. 'I gather you know all about this business of his daughter?'

Disappointed, Charles saw that the moment had passed. 'Oh yes, Simon had to tell me. The girl has been ringing the office saying she would like to talk to her father.'

Elizabeth sat back in her chair and sighed heavily. 'I thought we'd managed to get rid of her,' she said.

'She's out of the country, at any rate. I believe she's in Rome. At least that's where she said she was calling from.'

'Rome,' said Elizabeth in surprise. ' What's she doing there?'

'Having a good time, I imagine,' said Charles drily, as he caught the pained exasperation on Elizabeth's face.

'When will it all end,' she asked, not expecting an answer, but pleased at the comfort of having Charles there by her.

'Oh, well,' she sighed again, 'I suppose it's just going to go on and on, like the other women.'

'I hope not, for your sake.'

'If I left him, what would I do?'

There was a long silence. Finally Charles spoke, hesitating over the words. 'You could always come to me.' He did not look at her as he said this, but kept his eyes firmly fixed on the table, twisting his napkin with his left hand.

Elizabeth looked at him sharply. 'I do believe you're serious,' she said.

Charles continued in a low voice. 'I'm utterly serious. I know it's not very likely, but if you do ever leave him, I would like you to consider coming to me. I know I could make you happy.' He still did not look at her. He dare not. For the first time they both became aware of the rumble of traffic outside in Piccadilly.

Elizabeth did not move, but sat and watched him with an unfathomable expression in her eyes. Finally she answered. 'I wish it were possible.' And for a moment she almost believed it might be.

Charles looked up quickly, hope rising. 'I didn't ask you to my flat to make love to you, you must believe that,' he said earnestly. Elizabeth smiled at him with great affection.

'I believe you,' her voice was soft and warm. A long moment passed, then she looked at her little gold watch. 'I suppose I should go home now.'

'Yes.'

'And you should get back to work.'

'Yes, I should.'

Neither of them made a move. There was another long silence. Finally Charles spoke, 'You know you can ring me at any time.'

'Thank you . . . and you can ring me. But you will be discreet, won't you?'

'You know I will.'

'How bad is it?'

Derek Wilson, the production assistant, threw the insurance claim on to the desk in front of him, leant back in his chair and ran both hands through his hair before replying to Leonie's question. 'It's bad.'

Leonie, just arrived at the studio, was standing in the open doorway of his office. She looked cool and immaculate in white cotton jeans and a pistachio-green silk T-shirt, but inside she was fizzing with fury and frustration. When she heard his reply she came in, shutting the door behind her with a bang.

'Does he need surgery?' she asked.

'They're going to stitch him up as best they can,' said Derek tersely, 'but there's no way he's going to use that arm for some time.'

Leonie stared at him, green eyes narrowed. 'How long?'

Derek looked at her steadily for a moment before speaking. 'Leo, it's a question of recast or rewrite,' he stated. Leonie's heart sank. Derek was good at his job and there was no way he would tell her this if it wasn't absolutely necessary. But Carlo was one of their chief assets, a vital pivot for the film's action as well as a big selling-point for the continental market.

'We can't lose Carlo,' she said firmly, hoping to God she was right.

'OK, so we write around him,' replied Derek.

'How much footage do we have of the fight?' she asked, thinking furiously.

'Not enough,' he said, with a curiously blank expression.

'But we did a whole morning's shoot,' said Leonie. 'What about all the stuff you shot before the accident?'

Derek regarded her steadily, 'It was no good, Leo.'

'What do you mean?'

Derek hesitated and looked down at the desk, shifting the papers in front of him. 'Rob wasn't on form,' he said reluctantly. 'We can't use any of the stuff we got this morning.'

Leonie's mouth tightened. 'Well we're just going to have to salvage something.'

Derek sighed. 'You'd better come and have a look at the rushes. I don't think you're going to like what you see, but it's up to you.'

Leonie knew that this was the ultimate thumbs down. Bloody, bloody Rob, she thought. How could he have been so stupid. He should know by now that a serious actor simply did not go out and get pissed the night before a big fight scene. Keeping off the booze and making sure you got your beauty sleep was one of the fundamental tenets of a film actor's life – at least a successful one. Time enough to let rip when shooting was over and the film was safely in the editors' hands. If he hadn't the self-control and maturity to respect the rules . . . she loved him, for sure, but this sort of thing was unforgivable. He had let himself down, he had let her down, and worst of all he had let the whole cast and crew down – not to mention poor Carlo, whose wound, if it proved serious, might affect his whole career. She ground her teeth, thinking of what she would say to Rob as soon as she got hold of him. By heaven, she would make him wish he'd never touched a drink in his life, so she would. Meanwhile, the pressing problem was how the hell to rescue the situation.

She took a deep breath, forcing herself to be calm. 'All right, Derek,' she said, the dangerous sparkle in her eye the only hint of her inner turmoil. 'Get the writers in. Rejig the ending.'

'Problem,' said Derek. 'They're in Amsterdam on the Anne Frank mini-series.'

Leonie bit back her frustration. She knew that the Anne Frank project was very dear to the hearts of Ted and Eric, their writers. They had been trying to set it up for years; they certainly weren't going to drop everything just to rescue her little swashbuckling romance.

Derek read her thoughts. 'If you pay them enough, they might give us a long weekend to rewrite.' It would barely be adequate, they both knew, and the budget was already pared to the bone.

'When will Carlo be well enough to work again?' asked Leonie.

'A couple of weeks, ten days if we're lucky, only for close-ups, though.' Derek looked at her and, when she did not reply, went on,

·

'Leo, we both know we can't afford to wait for him. There's only one way around this, as I see it. We rewrite the ending, cut the fight and shoot round Carlo, then try to get his stuff in the can in a couple of days, the minute he can stagger on set.'

'No,' said Leonie firmly. 'We can't cut the fight, it's the climax of the whole movie.'

'In that case,' said Derek, 'it's going to cost a whole lot of dosh. I suggest you hop over to LA and sweet talk the money boys into giving us another two weeks' shooting money. In the meantime I'll get on to Ted and Eric and see if they can do anything for us.' He paused and looked at her enquiringly. 'Well, you're the boss, what do you think?'

'I don't like it,' said Leonie slowly, 'but at the moment I can't think of any alternative. I'll try and get the first flight out tomorrow morning.' She looked at Derek and grinned ruefully, 'God, what a balls-up.'

'Life's a bitch, innit?'

'Too right.' Leonie laughed briefly, then her expression hardened. 'And now,' she said, with no amusement in her voice whatsoever, 'I suppose I'd better go and have a word with Robert Fenton and find out what the hell he thinks he's been playing at all day.'

·

6

When the cast and crew of *Swords at Sunset* reassembled for the afternoon's filming, you could have cut the atmosphere with a knife. Everyone was nervous and on edge after Carlo's accident. They would miss him badly: as one of that select group of intensely professional actors who are always prepared to give of their best regardless of domestic upheaval, personal tragedy or ill health, he had always been a tower of strength both on set and off it. Then, word had filtered back by some mysterious process that there were likely to be money problems. If anyone had doubted the accuracy of the rumour, or the seriousness of Carlo's injury, the sight of Leonie's set, furious face as she stalked through the studios would have confirmed that something was very badly wrong indeed.

Just before the afternoon's rehearsal finally began, Leonie was seen to depart in a hurry, looking even angrier than when she arrived. Rumour, again accurate, said that she had been found a seat on an evening flight to LA and was off to try and sweet talk her co-producers into letting them extend their filming schedule. Shortly afterwards, Rob appeared from his caravan, pale-faced and monosyllabic. He sat hunched in a corner of the set, speaking to no one, waiting his turn to rehearse.

There were some shaky moments during the next few hours before the hurriedly rescheduled scene was finally safely in the can. Though Rob and the actor playing the Cardinal did their considerable best, the brief period that both had had to prepare inevitably showed. Fluffed lines and missed moves brought the tension near breaking point, and the number of retakes mounted inexorably.

Towards evening, the tension was lightened a little when Andy Berena, Carlo's stuntman, returning from visiting Carlo in hospital, reported that the injury was not as serious as had first been feared. The ligaments in the arm had not been severed and Carlo's sword-fighting prowess should be unimpaired, though he still would not be able to hold a sword for several weeks. The relief everyone felt at his news was reflected in the performances of the two principal actors. It began to look as if the afternoon's filming would be successful after all.

Andy Berena, a veteran of some eighty movies and though in his late fifties still able to throw himself from a horse, a tree or a building with apparent ease, stayed to watch the final takes. His muscle-packed frame was hunched and his lined face thoughtful as he looked about him, noting the still-subdued mood of the whole unit. When the director had called 'cut', for the last time, he stepped on to the set and held up his hand for silence. Everyone stopped what they were doing and waited expectantly wondering if there was more news of Carlo.

'Boys and girls,' said Andy, looking at the sea of sombre faces surrounding him, ' I know we're all upset by what happened this morning, and we're very sorry for both Carlo and Rob.' There was a murmur of approval. 'But we all know Carlo would want us to carry on and make sure this is the best bloody picture he's ever worked on. We owe it to him, don't we? So I think we should all cheer up and think positive, and to help us I'm going to have a party,' he looked around, grinning, 'and quite a lot of you have been to my parties before, haven't you?' The murmur of approval swelled to a roar. Most of the cast and crew knew that Andy was one of the film world's ace party-givers. 'OK, let's make it Friday night, most of you know where my place is, see you there about nine, bring a bottle and *lots* of girls.'

As people began to move off the set in little groups, talking and laughing, Rob walked away alone. He knew he had done something to redeem himself that afternoon, but he didn't feel like company. He was still sore from the tongue-lashing Leonie had given him earlier. She had made him feel like a whipped schoolboy and though he knew she was right to be angry her peremptory manner had infuriated him. There had been hard words said on both sides, words that both of them would regret, before Leonie had stormed out of the studios, leaving him feeling both angry and very resentful.

There was a gentle tap on his shoulder. He turned to see the cheerful, guileless face of Giovanni Frescaldi. 'Eh, Rob,' said Giovanni, 'is good news about Carlo. You want to come for a beer with me now, maybe a pizza after? I hear Leonie's gone to LA – you don't want to be alone.'

'Thanks, John, but no,' said Rob. 'I think I'd rather go home and get pissed on my own. I won't be much company tonight.'

'OK, fine,' said Giovanni easily. 'But you come to the party, Friday?'

'Sure,' said Rob glumly, 'why not. I'll be there. I've nothing better to do.'

It was two weeks since Amanda's visit to the Cinecittà studios and she had seen nothing more of Giovanni. She had visited La Mosca on several occasions, but had drawn a blank, learning only that the unit was out on location, filming somewhere south of Rome. She would have to wait till they returned to make her next move, she decided.

To fill in time on her Friday off, she decided to do some sightseeing. She had been in Rome for a month now and had hardly seen a thing. Like practically every other visitor to Rome she made her way first to the Piazza di Spagna, dominated by the Spanish Steps, that magnificent open-air staircase that is meeting-place, posing-place and tourist landmark all in one.

As she approached the steps, planning to climb them to enjoy the splendid view across Rome from the piazza at the top, she passed a newsvendor's stall. Her eye was caught by a photograph in the day's edition of *Il Messagero*, the Rome daily paper. Even in blurred newsprint and lying on its side in a rack, the subject was unmistakably Rob Fenton. Hurriedly, she bought a copy and, leaving the Spanish Steps unclimbed, she settled down at a table in a nearby pavement café to read the story attached to the picture. At first she struggled, but underneath Rob's photo was a smaller picture of an Italian actor, Carlo Fillippi, with the word *accidente* in large letters. Gradually she managed to make out that there had indeed been an accident, somehow involving Rob Fenton, and that the Italian was seriously wounded. Leonie O'Brien had apparently flown to Los Angeles and there was speculation that the entire film would have to be abandoned. The news was a blow to Amanda. She had been doing so well and now it looked as if the principal characters in her little drama were vanishing before her eyes.

Engrossed in her thoughts, she did not notice at first that someone was standing beside her. Then, sensing herself observed, she looked up and to her astonishment found herself face to face with her adoptive mother.

'Amanda,' said Beryl, smiling at her with genuine pleasure, 'I thought it was you. I didn't like to bother you at work, but I was sure I would bump into you sooner or later.'

Of course, Beryl had said she would be visiting Rome, but Amanda had been so taken up with her own plans that she had hardly given the news another moment's thought. She recovered quickly to make the best of the situation. 'It's nice to see you,' she said coolly. 'Won't you join me? I'll get you a drink. It's boiling, isn't it?'

'Yes,' agreed Beryl, 'I must say I could do with something. Is that lemon you're drinking? It looks delicious.'

Amanda regarded her with interest. She looked completely different – about ten years younger for a start – and, with her newly blonded hair, a light tan and wearing a simple but beautifully cut black and white summer dress, really quite glamorous. It was not a word that Amanda would have used to describe Beryl before.

'You look very nice,' she said, as Beryl sat down opposite her. Beryl stroked her blonde bob self-consciously. 'Yes, thank you, people seem to like the new hair-style.'

Amanda was surprised to find that she was genuinely pleased to see Beryl. She realized with a pang that she was really quite fond of the old thing – after all Beryl had always done her best for her – and yet at the same time she still could not help resenting the fact that she had taken the place of her real mother. But in spite of these mixed feelings, it was good to be with her again.

'How's the job going?' asked Beryl tentatively.

'It's all right,' Amanda shrugged. 'The little boys are vile, of course, but the parents aren't bad. And it's a nice place.'

'Oh dear, I'm sorry to hear about the boys.' Beryl laughed sympathetically, adding, 'Children can be so difficult, you know.' She stopped suddenly as she realized what she had said, but Amanda, ordering her drink, did not appear to notice. 'So, how are the Vander-bilts treating you?' she went on, moving quickly to a less contentious subject.

'Van der Velt,' corrected Amanda. 'They're rich, but not that rich.'

'Yes, of course.' Beryl smiled. 'But do you think you'll be happy there?' she persisted.

'I'm not planning on staying very long, you know,' said Amanda.

'Oh. So what are you going to do next?'

'I've got plans,' said Amanda enigmatically, her old arrogant self resurfacing. Beryl regarded her for a moment and wondered yet again where she had gone wrong with her.

'What do you think of Rome?' asked Amanda, after a brief silence.

'I think it's the most beautiful place I've ever seen,' replied Beryl simply.

'And where are you going next?'

'Vienna.' Beryl looked dreamy. 'But I'm here for at least a week.'

Blast! though Amanda. It may have been quite nice to see Beryl again, but she did not want her hanging around cramping her style.

'Have you made any friends?' asked Beryl, seeing that Amanda's attention was drifting away.

'No, not really. I'm so busy I don't get a chance to meet anyone,' said Amanda untruthfully.

At that moment a delighted voice hailed her from across the square, 'Signorina Amanda, buongiorno.'

It was Giovanni, who was now approaching rapidly, a happy smile on his face. Amanda was pleased to see him, but wished she could have been alone. However, there was obviously no chance of getting rid of Beryl for the moment. She was sitting there looking very comfortable, sipping her drink and surveying the handsome young Italian with a surprising amount of interest.

'Signorina, I am so happy to find you.' He stopped abruptly as he noticed Beryl, and his eyes gleamed. 'Oh, but please forgive me.' He bowed politely in Beryl's direction and Amanda decided to submit to the inevitable.

'Giovanni,' she said, 'this is a friend of mine – Beryl Willoughby.' She threw Beryl a challenging glance, daring her to contradict the relationship. Beryl caught her breath and looked at her sharply. Amanda continued the introduction, 'And this is Giovanni Frescaldi.' Beryl stretched out her hand. Instead of shaking it, Giovanni bent over it and kissed it gallantly.

'Enchanted, signora,' he murmured.

'How do you do, Signore Frescaldi?' said Beryl, blushing slightly as she spoke.

'May I join you ladies?'

Before Amanda could speak, Beryl answered for her. 'It would be our pleasure, signore.'

Amanda gasped. This was not the shy, quiet Beryl she knew. She was in a quandary: she wanted to question Giovanni about what was happening to the film, and to Leonie and Rob, but she did not want to do so in front of Beryl.

'Giovanni,' she said, 'I'm glad I met you. I think I might have heard of a job for your sister. If she hasn't found work yet, I'll get some more details. Perhaps we could meet again later?' It was a total fabrication, she had forgotten all about his sister until now, but she would be able to think of something; the van der Velts' friends were always changing their staff, there was bound to be a job going somewhere. The point was to arrange to see Giovanni alone.

'You are very kind,' said Giovanni, smiling at Beryl, 'but Sophia has a job now. No, I am glad to see you because I want to invite you to a party – tonight. It is for all the cast and crew, you know. Will be *very* good.'

Amanda's heart leapt. 'A party. I'd love to go,' she replied eagerly. She prayed that the newspaper report about Leonie being in LA was correct. It would allow her to get seriously to work on Mr Fenton.

'I am so pleased,' said Giovanni. 'And perhaps,' he gave Beryl a soulful look from deep brown eyes, 'perhaps your charming friend would come too?'

Oh no, thought Amanda. Please don't let her!

'That is very kind of you,' said Beryl shyly, 'but I think not.'

'Oh, but signora, it is just some friends of mine – actors, film people – Amanda knows them . . . they are very nice.'

'I'm sure they are,' said Beryl. 'It's just that I'm not very good at parties.' She smiled shyly at him again.

'That is so sad,' sighed Giovanni, then he brightened, 'but, signora, you will permit me to take you out – another time.' He gazed at her ardently.

Amanda watched them both in amazement, wondering what the hell was going on? Surely to God he couldn't fancy her own mother! She must be all of twenty-five years older than him. She waited for Beryl's reply.

'Do you like music, Signore Frescaldi?' Beryl asked, tentatively.

'Please call me Giovanni, signora . . . Yes, I like music very much.'

'I have a spare ticket for the opera tomorrow night. Perhaps you would like to come with me?'

Giovanni's face lit up as if no greater treat had ever been offered him. 'Oh, signora, that would be wonderful. Give me your address and I will come to your hotel before.'

'No,' said Beryl firmly, with a slightly panic-stricken expression. 'Perhaps it would be better if we met at the *teatro*.'

'Whatever you say, signora,' said Giovanni, with a gallant gesture.

Beryl, looking suddenly flustered, started to gather up her things. 'I think I'd better go,' she said hurriedly, rising from the table. 'It's getting rather late and I've promised to meet the others. So nice to see you, Amanda, I hope we meet again soon. And you, Signore . . .

Giovanni,' she went on self-consciously, 'I'll see you on Saturday, at the opera.'

'Of course,' Giovanni leapt to his feet, smiling brilliantly, 'it will be a very great pleasure. Arrivederci, Signora Beryl.' He stood gazing after her for a moment as Beryl hurried away down the Via Sistina, then sat down again facing Amanda. 'A charming woman, your friend,' he said with a grin. 'Don't you think so, Amanda?'

Amanda looked at him levelly. 'Very nice indeed, Giovanni. Now, what about this party . . . ?'

Leonie strode into the breakfast loggia of the Beverly Hills Hotel. The dark green décor and the lush foliage of the trees growing on the patio outside gave the cool, airy room a welcome sense of tranquillity. She had just driven there in rush-hour traffic through a blanket of Los Angeles smog. Now the relentless California sun was starting to burn its way through the haze and by lunchtime it would be blisteringly hot.

She was mildly irritated to see that, although she was on time to the minute, her breakfast guests were already seated at a round table in the corner of the loggia. Marvin Mandel, a sleek and prosperous-looking Californian in his mid-fifties, rose to greet her with a dazzling smile. His iron-grey hair cropped close to his head, his trim, svelte figure encased in a perfectly cut silver suit, he was the very picture of the successful American businessmen and one of the shrewdest producers in the movie business. He had enormous charm, but deep down he was as tough as old boot leather. Leonie knew that she would have to use every ounce of guile and determination she possessed to persuade him to come up with the further million dollars she now needed to complete *Swords at Sunset*.

His companion, Judd Taylor, also got to his feet as Leonie approached. He was much the younger of the two, casually dressed in a cotton polo shirt and chinos, a taupe linen Armani jacket slung over the chair behind him. The clothes suited his boyish good looks and easy, open manner. Judd's father, now dead, had been boss of a major film studio and Judd himself had inherited both his parent's ability and a great deal of his money.

Both men seemed delighted to see Leonie, which did not fool her one little bit. All of them knew that a major financial wrangle was going to take place before breakfast was over.

'What a pleasure, Leonie,' began Marvin, kissing her lightly on the cheek. 'You look wonderful as usual.' Leonie was certain that after the long flight from Rome and a snatched few hours of sleep she looked nothing like wonderful, but she smiled sweetly at the compliment and sat down. The two men followed suit.

'You don't look so bad yourself, Marvin. Business good?'

Marvin shrugged, as Leonie knew he would. Getting him to admit that he was making money was like pulling teeth. 'So, so.'

Leonie interpreted this to mean that he had probably made another couple of million in the past week. Her spirits rose a little. If Marvin was flush with cash her task might be made slightly easier.

Judd captured a passing waiter. 'Another OJ for Miss O'Brien,' he said, indicating his own half-finished glass of freshly squeezed orange juice. He looked at Leonie, smiling. 'Ready to order now? It's waffles and coffee if I remember rightly.'

Leonie laughed, remembering how she had been teased before about her passion for the hotel's superb waffles. 'I shouldn't, but I can't resist.' Besides, she could do with raising her blood-sugar level. She needed the energy for the negotiations ahead.

'Nonsense,' observed Marvin. 'You, Leonie, are lucky enough to have a perfect figure. I, on the other hand, must content myself with a small portion of lightly scrambled eggs on rye. What for you, Judd?'

'Ham and eggs, hash browns, coffee.' Leonie knew he would work off the extra calories later on the tennis-court.

While they waited for their food, they padded the time with the small change of conversation. The two men enquired about Leonie's flight, filled her in on a few snippets of Hollywood gossip and asked about one or two mutual acquaintances currently in Europe. Leonie answered their question with only half her mind on the conversation. The other half was preoccupied with what was to come.

When their food appeared, delivered at breakneck speed by a delightfully camp waiter, they all ate in silence for a while. Leonie was relishing the delicious indulgence of her waffles when Marvin suddenly spoke. 'Unfortunate, this duelling business.'

Leonie deliberately sipped her coffee before replying firmly. 'It was a genuine accident, Marvin. Every precaution had been taken.'

'Sure it had. I know you, Leonie, wouldn't be anything less than thorough. Still, you can't deny it's going to cause us a big problem.' He shook his head sadly at her.

'How exactly did it happen?' asked Judd.

'It was just one of those things,' said Leonie. 'You know fight scenes. An inch or two off line and . . .' she left the rest to their imagination. Though she was still angry with Rob, she certainly wasn't going to throw him to this pair of wolves.

'Wasn't the way I heard it,' said Judd bluntly. 'I heard Rob screwed up.' He gave her a hard look, every atom of boyish good humour vanished as if it had never existed.

'Then you heard wrong,' said Leonie, returning stare for stare. 'I've told you it was an accident. Do you want to argue?' Her green eyes flashed. Judd began to fidget uncomfortably as she refused to drop her gaze, daring him to disagree.

Marvin leant across and patted her hand lightly. 'Look you two, we're not here to blame anyone. We're here to try and resolve the situation. Although,' he added in a wry tone, 'it looks as though that young man of yours may have cost you a lot of bucks.' The venomous look that Leonie turned on him caused him to add hastily, 'Well I'm afraid the backing for another two weeks' shooting is going to eat into your profits, Leonie.'

So what, thought Leonie. It sounded as if, at the end of the day, they intended to find the money. At the moment she didn't give a damn about profits. She just wanted to get out of this whole mess.

'By how much?' she asked in a businesslike way, looking Marvin straight in the eye.

The two men glanced at one another. Marvin cleared his throat. 'You must understand, Leonie, it's not simply a matter of the cost of rescheduling that we are looking at here. There's a very real possibility of heavy damages to pay. How seriously was this guy wounded?'

Leonie discovered that her waffles had lost their appeal. She pushed the plate away from her and drank some orange juice. She knew that Carlo, nice guy as he was, would almost certainly sue the company for his injury. He couldn't afford not to. 'Bad enough,' she admitted. 'And you're right, he probably will sue. But surely the insurance policy will cover all that?'

'Sure,' said Marvin, 'but that's not quite the whole story . . .' He hesitated.

Judd spelt it out. 'The fact is, Leonie, that this sort of thing makes people nervous. The moment the news of this accident got out, we lost some of our backing for that big sci-fi movie we start production on next year. Now as I'm sure you are aware, a great deal of pre-production money has already been spent on it and we can't afford to pull out now. Nor can we find any alternative sources of finance. The bottom line is, Leonie, that if we are to rescue *Swords at Sunset*, the money will have to come out of our own pockets and the backing for *Jupiter Dawn* from the box-office receipts of your movie.'

Bastards, thought Leonie. Of course they could find the money if they really wanted to. But then people like Marvin and Judd didn't get rich by throwing away opportunities to turn a fast buck. They were going to use this accident as an excuse to screw her into paying for *Jupiter Dawn* and at the moment there wasn't a thing she could do about it.

'Of course, my dear, you're not obliged to agree to our terms. There is nothing to stop you seeking the money you require elsewhere.' Marvin's tone was kindly. 'But I don't think you'll find it easy.'

'There's very little money around just now,' added Judd. 'The crisis in the Middle East hit share prices and put interest rates up. We have no choice but to pursue this course.' Judd's voice sounded harsh. He was leaving her no escape route.

'We have every confidence that *Swords at Sunset* will be a box-office smash and we'll make a lot of money – eventually.' Marvin looked at her encouragingly.

Leonie knew she was powerless to argue. At this moment she could cheerfully have wrung Rob's neck. She decided there was nothing for it but to give in gracefully. 'Well, gentlemen, if that's the only way out, so be it.' She smiled at them both, insincerely but effectively. 'And now, if you'll excuse me, I'll be on my way. You can confirm the financial details with Derek in Rome, can't you?'

'No problem.' Judd's tone was brisk as he clicked his fingers to attract the waiter's attention. 'Check, please.'

'Well, I have to say, Leonie, it's been wonderful to see you again.' Marvin spoke as though the previous conversation had never taken place. 'We'll be over in Europe in a couple of months you know. We must all get together and see a rough cut of the picture.'

'Yes, of course,' Leonie knew the rules. 'And you'll have dinner with us, of course.'

More smiles, more compliments, and Leonie found herself outside in the blinding sunshine again, driving along the perfectly manicured roads of Beverly Hills. The traffic had eased off a little and it didn't take her long to reach Sunset Boulevard and the Château Marmont Hotel, where she was staying. When she got to her room she kicked off her shoes, flung herself thankfully on to the bed and reached for the telephone. It was time to talk to Rob. She had tried to call him the previous night when she arrived, but he had been out. Now, alone and lonely in her rather bare room, she needed the comfort of his familiar voice. She stretched out her hand to pick up the receiver, but as she did so the phone rang. She snatched it up eagerly. It must be Rob: he would be calling to find out how her meeting had gone.

'Hi, hon,' drawled an all-too-familiar voice. Leonie felt ready to weep with disappointment. Bill, bloody Bill, she thought. Jesus. How the hell had he found her? Very easily, she realized. Everyone knew she was in town and the grapevine in Hollywood was more efficient than probably anywhere else on earth. Oh well!

'Hello, stranger,' she tried to make her tone light and friendly, though she was seething inside. 'How did you know I was here?'

'You know me, babe, I can smell you a mile off.'

'Thanks a lot,' said Leonie drily.

'It's the nose – it's never let me down. Your scent came wafting over the airways to me, downtown here in West Hollywood.'

Bill Newman's tone was affable. Too affable, Leonie thought.

'Where are you?' She regretted the question almost immediately.

'On Laurel Avenue,' he replied. 'I'm renting Micky Rooney's old place for a few months. I'm working on a new project. Hot stuff.'

'Good for you.' Leonie was still trying to be friendly but distant.

'No really, honey, this is the big one. I finally cracked it.'

Bullshit. Leonie knew bullshit when she heard it, especially from Bill, the biggest bullshitter of them all. And she should know, after all she'd been married to him for eight years. 'Fantastic, Bill,' she said insincerely. I'm really pleased for you.'

'Hey, sweetheart, why don't you come over? I'd love to show you the outline – you always did know how to pick a good movie script.'

More bullshit, thought Leonie. I never knew how to pick a good movie script. If I had, I wouldn't be scrabbling around for money like this. Her better judgement told her not to go downtown to see Bill. She knew it would probably end up as an all-night drinking session. But it was a long time since she had seen him – and once upon a time they had been good friends, as well as lovers. 'OK, I'll see you around six this evening,' she said.

But Bill had other ideas. 'Why not come over now – join me in a working breakfast?'

'I've just had a working breakfast,' said Leonie wearily.

'So, have another one. Come on, hon, no time like the present. I can't wait till tonight to see you.'

Leonie laughed, disarmed in spite of herself. 'You don't change, do you? How long is it since we got divorced?'

'Eight years. But who's counting?'

'You, obviously,' said Leonie tartly. Then she went on, 'OK, give me time to change – I'll be right over.' There was something infectious about Bill's good humour – when he was sober. Leonie sighed. She could have stayed happily with Bill for the rest of her life, if only he had not been, let's face it, she thought, a drunk.

She had met him when she first arrived in Hollywood, nearly fourteen years ago. Still young for her age, insecure, except in her work, and very vulnerable after the trauma of Simon's rejection and the birth and adoption of Amanda, she was trying to escape from the harsh realities with which life had presented her until that moment. After the drudgery of rep, she had recently had a couple of small but significant successes on the West End stage and the offer of a season with one of Britain's most prestigious theatre companies. People were beginning to talk about her as one of the most promising of the younger actresses. It was, she knew, perverse to throw all this up and head for Hollywood almost on a whim, but at the time it seemed that only by leaving England could she leave behind the pain and grief she still felt.

She had met Bill at a Hollywood party; not the usual peacock parade, not just an excuse to see and be seen, but what was for LA an intimate gathering, thrown by an actor chum from London who was having a big, although as it proved brief, success in films. There were several theatre actors from the east coast; a well-known director who was running the Los Angeles Theatre Centre; a composer who had recently written a highly acclaimed score for a science-fiction movie; and several writers, one a distinguished poet who was working on a biblical epic. Bill was not out of place in this company. To Leonie he appeared good-looking, charming and wildly intelligent – and the immediate attraction was mutual. It wasn't until later that she learned of his reputation with women and drink.

The music that night had been Telemann, the conversation witty and erudite, and Leonie had been entranced. Bill himself was fascinated by the glorious creature with slanting green eyes, an abundance of copper hair and a troubled soul. He had held her hand on the battered old leather chesterfield as he talked to her, and she had found him both fascinating and immensely reassuring. He was quite a few years older then her, and the warmth of his interest in her had a paternal quality which, bruised and battered as she was, she found irresistible. In the months that followed, Bill painstakingly picked up the pieces of her life and made her whole. Shortly after they met, she moved into his house in Malibu. She remembered the many hours they spent walking on the seashore, watching the sandpipers and other people's dogs bounding joyously along the sand, as among the happiest in her life.

Bill's literary output at this time was prodigious. Leonie, he said, inspired him; she was later to discover that this was the case with all his new relationships. Leonie's career began to soar, largely thanks to the brilliant scripts he wrote for her first two movies. She also, at Bill's insistence, appeared at a couple of the Los Angeles playhouses in works by Ibsen and Sartre: totally uncommercial productions which nevertheless enhanced her reputation as an actress. It was important, Bill instructed her, to be taken seriously at the outset of her career and this was one way to achieve it.

Gradually, however, his creation began to succeed beyond his wildest dreams. Leonie rapidly become more famous and more sought after than Bill himself, and drink, so far kept under control, began to feature more and more largely in his life again. With the drinking, the affairs began, and the massive rows and sleepless nights as Leonie tried to make him realize what he was doing to both himself and their marriage. Always, the next day, he would be consumed with remorse, and lie, shaking and sobbing in her arms, muttering endless promises of reform. And, indeed, for a couple of months he would behave, but then one day she would return, full of high spirits from the studio and looking forward to walking with him along the beach in the ocean spray, only to find him gone. There would be no sign then of Bill for several days when she would become, in turn, hurt, worried, despairing, angry.

The pattern was always the same: an endless string of boozy nights spent with an ever changing cast of aspiring young actresses. For five years Leonie struggled to keep the marriage together, but eventually she came to realize that her own emotional survival depended on a life that did not include Bill. Even so, she had not anticipated quite the pain that she experienced during the divorce. There was an awful sense of failure in the knowledge that she was legally separating herself from him. However, once the divorce was over she suddenly experienced a feeling of freedom – of independence – that she had never known before. At last she was taking control of her own life and making something of it. But the affection she felt for her ex-husband never entirely disappeared, and she would always be grateful to him for all that he had given her in their early years together.

Leonie pulled up outside Bill's house on Laurel Avenue and sat for a brief moment considering the exterior. It was a comparatively modest-looking building by Hollywood standards, with a high-walled front garden and wrought-iron gates that kept out any unwelcome strangers. This part of Hollywood was renowned for its homosexual fraternity and there were a number of whores, of questionable gender, plying their trade on the street corner.

Bill had heard her car and was standing in the doorway, grinning at her. She was always pleased to see him but on this occasion she was shocked to see how much he had aged since their last meeting. They embraced warmly on the doorstep, then he led her into his apartment, which was cool and airy with something of the feel of Leonie's Rome *palazzo*. The rugs on the floor were Persian antiques, there were some choice pieces of eighteenth-century French and English furniture, and the paintings were all minor Impressionists. Leonie suddenly realized that it was Bill's experience of life and art that she missed in Rob. She had had to teach Rob everything that Bill had taught her – and there were times when she yearned for the older man. But then she remembered the drinking and the feeling soon passed.

'You're looking great,' he greeted her. 'You gotta picture in the attic somewhere growing old?' Leonie laughed appreciatively. Bill had always been generous in his compliments. This was another thing she missed.

Leonie wandered around, noting familiar objects from their time together; things they had chosen; things she had left behind. She had taken nothing with her – at the time she didn't want to be reminded of anything to do with her marriage – and as she stood in the middle of the living-room, she surveyed her surroundings in a sad contemplation of a past existence.

'Sit down, sweetheart. Make yourself at home,' Bill called happily from the adjacent kitchen. 'Why don't you put on some music?'

Leonie crossed to the music centre and selected a piece by Ravel. She always thought of Ravel as having a tang of sadness, bitter-sweet, appropriate at this moment.

Bill came in bearing two glasses with creamy-coloured contents.

'What on earth's that?' asked Leonie, who had expected the inevitable Californian orange juice.

'Don't kid me,' Bill looked hurt. 'Don't tell me you've forgotten your favourite drink?'

Leonie was puzzled for a moment then remembered. 'Of course, pineapple and coconut juice. Brilliant.' She was strangely touched that he had remembered an early favourite of hers. It was one of the novelties of California that had delighted her on her arrival. They both sat down opposite each other and smiled across their drinks.

'My God, Leonie, you look good enough to fuck.' Leonie froze. Then laughed to cover her embarrassment. She liked Bill, but she certainly didn't want to go to bed with him again.

'Don't even think about it,' she was smiling as she spoke but the message was clear.

'Well, here's looking at you, kid,' said Bill holding up his glass.

'So, tell me about your new project.' She was anxious to steer the conversation into safer waters. To her surprise, Bill said nothing. There was a long pause as he gazed down at the contents of his glass.

Finally he spoke. 'There isn't one,' he said simply.

'What do you mean?' Leonie was puzzled. 'I thought you said . . .'

'There isn't one – there's never been one. I haven't had any commissions for months.' It was the first time she had heard Bill sound really embittered. Of course, he had complained in the old days about his talents not being fully recognized, of how he was worthy of better stuff, of how he had never even been nominated for an Academy Award, but then there had always been the promise of better to things to come. Now she stared at him, surprised and concerned.

'Sweetheart, I need money. I'm broke.' Leonie suddenly felt angry. Was that why he had asked her here?

She looked at him for a long time, then made up her mind. 'OK, how much?' There was another long pause. Bill just sat there, humiliated, saying nothing. Looking at him, Leonie's anger died. She began to feel sorry for him. He looked old, and broken.

'What's happened to you?' she asked, tenderness creeping into her voice. 'Why haven't you been getting any work – you're a bloody good writer. Why?'

'I've, I've . . .' Bill began. He shifted uneasily and ran his fingers through his thinning silver hair. 'I've been drying out.' He laughed ruefully. 'And it costs a fortune.'

'Jesus, Bill.' Leonie simply did not know what to say. Then she had an brainwave.

'Listen, honey, I've got a wonderful, wonderful idea. Why not write a movie for Rob and me? Heaven knows we could do with a good scriptwriter – what about it?'

For a moment a spark of hope flickered in Bill's eyes, then died. 'I don't want your pity, Leo,' he said in a dreary voice.

Leonie felt justifiably annoyed. 'Sure, but you don't mind taking my money.' As she saw Bill flinch from her anger, she immediately regretted her words. 'No, I'm sorry – I didn't mean it – I'm sorry.' She knew that there was no point in prolonging the meeting. Opening her handbag, she wrote out a cheque to Bill Newman for $10,000, tearing it out briskly and placing it under her half-finished glass of fruit juice. Then she walked to the front door, and paused. 'Bye, Bill. Don't call me, I'll call you.'

Three hours later, she was boarding a plane for Rome at Los Angeles Airport.

When Amanda arrived at Andy Berena's apartment in a narrow street near the Tiber, the party was already well under way and the whole place was pulsating with noise and energy. Almost the entire film unit of some ninety-six persons was there and Andy's spacious split-level living-room was jammed with bodies.

Andy shared the apartment with his fellow stuntman, Gus Jones, a former boxer, and it was Gus who opened the door when Amanda hesitantly rang the bell. A slightly bemused look crossed Gus's square face, as though he felt he should know her but couldn't quite place her. Amanda took a deep breath and smiled a confident smile. 'I'm a friend of Giovanni's,' she said brightly, holding out the bottle she had brought.

Gus eyed Amanda, his expression registering approval. She had dressed with care for the evening in a skimpy black Lycra top that clung

to her young breasts and a short, hot-pink skirt. Her freshly washed
hair rippled down her back in shining waves and her long, tanned legs
were bare.

He nodded amiably. 'Oh, great. Come on in,' he yelled above the
din from the room behind him. 'Just a quiet little do we're having,' he
added rolling his eyes heavenwards. Amanda laughed nervously; now
she was here at last, she felt suddenly scared. If she could have turned
tail at that moment, she would have done, but Gus took her firmly by
the arm and ushered her inside. 'Thanks for the booze,' he said, steer-
ing her into the crowded, smoke-filled room, 'mind you, we've got a ton
already. What can I get you?'

'A glass of wine would be fine,' said Amanda. 'White, please.'

'Sure, I'll be right back.' Gus made as if to leave her, but Amanda
had a question for him first. It was one to which she had to know the
answer.

'Is Leonie O'Brien here tonight? I'd really love to meet her. She's
always been one of my favourite actresses.' Amanda looked at Gus
expectantly, wide-eyed and innocent.

He shook his head regretfully. 'No, it's a real shame. She's had to
fly over to LA for a meeting and she won't be back until tomorrow at the
earliest. I'm sorry, love.'

Relief flooded through Amanda. Though the newspaper had said
that Leonie was in the States, she wanted to know for sure before she
made her next move. As Gus disappeared to fetch her drink, she looked
around, scanning the crowd for a face that she knew. There was no
immediate sign of Giovanni, or indeed of any of the others whom she
had met in the restaurant. She pushed her way further into the room.
The lights were dim and no one took any notice of her. Most people
seemed rather drunk. She looked up at the room's mezzanine floor,
linked to the lower level by a handsome wrought-iron staircase, and saw
the back of a dark head which looked familiar. Giovanni, she thought. He
was talking to a pretty blonde girl whom she did not recognize. They
seemed to be very friendly.

At least it's not Beryl he's with, she thought thankfully, as she
made her way towards the stairs. It would have been so awkward if she

had decided to come to the party. Pushing her way through the crush on the stairs she wondered, again, what a good-looking guy like Giovanni could possibly see in her adoptive mother.

She reached the top of the stairs and made her way to where Giovanni and the blonde were standing, deep in conversation. She was hesitating, unsure whether to interrupt or not, when the decision was taken out of her hands as someone pushed against her in the crush and jolted her off balance. She swayed against Giovanni, clutching at him to save herself from falling. 'Oh, Giovanni,' she gasped, embarrassed, 'I'm so sorry.' Then, as he turned and she looked up into his face, her heart missed a beat. It was not Giovanni who was standing looking down at her with a bemused smile, but Rob Fenton.

Rob had been drinking for several hours. He had been in a black mood ever since Leonie had left for LA, furious both with himself for screwing up and with her for making such a big deal about it. If she had still been in Rome they would have made up their quarrel in bed as they had always done before; instead, another lonely night in the apartment fuelled his misery and resentment. By morning, he had begun to feel that the whole business was Leonie's fault. After all, if she hadn't left him on his own so much while she played the big producer, he would never have gone out with Giovanni in the first place, and the accident wouldn't have happened. He was the star of the film, he deserved some consideration too. It was Leonie's duty to look after him properly and she hadn't done. Meanwhile, there were plenty of other women who would be only too glad to give him their company – and other things.

Rob had started drinking before he left for the party. He was now quite pissed, but not too pissed to notice that the red-head who was now gazing at him with big green eyes that were somehow vaguely familiar was an exceptionally attractive girl. 'Hey,' he said, swaying slightly, 'I know you, don't I? Haven't we met before?' The blonde girl at his side clutched his arm, looking daggers at Amanda.

'Yes, we met at the studio a couple of weeks ago. I'm Amanda Willoughby, a friend of Giovanni's.' As Amanda spoke, she wondered how she could ever have mistaken him for Giovanni.

'Oh, yeah, I remember. Nice to see you again.' The blonde

intervened. 'Hey, Rob, honey.' She put her arms around his neck and twined herself round him. Rob pulled himself free.

'Lay off, Susie, I want to talk to Amanda.'

The blonde pouted. 'If that's how you feel, don't let me stop you.'

'Fine,' said Rob amiably. 'Push off then. I'll catch you later.'

'You won't,' said Susie, with another vicious glance at Amanda as she left them.

Amanda could not repress a feeling of triumph at her departure. Now she had Rob all to herself and he seemed to be interested in her. She looked at him, smiling shyly. 'Actually, for a moment there, I thought you were Giovanni.'

Rob laughed. 'That's a new one. It's usually the other way around. I must tell John, he'll be pleased.'

'Is he here?' asked Amanda. 'He asked me to come, but I haven't seen him yet.'

Rob looked her up and down, a predatory light in his eye. 'You mean you're all on your own. We can't have that. Let's find a drink for you, then we'll see.'

Two hours and a great deal of wine later, Amanda was thoroughly enjoying the party. She knew she was rather pissed but she didn't care. She had danced, and laughed, and talked and drunk and all the time, without any effort on her part, Rob Fenton had stayed close to her side. It was almost eerie to find what she had wanted coming to her so easily. Now the music was sweet and yearning, the tempo of the party had slowed, and she was dancing in Rob's arms, leaning close against him, feeling his hard body pressed to hers.

The track ended and they stopped, still locked together. Then the sound of the Rolling Stones came pounding into the room as someone turned the volume up several decibels. 'Shall we go somewhere quieter?' asked Rob, releasing her and looking at her intently.

Amanda nodded dumbly. It was going to happen, she knew it was. He put his arm around her and guided her out of the room. He was leaning on her heavily; Amanda knew that he was drunk but so far he had disguised the fact remarkably well. She hoped he would not be too drunk for what was to follow.

Rob opened one of the doors in the corridor leading off the main room, and pulled her inside, shutting the door firmly behind them. Amanda felt a quiver of excitement run through her body and, smiling, stretched out her arms to pull him towards her. Light from a street lamp outside the window spilled into the room and Amanda could see Rob's face clearly. He was staring at her with a strange, hesitant expression, as if he was wondering who she was. 'Rob, darling,' she murmured encouragingly, 'what are we waiting for?'

Suddenly Rob lunged forward and grabbed her, kissing her fiercely. 'All right, you bitch,' he muttered, 'you've asked for it, haven't you?' He rammed his tongue down her throat and, groping for her hand, thrust it towards his cock. Amanda, astonished by his sudden violence, tried to pull away, but he pinned her against the wall, hurriedly undoing his flies as he did so. Then, before she could utter a word of protest, he pushed her to her knees, tilted her head up roughly and forced his cock into her mouth. 'Is this what you wanted?' he murmured, slurring his words. 'Yes, that's right, baby, that's what you like.' He came suddenly, spurting his semen down her throat. Amanda choked, then retched, spewing it out.

Rob pulled her to her feet. 'What's the matter, can't you take it any more? But we've only just started, darling.' Limp with shock, Amanda allowed him to half drag, half carry her to the bed. As he laid her down on the slippery quilt, the bedroom door opened and someone stuck their head in. 'Sorry . . . thought this was free,' mumbled a drunken male voice. There was a high-pitched feminine giggle behind him. Amanda started to call out but Rob shoved his hand over her mouth, muffling her cry. 'Piss off,' he said threateningly, 'can't you see we're busy.' The door shut with a bang.

'Now where were we?' asked Rob, kneeling beside Amanda on the bed. He was breathing heavily as he fumbled under Amanda's skirt for her pants and tore them off. The he pushed her legs apart and plunged his tongue into her. Amanda tried to force him off with her legs. His rough treatment amazed and frightened her. There was a cold, ruthless anger in his actions that she could not understand. It was as if he was punishing her for something. His hands found her breasts and he started to pull at her nipples, pinching them with his fingers. Amanda gave a scream.

'Shut up, bitch,' he said, raising his head at last. He heaved himself on top of her and started to kiss her again. He tasted musky and she realized that she was tasting her own juices. Suddenly he seized her hair with both hands and yanked her head back hard on to the pillow. 'Bitch,' he repeated. 'Think you can treat me like a bad little boy. Well I'll show you how much of a man I am.'

Amanda screamed again and hit out at him, but her cries were drowned by the noise of the party outside and her resistance seemed only to madden him further. He hit her hard across the face, once, twice, and she started to whimper with fear. Then, as she lay, limp and unresisting, he seized her ankles, pulling her legs up to lie over his shoulders before he rammed into her with bruising force. She moaned and writhed in pain and outrage, but he clamped a hand over her mouth and continued to fuck her relentlessly for what seemed like hours. Then at last he came, suddenly and violently, collapsing on top of her with an anguished groan. Then he was kissing her, tender, passionate kisses, stroking her damp cheeks and whispering, 'Baby, I'm sorry, I'm sorry, I didn't mean it. Did I hurt you, sweetheart? Oh god, I know I shouldn't have done, but you made me so mad, oh baby I'm sorry, so sorry . . .' Drained of feeling, beyond even surprise at this turn of events, Amanda allowed him to kiss and caress her, mumbling his apologies until his voice died away and at last he slept.

The room was stuffy and airless. Wriggling from beneath Rob's sprawled body, Amanda lay, hardly daring to move, until she drifted off into an uneasy slumber. When she awoke, a dim grey light filtered through the window indicating that dawn was not far away. There was a pungent, unfamiliar, odour in the room, half-sweet, yet stale. She realized that it was the smell of sperm and sweat. She shifted slightly in the bed; her thighs seemed to be stuck together and her vagina was sore. The man beside her was sleeping soundly. He was lying heavily against her, his hands resting on her stomach, and his face pressed to her shoulder. She felt trapped and knew she had to get out of this suffocating room. As she shifted again, he stirred in his sleep and his hand crept up to fondle her breasts. She froze in horror. Oh, please God, she thought, not again. But he only snuggled closer to her and continued sleeping.

She hated him for the way he had treated her, but he had served his purpose. Soon she would find Leonie and tell her what her lover had done. The thought gave her strength. She longed to see Leonie's exquisite features contorted in grief and despair when she delivered her news. She had done it; she had fucked her mother's lover. Now Leonie would at last start to pay for the way in which she had ruined Amanda's life.

Rob muttered something and Amanda stiffened, listening with a beating heart. She heard Leonie's name – as though he had read her thoughts – and she froze in anticipation, but he only turned over and continued sleeping. She was able to escape now, sliding silently out of bed and crawling on all fours to where her clothes had been flung on the floor. She felt around for her shoes and instead found Rob's jacket. A sudden inspiration came to her and she put her hand into the pocket. Yes – keys – a clutch of assorted keys on a ring. One of these had to be his front-door key.

Slipping quickly into her clothes, she opened the door and, shoes in hand, crept down the marble-floored corridor and into the living-room. The smell of stale cigarette smoke was overpowering and someone was asleep on a sofa, snoring loudly. She picked her way carefully to the front door, slipped on her shoes and tiptoed out. Closing the door quietly behind her, she left the house.

Once outside she realized that she couldn't remember where she was in relation to Parioli and the van der Velts' villa. She walked for a while, through silent streets populated only by prowling cats until she reached what looked like a main road. As she stood, trying to find a familiar name on the road signs, luck was on her side in the shape of an early-morning bus, trundling up the street with its load of city workers. On the front it said *Termini*. Amanda breathed a sigh of relief. She knew she could find her way from Rome's main railway station. She stepped out into the road to flag it down and the bus ground to a halt near her, the automatic doors opening, and the driver gesturing her to climb aboard. Gratefully she scrambled on to the bus and sat down on a spare seat at the front. The bus lurched forward, and the driver crossed himself, mentally thanking the blessed virgin that the pretty girl with the mascara-stained cheeks was not his daughter. He shook his head and whistled through his teeth, determined to give his beautiful Maria another lecture on the ways of the world.

Amanda was clutching the rail in front of her, thanking her lucky stars that she was not in Britain, where she doubted that any bus would have stopped for her when she was nowhere near a bus-stop. It took some twenty minutes to reach the station. Most of the other passengers were getting off too, and several looked at her curiously and, so Amanda imagined, disapprovingly. As she left the bus, Amanda smiled her thanks to the driver. She knew where she was now. And she knew what she had to do.

7

The staff of the van der Velt household were up and about when Amanda finally entered the wrought-iron gates that shielded the villa from the gaze of the curious passer-by. Although she had her own front-door key, she decided that her late, or rather, early, return would be less likely to be observed if she went in by the back entrance. A smell of cooking wafted towards her nostrils as she approached the door. She glanced quickly in at the kitchen window and saw several of the domestic staff eating an early breakfast. For a moment she was tempted to join them – she was ravenously hungry – but she had no wish to attract comment and she knew she must look a sight. So, slowly and silently, she eased open the back door and slid inside. A steady murmur of conversation came from the kitchen, followed by a sudden rise in the decibel level as someone dropped a pan with a loud clang and called on their patron saint to cure them of their clumsiness.

Amanda took advantage of the diversion to dart past the kitchen and through the hallway. She raced up several flights of stairs, two steps at a time, and, gaining the comparative safety of her room, collapsed on her bed. For some time she lay there going over in her mind the events of the night. She had done what she had set out to do.

It had been extremely unpleasant in the end, but so far she was ahead. There was still much to be done.

She eased herself off the bed and peered at herself in the mirror above the hand basin. In the dim early-morning light, she could see that she looked appalling. Her eyes were puffy from tears and lack of sleep, her hair was tangled and what little remained of her make-up was streaked and blotched. She ran a basin of hot water to bathe her face. The water was soothing and she took her time, but as she washed, she began to feel a nagging sense of anxiety. She looked at her watch: it was 7 a.m. She had just three hours before she needed to be with her nasty little charges again. It wasn't really long enough, but she decided to chance it. There was a lot to do in a short time.

Amanda tore off her clothes, had a thorough strip-wash and began to feel better as she put on fresh underwear and a clean T-shirt, jeans and trainers. After cleaning her teeth and applying a little make-up, she pulled a brush hurriedly through her hair and grabbed the shoulder bag in which she had put Rob's keys. She crept once again through the household, which was beginning to show more signs of life; she could hear water gushing in Harmony's bathroom, and the boys noisily engaged in what sounded like an early-morning pillow fight.

She ran lightly down the stairs and towards the back door, only to collide with Patrizia as she emerged from the kitchen carrying a breakfast tray.

'Mamma mia!' exclaimed a startled Patrizia, barely managing to steady her burden.

'Oh, scusi, Patrizia,' said Amanda. 'Buongiorno,' she added, smiling brightly.

'Buongiorno, cara mia,' beamed Patrizia, who liked the pretty English girl. 'Che fa?'

'Oh, just going to visit a friend,' replied Amanda, knowing that Patrizia would not understand her. 'Ciao,' she said cheerily and quickly made her way to the covered porch where she kept her Vespa. In no time at all she was zipping along the half-deserted streets in the direction of central Rome.

Rob jolted awake and opened his eyes abruptly. The other half of the bed was empty, but there was a familiar smell of dried semen and stale sweat. He lay for a moment trying to gather his thoughts. What in God's name was he doing here – in a strange bed in a strange apartment? He sat up and groaned. He felt terrible: his head was thumping and there was a revolting taste in his mouth. He eased himself slowly off the bed and staggered to the adjoining bathroom, where he scrabbled around in the medicine cabinet above the basin until he found a packet of Alka-Seltzer. Filling a glass with water, he dropped in four tablets and gulped them down, only to feel immediately and violently sick. For some minutes he knelt beside the lavatory pan, retching until his stomach began to hurt. Then he struggled to his feet, took a towel, soaked it in cold water and laid it on his throbbing forehead. Suddenly he felt terribly cold. Grabbing another bath towel, he wrapped his naked body in it, staggered back into the bedroom and fell on to the bed in an uneasy sleep.

An hour later he awoke feeling delicate in the extreme but a little better. He tried again to take some Alka-Seltzers and this time succeeded. He showered, rubbed himself dry and dressed, but it wasn't until he was slouched against the stove in the kitchen, trying to drink a tepid cup of coffee, that he dared to think about the events of the previous night.

He had been to bed with someone, there was no doubt about it. And there was also, unfortunately, no doubt that it had not been Leonie, although he had a vague memory of somehow believing that it had been her – a Leonie with whom he was still very angry. He must have been very drunk indeed. Leonie was, as he knew all too well, probably in a plane right now on her way back from LA. And he hadn't even called her there to find out how her meeting had gone. Remorse flooded through him. He had tried so hard to be faithful to Leonie – and now, at this crucial moment, he had ruined everything. He had let her down and he had let himself down too. Could she ever forgive him? God, no. So he would be mad to tell her.

Leonie, thought Rob, I must get back to Leonie. She could even be home by now if she had got on an early flight. He was not sure whom he felt most worried about – himself, Leonie or the unknown girl – but he knew that somehow seeing Leonie would make things all right again. Leaving his coffee unfinished he put down his mug and walked quietly out of the apartment, thankful that no one else was stirring yet. Out in the street, the early-morning sunshine was brilliant. He groped in his jacket pocket for his sunglasses and put them on to shade his burning eyes. Then he hailed a passing cab, gave the address of the apartment, and sat slumped miserably in the back as the driver sped towards the heart of Rome.

Leonie lay soaking in the wonderfully old-fashioned bath-tub, looking round her with pleasure. The spacious room was tiled in Delft blue and white, the floor was marble and all the fittings were either mahogany or brass. She had emptied a liberal quantity of perfumed body shampoo into the steaming water before thankfully lowering her jet-lagged body into its warmly scented depths. She had managed to snatch a few hours' sleep on the flight back from Los Angeles to Rome, and she was pleased to be back so soon. but even travelling First Class as she always did, two transatlantic flights in the space of a couple of days could never be less than exhausting.

The bath was old – she imagined it had been in the apartment since the 1920s – and capacious and she could stretch out fully, her feet touching the end. As the soothing water lapped round her, spreading her hair out in fan-like fronds around her shoulders, she began to feel at peace at last. Her mission had been relatively successful, the movie had been saved. There was, of course, the question of the money, but she found she didn't care so much about that side of things at the moment. She just wanted to be with Rob. She was massaging shampoo into her wet hair, when she heard a key being turned in the door. Leonie's heart leapt. That must be him. She smiled to herself as she imagined how contrite he would be to find her already home. It had been surprising and rather unsettling to find the apartment empty when she returned, but she knew he did not expect her until later. Almost certainly he would have gone out with some of the cast the night before, had a bit too much to drink, and crashed in someone's flat. She could not blame him; he would still be worried about the results of her mission to LA and she could hardly expect him to wait at home, biting his nails until she got back. Well, now she would be able to set his mind at rest.

'I'm in the bath,' she called out happily, knowing he would not be able to resist the invitation. Silence. Silly bugger, she thought as she dunked her head under the water to remove the shampoo. He's going to get undressed and surprise me in here. With a delicious shiver she thought of the love-making in the bath that would follow. She eased herself down into the water, her nipples just peeping above the foam, and waited. Her desire was increasing by the second.

The door swung open slowly. A strange girl was standing there. Leonie froze for a moment, then outrage took over. 'What do you want?' she snapped. 'How the hell did you get into my apartment?' The girl said nothing. Leonie stared at her, recognition dawning. It was the red-headed girl on the Vespa whom she had seen once or twice recently outside the apartment. Oh God. Her mind raced as she began to put two and two together. The girl Nigel had mentioned who had called him repeatedly, trying to contact her; the letter with the lock of red hair. It had to be her.

Lying there in the bath she was at a distinct disadvantage, but she was determined to stay calm. 'Who are you, and what do you want?' she demanded.

The girl advanced into the room and regarded Leonie coolly. 'My name is Amanda Willoughby, and I am your daughter.'

Leonie felt suddenly light-headed, then a burning, nauseous sensation began to rise from her stomach. She had a horrible feeling that she was going to faint. Instead, she heard her own voice say with total sang-froid, 'I think you are mistaken. Could you pass me a towel, please?'

She had heard of people who had been involved in horrific accidents having conversations about very ordinary, mundane things, so as to blot out a scene which was too horrible to contemplate. It had always been very hard to believe, but now she seemed to be doing it herself.

Amanda did not pass a towel. Instead she stared disconcertingly as Leonie stepped naked and dripping from her bath. Wordlessly, Leonie stepped past her to reach for the towelling robe that was hanging on the back of the door.

She wrapped it round herself, then twisted a towel, turban-fashion, round her hair. 'You'd better come with me,' she said curtly, leading Amanda towards the drawing-room. For some reason she felt completely in control of the situation.

The west-facing drawing-room was still cool and she shivered involuntarily as the change in temperature hit her. She gestured Amanda towards the sofa. 'Drink?' she enquired briefly. Without waiting for a reply she went straight to the drinks cabinet. The truth was that she desperately needed a drink herself. She picked up the cut-glass decanter to pour herself a Scotch; her hands were shaking so uncontrollably that she spilled it on to the silver tray as she poured. She was glad that she had her back to the room and Amanda could not see her clumsiness. 'Scotch?' she said to Amanda without turning round.

'Thanks, that would be fine.' In Amanda's voice, she heard a tremor that belied her apparent composure. It made her feel better, and she managed to pour the second whisky without further mishap. She picked up the glass and carried it across to Amanda. Although she was clutching it in both hands, she could see that it was still trembling as she handed it to the stranger on the cream sofa. A complete stranger. And yet there was something familiar about her.

She went back to the cabinet and picked up her own drink, then seated herself opposite Amanda in an armchair and surveyed her with forced calmness. There was no point in panicking, after all this could be a put-up job, blackmail, anything. Just stay cool, she said to herself, be reasonable, hear her out, and phone the police if you start feeling really worried.

'How did you get in?' She repeated the question in the manner of someone merely asking for information. She was surprised at her complete lack of emotion. If this really was her daughter . . . Her daughter – it hit her like a blow to the solar plexus – that was what she was finding so unnerving. She suddenly realized that she was looking at a reflection of herself: herself, nineteen years ago. Amanda's face started to go out of focus, and the room began to revolve slowly. Please God, don't let me faint, she thought. She took a gulp of her whisky.

'I borrowed the key from your boyfriend. He said you wouldn't mind.'

'Oh, really?' Leonie's mind was starting to reel. Where the hell was Rob? If he'd got to know this girl while she'd been away, why hadn't he been here to soften the blow, to prepare her for what was, after all, the most traumatic meeting of her life? She wrenched her thoughts away from Rob and tried to focus on the girl sitting opposite her.

'His stand-in, Giovanni, and I are an item, as you might say.' Amanda laughed, but alarm bells started going off in Leonie's head. What was this girl after? If she was her daughter, and in the cold pit of her stomach Leonie knew that she was, why hadn't she revealed her identity sooner? She had obviously been in Rome some time. Leonie took two more gulps of whisky in quick succession.

'Why did you have me adopted?' The question was as direct as the flight of a bolt from a crossbow. Leonie felt her mouth go slack. She sat there staring stupidly at the creature she had spawned, not able to speak. Amanda twisted the barb. 'Why? Didn't you love me at all?'

Tears started to trickle down Leonie's stricken face. Amanda watched dispassionately. 'There's no need to get upset, I know it must have been difficult for you. I just wondered how you could bring yourself to do it, that's all.'

Leonie started to articulate a reply. Her lips moved, trying to form words that she had kept hidden in the most secret and private part of her heart, a tiny corner closed up so tightly that even she had not dared to prise open. A choked sound came from her throat.

'I . . . I,' she stammered, 'I c-couldn't, I couldn't, I couldn't do, do it, I couldn't,' she sobbed incoherently not able to hide her pain, not caring any more. The girl rose and came to her side. She sat on the arm of the chair.

'Perhaps you have some idea of how I feel now,' she said coldly, as her mother sat and wept uncontrollably, releasing years of pent-up grief. After a while the crying subsided in a series of convulsive shudders that seemed to wrack Leonie's whole frame. Her body started to shake.

'You're cold, you should put something on,' said Amanda, in a slightly relenting tone. Leonie allowed herself to be led out of the drawing-room. 'Is this your bedroom?' asked the girl, and Leonie nodded, not trusting herself to speak. Amanda looked around, taking in the huge gilt mirrors, the brocaded drapes, as Leonie shakily pulled a sweatshirt and leggings from one of the shelves in the carved oak cupboard. Suddenly shy, Leonie pulled on underpants with trembling fingers, then put on the other clothes. When she had finished, she climbed on to the bed and lay back among the scatter of satin cushions at its head.

'Can I fetch you something?' asked Amanda. Leonie nodded. 'More whisky?' Leonie nodded again.

A few minutes later, Leonie was sitting propped up among the cushions, sipping her drink. Then in a low voice, she started to relive the events that had taken place nineteen years earlier. The words tumbled and poured out, as though relieved to be free at last. It was the first time she had told the story aloud, although, God knows, she had gone over and over the nightmare countless times in her head. As the years had passed she had pushed it, forced it, to the very back of her consciousness. But it was always there. Not a day had gone by when the memory had not returned to haunt her, however briefly. At last Leonie came to the end of her story. The bedroom confessional was silent. There was a long, long pause. Without looking at Amanda, Leonie spoke in a low voice. 'Can you forgive me?'

Amanda hesitated for a second. When she spoke, her voice was hard, relentless. 'No, I'm afraid I can't.'

Leonie felt as though she had been struck across the face. Amanda saw the reaction and knew that she had won. Leonie stared at her in disbelief. 'Don't you understand anything of what I told you? What else could I have done?'

'You could have kept me, you could have loved me.' Amanda's tone was suddenly fierce.

'I did love you.' Leonie shouted the words in anguish.

'Then prove it.'

'Prove it?' Leonie whispered.

'Yes, go on, prove it. Take me in, give me a home, love me now.' Amanda's voice became strident. 'Give me what I never had, give me what I deserve.' There was no softness in her tone; her expression was menacing, frightening.

With a shock, Leonie realized that she had loved her baby, but that she had no love for this girl, this cold unnatural stranger for whom she had suffered nineteen years of torment. 'Get out of my home,' she hissed. 'Get out, you little bitch.'

'It's even easier the second time, isn't it?' sneered Amanda.

But Leonie's control had snapped. 'Get out!' she screamed.

'Don't worry, I'm going, *mummy dearest*,' Amanda spat back at her, 'but I think you should ask your precious boyfriend how I got his keys.' She tossed her auburn mane and swept out of the bedroom. Leonie heard the front door open, then the shrill sound of Amanda's voice shouting from the hall, 'And I'm going to the papers. I'm going to tell them everything about you and your sordid little secrets.' The door slammed shut with an almighty crash.

Tony Sneller's stay in Rome was proving fruitful. Trawling round Cinecittà for more gossip about Leonie and Rob, he could hardly believe his luck when he found himself outside the film studios as the ambulance arrived to carry Carlo off to hospital. He managed to locate an extra who spoke some English – he'd already had the sense to realize that none of the crew would be prepared to speak to him – and half an hour later had phoned through news of the accident to Trevor Grantley. Further digging brought hints of a quarrel between Leonie and her leading man, and of the picture's financial problems. It was clear that it would be in the newspaper's best interests for him to stay on in Rome a little longer.

A few thousand extra lire to his informant extracted the news that there was to be a party for the cast and crew at Andy Berena's apartment. Tony had great hopes of joining them, but his luck at last ran out when it was Andy himself who answered the door when he turned up on the Friday night. Andy recognized Sneller of old. Tony tried to bluff his way in, but Andy told him that he knew dung when he smelt it and that if he didn't piss off sharpish he'd find himself chucked out on his fat arse.

So Tony retired to the hire car parked just up the street and decided to wait out the evening, reckoning that sooner or later someone was bound to emerge drunk or that, with luck, there might be a fight.

For several hours nothing happened and eventually he fell asleep. Then, just as dawn was breaking, some sixth sense woke him in time to see Amanda making her get-away. Stiff and cramped from his night in the small Fiat, he watched with interest. He could see that the girl was very young and very pretty, and that she appeared to have no transport of her own. Intrigued, he started the car and followed her at a distance when she set off on foot. He had a vague idea that he might offer her a lift and get some details about the party. Then he saw her board a bus, and, sixth sense still working overtime, decided to stay on her trail.

The bus trundled slowly into Rome through half-deserted streets. When Amanda left it at Termini, Tony watched her board another bus for Parioli and, chugging patiently behind in his anonymous little car, followed until she was dropped off fifty yards from the van der Velt residence. The one thing Tony Sneller had acquired during all his years in journalism was a nose – a nose for a story – and this nose was telling him very clearly now that there was a story not far away. He was tired, crumpled, unwashed, and desperately in need of a drink. But he waited patiently, parked in middle of the exclusive residential area with no sign of a café anywhere and only a tree behind which he could relieve himself.

Half an hour passed before the girl emerged again. She shot out into the road on a Vespa, so quickly that Tony almost missed her. Then, pulling himself together quickly, he chased after her, following her as far as the Via Veneto, where to his disgust he lost her in the thickening traffic. He cruised around the area for an hour, cursing himself for incompetence, becoming increasingly tired and irritable. Perhaps this was a wild-goose chase after all.

He decided to call it a day and get some breakfast. Then, just as he was passing the Palazzo Barberini, he spotted a familiar flash of red hair emerging from a door on the other side of the road. The girl flung herself on to the Vespa again. I'll give it one last go, thought Tony to himself, and headed after her. To his surprise, she eventually pulled up

·

outside the offices of *Il Giorno*, a popular daily newspaper. He thought for a while, and decided that she must be one of the publicity girls on the movie, though he was still curious as to the explanation for her dawn exit from the party. Anyway, she should be full of information about what was happening on the film set, so he waited until she emerged from the building again and hurried up to her.

'Scusi, signorina,' he said in an appalling accent. Amanda turned and gave him a look of distaste. 'Fuck off,' she said.

'You're English,' he said, surprised. 'So am I . . . I saw you at Andy Berena's party last night, didn't I? I work for the *Chronicle*,' he lied, using the time-honoured ploy of hiding behind the up-market broadsheet. 'Can I help you?'

Amanda looked at him in disbelief as he ferreted in his jacket pocket and produced an NUJ membership card. She glanced at it and back at him.

'Sorry about the appearance,' he continued. 'I had to go on after the party to cover a political meeting and it went on all night.' Again she stared at him suspiciously.

'Are you a political correspondent?' she asked.

'I cover anything if it's news,' he answered, truthfully.

Amanda smiled. 'Then you might be just the man I'm looking for,' she said.

Tony smiled too. 'Shall we talk over breakfast?' he asked. 'I'm desperate for a coffee and something to eat.'

'OK,' said Amanda. 'That suits me. I can give you half an hour,' she added, glancing at her watch.

'That'll be quite enough,' replied Tony Sneller happily.

For breakfast, Amanda ordered coffee, and rolls with cheese and ham. Sneller's mouth felt like the bottom of a parrot's cage. He would have liked bacon, eggs, fried bread, and sausages, washed down by several cups of P.G. Tips. But he was out of luck, so he decided to settle for the same as Amanda. He produced a tatty notebook from the depths of a bulging pocket, and a rather superior gold pen.

'So, Miss, er . . .'

'Willoughby,' said Amanda. 'Amanda Willoughby.'

·

'So, Amanda, how did you enjoy the party last night?'

'I don't want to talk about it,' said Amanda with a sulky expression, 'it was very boring.'

'Oh,' said Sneller, disappointed, 'I was hoping you were about to tell me that Leonie O'Brien and Rob Fenton had a massive row. People say that all is not well between them, you know.'

'If you had been there,' said Amanda scornfully, 'which I doubt, you'd have known that Leonie wasn't even at the party.'

But Sneller was seldom put out by such accusations. He'd spent too much of his life covering his tracks. 'I thought that was because they'd had an enormous bust-up.'

'Guess again, smarty-pants. Everyone there knew that she was in LA raising more money for the reshoot.'

Sneller mentally filed this information away for later, but chose to pursue his main theme. 'But relations between them are strained, aren't they?'

Amanda saw the opportunity to stir things a little. 'They're not so idyllic as they were, that's true.'

'And are you her new rival?' Amanda looked sharply at Sneller, astonished that this grubby little man had got so close to the truth so quickly.

'No, I'm her old daughter,' she replied, watching his reaction closely.

'You're what?' Sneller did an amazed double-take. This was news indeed.

'Yes,' said Amanda, looking at him with innocent eyes. 'I'm her long-lost daughter. She had me adopted over nineteen years ago.'

Sneller was excited, but he kept his manner matter-of-fact. 'Are you on the level?'

'Of course, you can check it out if you like.'

'She's never mentioned you before,' he said suspiciously.

'Well, would you?' Amanda gazed at him pitifully. 'She is deeply ashamed of abandoning me.'

'But you say she had you adopted. That's not quite the same as abandoning you, is it?'

Amanda stared at him, tears beginning to form in her eyes. 'Have you any idea at all of the torment I have been through since I discovered I was her daughter?' Her lower lip started to tremble.

Sneller was unmoved. 'Sure, it must be hell for you. But how does it feel to be Leonie O'Brien's daughter? What's it like, suddenly finding out you have a famous mother?'

'What's it worth?' said Amanda, her tears remaining unshed.

'What?'

'I said, what's it worth?'

'Who to?' said Sneller, immediately wishing he'd said 'to whom'.

'Your newspaper, of course. Who did you say you worked for?'

'The *Globe*.'

'Funny, I could have sworn you mentioned the *Chronicle*.'

Caught out, thought Sneller irritably. That's what comes of spending the night in a car. 'Well, actually, I'm a sort of freelance. I work for them both. They're sister papers.'

Amanda appeared uninterested in his explanation. ' So, what would the *Globe* be willing to pay for this story?'

'We're not in the habit of paying for stories.'

'Oh yes you are. You paid the girl who was with that football player a lot of money.'

'That was different. She had a lot to tell us and it filled a double-page spread for three Sundays running.'

'So will my story.'

Tony sighed. 'With respect, Amanda, a story like yours would hardly make the front page. A nice little piece on the inside pages. Human interest, we call it. Nothing sensational, just a heart-warming account of a mother reunited with her long-lost daughter. O'Brien fans the world over will be touched by it.'

'It wasn't heart-warming. She threw me out of her apartment. She screamed abuse at me. It was like a nightmare.' A catch in Amanda's voice interrupted her speech.

Tony Sneller's eyes lit up. This was going to make the front page all right. 'This obviously wasn't what you were expecting. You were hoping for some sign of affection? Regret? Remorse?' He was helping her along, encouraging her.

'I was longing to meet my m-mother. I'd admired her all my life. It seemed incredible to me that Leonie O'Brien, my favourite film star, was actually my own mother.' Amanda started to cry.

'So it must have been a shock, a severe blow to you, when you saw her reaction?' he prompted.

'I was heart-broken.' She started to sob freely.

Sneller began to scribble furiously. 'When are you going to see her again?' he asked.

'She doesn't want to see me again – ever! She doesn't want me.' Amanda's sobs increased in intensity.

'It's just that it would be nice to have some pictures to go with the article. You know, mother and daughter stuff.'

Amanda voice rose to a wail and Sneller glanced round uneasily as people started to stare in their direction. 'She won't see me. She doesn't want to know me. She wishes I were dead.'

'How do you know that?' he asked, leading her on.

'She yelled at me to get out – my own mother.'

'And how do you feel about that?' he asked – unnecessarily, Amanda thought. Surely he could see how she felt. Wasn't she playing the distraught rejected daughter to perfection? And, in truth, her lack of sleep, the violence of the night, the meeting with Leonie, had all affected her more than she realized. The tears came easily; they were a release.

Sneller made no pretence at sympathy; this was all in the day's work. If she was upset it was all to the good. She was the more likely to give something away that would make good copy, but he would prefer her not to become hysterical. He would get nothing out of her that way and they would attract too much attention. Fortunately she seemed to have calmed down now and was crying quietly. He repeated the question.

'How do you feel about your mother now?'

'I'm shattered, devastated. My real father was at least civil to me.'

'Oh, so you know who he is then?' Sneller pricked up his ears. A tawdry affair with a struggling actor in the early days – this could make quite a nice little piece.

'Oh yes, he's very well known.'

'He is?' Sneller sat up, pen poised. 'Who is he?'

Amanda took a tissue from her bag to wipe her eyes. 'I wouldn't dream of revealing his name to you. It would do no good to his political career, it might even harm it.' She appeared to be preoccupied with her handkerchief.

Sneller was bristling with anticipation. Could it be that he was on the brink of a really hot scandal here? It hadn't happened to him for ages. An internationally famous film star and a politician, hopefully Tory. All that public school stuff, good copy that. He could see the headlines now, but best of all he could see his byline: 'Exclusive from our show-business correspondent, Tony Sneller.' He might even get his picture in.

'Oh, come on, surely you can tell me his name? I'll find out anyway.' Amanda shook her head slowly as though overcome with emotion. Sneller persisted. 'You say he was pleased to see you?'

'He was a bit distant. I think he was just shy, and awkward, but at least he didn't scream at me.'

The idea of a Tory politician being shy and awkward taxed Sneller's imagination. He decided to pursue it. 'Not like a Tory to be shy and retiring,' he joked. 'Still, as you say, at least he didn't shout at you. I expect he was proud of you, wasn't he?' Sneller was making a real effort now.

'Why?' Amanda gave him an innocent, questioning look. So she hadn't contradicted him. He was Tory all right.

'Well,' he replied, shifting in his seat, 'you're a good-looking girl and you're obviously intelligent. He'd be pleased to think you were his daughter. Any man would.'

'Do you really think so?'

'What?'

'That I'm good-looking?'

Sneller was irritated. What stupid questions women asked. 'Yes, and he must have thought so too,' he said wearily. 'Now, how did he react when he first saw you?'

'Who?'

'You haven't told me you father's name, so I don't know who, do I?' Sneller laughed at his own wit. Amanda remained silent. 'Come on,' he urged, 'who is he? We'll find out sooner or later, so you might as well tell me now.'

'How much is it worth to you?'

Sneller threw down his pen and pad. He didn't believe this was happening to him. The girl was slipperier than an eel. The waitress arrived with their order and Sneller gratefully gulped down some coffee. As he considered his next move, Amanda renewed her attack. 'Mr Sneller, I have just been through the most traumatic experience of my life. I have no money. I don't know what to do next.'

Her expression was pathetic, but Sneller had heard this line before. 'How did you get to Rome, then?' he protested.

'I took a job as an au pair, but my employers are American. They're going back to the States soon,' she lied, 'and they're not taking me with them. That was why I went to the newspaper offices. I thought they might be able to give me some financial help.'

'And did they?' Sneller wanted to know how much she'd said. He wanted to keep this story exclusive.

'No,' said Amanda, lying again. 'they weren't interested.' Actually, the features editor of *Il Giorno* had been extremely interested. He had promised to follow up the story immediately and was excitedly calling a colleague on his sister Sunday paper when she left him.

Sneller, blissfully unaware of this, tackled his breakfast with gusto. 'Would you be prepared to grant me an exclusive interview? It would mean complete coverage of your personal story, and would be serialized,' he said between mouthfuls. Trevor would be only too happy to pay her air fare for that, but he decided to cover himself. 'Of course, I'd have to speak to my editor first.'

'You won't regret it,' Amanda promised.

'I'm sure I won't. Did you meet her boyfriend, by the way?'

'Oh, yes, he's very handsome, isn't he?' Amanda looked starry-eyed.

Now this was a good angle, thought Tony. Long-lost daughter has crush on Mum's boyfriend. Nice one. 'You think so, do you?'

'I think he's wonderful,' she breathed.

He was going to enjoy writing this piece. 'Well, Amanda,' he said briskly, 'I'll get on to my editor as soon as we've finished breakfast.' He started bolting down his food. He couldn't wait to phone Trevor.

'Tell him,' said Amanda coolly, 'that I'll do it for £75,000.'

Tony Sneller choked on his bread roll. For a long moment he was quite incapable of speech.

8

By the time Amanda returned to the van der Velt villa shortly before lunch, it was obvious that the man at *Il Giorno* had done his work all too well. The normally quiet road outside the house was blocked with cars and scooters; the area immediately outside the tightly shut wrought-iron gates was a seething mass of journalists, photographers and news cameras. Amanda took one look and knew that she would never get through them. Swiftly, she spun her Vespa round and headed up a little lane that led to the back of the villa's grounds. There she abandoned the Vespa and, after clambering painfully over a rough stone wall, made her way up to the house through the garden.

As she came in through the back door she met Patrizia, who greeted her with an anxious frown. 'Amanda,' she said excitedly, 'where you been? Everyone want you. Signore van der Velt, he very angry. You see him now, OK?'

Amanda smiled at her. 'OK, Patrizia, I'll go and see him. I'll see you later – perhaps.' She might as well get it over with, she thought, making her way towards the library where, when he was at home, Livingstone van der Velt was usually to be found at this time of day.

She found him seated at his desk, deep in contemplation of a small Leonardo drawing which he had acquired the previous day. It seemed the barbarian host outside was marring his enjoyment of his new treasure, for he looked very solemn when she entered. Harmony was there too, gazing gloomily out of the window at the baying mob beyond their gates.

There was a long silence before anyone spoke. Finally Livingstone cleared his throat. 'Now, see here Amanda,' he said, 'we can't have this sort of thing going on. The press are all over the place. What the hell have you been up to?'

'I'm sorry,' said Amanda, 'it's rather a long story.'

'It's so awful for the boys,' said Harmony regarding her sorrowfully, 'such a bad atmosphere. And poor Livingstone can't possibly work. You'll have to get rid of them, you know.'

'I'm sorry,' said Amanda again. 'I suppose you want me to leave?'

Relief dawned in both their faces. 'We think it would be best, for all of us,' said Harmony.

'All right,' said Amanda, 'When do you want me to go?'

'Your belongings have been packed up. Georgio is waiting to take you to the Hotel d'Umberto,' replied Harmony briskly.

Amanda was taken aback; she had been expecting something like this, but she had anticipated at least a week's notice.

'Your bill will be paid for a week, to give you time to seek new employment,' said Harmony, as if in answer to her thoughts.

'Very well,' said Amanda, secretly relieved to be released so quickly. 'I'm sorry to have brought you so much trouble. Thank you for all you have done for me,' she added.

'The boys will be sorry to see you go,' said Harmony vaguely, turning back to the window as if she considered the interview over.

No they won't, thought Amanda. Not those little savages. And I certainly shan't be sorry to see the back of them. Half an hour later she was being driven through the gates in the back of the van der Velt's big black BMW, surrounded by dozens of peering, leering faces, all trying to mouth questions at her through the tightly closed smoked-glass windows. The car forced its way through the mob and drove quickly and smoothly away, leaving the mass of bloodhounds to try and puzzle out her trail.

When the car glided to a halt outside the Hotel d'Umberto a uniformed commissionaire stepped forward to open the door and help Amanda out. A porter appeared at once to unload her luggage and she was ushered through glass and gilt doors into a high-ceilinged vestibule, thickly carpeted, with comfortable armchairs, glass-topped tables and banks of fresh flowers. Amid a quiet buzz of activity, Amanda watched the parade of expensively dressed women. They were chic in a uniquely Italian way, with an almost nonchalant approach to their beautiful clothes and perfectly chosen accessories. Amanda looked down at her own outfit of jeans and T-shirt, which suddenly seemed cheap and tawdry by comparison.

To one side of the vestibule there was an arcade of elegant shops selling perfume, jewellery and other luxury items. In the window of one, Amanda noticed a beautiful suit of ecru linen. She gazed at it covetously. As she waited to be checked in, she felt a tide of resentment rising inside her. All this glamour and luxury that only money could buy was hers by right and, if her mother had kept her, had not cast her off for adoption, she could have lived like this for most of her life. Not for the first time, she made a silent vow to have what she believed was right-fully hers: she was determined to have the money to dress like these women.

'What name, please, signorina?'

Amanda roused herself from her reverie. 'I'm not sure. The reservation was made by Mr Livingstone van der Velt . . .'

The receptionist's face became wreathed in smiles. 'Ah, Mr van der Velt. Yes indeed. A pleasure to have you here, Signorina . . .' and he checked the name, 'Willoughby?'

'That's right,' said Amanda, with mild irritation. The day would come, she was resolved, when people would react with equal enthusiasm to her name. She stopped. Not if it was Willoughby. That wasn't her name. What was her name? It was the first time she had really thought about it. Willoughby would not do and she could not use O'Brien. Her bitch of a mother did not want her, that was plain to see, and, in any case, she would simply be accused of trading on her fame. No, she would have to think up something else, something that told the world that she was her own person. She would have to do it soon though; by the time she hit Hollywood she must have her identity settled.

'How long will you be with us, Signorina Willoughby?'

She started. 'How long has Mr van der Velt booked me in for?'

'One week, signorina.'

She glanced around the lobby again. Could they really mean her to stay here all week at their expense?

'Excuse me,' she said to the receptionist, ' but Signore van der Velt – is he paying for everything?'

'*Everything*, signorina,' said the receptionist, with what seemed to Amanda to be a meaningful smile. Perhaps he thought she was van der Velt's mistress. Bloody cheek! Well, whatever he thought, she would certainly make the most of it.

She signed the register and a porter picked up her shabby suitcases. As she followed him towards the lift, she sniffed the perfumed air. The hotel even smelt good: it was a far cry from sad aromas of overcooked cabbage and stale cigarette smoke in the dreary English hotels that she had stayed in with Arnold and Beryl. No more of that, she vowed; she was going to live like this from now on.

The porter sent the lift winging to the fourth floor, where she was shown a room so magnificent that it almost took her breath away. It was decorated in the style of a *cinquecento* Florentine *palazzo*, with frescoed walls depicting a fairy-tale landscape of hills crowned with little walled towns, surrounded by vineyards, flowering meadows and lines of cypresses. She stood in the centre of the room, gazing around her with delight. Her battered suitcases had been carefully placed by the porter on an ornate gilt stand and now the man was hovering by the door. She had an idea that she was meant to tip him, but had no clue as to how much. Hastily she took some bills from her purse and thrust them at him. This seemed to do the trick as he bowed deferentially and left. Luxury was all very well, but it was costly and if she had to part with all this money every time she wanted anything done, she would be out of pocket very shortly. She wondered how much this room was costing van der Velt, then remembered that it was in lieu of a month's wages.

Of course, they were buying her off. Amazing to what lengths people would go to disassociate themselves from scandal.

She surveyed herself in the huge mirror that dominated the room and was dissatisfied with what she saw; her clothes especially were impossible. She started to undress slowly, mulling things over as she sauntered into the bathroom to take a shower. As she doused herself under the steaming-hot jets of water, she scrubbed her skin thoroughly in an attempt to wash away the memory of her night with Rob. Sex with him had been so inexplicably violent. Was he always like that, or was it simply something about her that had caused him to behave in such a way? Well, she wished her mother joy of him. He might as well have raped her for all the pleasure he had given her. As she stood there under the shower, the warm water running in soapy rivulets down her back, an idea began to form in her mind. Rape – it was a very nasty word. It was also a word which Tony Sneller would find irresistible.

She stepped out of the shower and wrapped herself in a huge, velvety bath towel. She liked the feel of it. One day she would have towels like this. She would have a bathroom like this, all mosaic tiles and smoky mirrors, with subdued inset lighting. As she rubbed herself dry she saw her reflection in the mirror; she looked all pink and fresh and vibrant, with no hint of the emotional turbulence she had undergone. She knew she was pretty. She could tell by men's reactions. But if she was to succeed as a film actress she needed the right clothes too.

Back in the bedroom, she opened her case and rifled through the contents. Hopeless. She remembered the women downstairs in the lobby: one in a silk dress with a cashmere jacket slung casually around her shoulders, another in natural linen slacks with a matching loose cotton sweater. Both were wearing beautiful Italian leather shoes and carrying smart handbags. She thought of the delightful little suit in the boutique window and slammed the case shut in disgust. There was nothing here that she could possibly wear. She couldn't face the women outside in her cheap chainstore clothes. They were attractive enough, but they had no class, no style. Still enveloped in the towel, she picked up the phone.

'Could I speak to the manager, please?' she said. There was a considerable pause before she was connected. Finally he came through.

'How can I help you, signorina?'

'I have a pressing engagement this evening. I'm meeting an important film producer and I need an outfit quickly.'

'You need it pressing, signorina? I understand. I will send the valet service to you.' The manager was puzzled, but polite.

Amanda tried again. 'No, I'm sorry, you don't understand. You have an outfit downstairs in the boutique. I want to buy it to wear this evening.'

'Very good, signorina. The boutique is now open and ready for your inspection.'

'I've already seen what I wish to buy. It's in the window. Could you send someone up with it?'

'You do not wish to try it on, signorina?'

'Yes, here in my room.'

'I see, signorina.' The penny finally dropped. 'You do not wish to come down?'

'I have no clothes on.'

'Very good, signorina.' The manager betrayed no hint of surprise at Amanda's information. Perhaps it happened all the time.

'If it fits me and I like it, you can put it on my bill.' Or rather on Livingstone van der Velt's bill, she thought gleefully.

Half an hour later, she was examining her reflection again. The little ecru linen suit fitted her like a glove, as she had guessed it would. Its short-sleeved jacket was nipped in tightly at the waist and the brief skirt ended well above the knee. The price, in lire, looked astronomical for such a small amount of material. The unusual sight of herself in such an expensive new garment for some reason made her think of Beryl. Funny, since that meeting in the square, she had barely given her a second thought. She really had no feelings about her at all. What on earth Giovanni had seen in her, she couldn't imagine. Perhaps he thought she had money. It seemed the only possible explanation.

She had brushed her auburn hair back into the nape of her neck and secured it with a clasp, a rather pretty clasp in tortoiseshell and gold that Beryl had given her for her last birthday. Antique, she had said it was. It certainly went very well with her hair, and it looked classy. Fortunately she had just bought a pair of wedge-heeled espadrilles. They were only cream canvas, but at least they were new and clean and they would look quite good with the suit. As she was slipping them on, the phone buzzed. She ran to pick it up.

'Yes?'

'Amanda? It's Tony Sneller.'

'Who?' she said, pretending not to recognize the name.

'Tony Sneller. We met this morning.' His voice sounded irritated.

'How did you know I was here?'

'I made it my business to find out. Not much gets past me, Amanda. For instance, I know you've left your employment, and that you're here as the guest of Livingstone van der Velt.'

'So what?' said Amanda. 'Don't think you can make anything of that.' Tony's voice had implied that there was something dubious about the arrangement.

He ignored her reply. 'Can I buy you a drink, Amanda? I think it's time we had another little chat.'

'Have you talked to your editor about the money?' asked Amanda sharply.

'Yes, and he's sure we can work something out,' said Tony in what was intended to be a reassuring tone.

'All right,' said Amanda, considering the situation. 'I'll meet you downstairs in the bar in half an hour.' When she had replaced the receiver she sat down at the dressing table and began to apply some make-up. Sneller was not a very nice man, she thought as she stroked mascara on to her long lashes; she didn't ʾike or trust him. But he was her only contact with the British press anᵾ she needed him to sell her story, sleazy though he was. If only he wasn't so physically unappealing. The thought of another session with him made her cringe.

A thought struck her, and she picked up the phone again.

'Hello. It's room 434 again. I'd like to have perfume delivered to my room.'

'Very good, signorina. Which perfume you would like?'

'The most expensive you've got.'

'That is, er . . .' there was some whispering in the background, '*Joy* from Patou. It is the most expensive perfume in the world.'

'Fine,' said Amanda, 'I'll have the largest bottle you do.'

Tony Sneller was a stinking bastard in more ways than one, but at least she'd smell nice and look good when she met him. It would all help give her the confidence she needed to get the best deal she could. A few minutes later the scent arrived, delivered by a grinning page-boy. Amanda unstoppered the big crystal flagon and took a sniff. Mmm, delicious, she thought, splashing it liberally over herself. When she went downstairs, she was feeling like a million dollars, and the covert glances of one or two women and frank stares of admiration from several men as she passed through the lobby told her that she was looking pretty good too.

She walked serenely into the bar, and looked around for Sneller. There he was in the corner, a greasy blot on all this gilded splendour. The walls of the bar were decorated with delicate murals in the style of Tiepolo, and the lighting was subdued. In the background gentle music played: definitely Monteverdi rather than Mantovani, Amanda thought.

'Amanda, good to see you, what can I get you?' Tony Sneller looked utterly out of place in this haunt of the rich and beautiful, but he was still trying hard. He had not commented on her transformed appearance but Amanda could tell by his startled expression that he was impressed.

'A champagne cocktail, please,' she said blithely.

Sneller looked stunned for a moment, but recovered quickly. He liked a drop of champagne himself, and it all went on the expense sheet.

'Good thinking. Er, waiter!' He snapped his fingers, but a waiter was already gliding towards them.

'I'm glad you approve. I thought we should celebrate.'

Sneller paused in the middle of giving his order and looked at her suspiciously. 'What are we celebrating?'

'Our new deal.'

Tony's nose started to send out warning signals. Not only was it as good at tracking down stories as a pig snouting truffles, but it also informed him when he was about to be taken for a ride. His boss,

Trevor Grantley, was a sarcastic bastard and his wit was all too often directed at Tony himself. Now he could hear something in Amanda's voice that reminded him of Trevor, of whom he did not wish to be reminded just now. One of the better things about Rome was the distance it had put between him and his boss, but he still had to endure him on the phone from time to time. This morning Trevor had told him in no uncertain terms to get his arse in gear and ferret a fucking red-hot story out of this Willoughby tart, or he'd be paying his own airfare home. And he needn't bother to check in to the office on Monday either; someone would clear out the empty vodka bottles from his desk and take them to the bottle bank for him.

Playing for time, Tony ordered the champagne. Then he turned to Amanda again. 'And what new deal would that be?'

'I assume the reason you've bothered to track me down again is that you've spoken to your editor, and you want to publish my full story?'

Well, that was more like it. At last the girl was beginning to show some form.

'At the right price, of course,' Amanda went on sweetly.

Tony groaned inwardly. Various other parts of his anatomy might let him down from time to time. But not his nose. He took a deep breath. 'I'm instructed by my editor to offer you £5,000 for your story,' he said.

'Tell him to get stuffed,' said Amanda. 'I want £75,000 or I'll take it somewhere else.'

'No other paper will offer you any more, don't you understand?' Tony felt exasperated. 'Until they know what the story is, they won't buy it. How can anyone tell if it's worth that amount?'

'It's worth it all right,' she said smugly.

'I'll be the judge of that.' Tony was now beginning to find the girl extremely irritating; she was so high-handed, so arrogant. Thick-skinned as he was, she was getting to him.

'Look,' he said, spelling it out, 'the story has to be sensational to warrant that kind of money. We have to be able to serialize it for at least three Sundays.'

Amanda surveyed him in a way which did not hide her contempt. 'As you know, my mother, an international film star, gave me away when I was born. My father, a prominent Tory MP, would have nothing to do with me. What more do they want?'

'The juicy details.'

'Well, I can give them those.'

'Then take them to the *Guinness Book of Records*,' said Tony in a rare moment of wit. 'There can't be too many people who can remember what happened when they were still in the cradle.'

'No,' said Amanda crossly, 'I mean what's happened recently, you stupid man.'

Sneller's nose twitched. He ignored her rudeness; it was all part of the job. 'Like what?' he scoffed, trying to draw her out. 'I can't believe anything could have happened that's worth £75,000.'

'How about rape?' asked Amanda in a cool voice.

Sneller's brain went into overdrive. 'Whose?' he sneered trying desperately to conceal his interest.

'That's for me to know, and you to find out,' she teased. 'I'd like another drink, please.'

'I'm going to make a phone call,' said Tony, heaving himself up. 'Order what you like. I'll be back.' And he hurried off to call Trevor Grantley.

'It's no good, Trev,' he said, a few minutes later. 'She won't spill the beans. She won't tell us who her father is. I'm quite sure there's more there – she mentioned something about rape – but the little tart has gone all tight-arsed about it.'

'What!' Trevor's voice sounded distorted over the phone, but his excitement was clear, and it took quite a lot to get Trevor excited. 'Did you say rape? Do you mean to say that her father, a prominent Tory MP, raped her?'

'That's what she's just implied. And I think she's on the level.'

'Well, for fuck's sake find out who he is,' Trevor bellowed.

'I'm trying, Trev, but she wants more money. A lot more money.'

'All right,' said Trevor wearily, 'offer her thirty grand. But it had better be bloody worth it. Let me know how you get on.' He slammed down the phone without waiting for a reply and Tony was left staring down at a mute receiver. He replaced it and returned to the bar, to find Amanda happily sipping another champagne cocktail.

'You might have got me one,' he said grumpily, staring at his empty glass. Then he looked at her. 'All right, thirty grand. It's our final offer – take it or leave it.'

'I'll take it,' she said immediately. Sneller couldn't believe his luck. Quickly, before she changed her mind, he pulled himself together and took out his mini tape-recorder.

'OK,' he said, 'I'm ready.'

'How do I know I'll get the money?' asked Amanda.

'You'll get it, don't worry.'

'I was raped by my mother's boyfriend,' she said calmly. Tony Sneller nearly fell out of his chair in astonishment. 'What! Not Rob Fenton?'

'Yes, Rob Fenton.'

This was a hundred times better than Sneller had dared hope. He hid his glee with an expression of pained sympathy.

'How terrible for you,' he said.

'Yes, it was. I doubt if I shall ever get over it.' Amanda's lower lip trembled as she spoke, and she made a conspicuous effort to control herself. She was very pleased with her performance, though it was not hard for her to play the shattered victim. She had indeed found the experience genuinely distressing, even if she knew in her heart that she had led Rob on.

By the end of an hour, Tony Sneller had heard Amanda's version of the events at the party and had got his third scoop in a fortnight. What he had not got, however, was the name of the Tory MP. Amanda had broken down and wept uncontrollably as she recounted her ordeal, and as Sneller sat there, tape-recorder whirring away, he began to feel distinctly awkward. Eventually he dug into the sagging pocket of his jacket and pulled out a crumpled, grey handkerchief. Amanda took it, wiping away her tears as they continued to pour down her face.

'Please excuse me,' she whispered at last, thrusting the handkerchief back at him, 'but I really can't go on any longer . . .' Abruptly she rose from her chair and walked quickly away, leaving him sitting there staring after her departing back.

Oh well, he thought philosophically, let her have a good cry. I'll talk to her again tomorrow. And he ordered himself another champagne cocktail before going off to phone Trevor with the good news.

'We're going to have to tread very carefully on this one, Tone,' observed Trevor. 'Rape is not a pretty word.'

'But Trev —'

'Although, funnily enough, it is, of course, also the name given to the bright yellow crop you see all over the country in spring – very un-English in my opinion. It provides oil and animal fodder, I believe.'

What for fuck's sake was Trevor burbling about now? thought Tony. 'Listen Trev,' he said urgently, ignoring entirely his editor's last remarks, 'this is a really hot story, it could get us several jumps ahead of the competition —'

'No, Tony, you listen to me. This girl has got you all gee'd up, but it's a dodgy business. I think we hold back for a bit; get the low-down, by all means, but let's be sure of facts first.' This was a fine time for Trevor to have developed integrity. 'You said something about problems with the film?' Trevor continued.

'Yes,' said Tony. 'I understand this accident has totally buggered things up for them. They might have to abandon production.'

'Couldn't suit us better. We wait for the word to become official and time our rape story to coincide. Should make them really sweat.' Sneller breathed a sigh of relief. For one ghastly moment there, he thought Trevor had acquired a social conscience.

'I like your style, Trev.'

'Well, get on with it then and try to get it wrapped up – your hotel is costing us a small fortune.'

'Yes, Trev.'

'And watch those bar bills.'

Rob lay back in the taxi, his head lolling from side to side as the sun's warmth filtered the rear window. He started to feel sick again. The noise and bustle of the busy Roman thoroughfare was crashing though his head. He just wanted to be lying in Leonie's arms, between cool sheets, where everything would be all right again. The taxi jerked to a halt and Rob pulled himself together and crawled blearily out into the sunshine. He paid the driver, then dragged himself up the steps to the apartment. Outside the door, he fumbled in his jacket pocket for his keys. Damn, they weren't there. He searched all his pockets but in vain. They were definitely gone; he must have dropped them somewhere at Andy's. He had hoped to get back before Leonie's return, but now he prayed that she was early. He didn't think he could face another taxi journey across the city to retrieve his keys.

He rang the doorbell and waited. The sound of hurrying footsteps came towards him from inside. Then there was the noise of a bolt and a chain being drawn back. The front door opened a fraction and the next moment Leonie was in Rob's arms, sobbing.

'Darling, what on earth is going on?'

'Oh, Rob, it's dreadful, I can't bear it.' Leonie was almost hysterical. 'She's been here – that girl we saw on the moped.'

'What are you talking about, Leo?'

'She's been spying on us, Rob. She's been watching us, our every movement. She's been here. I've met her. Oh, Rob, it was horrible.' Here Leonie burst into tears again. Rob felt a cold hand creeping up his spine. He thought frantically for a moment.

'You mean the red-headed girl we saw driving past here on a Vespa,' he said carefully, as though trying to get the facts clear in his mind. 'You mean the girl, the same girl I met later that day at the studio. Leo, you're not trying to tell me that – she's – something to do with you?'

'Yes, yes, yes.' Leonie sobbed uncontrollably.

'Leo,' he was holding her tightly in his arms, 'Leo, what is she – to you?' He hardly dared ask the question.

'She, she . . . she's my daughter.'

Oh, God, no, he thought desperately. No, please. Anything but that. 'You mean, your real daughter, your own natural daughter?' he asked, still hoping there might have been some misunderstanding.

'Yes,' she wailed. He still held her closely, pressing her head into his chest so that she could not see his face.

'Not by Bill, though?' Rob was fairly vague about Leonie's past and preferred to keep it that way.

'No.' She was quieter now, as though his embrace had calmed her. 'It was before I met Bill, several years earlier.' She was speaking in a low voice. 'I had an affair with someone and I got pregnant . . . I wanted to keep the baby, but I couldn't – he abandoned me – and I was persuaded, against my better judgement I know now, to have the baby adopted. I was heart-broken, but there seemed to be no alternative. It is the worst thing that has ever happened to me. Now, more than nineteen years later, she's found me. She came to Rome looking for me.'

Rob stood rooted to the spot. Time for him seemed to stand still and he didn't dare to move, afraid that somehow he might give himself away. He had been feeling queasy before; now he was afraid he would be physically ill again. His brain was in turmoil. Had he really spent the night with that girl? It had seemed like a dream ever since he woke and now it had become a horrible nightmare. If indeed he had fucked her, as he had a dim memory of doing, then he had fucked Leonie's own daughter. Jesus, it was practically incest. What to do? He was trying to think clearly, quickly, but seemed incapable of doing either.

Leonie raised her tear-stained face and looked up at him. 'Rob, what are you thinking? You're not angry with me are you?'

He felt slightly better at her question. She was not, after all, able to read his thoughts. 'What is there to be angry about? I just feel desperately sorry for you. Anyway, it all happened so long before we met.' He tried to laugh reassuringly, but it didn't quite work.

'No,' said Leonie slowly, 'I mean, are you angry I didn't tell you about her? It's not that I didn't want to, it's just that I couldn't. I haven't been able to tell anybody, ever. Even my parents never knew.' She was gazing up at him, eyes drowned in tears. 'Please forgive me. It's just that it had become a very private, very secret part of me. I tried never to think about it myself, but it's always been there. It's haunted me all these years. There were times when I nearly said something. The other day, when that message came through from

Nigel, I wanted to tell you then . . .'

She broke off and looked at him anxiously. 'What's the matter – don't you believe me?'

Rob kissed her gently on the forehead. 'Darling, Leo, of course I believe you. I was just thinking how wonderful you are, that's all. To have carried this burden all these years on your own. I wish I'd been able to share it with you.' He stroked her hair and guided her towards the drawing-room. 'Come and sit down, now, and have a drink. Then you can tell me about LA. To be honest, I'm much more interested in that than your daughter. After all, that's all in the past now.'

Leonie allowed herself to be installed on the sofa. Rob sat down beside her. Then she turned to him, eyes wide and serious. 'Rob, I don't think you understand what I'm saying. It's not all in the past; she's just been here.'

Yes, that's what he thought she had said. He had prayed that he had misheard her. 'What do you mean?' He pretended to be confused. 'Who was here?'

'Amanda. The girl. My daughter.'

Dear God, there was no escape. What if she'd said something?

'She's been here?' his voice was incredulous.

'It was awful,' replied Leonie shakily, 'she was . . . like a vulture,' and she started to sob again.

'Why did you let her in?' He had to bluff it out now. It was the only way.

'I didn't. She let herself in. She said she had your keys.'

'My keys! She must have nicked them out of my jacket pocket. Stupid girl, why didn't she ask me? I could have brought her round to see you if I'd known who she was. Why didn't she say something?'

'What do you mean? When did you see her?' Leonie was perplexed.

'At the party,' said Rob in a matter-of-fact tone, trying to make everything sound ordinary.

'Which party?' Leonie was still puzzled.

'At Andy's place. He threw a party last night. He wanted to cheer us all up after Carlo's accident. That's why I was out so late,' he added with a rueful grin.

'That was good of Andy. What a lovely idea.' Leonie was genuinely appreciative.

'I thought you'd be pleased when you heard.' Now that the subject of the accident had come up, Rob decided to seize his moment. 'Honestly, darling, it really was an accident, you know: the sun was so bright and someone got in my eyeline and . . .'

'Yes, I know, sweetheart,' Leonie was dismissive. Then her eyes narrowed in thought. 'But what was Amanda doing at the party – what the hell was the little bitch doing there?' Her voice was rising again.

'Darling, darling, don't . . . ' Rob put his arms round her in an attempt to soothe her.

'Rob, it's so awful. I loathe her, I absolutely loathe her.' She started to shake uncontrollably as though she were freezing cold.

'Come on, angel, you've been to hell and back today. I'm going to put you to bed.' Rob picked her up and, cradling her in his arms, carried her into the bedroom. There he laid her gently on the bed and pulled the covers over her, then sat beside her gently stroking her hair.

Calmer now, Leonie still would not be put off. 'Rob, I want to know, how did she get to the party?'

'Someone must have invited her, of course. Probably Giovanni, the stupid sod,' he said between gritted teeth.

'Probably,' she agreed. There was a pause, then, 'Rob?' she said in a puzzled voice. He knew what was coming next. 'How did she get your keys?'

Rob took a deep breath. 'Leo, you know what I'm like at a party – I like to have a good time. The jacket comes off almost as soon as I'm inside the door. This wretched bimbo – I'm sorry, I know she's your daughter, but even so I didn't take to her much myself – anyway, this Amanda obviously knew who I was, because she made a bee-line for me and tried to chat me up. When I wouldn't play along she was obviously pissed off, so she nicked my keys to get back at me. It wouldn't have difficult. I'm afraid I'd had rather a skinful as you can probably tell.' He stopped. Leonie obviously wasn't listening any longer.

As he looked at her, trying to make out how his explanation had been received, her lip started to quiver again. 'She said she was going to the press,' she whispered.

'Why on earth?' he demanded angrily. 'What's the matter with her for Christ's sake?' Please God, she didn't say anything about their night together.

'It's my fault,' said Leonie miserably. 'I told her to get out. Rob, I simply don't want to have anything to do with her. I can't bear her, she's my own daughter but I can't bear her. Do you think I'm unnatural?'

'Of course not, darling. You didn't bring her up, she's nothing to do with you.' Rob's voice was reassuring.

'I brought her into this world.'

'Be honest, if you had to pick her out of a room of a hundred girls her age, would you have known her?' asked Rob, trying to put the situation in perspective.

'Probably. She has my colouring and bone structure.'

'All right then, out of a roomful of red-heads with high cheek-bones? It's only her appearance, not some kind of buried maternal instinct, that makes you recognize her.'

'No,' said Leonie reluctantly. 'I suppose not.'

'Well, there you are then,' said Rob briskly. He took her hand and kissed it, trying again to distract her. 'Now come on, don't worry about her. I don't suppose she'll go anywhere near the papers. Tell me about LA? How was it?'

Leonie sighed. 'I hope you're right, that's all.' She smiled at him for the first time. It was a small smile, but a hopeful sign. 'LA was much the same as always: airless and manicured, sleazy and tawdry, bright and beautiful.'

'What about Judd and Marv? Were they bright and beautiful too?'

'Too bright,' said Leonie grimly, remembering the meeting, 'but we've got the money. Though there are some strings attached. Now all we've got to think about are the rewrites . . . and who the hell we're going to get to do them.' She sighed. Rob looked away awkwardly and Leonie could have bitten her tongue off.

One of the aspects of her husband's job that really irritated Elizabeth

Brentford was the mountainous heap of newspapers that littered her otherwise perfect drawing-room each Sunday. Thankfully, she was spared them during the week, as Simon read them at his office. She sighed heavily as she came down the stairs and, as usual on a Sunday morning, saw the pile of newspapers lying on the rather charming eighteenth-century hall table. She was very proud of her home and the papers, with their lurid colour pictures and glaring headlines, completely destroyed the symmetry of her carefully arranged room. The whole house was a masterpiece of discreet good taste: the colours were subtle, the furniture classic and comfortable, and the antiques carefully chosen. Elizabeth herself was dressed with equal care in an oyster silk négligé trimmed with a froth of Brussels lace.

The telephone that also sat on the table rang abruptly. She looked at the papers again and made a small sound of annoyance as she picked up the receiver.

'Mrs Brentford?'

'Yes?'

'This is Charles, Charles Pendlebury.' Her heart leapt. But what the hell was he doing phoning her at home on a Sunday? She thought she heard the sound of Simon stirring upstairs. Of course, it was Simon he was ringing. She glanced at the grandfather clock on the opposite wall. Eight o'clock. Almost. She tried to sound unconcerned.

'Good God, Charles, it's awfully early for a Sunday.' Another crisis, she thought wearily.

'Yes, I realize that. I am most awfully sorry to disturb you . . .' Charles paused.

'Don't worry about that. What is it?'

'Mrs Brentford . . .' Another pause. There was something in his tone that she did not like. The clock started chiming the musical pre-amble that lead up to the strokes telling the hour. She put a hand over her free ear to block out the noise.

'Charles. What's happened?'

'Mrs Brentford, I don't quite know how to tell you this . . .'

'What is it?' Elizabeth shouted down the phone. The clock started chiming loudly.

'Have you seen the papers . . ?' The rest of Charles's words were drowned in a cacophony of reverberating chimes. The clock had been a wedding present from Simon's mother and, like its donor, had a tendency to make itself heard at inconvenient moments.

'Hang on a minute!' she yelled.

'I can hear some sort of noise . . .'

The clock finally exhausted itself and reverted to a loud, relentless ticking. 'It's finished. Now, what is it?' She tried to sound confident and in control.

'Have you seen the papers?' repeated Charles. She glanced down at the pile in front of her. The heavies were on top. There were the usual articles about the state of economy, even an unflattering picture of the prime minister's wife in protective headgear visiting a factory. Scanning the front page, she could see nothing about war having been declared, or an IRA bomb having blown up the Houses of Parliament, or a crash on the stock-market.

'No, I've only just got up. What's the matter?'

'I'm afraid, it's not awfully good news. I think you should take a look at the *Globe*. You do get it, don't you?'

'Yes, of course we get it,' she replied tartly. We get every piece of bilge going, Elizabeth thought to herself savagely, trying to extricate it from the bottom of the pile. She found it. *Leonie O'Brien abandoned love child shock*: the words were huge, occupying most of the front page. They were accompanied by a full-length photograph of Leonie in a bikini, showing off her splendid figure. Elizabeth gasped and almost dropped the phone. Her eyes raked the small print at the bottom of the page that gave further details.

'LEONIE O'BRIEN, 43, SULTRY STAR OF THE BLOCKBUSTER MINI-SERIES *Wings of Love* IS MY MOTHER,' CLAIMED A SOBBING TEENAGER YESTERDAY.

She couldn't see Simon's name on the front page, but the story went on inside. She turned the pages in horrified anticipation.

'Elizabeth, are you all right?' Charles's disembodied voice came down the phone. Elizabeth read on, appalled:

AMANDA, 19, TEARS STREAMING DOWN HER FACE, SPOKE YESTERDAY OF
HOW WEALTHY, HEARTLESS ACTRESS LEONIE, 43, HAD ABANDONED HER
AS A TINY, HELPLESS BABY . . .

She flicked through the rest of the article.

LAST NIGHT, CURVACEOUS ACTRESS LEONIE, WAS IN HIDING AT HER
ROME APARTMENT AND WAS NOT AVAILABLE FOR COMMENT.

No mention of Simon up to now, she thought.

SO FAR, DISTRAUGHT MANDY HAS DECLINED TO REVEAL THE NAME OF
THE FATHER.

Elizabeth's heart was pounding. 'So far' it said. She made a determined
effort at self-control. 'Hello, Charles, are you there?'
    'Yes, I'm here. Elizabeth, are you all right?'
    'Yes.' She tried to sound calm. 'I'm all right.'
    'You've seen the article?'
    'Yes.'
    'I'm sorry, Elizabeth, but I thought you should know.'
    'Yes, you were quite right.'
    'Elizabeth,' Charles paused, 'I think it's only a matter of time
before she involves Simon.'
    'I know.' She was trying hard to think clearly. 'I think I can hear my
husband,' she said, needing time to collect herself. 'I'll get him to call
you back. Goodbye, Charles. And thank you.' Without waiting for his
reply, she put down the receiver.
    She stood there in the hall, rooted to the spot. So, it had happened,
Charles was right. It was only a matter of time before all was revealed.
Amanda was obviously keeping that ace up her sleeve; she would play
that card when she was good and ready – little bitch! At that moment
Elizabeth would have given almost anything to be married to Charles

Pendlebury and comfortably settled in his flat in Albany, enjoying a peaceful Sunday breakfast.

She picked up the paper and carried it into the breakfast room. The table was already laid, the Georgian silver sparkling in the early sunshine that filtered through the crystal-clear windows. She gazed with unseeing eyes across the green sweep of the lawn; somewhere a thrush was singing furiously. It was going to be a perfect day – she seemed to remember it was always a perfect day when there was bad news. Her beloved mother had died on such a day, and she felt tears prick the back of her eyes as she remembered her mother and thought how she missed her more than she ever dared admit. God, she needed her now. She would have known how to deal with the impending disaster.

Time stood still for a moment as she suddenly realized with a shock how her carefully constructed world might soon be shattered. Simon's career would be ruined, and with it everything that she had worked for. And the children – they would suffer, too. Although perhaps, being away at school, they might escape the worst of the scandal. No, she thought with a heavy heart, she knew she was lying to herself. They would suffer too. An involuntary sob escaped her. She immediately pressed a hand over her mouth to stifle the sound.

'Can I get you some coffee, madam?'

Elizabeth was startled by the housekeeper's words. Janet was hovering in the open doorway looking concerned. Their eyes met and for a moment they looked at each other. Not a word was spoken, but there was a tacit understanding.

'That would be lovely, thank you, Janet. No, on second thoughts, a strong cup of China tea would be even better.' She smiled bravely.

Janet wished privately that protocol did not prevent her from putting her arms around the unhappy woman to comfort her. 'Very good, madam,' was all she said, however.

It was not often that Elizabeth allowed herself a public demonstration of emotion. She had remained impassive throughout her mother's funeral and had mourned her later in the privacy of her little sitting-room, with only the cat to witness her distress. The bewildered animal had sat watching her with unblinking eyes, disturbed by her grief. She had clasped the creature to her and he had submitted to the embrace without fuss, calmly returning to wash himself afterwards, his fur drenched in her tears. Similarly, when she had been told by a well-meaning girlfriend about one of Simon's frequent infidelities, she had been apparently unmoved, but had later wept silently and alone in a quiet corner of the grounds.

Now she straightened her shoulders as if to brace herself for the trial to come. She heard footsteps on the stairs. Simon was up. She swiftly considered the options open to her and made her decision.

Simon entered the room looking tired and unusually dishevelled. 'Good morning, darling,' she said brightly. 'Tea is just coming. What would you like for breakfast?'

He yawned loudly. 'Oh God, just toast or something – I've had a terrible night.' He kissed her perfunctorily on the cheek and sank into the Chippendale carver at the head of the table. 'Where are the papers?' he demanded.

Elizabeth hid the copy of the *Globe* behind her back.

'They're in the hall. Didn't you see them?'

'No, I did not. I had a ghastly night.' He was clearly in a foul mood.

'I'll get them.' She turned away so that he couldn't see the paper she was holding and quickly left the room. Once in the hall, she took a copy of the *Mail on Sunday* and slipped the other paper inside.

When she returned to the breakfast room, Simon was slumped in his chair, a sullen expression on his face. Removing the *Mail* from the top of the pile and putting it on her own plate, she placed the rest of the heap of newspapers in front of him. He grunted in acknowledgement. Elizabeth then allowed him to drink a cup of steaming tea, munch a piece of toast and marmalade and glance through the main headlines, before she spoke to him.

'Darling . . .' she said.

'What a simply frightful picture of the PM's wife,' said Simon happily.

'Yes, isn't it,' replied Elizabeth. She hadn't even seen it. 'Darling . . .' she tried again, more firmly this time. There was something in her voice that made Simon look up.

'What? What's the matter?' He saw her face. 'Oh God, Jamie's not ill again is he?'

'No, darling, he's fine. There was a letter from him yesterday. Didn't you read it? I put it on your desk.'

'Did he get into the first eleven?'

'He still hasn't heard . . . Darling, I'm afraid this may be serious.' Elizabeth took the bull by the horns. 'Amanda has gone to the papers. She hasn't actually mentioned your name yet, but Charles feels it's only a matter of time.'

Simon stared at his wife in disbelief. The paper he was reading fell from his grasp. 'Jesus Christ,' he said slowly.

'Simon,' Elizabeth continued, 'the girl means business. You've got to do something, and quickly. Just take a look at this!' Elizabeth handed him her copy of the *Globe*. Simon read the cover and inside pages in grim silence. The birds sang on outside.

'She could wreck our lives,' Elizabeth said.

Simon laid down the paper and looked at his wife across the table. 'You don't deserve this, Liz,' he said quietly.

The gentleness of his voice surprised and disarmed her. She rose quickly and moved round the table to stand behind him, gripping his shoulders lightly with her hands.

He leant his head back against her and sighed. 'I'm sorry about this. It isn't fair on you.'

'We're both in this now, and we're going to fight it together,' said Elizabeth gently.

'Do you think she'll . . . ?' He left the question hanging in the air.

'Talk? Yes, I do.'

'But why? She's had money. What else does she want?'

'Attention, revenge, acceptance, love – who knows?'

'God, what a mess,' he groaned.

'What's the worst that can happen?' Elizabeth asked, though she already knew the answer.

'The worst? Oh, that's easy. If it all gets out, I'm deemed morally unsound, irresponsible and generally unfit to represent the people of this green and unpleasant land. The press have a field day, I resign from my job and spend the next five years repenting my sins on the back-benches.'

Elizabeth closed her eyes to blot out the awful prospect and hugged her husband closer to her.

'Do you know what I say, Liz?' he murmured from among the soft folds of oyster-coloured silk.

'No, what?' she whispered.

'Publish and be damned! She's going to and I will be!'

9

Early morning in Rome. The start of another perfect day. Leonie and Rob were in bed, sleeping the sleep of the exhausted. After the emotional upheavals of the previous day they had been too wrung out for anything more than a snack supper in the apartment and a very early night. Both looked forward to a peaceful Sunday and a chance to unwind.

Leonie woke first, her body-clock still confused by the rapid time changes of her trip to LA. Gradually she became aware that something was wrong. It was Sunday, the one day when peace descended on central Rome. It should be quiet, but instead there was a buzz of activity in the street outside. Puzzled, Leonie slipped out of bed, pulled on her robe, and went to the window to see what was happening. She took one look and drew back in horror. The pavement was heaving with journalists and photographers. Amanda had wasted no time.

Too late, she had been spotted. The babble of English, American and Italian voices rose to a crescendo, like the howling of wild beasts baying for blood. The doorbell began to ring insistently. Then the telephone started to shrill.

'Jesus wept.' Rob was by Leonie's side, gazing out in awe. 'What the fuck's going on? Is it us they want? I'd better get the door.'

'No', said Leonie sharply, 'ignore it. They'll give up eventually.' She reached for the telephone and made as if to take it off the hook without answering. Then she changed her mind at the sound of a familiar voice. 'Nigel,' she said, 'thank God it's you. All hell's broken loose here . . . What? In the British papers? No, of course I haven't seen them . . . Well what on earth am I going to do about it?' A long pause. 'You're not serious? I can't, Nigel, truly I can't.' Looking at Rob, she covered the phone with her hand and said, 'He wants me to give a press conference . . . to make a statement and tell the whole world about Amanda.' Then she burst into tears.

'You've got to face them, Leo.' Rob's tone, a few minutes later, was tender but firm. Leonie turned a tear-stained face towards him.

'No, no, I can't,' she whispered.

'Darling, listen to me.' He gripped her upper arms and held her tightly. 'It's the only way you'll exorcise the whole business for good.'

Shocked, Leonie pulled away. 'I thought you'd understand, Rob, I can't believe you're telling me this.'

'I do understand, baby.'

But Leonie was talking rapidly. 'No, you don't, you don't understand – this is my own private grief. For nineteen years, it's been part of me. You can't know what it's like. It's . . . it's as though the baby had died and I've been in mourning for it all those years. And now . . . those vultures, those harpies,' she spat out vehemently. 'I don't want people like that exposing my bereavement to the public gaze, just for people to pore over while they're munching their cornflakes. It's too precious, it's too personal . . . it's *mine*.'

'I know what it means to you, Leonie,' said Rob quietly. 'I know what you've been through and I think I understand what you've been suffering all these years. Now you've got to go out there and face those bastards – it's the only way to purge yourself of the guilt. It's not going to hurt the girl – she's a little cow anyway . . .'

'I hate her, Rob,' Leonie whispered miserably. 'How can I hate my own daughter?'

'You didn't bring her up, darling – and remember who her father is.' Rob sounded bitter. Now he knew, he was envious of Simon. Not for the first time, he wished that he had known Leonie when she was young. 'If this gets out he'll be the one to suffer. After all, you've done nothing wrong. You did the best you could for the child by having her adopted. He's the one who abandoned you.'

Leonie's face hardened. 'I've paid the price once. Why do I have to pay all over again?' Her fists clenched.

'Do it, baby – then it'll be gone for good.' His tone was firm. 'Go and wash your face, get dressed.' A pause. 'I'll get them up here. It will be hell for an hour or so and then it will all be over. For good.' Another pause. Leonie took a deep breath and said quietly.

'You're right, it is the only way.'

'Now?'

'Yes, now.' She smiled bravely. 'Let's get it over.'

'How long do you need to get ready?'

'Ten minutes, that's all.'

'Good girl.' Rob pulled on jeans and a T-shirt and left the bedroom. As he went through the door he paused, smiled back at her, and winked, saying, 'This is your ten-minute call, Christians. Ten minutes, please.' Then he was gone. And the lions are ravenous, thought Leonie.

She went to the bathroom, washed and bathed her swollen face with a hot flannel. Then she dressed quickly in a plain white cotton shirt, cut like a man's, and a pair of black Levis. This was one occasion when she definitely did not want to look sexy. She combed her hair, sprayed herself with scent, brushed a little blusher over her pale cheeks and braced herself to face the toughest audience of her life. Thoughts of Saint Barbara and Saint Catherine and other female Roman martyrs flashed through her mind. They gave her strength. I'll show them, she said to herself, I'm tougher than they are. I'll show them. She wondered for a moment whether those brave Roman women had had similar thoughts almost two thousand years ago. Their physical suffering had been appalling. And they had died. Hers was, after all, only mental anguish and she would live to see another day.

She left the bedroom, went into the kitchen and switched on the electric kettle. She could hear a noise on the stairs outside – it sounded like hundreds of people tramping, a babbled confusion of many voices. It came nearer and nearer, and finally burst through the front door. She could hear Rob yelling at everyone, telling them to calm down, trying to get them into some sort of order. A belligerent voice was arguing with him, but Rob topped him vocally and the man subsided. Leonie smiled to herself. Being an actor had many advantages, she thought, even in real life.

Real life. What the hell was that? Was this real? The whole thing seemed like a ghastly horror movie. Automatically she took a mug from the cupboard and made some coffee. She took milk from the fridge and spooned in sugar from the terracotta container, scarcely aware of what she was doing. Rob appeared in the doorway. 'Darling, are you ready?' he asked tensely.

Leonie looked up, her eyes bright and fearless. 'Yes, I'm ready.' She took a gulp of her coffee.

'Then let's go get them,' said Rob. And they moved together to face the ordeal.

A sea of faces greeted Leonie on her entrance into the drawing-room, and the place was packed with a forest of cameras, lights and sound booms. The room exploded with flash bulbs as soon as she appeared; cameras clicked, film equipment whirred. Leonie allowed Rob to lead her to one of the two chairs placed facing their tormentors. There was silence. Leonie realized that they were waiting for some sort of greeting.

Almost automatically, she began to talk: 'I beg permission, gentlemen, to speak freely and to say all that I think is necessary and without being interrupted according to the promise made to me.' The words came easily and unbidden. What the hell was she saying? The wall of faces before her looked blank. Suddenly she realized that she was quoting Mary Queen of Scots at her trial. The speech had featured in a play she'd done years ago in rep. God almighty, she thought to herself, I've got to pull myself together.

Rob took over. 'Miss O'Brien is going to make a statement,' he said. God, am I? thought Leonie wildly. 'If you require any clarification of that statement, please raise your hands afterwards. Thank you.' Rob sat down beside Leonie, and leant towards her. 'You're on,' he murmured in her ear. 'Just tell them what you told me and there won't be a dry eye in the house.'

Leonie told her story simply and unemotionally. She said that it was true she was Amanda's mother and that she had given her up for adoption. That the sacrifice she had made nineteen years ago had been the hardest decision of her life. That it had not been taken lightly. That she had regretted it ever since. That the giving up of her child had been as though that child had passed away. That she had mourned for that child. That it was a private grief. She felt it was of no concern to anyone else and she would now like the matter closed. She sat back and waited. At least twenty hands were raised. Their owners did not, however. wait for permission to speak.

'Is it true that the father is a well-known personality?'

'What do you plan for your daughter now?'

'Who is the father?'

'How are you going to make amends to your daughter?'

'Has she met her father? Are you still in touch?'

'Mr Fenton, what's it like having a stepdaughter around?'

'How do you feel about all this, Rob? Are you planning to marry Miss O'Brien?'

The questions came thick and fast. There was no opportunity for Leonie to answer, nor did she want to. Eventually Rob stood up and held up his hands for silence. 'Miss O'Brien has made her statement,' he said. 'We have no further comment to add. Good day, ladies and gentlemen.'

Leonie sat there dazed. 'Come on,' said Rob. 'You've had enough.' And Leonie allowed herself to be led from the room. Rob pushed her into the kitchen. 'Well done, darling. Now you have a stiff brandy and I'll get rid of that mob.' He shut the door firmly, then Leonie heard him trying to persuade everyone to leave. He seemed to be having trouble keeping his temper, and the whole process took the better part of thirty minutes.

When he finally returned, Leonie was still standing where he had left her. 'Is it over?' she whispered, gazing at him with shadowed eyes.

Rob looked wrung out. 'Yes, it's over. They've had all they're going to get. It's "no comment" from us from now on.'

The foyer of the Teatro dell'Opera was starting to fill up rapidly and the subdued hum had now risen to a clamorous babel of voices, mainly Italian, but mixed with American, German, Swedish and Japanese. Beryl was to bless the saleswoman in Cassandra's on more than one occasion during her holiday, and this was one of them. This was a smart and sophisticated occasion, but in her new clothes she felt equal to it. Standing alone in the midst of this confusion of opera buffs, trying to look at ease, she caught sight of herself in one of the huge gold baroque mirrors that lined the walls and was startled to see that her reflection showed her to be a slim, elegant woman, younger than she had imagined and, she had to admit, more glamorous that she had dared hope. Her midnight-blue silk jersey dress – another Jean Muir extravagance – fell to her ankles in graceful folds and a double strand of creamy pearls gleamed on her tanned neck.

A sudden spasm of nerves assailed her: would Giovanni turn up? Why hadn't she arranged to meet him at her hotel? What on earth had made her plump for the opera-house foyer? The answer came in a flash. Of course, that's what she had always done in the old days with Arnold. He would drop her at the theatre doors and she would deposit her coat in the cloakroom and buy a programme while he parked the car. It was a monthly ritual. At that moment she experienced, for the first time since his death, twinges of affectionate remembrance. There had been good times, always connected with music, but if only he hadn't spoiled it all. She realized again how her feelings for Arnold had gradually diminished during the tumultuous years spent coping with Amanda. Instead of facing the problem together, they had retreated into isolated misery.

She supposed the lack of sexual contact was also to blame; that had certainly led to a breakdown in communications. She was beginning to think that sex was rather more important than she had hitherto supposed. And – the revelation came as a shock to her – if she was honest with herself she was forced to admit that the main attraction she felt for Giovanni was sexual. Was it mutual? She hardly dared hope so – he was after all considerably younger than her. Perhaps she had entirely mistaken the nature of his interest in her, and he was just missing his mother. She knew he must care deeply for his family, as all Italians did. Yes, that was it – he missed the reassurance of an older woman – and she felt relieved to have reached this conclusion. Yet she realized also that she felt a pang of disappointment – no, she could not escape the truth, she wanted him to desire her.

She stood rigid with shock as the idea penetrated her mind. Was she, Beryl Willoughby, stalwart of the Ashebourn Choral Society, reliable member of the Meals on Wheels rota, church-goer and tennis player, actually contemplating going to bed with a young man not much older than her adopted daughter? She was terrified yet thrilled by the idea and she felt that people were giving her curious and interested looks, as though able to read her thoughts.

Feeling conspicuous, she pretended to touch up her hair in the mirror. Then her heart lurched and she caught her breath as she saw Giovanni, reflected in the mirror, pushing his way through the jostling throng. For a moment she panicked and was tempted to run away; she turned, hoping Giovanni had not seen her yet, and started to walk quickly towards the cloakroom.

'Signora. At last I find you.' Giovanni caught her arm.

'Oh, there you are.' She laughed nervously. 'I couldn't see you anywhere, so I just thought . . .' she trailed off.

'I was by the stairs as we agreed,' he replied, sounding hurt.

'I'm sorry – I forgot.' She felt like a simpleton – why was she so nervous?

Giovanni looked her up and down appreciatively. 'But you look superb.'

Unused to admiration, Beryl blushed and shyly acknowledged the compliment. 'Thank you, thank you so much.'

'This dress – this colour – it suits you so very well.' Giovanni gazed at her admiringly. 'You look so beautiful, so young.'

Beryl was overwhelmed, Arnold had never complimented her on her appearance. Giovanni inclined slightly towards her and as he bent his head to kiss her cheek, she was engulfed in an overpowering aroma of expensive aftershave lotion. She felt her senses reel. She was quite unable to speak. 'You have the tickets, yes?' asked Giovanni, taking her by the elbow and starting to steer her through the crowds of people who were already moving to the auditorium.

Beryl fumbled with the catch of her little black-velvet evening bag. 'Yes, yes, of course. Here they are,' she stammered, hastily pulling them out. She feared that everyone was looking at her, that she was the object of a hundred pairs of eyes, and she became aware that she was clinging on to Giovanni for dear life. He didn't seem to mind. Taking charge, he pried the tickets from her hand and gave them to the usherette. She had been through this routine a thousand times before with Arnold, but somehow it felt new and exciting with a handsome young man beside her.

Their seats in the dress circle were good ones. Still feeling unsure of herself, she devoted herself to her programme as soon as they were safely ensconced. As it was entirely in Italian, this was a daunting task.

'Shall I read it for you?' Giovanni offered, *sotto voce* in her ear. He was so close she could feel his warm breath on her cheek. There was no escape: she had to lean towards him in order to hear what he was saying about the cast and the staging. Fortunately, the lights soon began to dim and she could hide her blushes in comforting darkness.

The opera was *L'Orfeo* which Beryl knew well. It was performed in the seventeenth-century manner with the backdrops on rollers, unfurling to reveal each charming new scene. The singing was superb, and soon Beryl was completely caught up in the story. She forgot herself and where she was and became enthralled. However, when the scene changed to Hades and the River Styx, Giovanni took advantage of the supposed horror of the scene to put his hand gently on top of hers. She froze, hardly daring to breathe, and for a while her enjoyment of the music was marred, especially as he made no attempt to let go of her hand and, if anything, clasped it tighter. Then, as she became used to the situation, Beryl began to relax imperceptibly, the music carrying her ever onwards. The piece was continuous, with no interval, and Giovanni did not release her hand until the performance was over and it was time to applaud.

He looked at her, flushed with excitement. 'That was superb, yes?'

he asked. Beryl soon found out that superb was Giovanni's favourite word, one of the few adjectives he had acquired. She was determined to teach him some others. Now she turned to him, her eyes shining, her skin glowing. 'It was wonderful,' she breathed. Giovanni gazed at her admiringly for the second time that evening.

'We go for some food now, yes?' Beryl also determined to teach Giovanni some grammar.

'Yes,' she said simply.

'I know of just the place,' he confided, as they slowly left their seats, pushing towards the exit with the throng of people. Beryl said nothing. She was starting to feel apprehensive again. When and where would this evening end? She shook herself impatiently. For heaven's sake, she was a grown-up woman and she could take care of herself.

Giovanni took her elbow as he guided her towards the doors and as soon as they were outside he said, 'We walk? Yes?'

Beryl laughed. 'Shall we walk?' she corrected him teasingly.

'Yes, that is what I say,' agreed Giovanni.

'I know,' she smiled. 'I am just giving you a different way of saying it.'

'OK, I see.' He realized she was laughing at him. 'Passeggiamo, all right, I give you a different way of saying it too.' Beryl's laughter was completely spontaneous.

'Passeggiamo,' she echoed quietly. 'Yes, why not?'

Giovanni took her hand. They crossed the street. 'OK, now shall we eat?' he asked carefully.

'Yes, please,' said Beryl happily.

It was not far from the Teatro dell'Opera to George's, just off the Via Veneto. The restaurant seemed to expect them and Beryl was touched at Giovanni's thoughtfulness in booking a table. They dined outside in the balmy evening air. Giovanni chose the food and the wine. He would give her the very best the Italians had to offer, he insisted. For most of the evening, they chatted easily and happily about music. Beryl was surprised how well-informed Giovanni was on the subject. He was quite astonished that she had only ever listened to opera in English, and protested that she could not possibly appreciate the full romantic lyricism of the music. No, Italian was the language of music, and rightly so. He hadn't much time for German, either, insisting that even the German composers sounded better in Italian.

The wine had gone to Beryl's head and she was prepared to argue with him, although she had to admit that she had never actually heard opera sung live in German, only on recordings or the radio. Giovanni was adamant, Italian was best, Italy was best, Roma was best, OK? Beryl giggled uncontrollably. 'Why do you always say OK at the end of every sentence?' she asked.

'OK is the first English word I learn,' he explained proudly.

'But it's not really English,' said Beryl, still giggling. 'It's American.'

'No, really?' Giovanni was puzzled.

Beryl laughed openly at the amazement on his face. 'Yes, really.'

Quite unexpectedly, Giovanni leaned across the table and took Beryl's hand in his. 'You see, signora, you could teach me so much,' he said simply, gazing into her eyes. Beryl sat, frozen, gazing back at him.

'What could I possibly teach you?' she said at last, looking downwards to avoid his gaze.

'You are a woman of experience – you know things – you could teach me much.' Giovanni's tone was insistent.

Beryl did not dare to look at him. She had no idea what to say. Instead she just sat, her hand in his, eyes fixed on her plate, not saying a word. Giovanni was immediately contrite.

'I am so sorry, signora. I have said too much and you must forgive me.'

'Please,' she said slowly, 'not signora. My name is Beryl.'

Giovanni smiled broadly at her words. 'Come then, Beryl, we will now see the beautiful city.' He clicked his fingers at the waiter and gestured for the bill. 'Have you seen Roma?'

Beryl thought of the endless sightseeing she had done in the last few days. 'Well, yes, I think so.'

'But not like this, not at night.' The waiter arrived with the bill. Without any hesitation or sign of embarrassment, Giovanni handed it to Beryl. She gave him a startled look, hesitated for a second, then finally realized what was expected of her. She covered her confusion by leaning down to pick up her handbag from the floor, searching in its depths for her purse. Never in her life before had she been out for a meal with a man and paid. She counted out the thousands of lire – the meal was expensive, though it had been delicious – and placed the money on the plate with the check.

As the smiling waiter bore it away, Giovanni took her hand again, frowning slightly. 'Your name,' he said, 'Beryl . . . I do not like it.'

Beryl gasped and laughed at his audacity.

'Oh dear,' she said finally.

He looked at her thoughtfully. 'I shall call you Carina – in Italian that means "darling".'

Beryl gazed at the good-looking young man, and could hardly believe what was happening. 'If you like,' she whispered. It sounded inadequate, but it was all she could think of saying.

The waiter reappeared with the change. As Giovanni downed the rest of his wine in one gulp, Beryl detached her hand from his and, taking a compact from her handbag, checked her appearance in the mirror. Cheeks a little flushed, she thought, and hastened to apply a little more powder.

Giovanni regarded her with amusement. 'Why you do that, Carina? You look beautiful,' he said in open admiration. Beryl blushed, making the situation worse.

'I'm afraid the wine has gone to my cheeks,' she said, smiling shyly. 'I can't go around with a pink face.'

'But, Carina, you waste your time. Soon I kiss it all off you again.'

Beryl reddened even more, embarrassed by his candour. She looked at her change. 'How much should I leave?' she asked.

Giovanni counted out some money. 'That is sufficient. Come, we go now.'

As Beryl and Giovanni wandered hand in hand through the streets of central Rome, Beryl wondered if she had ever been so happy in her life. She glanced at Giovanni with a questioning look when they came to a square where ponies and traps stood at ease with their drivers.

'Of course, Carina, we go for a ride.' He led her over to a trap with a dozing grey pony between the shafts and muttered some instructions to the bored-looking driver. Then he gestured to Beryl to mount the steps, helping her up as she gathered her skirts about her. With an agile leap, he joined her; when they had settled into the seat Giovanni was insistent that she should tuck a rug around her knees, even though the late-evening air was warm. A ride around the Eternal City – seeing the sights of Ancient Rome on a balmy June evening, with a handsome young man by her side – it was beyond her wildest imaginings, and Beryl knew she would never forget this night. At one point, when Giovanni was not looking, she even pinched herself, just to make sure that it was real.

Giovanni was a charming and knowledgeable guide, but there was far more to her enjoyment than that. As they clip-clopped past the moonlit Forum, Beryl felt that her experience was surpassing even the most exotic of the romantic novels she had devoured at home. Relaxed and happy, she instinctively allowed herself to snuggle up against her companion, and he put his arm around her and held her close. It all seemed so natural to be sitting there, with her head on his shoulder, gazing in wonder at the marvellous sights they were passing and noting with amusement that the horse's ears twitched back every time Giovanni spoke to her, as though trying to overhear their conversation. She hoped this ride would go on for ever.

'You are tired, Carina,' murmured Giovanni tenderly after what seemed like hours. 'It's time for bed, yes?'

As he spoke to the driver in rapid Italian, Beryl became suddenly very wide awake. Bed. What did that mean? Was he intending to take her back to her hotel and leave her there? Or had he something else in mind? He might even want to accompany her to her room. Her mind raced feverishly over the various possibilities and she was astonished to find that, rather than being frightened, she was stimulated, even thrilled, by the prospect of being bedded by this attractive young man. She felt reckless and uninhibited, with a strange feeling that this was going to be her one chance to make a grab at life. Of one thing she was certain – she must take it. A montage of images flashed through her mind: Amanda's contemptuous laugh as she told her adoptive parents of her sexual conquests; Arnold's fumbling and infrequent attempts at love-making ; and, finally, most vivid of all, the lurid pictures in the porno-graphic magazines that she had found secreted in Arnold's study.

The pony had turned and they were headed back into the centre of Rome. Giovanni was murmuring sweet nothings to her in Italian, and the horse's ears swivelled ever more rapidly. Beryl started to laugh and Giovanni drew back from her, looking hurt. 'What is it, Carina? I am funny?'

'No, of course not,' Beryl replied hastily, putting a reassuring hand on his arm. 'You were just tickling my ear, that's all.' She giggled, then added, 'I'm very happy.'

Finally the pony and trap pulled up in a back street of central Rome. Beryl didn't know where on earth she was and didn't care – she felt reckless and daring. As she attempted to pay the driver, Giovanni, looking outraged, produced the money from his own pocket, and Beryl laughed again, unable to understand the logic of this. Presumably the arrangement was that she paid for the most expensive treats and he for the inexpensive. Fine, she thought, anything goes – tonight I'm going to break all the rules.

Giovanni ushered her through a doorway into a small, dark, stone-flagged hall. 'It's a long way to the top,' he said. 'Shall I carry you?'

Beryl was beginning to feel slightly hysterical. 'Of course not,' she giggled, 'I can manage.' And holding up her long skirt, she started to climb the stairs.

Giovanni had not been mistaken when he had said it was a long way, and as she climbed higher and higher Beryl fleetingly wondered if she was being foolhardy. Then, quickly dismissing the thought from her mind, she pressed on until they had reached the landing at the very top of the building. Giovanni went on ahead to open the door and turn on the light, re-emerging to usher Beryl inside. The apartment seemed to comprise just one room with minimal furniture. There was a low sofa against one wall, a small table, a couple of chairs, a cupboard. A tiny kitchenette was partly screened off by a trellis-work partition, covered with foliage.

Giovanni went straight into the kitchenette and took glasses from a cupboard above the sink. 'Carina, I make you a very special drink,' he announced dramatically.

'How lovely,' Beryl said. Then, looking around for another door in vain, she asked, 'Could I use your bathroom?'

'Of course. Come, I show you the way.' To her surprise, he took her outside the front door again and indicated the floor below. 'The bathroom is that door there. I share with some other people, but I expect it is free,' he said airily. 'Don't be long now,' he added as he turned back into the apartment.

Beryl tentatively made her way down the stone stairs. The bathroom was old fashioned, but quite clean and functional. As she washed her hands she stared at her reflection in the small mirror. Beryl Willoughby, just what do you think you're doing? she wondered as she searched without success for a towel. Shaking her hands dry, she did not bother to reply to the question.

When she got back to the room, Giovanni had placed their drinks on the table. 'A special drink for a very special occasion,' he said, handing her a glass and raising his own. 'To us, Carina.'

Beryl wordlessly raised her glass in return and took a sip. It was champagne and some fruit juice – peach, she thought. As they drank, he gazed into her eyes. Then he leant forward to kiss her gently on her mouth, and Beryl felt a thrill of pleasure shiver through her. Giovanni took her glass from her hand and put it on the table with his own. With a deft movement, born of long practice, he swept her into his arms and kissed her passionately. Beryl was overwhelmed; she had never been kissed like this before in her life, even in the early days of Arnold's courtship. She made no attempt to resist, but abandoned herself completely to the experience.

Giovanni was becoming increasingly ardent. 'Oh, Carina, Carina,' he breathed in her ear, fervently kissing her neck. Suddenly he scooped her up in his arms and carried her towards a doorway which had been hidden by a beaded curtain. Behind it was a small bedroom almost entirely filled by a large double bed. Dizzy with wine and excitement as she was, Beryl was glad to notice with some last gleam of sense that the sheets were clean and it appeared to be freshly made.

Tenderly he laid her down on the bed and bent over her, covering her face and neck with kisses. His hands moved behind her back, he eased down the zip of her dress and slid it gently from her shoulders, taking her bra with it. She lay there unmoving, breasts revealed, and he gazed at them for a moment, face expressionless. Then with an almost reverent movement he bent down again and kissed them gently, cupping them in his hands. Beryl began to experience the stirring of feelings she had long since forgotten as he caressed her expertly. Then she felt cool air on her skin as Giovanni slid the dress lower still, printing burning kisses down the line of her body. She closed her eyes and abandoned herself to a world of rapturous sensations.

When Giovanni penetrated her she screamed out loud in a kind of ecstasy. She clasped him to her joyfully as he plunged into her with powerful strokes that made her shudder with excitement. 'Say you love me, Carina,' he gasped, 'you love me, don't you? Say you love me.'

'Oh, God, yes,' screamed Beryl, all her nerve-endings on fire as she trembled on the brink of ecstasy. Faster, deeper he thrust, until with a great shuddering cry he came, toppling Beryl over the edge with him into an undreamed-of ocean of pleasure.

The sound of church bells awoke Beryl next morning. For a moment she had no idea where she was. She glanced around the tiny bedroom with the curtains shut tight against the glare of the sun. Then she stretched contentedly, smiling as she remembered the events of the night before. She felt wonderful. Giovanni was nowhere to be seen, but she could hear some sort of activity going on next door. She had an overwhelming desire for a cup of tea.

The door opened and Giovanni appeared, smiling and bearing two cups. He was clad in a black and red paisley-silk dressing gown, which suited him admirably. 'Ah, you are awake, Carina. You see, I bring you some tea. I know you English ladies like tea. I hope this is right.' Beryl felt that if she hadn't loved him the night before, she certainly loved him now.

'How lovely, I was just thinking how much I would like some.'

'And, you see, you have your wish,' he said handing her a steaming cup. Beryl sipped it gratefully. The liquid was recognizably tea, but it had a taste that was strange to her.

Giovanni watched her drink it with satisfaction. 'You see, I know about these things.' He sounded smug.

'But how?' She smiled back at him. Giovanni averted his gaze and changed the subject.

'You look very beautiful this morning, Carina,' he said. Then, as though suddenly remembering something, he added, 'Of course, Leonie, she tell me these things. She is very fond of tea.'

Beryl started. 'Leonie?' she asked, astonished.

'Miss O'Brien,' he explained. 'I work for her.'

'You know Leonie O'Brien the film star?' asked Beryl incredulously.

'Yes, I know her very well. She is a very nice lady. She is my boss,' he said proudly.

'Is she here in Rome?' asked Beryl.

'Of course. She make film here with Rob Fenton.' He sat himself down on the bed by her side.

'Who is Rob Fenton?' asked Beryl.

'Her boyfriend,' he said sipping his tea.

'Of course, I forgot,' replied Beryl. 'Yes, I've read about them.' She looked thoughtful. 'Does Amanda know Leonie O'Brien?'

'No, but she wants very much to meet her.'

'Oh yes, I'm sure she does,' said Beryl.

'Now,' said Giovanni happily, 'I know another thing English ladies like is English newspapers. I go out and get some, and some rolls for breakfast. Then we decide what to do today.'

'That would be lovely, Giovanni,' said Beryl, sinking back into her pillows with a happy sigh.

It was late afternoon when Leonie awoke to the sound of buzzing. She ignored it and stretched out luxuriantly, suffused with a wonderful sense of well-being. She lay on the bed, rethinking the events of the last few hours. God knows, the experience had been traumatic, but the relief of having faced the unfaceable was indescribable. She tried to analyse it – it was as if a great burden had been lifted from her – and she saw with blinding clarity that she had been struggling alone for years under a load of self-loathing. Now it was gone and the feeling was extraordinary, as though she had finally exorcized an unwelcome ghost.

The buzzing sounded again and Leonie realized it was the intercom. Why didn't Rob answer it? She turned her head to find a note wedged beside the pillow scrawled in Rob's large hand: 'Darling – gone shopping – love you – R.' She smiled, and reluctantly swung her legs off the bed to go and pick up the front-door intercom phone.

A strange female voice spoke in English. 'Hello. I'm sorry to bother you – my name is Beryl Willoughby.'

'Yes?' Was it another reporter, Leonie wondered? She prepared to choke her off.

'I'm sorry to be a nuisance, but I need to talk to you. You see, I'm Amanda's mother.'

'What?' Leonie could not believe what she had heard.

'I must see you,' continued the voice desperately, 'please. There are reporters hanging around out here – please let me in.'

'All right – come on up,' said Leonie briefly and hung up. This woman could be a reporter herself, but her instincts said not. She hoped she was doing the right thing.

She went back into the bedroom and checked her appearance in the mirror. A bit crumpled, but not bad. She looked younger, she thought – maybe because she wasn't wearing make-up. The doorbell rang and Leonie crossed to the door and cautiously opened it a fraction. The woman standing on the doormat looked respectable enough, simply, but tastefully dressed in a lilac cotton shirtwaister, her slim waist accentuated by a wide, deep-violet suede belt. She had an attractive, lightly tanned face with wide-set grey eyes, and platinum-blonde hair. Late-forties, Leonie guessed. She opened the door slightly wider.

'Hello.' Her tone was cool but friendly. She didn't want to antagonize her, just in case she was a reporter. Leonie always prided herself on being polite to the press, no matter how objectionable they became.

'I'm sorry to bother you,' said the woman shyly. Leonie was quite convinced she had never seen her before.

'Not at all.' She smiled. 'Please come in.'

Beryl stepped over the threshold. 'Oh, what a beautiful place,' she breathed, looking around her with obvious pleasure. 'You must have very good taste,' she said in a voice that was tinged with envy.

'You're very kind. Can I get you a drink?'

'Yes, that would be lovely. A sherry if you have it.'

'Certainly,' said Leonie. She crossed briskly to the drinks cabinet, gesturing Beryl to follow her into the room. 'Please make yourself comfortable,' she said indicating the sofas, 'do sit down.' Beryl sank into the luxurious plumpness of cream Italian leather and looked around her as Leonie filled a crystal sherry glass to the brim. She handed it to her guest, who appeared ill at ease. In contrast, Leonie felt absolutely in control of the situation. The sleep had done her good and she was still feeling elated from the press conference.

She gave Beryl a penetrating glance. 'I never expected to meet you,' she said slowly, 'least of all in Rome. What are you doing here?'

Beryl chose to take the question at face value. 'I'm here on holiday. My husband died and I needed to get away.'

'I'm sorry.' Leonie said briefly.

Beryl was lost for words. How could she say what she needed to say now that she was face to face with Amanda's real mother. She had known that Leonie was good-looking, but she had been unprepared for the poised and beautiful woman who sat opposite her. Like many film stars, there was an unreal, intangible quality about her when viewed in the flesh. She was also much smaller than Beryl had imagined. Almost frail. 'It's so difficult . . .' she began, taking a sip of her drink. She looked up at Leonie again. There was something almost vulnerable about her, she thought. In a flash, she remembered her joy at holding the new baby, and her wonder at how the mother could possibly have parted from the tiny thing. She suddenly knew the anguish it must have cost her and, at the thought, tears began to rise in her eyes.

Leonie watched anxiously as a tear slid down Beryl's cheek. 'You're not well. Would you rather have some tea?'

'No, you don't understand,' Beryl said quietly. 'It's just that I've looked after Amanda ever since . . .'

Leonie sat absolutely still letting the news sink in at last: this woman had cared for her baby, brought her up, loved her, nursed her.

Beryl went on earnestly, 'I can't tell you how grateful I am to you for giving me Amanda all those years ago. I'm just so terribly upset at how things have turned out. We gave her everything – that was probably where we went wrong. When my husband died last year – he'd had a stroke – it was really her fault in a way. There was an awful row . . . and . . . well, he died eventually.' The words came tumbling out as though a stopper had been removed from a tightly sealed bottle that had sat for a long time on a forgotten shelf. Beryl looked mutely at the younger woman as Leonie smiled, her eyes brimming over with tears.

'Of course it's not your fault,' she murmured. 'I should be grateful to you . . .'

'No,' Beryl insisted, 'you gave me so much happiness, you can't imagine the joy that little girl . . .' She trembled visibly, but kept herself in check. Leonie began to contemplate again all she had sacrificed and thoughts that she had put firmly to the back of her mind started to surge forward: images of the last view she'd had of the baby bathed in golden sunlight in the cradle; the cry of a small child in a push-chair that had made Leonie start in anguish in a shop – supposing it was her child?; watching a little girl playing with others in a children's playground. She had stood for ages, staring, trying to decide which one might have been hers and had finally dragged herself away, the sound of childish laughter ringing in her ears.

'I've brought some photos. I always keep them with me – would you like to see them?' Leonie nodded, not able to speak as Beryl opened her handbag and took out a thick wallet. Inside, under some yellowing plastic, were half a dozen or so dog-eared snaps. Leonie took the photographs with shaking hands, though at first she could hardly focus on them through her tears: a baby in Beryl's arms; a small girl crouched on the sands with bucket and spade; a stiff little figure in a Brownie uniform, gap-toothed and grinning; a schoolgirl in pigtails giggling with a best friend; a beautiful smiling teenager leaning against the bonnet of a car with an older man.

'That's Arnold, my late husband,' explained Beryl. 'He adored her,' she added simply.

The final photograph showed a transformation. It was in colour and depicted a solemn creature with a stark white face, the eyes almost obliterated by black eye make-up. The beautiful auburn tresses had been dyed raven and turned into dreadlocks, and laddered black tights, pointed black boots, a black leather miniskirt and a heavily studded denim jacket completed the outfit.

'She wanted me to take that. It was her seventeenth birthday,' Beryl explained. The creature in the photo looked about thirty-five. 'That phase lasted nearly three years,' she added tightly.

There was the sound of a key turning in the door. It opened and Rob came in bearing a brown carrier bag in one arm. He viewed the scene with interest.

'Rob, darling.' Leonie jumped up. 'This is Amanda's mother – I mean, her adoptive mother . . . Beryl, this is my, friend, Rob Fenton.'

Rob came forward, hand outstretched, and Giovanni appeared in the doorway behind him. 'I'm delighted to meet you, Beryl. I believe you already know my friend John here,' Beryl smiled and blushed slightly. Leonie looked from one to the other and back again.

'You know Giovanni?' she asked in astonishment.

'Yes.' Beryl was going pinker and pinker.

'It's a long story, Leo,' Rob said, kissing her, 'perhaps John will fill you in later. Now he and I are going to cook you two a meal, aren't we?' he said, with a pointed glance at his friend.

'OK,' replied Giovanni cheerfully. He blew Beryl a kiss before following Rob into the kitchen.

'I should have explained,' said Beryl. 'Amanda introduced Giovanni to me. We went to the opera together last night and this morning,' she glanced at Leonie self-consciously, 'this morning we saw what Amanda had told the newspapers about you. I felt I had to come and talk to you and, of course, Giovanni knew where you lived. He was going to wait outside for me.'

Leonie gave her a mischievous smile. 'He's a nice boy, Giovanni, don't you think?'

'Very nice,' said Beryl. 'He's been very kind to me.' She giggled.

'Do you know, he calls me Carina. Isn't that silly of him?'

In the kitchen, Rob murmured to Giovanni, 'Keep your mouth shut about the party, will you? Nothing happened with Amanda, you know. We were just messing around – I was pissed, anyway.'

'Nothing? You sure?' said Giovanni innocently.

'You must be joking. Would you, with Leonie at home? Anyway, she's far too young. You're not the only one who prefers older women.'

Giovanni laughed, showing perfect white teeth. 'She a sweet lady, Beryl. Anyway I tell nothing because I see nothing. You know that Laura in make-up? She take me back to her place, early, and we have very nice time.'

'OK, fine,' said Rob, his expression clearing. 'After all,' he added, 'this is all your bloody fault anyway.' He was smiling as he spoke, but there was a threatening undertone in his voice.

'Me?' said Giovanni, his face stricken.

'Yes, you. You brought her to the studios in the first place, didn't you?' Then Rob grinned, and Giovanni relaxed. 'No, don't worry, John, I'm only joking. She was determined to get at us, one way or another – God, you're taking your time with those onions, aren't you?'

'Sorry, yes.' Giovanni resumed his task at the chopping board. 'But Rob,' he asked, as he sliced away busily, 'what happened to the man? You know, the father. Who is he? Beryl say he is in the government in Inghilterra.'

'What, the Right Honourable Simon Brentford, the member for South Molding, or wherever it is?' asked Rob sarcastically. 'Him? Oh, he's for the high jump and no mistake.'

10

Elizabeth sat calmly at her dressing table, fixing a panama hat of periwinkle blue on to her sleek, blonde head. The hat almost exactly matched her eyes and she was wearing a blue linen suit of a similar hue. Her reflection in the mirror showed a pale, serious, yet serene-looking woman. There was no evidence in her features of her inner turmoil nor indeed of the impending ordeal. She was a little too pale though, she decided, and she brushed on the faintest tinge of rose-coloured blusher, leaning back in her chair to survey the results. Yes, that was better. Now she looked the epitome of a true blue wife – loyal, dependable, unflustered, able to cope with any crisis, any emergency, any challenge. She was, after all, about to face the biggest challenge of her life, but she was confident that she could cope. How many of the other women in Simon's life would have been able to handle this situation? Not one, she felt quite sure. She allowed herself a small, confident smile, and picking up her gloves and handbag from the bed, gave her appearance a final check in a full-length mirror. Thus reassured she felt as ready as she would ever be to leave the safety of her home.

This Saturday was the day of the local annual Conservative fête. What timing, Elizabeth reflected bitterly. It was just under a week since the news had broken about Leonie O'Brien's illegitimate daughter, and the fear that Amanda would soon reveal the name of her famous father was hanging over them like an ugly black cloud. Simon would, as always, make a splendid speech, she would be smilingly supportive by his side and, at any moment, the scandal would become public knowledge. Well, at least the boys hadn't broken up yet from school. They were due back next week, when it would be best to pack them off to her sister in Gloucestershire, she thought wearily. The front-door bell rang.

'Simon, are you ready?' Elizabeth called along the passage. 'The car's here.' Simon emerged from the little room he used for dressing and, as he walked towards her, it struck her forcibly that he suddenly seemed much older.

'Yes, ready,' he replied and barely glancing at her, added, 'You look nice.' He started down the stairs. She followed him silently. Yes, she thought to herself, definitely older. His hair seemed to be flecked with more grey, he seemed heavier about the jawline and his posture was not as upright as it had been. Janet was already crossing to the front door as the two of them descended the stairs. She opened it to admit Charles Pendlebury, who stood there looking anxious and concerned, but in control.

'Morning, Charles,' Simon greeted him. He looked briefly in the hall mirror as he passed, smoothing down his hair with one hand.

'Good morning, sir. Mrs Brentford.' He smiled at Elizabeth reassuringly. 'It's a fine day,' he added. It would be, thought Elizabeth to herself resignedly.

'That's a matter of opinion,' muttered Simon as he passed Charles and went out of the front door.

They were bowling along in the Daimler towards the village before Charles spoke. 'There's been no word from Downing Street, sir,' he said quietly.

'There will be,' replied Simon tersely. 'Have you got my speech?' He thrust out his hand. Charles opened his briefcase and took out some sheets of paper. He caught Simon's look as he handed over the speech, 'I think you're doing the right thing, sir,' he murmured.

Simon returned the look, leant back in his seat and gave his attention to the typescript in front of him. 'Of course,' was all he said.

Charles glanced covertly at Elizabeth. She was staring out of the car window, her thoughts obviously far away. He began to say something, thought better of it, and sat back feeling, for the first time in his life, powerless to help. He noticed how bright everything looked in the sparkling sunshine and became aware that Elizabeth was looking at him. They exchanged a glance of mutual warmth and he felt the strength surging back into his veins. She needed him today – all be it in the background, playing a supporting role – and he wanted her to know that he was there, with her all the way. They looked at each other and, uncharacteristically, he winked at her.

The day was scorching hot and people flocked in their hundreds to the gardens of Audleigh Manor, home of Sir Edward and Lady Audleigh, who opened their house and grounds each year for the Conservative fête. It was opened officially by Lady Audleigh, a landscape artist of some repute, clad in an ancient tea-gown of prune-coloured chiffon. From the podium on the lawn, she was inaudibly effusive as she referred to their charming and handsome MP who would be addressing them later. He would of course, she gushed, be accompanied by his exquisite wife. Here she turned and wafted her hand in the direction of Elizabeth, who looked suitably modest. Then she stepped down and the crowd, even those who hadn't heard a word that she said, applauded loudly before surging in the direction of the refreshment tent.

Simon was immediately surrounded by a bevy of handsome middle-aged women, whose pin-up he had been for several years, and Charles took advantage of the temporary diversion to guide Elizabeth into the cool interior of the house. This took some time as they had to return the salutations of the dozens of supporters, who greeted her on all sides. They finally found sanctuary in what had once been the butler's pantry, a dark and quiet room tucked away behind the kitchens. Charles glanced around to ensure their privacy before speaking. 'Elizabeth, are you all right?'

'It's going to happen, isn't it?'

'Yes, I'm afraid so. Are you all right?' he insisted, touching her arm lightly.

'Yes, I'll manage. Do they know?'

'Yes. I spoke to the office on the car phone before I got to you. The girl's said that Simon is her father. It's going to be all over the front page of the *Globe* tomorrow. The rest of Fleet Street has been ringing non-stop and our people have been stalling like mad – you know, saying "no comment" and promising statements. But they are on to it all right.'

She moved towards him and laid her hand on his chest. 'Charles, will you do something – would you hold me for a moment?' She looked up at him almost imploringly, but Charles needed no second bidding and took her in his arms. For several wonderful moments, she was his. He held her close, tightly yet gently. He could hear her heart thumping, like an animal frightened by fireworks. He kissed her forehead lightly – she didn't seem to mind – but she still remained motionless. Footsteps crunched on the gravel outside and, reluctantly, they separated. Both had derived some comfort from the moment.

'Thank you, I'll be all right now.' She smiled at him, and automatically straightened her skirt and smoothed her hair, ready to face the world again, whatever it threw at her.

'The press will have to be dealt with,' he said, sensing this. 'They'll descend – probably tonight when you get home – are you ready for them?'

Elizabeth tossed her head defiantly. 'I'm ready for anything.'

'I love you, Elizabeth.' He heard himself whisper the words. She said nothing in reply, but the look she gave him told him plainly that if it were possible, she would return that love. She walked out into the sunlight and he followed at a discreet distance, watching as she crossed the courtyard and rounded the corner of the house. There were several people wandering around, and heads turned as she passed. Charles smiled with a mixture of pride, sadness and longing; a moment ago she had been in his arms and he had declared his love for her. It didn't matter what happened now. He could live happily in the knowledge that she returned at least some of that feeling. He waited for her to disappear, then set off in search of Simon.

Elizabeth felt strangely calm in the face of the impending storm. Charles's comforting embrace had given her untold strength and anyone observing her progress around the gardens, as she made her way to the orangery to find the crafts stalls, would have seen a beautifully poised, svelte woman completely in control of herself and at ease with the world. The orangery was a Victorian addition to the house, built along the lines of a mini Crystal Palace. The interior with its abundance of ferns, palms and other greenery was still relatively cool; the sun had not yet reached its glass dome. Elizabeth knew she would have to purchase one of Lady Audleigh's local views, and had also promised to visit her friend Angela's stall, a veritable cornucopia of cushions, but for the moment she was waylaid on all sides by the greetings of friends and acquaintances, and somehow managed to exchange a word with all of them. Soon, however, she found herself in a quieter corner, where a smiling Angela was installed among an array of rich fabrics, hanging tassels and braids, the prerequisites of her trade. There was only one other customer, a woman who was browsing happily among the gorgeous brocades and tapestries that were strewn across the trestle-table.

'Angela, what a superb display. You must have worked like a Trojan to get this done in time.' At the sound of her voice, the woman customer looked up and turned away abruptly

'Elizabeth! How good of you to come so soon. Look, you're already starting to attract more trade for me.' And Angela indicated a little group of people who had spotted the MP's wife and were heading in her direction.

'Oh, Lord,' laughed Elizabeth. 'Quickly, show me the cushion you were talking about.' Angela indicated the pile of cushions that the other customer was examining.

'It's the one at the back there,' she said.

Elizabeth moved to the customer's side. 'I'm so sorry. Can I just stretch across you?' she asked, smiling politely.

'Of course,' the other woman murmured, trying to edge away, but with Angela now standing on her other side, her exit was blocked. The three of them were forced to examine the cushion in question together.

'Oh,' exclaimed Elizabeth in genuine admiration. 'It's quite beautiful.' Because of her proximity and out of politeness, Elizabeth also addressed the unknown woman. 'It's exquisite, isn't it?'

The woman fingered it gently. 'Yes, it's lovely,' she agreed. She was wearing some scent that seemed familiar to Elizabeth, but she couldn't place it. Then she looked up and, as their eyes met, Elizabeth knew as clearly as if it had been stamped on the other woman's forehead that she was looking at her husband's current mistress. And she knew that the woman knew too. Their eyes locked for several seconds.

'Where did you find this piece of tapestry, Angela?' she asked with keen interest, taking the upper hand.

'Believe it or not, it's late-seventeenth century and very rare,' Angela replied unaware of the drama that was being enacted in front of her. To Elizabeth's surprise, she felt no animosity in her heart for this woman. In fact, quite the reverse. As she looked at her, there seemed to be some sort of tacit understanding between them, a mutual sympathy. She instinctively liked the woman, with her bright, intelligent eyes and lovely chestnut hair. She was not a beauty like Elizabeth, but she had an open and attractive face.

'How much is it?' she asked, turning her attention back to the cushion once more.

'I'm afraid . . .,' hesitated Angela, 'I'm afraid it's £250.'

'I'll take it,' said Elizabeth immediately, and she opened her hand-bag and took out her cheque book and pen. The woman lingered on, obviously determined not to be fazed by the encounter. 'It will go perfectly with the colour scheme in our living-room,' she said calmly as she wrote out the cheque. The woman's perfume wafted past her again, and she suddenly remembered the other scent, the scent she had smelt on her husband's fingers.

'Well, Elizabeth,' said Angela happily, pleased at having started the afternoon's sales so well, 'I hope Simon likes it.'

'I doubt it,' replied Elizabeth brightly as she handed over the cheque. 'He doesn't really appreciate beautiful things.'

'Oh?' said Angela, somewhat surprised, as she gave the cushion to Elizabeth in a plastic carrier-bag.

'No,' said Elizabeth, taking the bag from her, 'I'm afraid his taste is deplorable,' and she smiled a charming smile that included both women, and turned on her heel.

Once out in the main body of the orangery again, she found that she was trembling and wanted badly to sit down. She needed to get away from this place, but when she made her way outside again into the blazing sunshine, the heat was so overpowering that she felt quite certain she was about to faint. She half-ran, half-stumbled towards the refreshment tent, her mind seething with confused thoughts. She hated herself for having behaved so badly. It was so uncharacteristic of her and she had never said anything quite so bitchy in her life before. What on earth had possessed her? She tried to comfort herself – perhaps it wasn't quite as bad as she had imagined, perhaps it had just seemed like small talk, perhaps the woman hadn't realized that she knew? Yes, that was it. After all, how could she have guessed?

'Why, Mrs Brentford, you look done in,' remarked one of the ladies serving tea. 'Are you all right?'

'Yes, thank you,' said Elizabeth a little breathlessly. 'Thank you, Mrs Durrant, I just can't take this heat.'

'A nice cup of tea is what you need,' said Mrs Durrant knowledgeably. 'Come on, dear, you sit down here, and we'll have you right as rain in no time.' And she suited her actions to her words, urging Elizabeth to relax on a nearby chair and giving her a cup of hot, strong tea into which she liberally spooned some sugar. Elizabeth did not take sugar, but she did not say anything, feeling strangely comforted by this woman's attentions. People were milling around the tea-urns, but, to her relief, no one seemed to have noticed her. To her surprise the sweet, hot tea made her feel much better, and she soon felt able to cope again. She stood up and handed the empty teacup to her benefactress.

'Thank you so much for your kindness,' she said in the charming way that had won so many hearts. 'I must go now and find my husband; he'll wonder what on earth has become of me.' She smiled and left the tent, only to be accosted immediately by Lady Audleigh.

'Ah, Elizabeth, my dear, just the person I was looking for. Mrs Burton feels we ought to hold the children's dance-group demonstration on the front lawn, where the cedar of Lebanon will afford them some shade. Don't you agree?'

'A very sensible idea,' Elizabeth replied briskly, her old self resurfacing.

Lady Audleigh smiled approvingly. 'And we were wondering if you would be kind enough to draw the raffle afterwards?' she asked.

'Of course, I should be delighted.'

'Excellent. I'll go and tell Mrs Pearson, she'll be so pleased. The children are dancing to "In an English Country Garden", you know,' she added inconsequentially.

'How appropriate,' replied Elizabeth, hardly listening. 'Lady Audleigh, please excuse me, I have to find my husband's secretary. I have something rather important to tell him.'

'Oh!' Lady Audleigh looked startled and disappointed at this abrupt dismissal. She had been hoping to have a nice, cosy chat with Elizabeth. 'That's that nice Mr Pendlebury, isn't it?'

'Yes. Have you seen him?'

'He's with our husbands. They're planning a game of croquet for the benefit of the local press photographers.'

'Thank you.' Elizabeth started to move away, then turned back. 'I hope to buy one of your paintings later, Lady Audleigh,' she added.

Lady Audleigh immediately looked much more cheerful. 'Do you? I'm so glad. I've devoted myself to the marshy swampland which surrounds Ilsley Castle. Rather successfully, I think you'll find.'

'That sounds lovely,' said Elizabeth politely and made her get-away.

She found a considerable number of people gathered around the croquet lawn to watch the spectacle in progress. Charles was standing on the fringe of the group, keeping an eye on things, ready to intervene when he felt the photographers had been given enough scope for candid shots. But Sir Edward and Simon appeared to be genuinely engrossed in their game and were content to go on playing. Of course, thought Elizabeth to herself, Simon wants to win. She watched him, brow furrowed in concentration as he tried a difficult shot.

She moved to stand beside Charles. 'I've met her,' she said quietly.

'Who?' asked Charles amiably, watching Simon's progress.

'Her. Simon's other woman,' replied Elizabeth *sotto voce*.

Charles swung round sharply. 'What!' he hissed under his breath.

Elizabeth looked at him blandly. 'You know who I mean.'

Charles tried to hide his agitation. 'Your husband plays croquet rather well, don't you think, Mrs Brentford?' he asked, his voice raised slightly, so that the nearby bystanders could hear.

'Brilliantly,' agreed Elizabeth still looking at him. 'What does she do, by the way?' she asked, drawing Charles away from the group of people to where Simon could not avoid seeing them. 'I mean apart from bedding other people's husbands,' she added in a stage whisper. She waved at Simon. 'Hello, darling,' she called gaily. Simon, distracted by her movement, muffed his shot.

'Oh, bad luck,' said Sir Edward happily.

The photographers noted Elizabeth's arrival. 'Mrs Brentford, can we have a picture of you with Mr Brentford and Sir Edward?'

'I've never played croquet before,' laughed Elizabeth, stepping confidently on to the lawn.

Sir Edward gallantly handed her his mallet. 'You can play my shot for me, my dear.' Elizabeth moved into position to take a swing at the ball.

'This way, Mrs Brentford.' The little group of local photographers jostled around her, trying to get a good view, and Elizabeth obliged, throwing them a dazzling smile. She grasped the mallet with both hands and swung, hitting the ball fairly and squarely. It sailed through the hoop. A cheer went up and Charles shouted his approval. 'Bravo!'

'Well done, Liz,' smiled Simon through gritted teeth.

'One more please, Mrs Brentford,' begged the photographers, but Charles intervened.

'Mrs Brentford,' he said coming forward, 'Mrs Burton was asking for you. It's about the children's dancing display.' He took her by the elbow and led her away from the crowd into safer waters.

'I know all about Mrs Burton,' protested Elizabeth as she was propelled in the direction of the house.

'Very possibly,' replied Charles with a grim expression on his face. 'But you must be careful, there are journalists everywhere.' Elizabeth allowed herself to be overruled and found that she rather liked it. Charles was being very masterful.

'You still haven't told me what she does,' she said as soon as they were out of earshot.

'She's a secretary in our department,' he said, realizing that she would not be deterred.

Elizabeth stopped in her tracks and roared with laughter. 'A secretary!'

Charles looked round to see if anyone might have overheard them, alarmed at Elizabeth's uncharacteristic behaviour. 'Yes, Mrs Brentford. Please try to control yourself,' he said, using her full name in an effort to calm her. Elizabeth stopped laughing.

'A secretary,' she repeated contemptuously. 'Well, what's she doing here? It's a long way to come to take shorthand.' Charles looked embarrassed.

'Oh, I see,' said Elizabeth sarcastically, 'this is a cover for a secret assignation, is it?'

'No,' said Charles eventually. 'She lives locally.' He saw no point in lying any further. Elizabeth stared at him in astonishment.

'Oh, how very convenient,' she said finally, then added in a small voice, 'I think I'm going to be sick.'

'No, you're not,' said Charles firmly, 'you're going to tour all the stalls with me,' and he took her by the arm and led her determinedly in the direction of the coconut shy. For the next hour or so, Charles was as good as his word. He and Elizabeth threw coconuts, played hoop-la, bought home-made cakes and fresh eggs, and even had their palms read. The gypsy told Elizabeth that she would receive some surprising news. Could there really be any more to come? thought Elizabeth wryly.

When the public-address system announced that Mr Simon Brentford, their MP, would be addressing them in five minutes, Elizabeth and Charles made their way back to the podium. As they were crossing the lawn, Angela appeared beside Elizabeth. 'I'm so glad you had the cushion,' she said confidentially. 'That other woman was very keen on it.'

'Was she?' Elizabeth's voice was cold. 'Well, she can't have it, it's mine.'

Angela laughed at the vehemence in her tone. 'Quite right,' she agreed. 'First come, first served.'

Elizabeth did not reply.

Simon's speech went off brilliantly, as expected. He was a good speaker, with his wit and dry humour, and he spoke lucidly on the world situation, the environment and his hopes and aspirations for the future welfare of his constituency, especially his efforts to improve its public services. Throughout the photographers snapped away happily, and Elizabeth sat serenely beautiful in the heat of the afternoon, glad of her periwinkle-blue straw hat. After it was over, Lady Audleigh rose and thanked Simon for his eloquence, urging everyone to gather on the front lawn where the children's dance display would shortly take place.

Something was gnawing away at the back of Leonie's mind. She felt sure that she had the answer to their present dilemma, but, infuriatingly, the solution remained just out of reach. She was sprawled on the floor of the production office, surrounded by a sea of paperwork, a tray of half-eaten sandwiches and a pot of coffee, now almost empty. Derek sat hunched in a leather armchair nearby, assessing the script rewrites, and Gareth George, the new scriptwriter, sat opposite them both, cross-legged on the floor. There was nothing wrong with Gareth's ideas – they were competent enough – but Derek and Leonie both knew that they were bland, prosaic and predictable. It would be a patched-up job, Derek thought privately.

Leonie sighed heavily and bit absentmindedly into the crusts of her sandwich, which she had left until last. Such a bad habit, she thought. God, these rewrites were so uninspired! She shifted listlessly through the pieces of paper scattered in front of her and was almost inclined to feel that she could do better herself. After all she had come up with a few ideas and suggestions when she had been with Bill and he had been stuck for ideas. She sat up with a jolt. Of course, Bill! He was the answer. Why the hell hadn't she thought of him before? There was nothing Bill didn't know about scriptwriting. He'd come up through the old hard school, writing second-rate scripts for second-rate actors in B movies. And then rewriting them overnight, ready for the next day's shoot – they were never crass enough for the studio bosses – using whole chunks of bowdlerized extracts from the gospels and the Old Testament for biblical epics, providing crisp, spare action-packed dialogue for television cop shows, always with a wryly humorous touch. Bill would work to a deadline, week after week, churning out escapist garbage for prime-time and then daytime soaps. Latterly he'd had a spell on a team of comedy writers, supplying sketches to some of the top sitcom television shows, and among all of this graft were the half a dozen or so really fine screenplays that he had produced during the years he'd spent with Leonie; there was no doubt she had been his muse, way back then. Oh, well, that was years ago. Tough shit. Now Bill was the man for this job. The more she thought about it, the more convinced she was.

'Why don't we call it a day?' she said. 'My brain is reeling, I can't focus any more.'

Derek unfolded himself gratefully and stretched, glancing at his watch. 'Good grief, look at the time,' he yawned. 'We'll just manage to get a few hours shut-eye before we can start all over again.'

Oblivious to the world, Gareth was still poring intently over a couple of pages and Leonie shot Derek a meaningful look, indicating that they should get rid of the boy and talk privately.

'See you tomorrow, old son,' said Derek to him cheerfully. 'Give it a rest now,' he added as Gareth seemed reluctant to get the message.

'What? Sorry. It's just that I think I may have cracked it.'

'Good. Great. Home now. Tell us about it tomorrow.'

'No, really —'

'Home,' said Derek sternly. 'I can't take any more in at the moment. I'll only reject it out of hand if you try to sell it to me now.' Gareth took the hint and started to gather up the pieces of script, looking disconsolate.

'The kid's useless,' Derek observed to Leonie as soon as they were alone. 'We've really got to think some more now. This is going nowhere fast.'

'I know,' she agreed. 'Listen, Derek, you remember Bill?' asked excitedly.

Derek looked puzzled. 'What, lighting cameraman Bill?'

'No, Bill Newman – my ex-husband.'

'Oh, that Bill,' said Derek dubiously.

'Well he's our man!'

'He is? Our man for what?' Derek gave Leonie a sideways look.

'He's the man for this job. You name it, he's written it. He's a brilliant writer – should have won a couple of Oscars at least – this is right up his street!'

'If he's that good, he's hardly going to chuck up a lucrative income in Tinseltown and hike over here to rescue a low-budget costume drama,' said Derek drily.

'He will, if I ask him.' Leonie's voice was firm.

'Ah, for old times' sake, you mean. Is this wise, Leo, working with your ex? What's Rob going to say?'

'There's not a lot Rob can say. It's because of him that we're in this mess,' Leonie said briskly.

'Yeah, well, he's under a lot of pressure, you know.'

'From me, you mean?' Leonie's green eyes sparkled dangerously.

'Not exactly from you, but because of you,' replied Derek bluntly.

There was a small pause. 'Well, since it seems to be my problem, it's up to me to sort it out, isn't it? What time is it in California at the moment?'

'Early evening,' replied Derek, resigned. He'd seen Leonie in this mood before and knew that there was no point in trying to distract her from her objective.

'Good, he should be in.'

Leonie hunted in her handbag for her address book and looked up Bill's number. Blast! It was the old one. Of course, he'd rung her before their most recent meeting. She hesitated, reluctant to ring Marvin, who'd suss her motives immediately. He was much too sharp. She remembered the house had been on Laurel Avenue, but what the hell was the number? It was no good. She rang Marvin's home and his boyfriend, Tommy, answered.

'Hi, Leonie! Good to hear you. Marv's not home right now – can I help?'

Leonie had always liked Tommy. Unlike Marvin, he had never tried to disguise his homosexuality and he always got on well with women. She was relieved and chatted easily with him for a few moments before asking for Bill's new number.

'No problem, honey!' Leonie could hear him flicking through an address book. 'I have to say, sweetie, that Marv says that you looked adorable when he saw you last week! I was quite jealous!' Leonie laughed appreciatively. 'Incidentally, did you hear about Nora Headingly?'

'No, I did not.' Leonie controlled her impatience. It was obvious she wasn't going to get the number without a bit of gossip.

'Where is it? Oh, nearly there . . . Well, my dear, she's had everything done again. She looks thirty-six and she has to be eighty-four – it's grotesque! Oh, here we are,' and Tommy recited the number to her.

'Thanks, Tommy, you're an angel. Are you coming over for the showing of the rough cut?'

'Would I miss that? Certainly I am. That is if I'm permitted.'

'We look forward to seeing you,' she said firmly. 'I'll tell Marvin he's not to come without you.'

'Oh, good! Now tell me, how's that child you're living with treating you?'

Leonie laughed. 'Tommy, for heaven's sake, Rob is twenty-five!'

'Well, aren't you the lucky one.'

'And what about him? He's lucky too, don't you agree?' she asked playfully.

'Darling, I would die for you, you know that, but I must admit I'd walk barefoot over burning coals for Rob.'

'I'll tell him, if you don't watch out,' Leonie threatened. She was still laughing as she hung up. Tommy was certainly a tonic and it would be fun to see him again, when this mess was sorted out.

Derek, meanwhile, had fetched a bottle of Scotch from a cupboard and was pouring himself a drink. 'Get me one, Derek, there's an angel. I'm going to ring Bill now,' she added, looking at him hard.

'Leo, are you quite sure about this?' Derek hesitated.

Leonie had been expecting this reaction and was ready for it. 'Absolutely sure. He's a great writer and he needs a challenge.'

Derek handed her a tumbler half-full of amber liquid. 'Go on then, you know the man.'

Although Derek had known Leonie for years, Bill had been part of her Hollywood experience and he had only met him once on a rare visit to London. He had liked him well enough on short acquaintance; the man undoubtedly had charm. The man also undoubtedly had an alcohol problem. Derek took a swig of his whisky.

'I know what you're thinking, Derek,' said Leonie, watching him, 'but he needs this. He needs this job.'

'Yes, and we need another problem on this picture like we need a hole in the head.'

'Trust me,' Leonie pleaded.

Derek smiled at her. 'You're the boss.'

Leonie tapped out the number and waited. 'Hello, Bill?'

'Pussycat! What a surprise. Where are you?'

'Bill, I'm in Rome. Listen, I want you to finish this picture for us. Bill, I'm in trouble and I need you. Please say you'll do it.' The words tumbled out. Leonie prayed he would not think it was another attempt to help him without hurting his pride.

There was a lengthy pause.

'Is this Christmas or what?' said Bill eventually.

'It's serious, Bill. We need you here.' She held her breath.

Another pause, then, 'Lioness, I'll do anything for you. I'm on the next plane over.'

'Bill, I love you!' cried Leonie exultantly.

'So you used to say,' observed Bill drily. But Leonie only laughed.

'I'll get you a smashing room at the Excelsior as from tomorrow!' Derek winced visibly. Only the most expensive hotel in Rome. 'I'll tell you all about it when you get here.'

'Let me guess. It's a rewrite job, right?'

'Nearly – it's a bit more than that.'

'OK, OK, I get the scenario. Or rather you'll get the scenario. This is the costume drama, right?'

'Yes, that's the one.'

'Great. I've got an idea already. Domani at the Excelsior. Don't call me, I'll call you.' And Bill hung up.

Leonie turned a flushed and excited face to Derek. 'He's coming!' she announced triumphantly. 'Derek, we're saved.'

Derek raised his glass. 'Here's to Bill!' he said. 'And let's hope the old saying is true,' he added.

'And what saying would that be?' asked Leonie, also raising her glass.

'That the pen is mightier than the sword.'

Chairs had been set out on the grass for the celebrities, while most people just flung themselves on to the dry lawn to await the dancing display. Elizabeth was sitting next to Simon, with Sir Edward on her right and Charles seated next to him.

'Your husband's a fine speaker,' observed Sir Edward, while they sat waiting for the dancing to begin. 'Very eloquent.'

'Yes,' agreed Elizabeth drily, 'he has a way with words.'

Lady Audleigh was talking to Simon about his speech, while Simon listened politely, nodding from time to time. Suddenly the music started and children appeared from the side of the house. They were all under seven and were dressed as assorted elves, fairies, rabbits, squirrels, and birds; there was even a mushroom and a hedgehog. Their appearance was greeted by oohs and ahs from the audience and the dance began. The children were adorable, the music delightful and the whole thing seemed so civilized, thought Elizabeth to herself. She recognized the jaunty tune as Percy Grainger's 'In an English Country Garden'.

Suddenly, beyond the lawn, through the haze of the afternoon's sunshine, she noticed a line of cars coming rapidly up the drive. The sun glinted on their chromework and she watched, horrified, as the occupants got out and started to crunch across the gravel drive towards them. Yet more cars appeared and parked haphazardly on the grass. Doors slammed and more people emerged carrying heavy equipment.

She saw that they were film-camera crews and photographers.

The charming scene on the lawn continued. The mushroom squatted, and a fairy sat on top of it, getting a sympathetic laugh as the mushroom collapsed underneath it. The little squirrel mimed eating a nut. The rabbit hopped about and bumped into the hedgehog, which curled into a ball and rolled away, to enthusiastic applause. Then other people began to notice the posse of press running across the lawn towards them. Elizabeth felt Simon tense beside her as Charles rose to his feet and set off to intercept them. She watched him halt the invasion party, waving his hands about as he indicated the children's dance, obviously trying to reason with them.

'What's going on?' demanded Lady Audleigh imperiously. 'Who are these people?'

'They've come for me,' was Simon's brief reply. Elizabeth instinctively reached out and took her husband's hand. He squeezed her own reassuringly.

'I'll deal with this,' he said tersely. Then he left to meet the press.

'Harpies,' said Elizabeth to herself. 'Harpies despoiling the feast.' But the entertainment was coming to a close in any case. The hedgehog, in its enthusiasm, had rolled into the trunk of a tree and was crying loudly. Several squirrels joined in and, as the music died away, the little group of sprites and woodland creatures took an uncertain curtain-call. The applause was perfunctory because everyone's attention was now riveted on the horde of cameramen, journalists and photographers who had by now engulfed Simon and Charles.

Elizabeth watched Charles detach himself from the crowd and hurry over to where they were sitting. He addressed his host and hostess in low tones. 'Sir Edward, Lady Audleigh, would it be possible, to accommodate these – ' he searched for an appropriate noun, 'people in the library?'

'Who are they?' demanded Lady Audleigh again.

'They're . . . from the BBC,' Charles lied valiantly, 'and the newspapers. They want to interview Mr Brentford and I feel it would be better done in private,' he added quietly.

'Oh, press johnnies,' said Sir Edward gruffly. 'Yes, by all means, shove them in the library.'

'Thank you,' said Charles. 'I hope it won't take long.'

'I don't know whether there's going to be enough tea for them all,' said Lady Audleigh querulously. Charles smiled a wan smile.

'I shouldn't worry about that, Lady Audleigh,' he replied. 'I'm sure they've had plenty to drink already.' Charles hurried away and a few seconds later was to be seen ushering the press and Simon into the house by the side door. Elizabeth and her hosts rose to their feet.

'What do they want?' demanded Sir Edward of Elizabeth.

'Blood,' replied Elizabeth, matter-of-factly, as she gathered her things together.

'Eh? What?'

'Blood!' Elizabeth repeated loudly. She didn't wait for his reaction, but started across the lawn to follow the house-bound party.

The audience had broken up into little groups and people were chattering among themselves, asking each other what the unexpected arrival of the press could mean. From out of the crowd, a woman walked towards Elizabeth. It was Simon's mistress. As she came near, she opened her mouth to speak. Elizabeth interrupted her. 'It's over,' she said. The woman stopped in her tracks. Elizabeth glanced down at the plastic bag containing the cushion that she was still clutching. She held it out to the other woman. 'Here, you may need this.' The woman took it automatically, a bewildered expression on her face.

'It's over,' said Elizabeth again, as if in further explanation. Then, with her head held high, she strode off in the direction of the house to be by her husband's side in his hour of need.

'How the hell can you have someone like Leonie O'Brien around and not use her?' demanded Bill disbelievingly. He was sitting on the leather sofa in the production office. Opposite him and ranged round the room were Leonie, Derek, Colin and Rob, all staring at him expectantly. Bill looked at them all one after the other. 'For Christ's sake, she's hot, she's box-office, she's the best you've got!'

'Not any more, she ain't,' remarked Leonie drily.

'Baby, look at you, and look at the young man beside you. Now what does that tell you?' Rob looked puzzled and Leonie shifted uneasily in her seat. Colin spoke for the first time.

'I think I'm on to you,' he observed briefly.

'Well, what does it say to you?' asked Bill.

'Well, I think that you are trying to say . . .' Colin began tentatively. 'What it says to me is that these two kids are crazy about each other, right?' The two 'kids' glanced at each other in an embarrassed way and smiled.

'I'm hardly a kid,' muttered Leonie. Bill pushed on regardless.

'What I see is a handsome young guy, and a beautiful, sophisticated, classy woman. OK, so she's a bit older than he is. Right – there's your spice!' The other members of the party looked at him with new interest and Leonie's eyes began to narrow. She could see the way this was heading and she liked it. In spite of the bumpy ride they were having, she was enjoying herself producing this picture, but she had to admit to a secret longing to be a part of it all, to be out in front of the camera again. She had watched Rob playing love scenes with the heroine – a pretty, charming girl in her early twenties – and she had longed to be in her place. But she knew how important it was for Rob to prove himself, not just to her, but to himself and the world. This was his picture, his big break. Still, she had longed to be part of it with him. She glanced at him, he was leaning forward in his chair, a half-smile on his lips. He liked the idea, she could tell.

'Come on, you guys,' exclaimed Bill impatiently. 'OK, here's how it goes.' He leant back into the sofa and examined the contents of his glass.

'Let me fill you up,' offered Derek, taking the cue. He rose and took Bill's glass.

Leonie sat looking at Bill expectantly. He had arrived in Rome as scheduled, and she had gone to meet him at the hotel. To her surprise, it had been an emotional reunion, Bill had been almost embarrassingly effusive in his greetings and gratitude. Leonie herself had been grateful to him for responding to her plea for help so promptly. When they took tea together in the hotel, Bill had refused to be drawn on his projected scenario. No, he was not going to spoil his moment, he was going to drop his bombshell in front of a full house. She had given him a brief run down on the current situation, both artistic and financial, and he had mulled it over, nodding every now and again. She sat there in the cool of the palm-fringed, marble-floored lounge, feeling wonderfully reassured and comforted. When it came to writing, Bill knew his job. The count-less years of experience showed and he became again the attractive man whom she had first fallen in love with, all those years ago. He was strong and confident about his work and, she knew, very talented. Why, oh why, had he thrown it all away?

'You've got to rethink the whole goddam picture,' Bill began firmly.

'Jesus,' said Colin.

'What with?' This came from Derek.

Rob laughed hopelessly, but Leonie just sat there smiling. She had supreme confidence in Bill.

'Forget your villain, he's unimportant,' continued Bill. 'Lose him, you don't need him.'

'What!' said Rob. Bill waved him aside impatiently. 'You have your hero in love with your heroine and your villain who is trying to seduce your heroine, right?'

They all nodded in agreement.

'OK, so, you have your hero in love with your heroine. Enter your villainess, who falls in love with your hero, persuades your villain to seduce your heroine. Your hero fights your villain to save your heroine's honour, wounding him severely. Re-enter your villainess, who seduces your hero, and successfully arranges your heroine's seduction. Dis-traught, your heroine kills herself. Your hero, thinking your villain has done the deed, challenges him to another duel. Re-enter your villainess for the third time, who dresses up as your villain, accepts the challenge of the duel. There is a fight to the death – of the villainess. End of story.' There was a long pause.

'I think you lost me somewhere around re-enter your villainess,' said Colin eventually.

'I like it,' said Derek in a surprised voice.

Leonie looked at Rob. It would mean, of course, that his would no longer be the leading role, that he would be sharing a considerable amount of screen time with her. How would he take it?

Rob leant back in his chair, his face unreadable; his brain was reeling. He was totally aware of what the rewrite would mean. It was a blow, there was no doubt about that, but he knew in his heart that this was a heaven-sent way of making amends to Leonie – for Amanda. She had said nothing more about her, but he was sure that she must suspect something. He would just have to swallow his pride and get on with it. Also, he had to admit, it was a bloody good idea.

'It's brilliant,' said Leonie. Bill smiled back at her.

'I thought you'd go for it, Leonie.' A pang of jealousy shot through Rob as he watched them.

'It's perfect,' he announced, cutting in on their moment of unspoken communication.

Leonie turned to him. 'You really think so, darling?' she asked quietly.

Rob put his hand over hers reassuringly before he replied. 'It's perfect, Leo, for all sorts of reasons.'

Leonie gazed at her lover fondly. She knew what it would cost his pride and she was proud that he was able to show such generosity. Maybe things would work out after all.

Soon they were all completely sold on the idea. Rob began to like the thought of the new twist to his role: it was, in the end, a more interesting part to play than the conventional hero. Leonie was already imagining herself dressed in the fabulous silk and lace dresses of the seventeenth century; her eyes were shining, she was feeling elated. It was a chance to triumph, a chance to get in front of the camera again!

'It'll take me back to my youth,' mused Colin. 'I was clapper boy on a picture like this one, *The Devil's* . . . something or other, it was called. What was it, Derek? Do you remember?'

'*Devil's Creek*?' offered Derek helpfully.

'Yeah, something like that . . . *Devil's Bay, Devil's Point, Devil's Cliff*? Smugglers, wasn't it?'

'Yes, smuggling . . . and, um, what's his name was in it. You know, Lee somebody or other.' Derek was racking his brains.

'Lee?' asked Colin incredulously.

'Yes, Lee – the Australian.'

'You know, I believe you're right. Whatever happened to him?'

'Went to Hollywood; never heard of again.'

The other three paid no attention to them. Leonie was still watching Rob, trying to gauge his mood. He seemed to be taking the proposed changes very well. She hoped a reaction would not set in later.

'Bill, I really do think it's great,' said Rob earnestly. 'Can we have a drink tonight to discuss the script in more detail?' Leonie smiled a little to herself; Rob was now trying to get the reins back into his own hands.

'That would be my pleasure.' Bill's reply was courteous, if a little wary.

'Why don't we meet later at your hotel?' Rob suggested. Leonie was interested to note that she was not included in this invitation, but she did not dislike the idea of her ex-husband and her current lover getting together. It was far better this way than that there should be any rancour between them.

'So, when do you think you're likely to come up with this little gem, mate?' Colin asked Bill.

'Give me till the weekend. I'll have it ready for shooting Monday morning,' replied Bill.

'I think we're all going to have to get off our backsides, if we're going to get this picture in the can on schedule,' observed Derek. They all looked at him. 'But,' he added reassuringly, 'I've got the ideal team to do it.'

'Then let's get started,' agreed Colin. 'Do you have any of the bunny yet?'

'He means dialogue,' said Leonie to Bill.

'It's OK, hon. I remember the lingo.' Bill smiled back at her.

Rob observed the look that passed between them and stood up abruptly. 'Why don't you go back to the hotel and freshen up, Bill? Leo, we could have everyone over to our place for a working supper tonight, yes?'

'Good idea,' agreed Leonie, pleased to see him showing such enthusiasm.

'Do you think you will have anything to show us by then?' Derek asked Bill.

'What the hell do you think I was doing during that goddam flight?' Bill replied.

Beryl sat on the bed in her hotel room. What had she done? Taken leave of her senses, it would seem. She had just agreed to spend a year in the company of a young man, Giovanni, whom she hardly knew. She was going to keep him: she would pay his fares, expenses, hotels, buy his clothes and feed him. For a whole year. Yes, there was no doubt about it, she was quite, quite mad. She sat there in a sort of stupor. She was supposed to be packing. They were going on to Vienna together soon.

There had been no problem with fitting Giovanni into the tour group. A couple of people had dropped out at the start through ill health and the organizers had not been able to fill their bookings at the last minute. So there was a place for him now, paid for by Beryl; the seat on the coach next to hers would no longer be empty. What the others would say, she hardly dared think. Did she care? She wasn't sure. She didn't want to seem a fool, but she knew in her heart that Giovanni was using her. She also knew, though, that he was genuinely fond of her, that he enjoyed her company. Well, that was good enough reason.

Still, it was a mad scheme. What would happen when the year was up? Would they just go their separate ways? Suppose she fell in love with him? That would be disastrous. She knew very well that his present declarations of love were to be taken lightly, enjoyable and flattering as they were. But she decided she didn't wish to look into the future. She would just let it happen. At the very least she'd have an entertaining time and enough sex to make up for all the barren years with Arnold. Giovanni made her laugh, and he flattered her all the time, which was very good for her confidence. She also suspected that he possessed a volatile Latin temper, but at least life wouldn't be dull with him.

She was leaving Rome and she was leaving Amanda too. When she and Giovanni had seen the newspapers with their lurid headlines about *la figlia inglesa* and her famous mother, she had been horrified. She telephoned the van der Velts in an attempt to talk to her and was told curtly that Miss Willoughby was no longer with them – she could be contacted at the Hotel d'Umberto. When Beryl finally got through to Amanda at the hotel, their conversation was brief and unsatisfactory. She had hoped strongly to persuade Amanda not to make any further disclosures, but Amanda was far from co-operative. 'Fuck off, mother – sorry, I mean Beryl. Get out of my hair, will you,' was all she had said, slamming down the phone before Beryl had a chance to utter another word.

Beryl did not attempt to contact her again. This was too unpleasantly like the old Amanda, and she had no wish to renew *her* acquaintance. No, she had to admit that although she had always done her best for the girl, somehow she had failed. She had failed with Arnold, too, and she looked bleakly back down the years and wondered why. Then, with a shrug, she pulled herself together and continued her packing. It was time to stop worrying about the past. She was bloody well going to make a success of her future instead. She was going to start living for herself, beginning right now.

It was half past eight in the morning and Leonie was dressed, ready to go on set. She surveyed herself in the dressing-room mirror, and was delighted with what she saw. She was clad in an off-white silk taffeta dress, edged with frothy matching lace and encrusted all over with seed pearls, which perfectly complemented her lightly tanned skin and cascading auburn curls. On her head, she wore a matching cavalier hat of velvet and curled feathers. The outfit showed off her figure superbly: emphasizing her tiny waist and full bosom, it was cut very low to exhibit a considerable amount of cleavage. Her green eyes were sparking with anticipation and excitement.

Could she be, Leonie wondered, the same woman who a few days ago was so distraught with grief, guilt, hate and self-disgust? Well, she was going to put all that behind her now. Nineteen years ago she had done what she had considered best for the child; in the process she had lacerated her own feelings and instincts. The sacrifice she had made then had caused her the most appalling pain she had ever known, and now she had been asked to pay the price all over again. Her own private tragedy, her personal grief, had become public property. It was unthinkable, but she had survived, she had come through it. She was back on course.

She began to murmur her lines over and over again to herself, nervously touching up her make-up a dozen times. There was a tap on the door.

'Miss O'Brien, we're ready for you on the set,' called Jim, a second assistant-director.

'Coming,' she replied, casting a final glance at her reflection. She flung open the door, almost dislodging Jim, who was hovering outside. Jim was twenty-two and highly impressionable, and he gaped at Leonie with a mixture of open admiration and lust.

'Wow! Miss O'Brien, you look fantastic.'

Leonie was pleased. 'Thank you, Jim. How kind you are.'

'No, I mean it. All that young crumpet on the set won't stand a chance with you around.'

Leonie had forgotten that she was considerably older than the other girls on the set, and the remark took the edge off her elation for a moment. They made their way down the corridors to the sound stage, the rehearsal bell sounding as they approached. Jim wrenched open the door and Leonie made her entrance. The silence and stunned looks on the faces of the cast and crew as she appeared more than made up for Jim's tactless remark and her confidence soared again.

Colin Scott rose from his canvas chair to greet her. 'Well, you look a bit of all right,' he commented quietly. As she looked around at the familiar faces – many of whom she had first worked with years ago – she saw that they were all gazing at her with affection and admiration. She smiled back at them happily and noticed with delight that they had given her a canvas chair with her name printed on the back. It was obviously a special, as it was black canvas with a chrome frame, while all the other chairs were pale green canvas and wood. Her name was picked out in dazzling white letters on the black canvas. She looked at it, tears pricking at her eyes, then turned to them.

'You are darlings – all of you – you can't imagine, how happy this makes me.' She was half-afraid that she might start to cry in earnest. To cover her confusion she quickly crossed the studio and sat down in the chair, feeling for all the world like a reigning monarch of the seventeenth century.

Dave Kelly allowed her a couple of minutes' grace, then it was on with the business of the day. 'OK, everyone, quiet for the rehearsal,' he bellowed, rather more loudly than was necessary to conceal his own emotion. The rehearsal bell clanged again and Leonie rose from her seat and approached the brilliantly lit set that stood isolated amid the dark of the studio.

Everyone watched in anticipation as Leonie swung into action, all her years of experience immediately apparent. She was confident, technically accomplished and word-perfect; she moved round the set with ease. Her first scene with the Cardinal was also well prepared this time. The dialogue flowed and Colin was delighted, though the only evidence of this was his decision to go for a take immediately. The first master was marred by a boom shadow, although the actors were on form, but Leonie was glad – she felt she could still improve. The second take was perfect and there was a huge collective sigh of relief: the picture was back on course again. By the time they came to the close-ups, in the middle of the morning, Leonie was well into her stride and wondering why she had ever stopped acting. Her only disappointment was that Rob was not there to witness her triumph. Later, though, while sipping a coffee during a break, she realized that his absence was fortunate. She would have to play down her personal successes until he had matched them with his own.

By lunchtime they had completed the scene and the atmosphere on set was one of immense optimism. Leonie returned to her dressing-room, flushed and pleased with her efforts. Her dresser removed her beautiful costume, and she put a silk gown on over her undergarments. The scene to be shot that afternoon was on a different set and required her to be in her bedroom, dressing with her maid; it contained little dialogue. The scene was not until the middle of the afternoon, so Leonie decided to go to the studio restaurant for lunch. As soon as she was ready, she left her room and started to make her way along the maze of corridors that led to the commissary The route took her past the production offices. Derek's door was ajar and, as she approached, she could hear him talking to someone.

'Pity Rob wasn't there to see her, she looked stunning, didn't she? Hand me that schedule, Dave, will you? Thanks. Nah, I can't think why he would look twice at the other girl – what was her name?'

'I dunno,' said Dave in a bored voice. 'You mean that little red-headed tart at the party.' Leonie froze in her tracks, her heart thumping.

'That's right. They disappeared together half-way through the evening. Silly bugger, she's not a patch on Leo.'

'No,' agreed Dave. 'Hang on I've got an amendment here, can you check it?'

'What's this?'

'I don't know. Colin's brainwave, I suppose.'

'He's mad. We'll never get all this done.'

'Well, if we go on like this morning, we very well might. She was really on good form, wasn't she?'

'She's a pro,' stated Derek matter-of-factly.

'Yeah, he doesn't know when he's well off, that boy. What on earth did he see in the girl?' asked Dave contemptuously.

'Just that. A girl. If you think about it, she did have a sort of O'Brien look about her. I suppose she could have reminded him a bit of Leonie when she was young,' replied Derek. Leonie stood rooted to the spot.

'Sure,' said Dave. 'I wonder if it'll work out between them.'

'Chi sa, mio amico,' said Derek.

Leonie had heard enough. She tiptoed past the door and, as soon as she was out of earshot, ran the rest of the way to the canteen. Her mind was in a daze. She couldn't think clearly. Could it be Amanda they were talking about? Had Rob really fallen for her? Had he, and the thought sent a shiver of horror through her, even been to bed with her?

During lunch, she tried desperately to behave normally, keeping up an overanimated conversation with the Cardinal while hardly touching her salad. She returned to her dressing-room to lie down and try and rest. Instead she tossed on her couch, mind racing. At three o'clock it was time do her next scene. She looked at herself in the mirror – face flushed and feverish, eyes too bright – and tried to pull herself together. You are not going to let this affect your performance, she said to herself. You will put it out of your mind and get on and play the scene. You are a professional and you will damn well behave like one. Then she went out to follow her own advice. It was not easy because scraps of the conversation kept resurfacing in her mind at the most inconvenient moments, but she gritted her teeth and ploughed on, priding herself that no one would have suspected that there was anything amiss. When she left the set at six o'clock, there was only one thought in her mind: she must confront Rob, and soon.

11

When Sheila returned to her tiny cottage in the hamlet of White-wood, about six miles from South Molding, she was in a fever of anxiety. It seemed obvious from Elizabeth's actions that she knew of the affair; she had been shocked by Elizabeth's apparent recognition of her at the cushion stall. Simon seldom mentioned his wife, and only in an offhand way – 'I can't see you Tuesday. Liz has some people coming over,' or 'Liz has gone to meet the boys off the train and I ought to get back' – and she had accepted her role as that of the mistress who had to take second place to domestic priorities.

After the dancing display, she had been determined to take her courage in her hands and introduce herself to Elizabeth as an employee in Simon's Ministry. She would offer help in the impending crisis, ask if she could be of any assistance to her in dealing with the press. Inside she nursed a gnawing fear that if Elizabeth knew for sure that she was Simon's mistress, then her relationship with Simon would be over. The idea was unthinkable: she could not exist without him. Her only hope of averting such a disaster was to convince Elizabeth that there was nothing going on, that she was just a professional colleague of Simon's. She had seen what looked like recognition in Elizabeth's eyes but perhaps, after all, it had been merely suspicion. Sheila knew she had to allay that suspicion. She had always believed that attack was the best form of defence, and when she had approached Elizabeth across the lawn, she knew what she intended to say.

'Mrs Brentford, I should have introduced myself before. I work in the Ministry. Can I be of any help? There seems to be some trouble.' Those were the phrases she had been rehearsing to herself as she had walked towards Simon's beautiful wife. But when she drew near Elizabeth, she had seen her face and the carefully constructed sentences had died on her lips. All she could think of as she drove back to her cottage, down the narrow country lanes, were Elizabeth's words to her: 'It's over. It's over.'

What had she meant? The marriage, his career, their affair – please, please, God, don't let it be the affair. She was driving recklessly, much too fast, and she knew it. There was really only room for one car on these narrow lanes and if she met another, travelling over the speed limit as she was, she knew there was no way to avoid an accident. Still, she hurtled on regardless, desperate to get home. She needed to think clearly. She just needed to sit down and think. Why on earth had Elizabeth given her the cushion? If she had meant that the marriage was over, she had presumably deduced that Sheila would need it in the home she was setting up with Simon. If she had meant the affair was over, then presumably Sheila was meant to sob into it. The gift was peculiar, and disturbing.

She drove back to the cottage without mishap and, clutching her bag and the cushion to her, ran inside and slammed the door behind her. Only then did she manage to breathe more evenly. She made her way slowly to the kitchen and put on a kettle. Automatically she made some tea, then leant for ages against the Aga, sipping it slowly. Surely Simon would ring her as soon as he could, even in this crisis? She knew he would make some excuse to get away before getting into the car and going home with Elizabeth. He would plead ministerial business and disappear into a private study somewhere in the Audleigh mansion. She knew Elizabeth would not argue; she was sure that Elizabeth was always the perfectly dutiful wife. The phone rang, making her jump and spill her tea. She raced into the next room to answer it.

'Yes?' she said, out of breath.

'Hello. Is that Ms Mackenzie?' It was an official-sounding voice. Her heart froze.

'Yes. Who is that?'

'This is Charles – Charles Pendlebury. Do you remember me? I'm Mr Brentford's private secretary now. I believe you were at the fête this afternoon?'

'Yes, I was. Has something happened?

There was a pause. Sheila felt her heart tighten. Her breathing became constricted. Jesus, what was he going to say to her?

'Ms Mackenzie, I'm afraid I have some rather bad news.'

Sheila felt as though she was going to faint. She sank into an armchair.

'Yes,' she said again, trying to sound as calm as possible.

'Mr Brentford asked me to telephone you.' Oh God, she thought.

'Ms Mackenzie, I'm afraid Mr Brentford has asked me to tell you that there will be no further contact between you. I am so sorry. If I can be of any assistance, please let me know.' His tone was kindly but very firm.

'I see,' Sheila heard herself say. 'Does that mean . . .' Her voice tailed off miserably.

Charles answered her unspoken question. 'Yes, I'm afraid so. He was quite specific. He asked that there should be no further contact of any sort between you.' Sheila started to shake uncontrollably. She felt the sobs starting to rise in her throat.

'May I not even say goodbye?' she asked tremulously.

'No, I'm so sorry, I'm afraid not.' There was another pause. 'I really am very sorry, Sheila.' His voice sounded genuinely sympathetic. It was more than Sheila could bear.

'Thank you. Thank you for telling me. Goodbye.' She put the phone down hurriedly. She wanted to retain some shreds of dignity and it would have been unbearable if she had broken down in Charles Pendlebury's hearing. She sat motionless for what seemed an age, staring at the opposite wall, seeing nothing. What she had dreaded most in the world had happened. He'd finished it. She felt numb, empty, and disbelieving; soon the pain would come, and she knew it would be insupportable. She started to cry, at first quietly, then hysterically, then violently, until her whole body was convulsed with sobs. She had always known that it would have to end sometime, of course, but somehow she had always managed to put the idea out of her mind, never allowing herself to confront it.

'What shall I do? What shall I do? Oh God, what am I going to do?' she asked herself again and again. Finally she rose from the chair and wandered restlessly into the kitchen, making herself another cup of tea, scarcely aware of what she was doing. She started to pace up and down, asking herself the question over and over again, 'What am I doing to do? Oh God, what on earth am I going to do?' She leant against the Aga and rocked herself backwards and forwards, hugging herself as if to protect herself from the world which had dealt this blow. She tried to think of Elizabeth and the pain that she must have felt, but all she could see was Simon's arrogant, smug face; all she could remember was the way he had lusted after her and taken her. She threw her teacup with all her might across the room. It bounced off the wall and shattered in several pieces on the floor. Bastard! The bastard! The unspeakable bastard! she thought savagely to herself. She went to the telephone and picked up the receiver. She had to talk to someone. This was too much to bear alone.

The number she dialled was that of Lorna, a friend from work. Lorna was a couple of years older than Sheila. She had been married early, then messily divorced a few years later and now she lived alone. Since her divorce she had had a series of unsatisfactory love affairs. She was one of the few people whom Sheila had told about her affair with Simon; she would understand, if anyone would.

Sheila dialled her number. Please God, let her be in, she prayed as she listened to the ringing tone.

'Hello,' said a brisk voice at the other end of the line.

'Lorna?' She tried hard to make her voice sound normal, but it was impossible.

'Sheila. What's wrong?' Lorna's voice was concerned.

'Lorna?' The tears started to flow again. 'Lorna, it's over, it's over.

He doesn't want to see me again.' The rest of her speech was drowned in sobs.

'OK. Hold everything, I'm on my way down.'

'No, it's all right,' Sheila gulped. 'I'll be fine, don't worry, I just wanted to talk to you — '

'I'm on my way down. Don't do anything, I'll be right with you.' Lorna's tone was firm and commanding.

Sheila breathed a sigh of relief. 'Thank you. It's a comfort just to hear your voice, but it would be even better to see you.'

'Give me an hour. I'll be there.'

Charles stirred uneasily. He had fallen asleep on the train. And no wonder, he thought: after all, this had been the longest day of his life. But in spite of everything he felt strangely happy. He wondered why, then remembered with a jolt that he had been dreaming about Elizabeth. He stared out at the twilit Berkshire countryside that was hurtling past the train window. He had been dreaming that they were in bed together and that she was in his arms again. He stifled a moan as he remembered her nestling against his chest in the cool dark study, then glanced across apprehensively at his travelling companion to see if he had heard. But the tweed-jacketed elderly man sitting opposite him was deep in the *Angling Times*, oblivious to the outside world.

Charles readjusted his position and rubbed the crick in his neck. What would happen next? he wondered. He doubted that Simon would resign if he could possibly avoid it. He was almost certainly destined for the Cabinet at the next reshuffle and with luck he would eventually make Foreign Secretary. It would be too cruel if his chances were to be thwarted by something that had happened nearly twenty years ago. Good God, we all make mistakes in our youth, thought Charles, nostalgically remembering an incident on a warm summer's night like this many years ago, when he had been caught in a hay field making love to the local vicar's daughter – a girl whom everyone had believed to be highly respectable. What the hell was her name? Sybil? Sylvia? The smell of grass always conjured up that memory. So long as they didn't find out about the mistress as well. That, unfortunately, would compound the offence.

Charles shifted uncomfortably again. He had hated making that phone call. Why the hell couldn't Simon do his own dirty work? Silly question. That was his job, doing Simon's dirty work. It was a bit like being a fag at Eton again; funny how the pattern of life didn't really alter. Even when one was supposed to be adult, one still existed in a sort of feudal system, answerable to an overlord and in charge of a host of underlings. No, it hadn't been pleasant. He had tried to do it as decently as possible, but he had heard her trying to keep back her tears. He'd almost offered to go over and comfort her. It was out of the question of course, but it had been difficult, listening to someone in an unhappy situation which was not so far apart from his own. Ironic really. There they were, both he and Sheila, two unhappy people who wanted two other people, who were just as unhappy and certainly did not want each other. What would happen next? He had an idea that Simon's good looks, charm and eloquence would probably win over the Conservative matrons on his local committee, who might be prepared to overlook a youthful indiscretion. But a current mistress would be quite a different kettle of fish: that would brand him a womanizer. Elizabeth was well loved and it would undoubtedly lose him a lot of constituency support. Simon would never be content on the back-benches. He wanted a seat on the Cabinet – that was what he had worked for all his life. His ambition would overcome any qualms of conscience, but could Sheila be counted on to keep quiet? Charles was almost sure she could.

He cast his mind back to Elizabeth's behaviour that afternoon and reluctantly had to admit to himself that she had been exhibiting all the signs of a jealous wife. Charles sighed heavily and returned to his favourite day-dream, the one in which Elizabeth, finally fed up with Simon's continual infidelities left home for good and came to him in Albany. Of course, he'd have to sell his apartment and buy a place in the country for her and the boys. The boys – he had forgotten about them. Well, they were nice children and they would be grown up before too long. The scenario was not completely improbable.

He became misty-eyed as he remembered her impeccable behaviour at the press conference. What a three-ring circus that had been. Her answers to the ruthless questions thrown at her had been discreet, truthful and dignified, and he had never admired her more. Afterwards she had been whisked away in the Daimler by Simon to 'an unknown destination'. Charles, of course, knew it to be Elizabeth's sister's home in Gloucestershire. They had requested the press to leave them alone, and with luck they might snatch a couple of days' peace there. Simon would be reporting to Downing Street before long to explain his version of events. But Elizabeth, he knew, would remain with her sister. The boys were due home from school and she would not want them to be exposed to the vultures of the press.

He had been offered a lift back to London that evening, but he had wanted to be alone with his thoughts, so asked to be dropped off at Reading station. It had taken him the better part of two hours after Simon's departure to explain things to the Audleighs and the local Conservative committee. Better that they heard the simple facts of the case from him, he had thought, rather than have to make what they would of the garbled, sensationalized versions that would doubtless appear in the tabloids. As the train pulled into Paddington, he took his briefcase down from the overhead rack and peered out of the window. It was pitch dark.

At the station news-stands the first editions of the Sunday newspapers had just been delivered. He bought them all and, clutching the bulky bundle, he took a taxi to his club in St James's. There he sat and quietly sipped a Scotch and soda, methodically working his way through them. The story was on every front page. The tabloids carried shrieking banner headlines and several of them reprinted the previous week's article, adding a picture of Simon next to the one of Leonie, clad in the briefest of bikinis. The quality papers had pictures of Simon at the press conference, Elizabeth by his side. Charles gazed fondly at her. She looked tense but so beautiful. Finally he rose and walked home to his flat. Once inside, he slung the pile of newspapers into a corner. He intended to forget about them until he went in to work again. Tomorrow was Sunday; he would spend the day rereading a favourite book and listening to music and the world could go hang.

Leonie lunged towards Rob. She wasn't sure what she wanted to do, but she had an idea that she would like to kill him. Rob was reading in an armchair when she let herself into the flat, and she had caught him off guard.

'For Christ's sake, Leo, cut it out, will you?' he yelled as she started to smack him about the head with her heavy bundle of scripts. 'What are you trying to do – kill me?'

'Yes!' she screamed, hitting out wildly. The odd blow continued to find its mark as he raised his hands to defend himself. Then he grabbed her wrists and held them tightly; she started to kick at him and stamp on his feet. He yelled in pain.

'Did that hurt? Good! You're going to hurt everywhere by the time I've finished with you – you're going to pray to die!' Beside herself, Leonie struggled to free her hands, succeeding in wrenching one loose when she kicked him sharply on the shin. She went for his face with her nails. He ducked swiftly, just in time, and she began to yank hard at his hair.

Finally, Rob managed to grab hold of her, pinning her arms behind her. He was breathing hard as he said, 'I don't know what I'm supposed to have done, but I can't believe I deserve this.'

Leonie stared at him furiously. 'Then you promise me it's not true,' she snapped.

Rob felt an icy sensation in the pit of his stomach. 'What the hell are you talking about?'

Leonie's eyes never left his. 'I didn't believe her, you see. I trusted you so completely . . . I thought she was lying.'

'Who? Who was lying?' A hideous fear was beginning to form in Rob's mind and he was playing for time.

'Amanda,' whispered Leonie, as if she could hardly bear to let her lips speak the name.

'Amanda?' said Rob, allowing a puzzled expression to cross his face. He was a good actor, but he knew now that he had to give the performance of a lifetime. 'So what am I supposed to have done to her? What's the latest story the little bitch has come up with? Hasn't she caused enough trouble yet?'

Injured innocence was written all over him. Leonie relaxed slightly and he let go of her arms. 'You promise me it's not true,' she said slowly, a note of pleading beginning to creep into her voice.

'Darling, what can I say? You've got to tell me what the problem is.' Rob knew he would have to lie through his teeth to preserve his relationship with her. Was it worth it? He looked longingly at her lovely, intelligent face with the faint lines of experience etched on it, at her still-perfect figure. He thought of how good she was in bed, of the film and the chance she had given him. Of course it was worth it. Besides, it was his word against Amanda's, and who would believe a girl half-crazed with revenge? She'd say anything to hurt her mother, and Leonie knew it.

'Come on, darling.' Gently he put his arms around her and pulled her to him. 'Come on, tell me all about it.' She rested her head on his shoulder for a moment. Then she spoke.

'When Amanda came to see me on that ghastly day – the day she went to the newspapers . . .' she began. She was still not looking at him, as if she were now embarrassed by what she had to tell.

'Yes, darling, yes,' he murmured encouragingly. Fucking hell, he thought to himself, what had the bloody girl said?

'She implied that you'd screwed her.' She forced out the words, her whole body tense in his arms.

'I don't bloody credit it!' Rob exploded. He pushed Leonie away, holding her at arm's length. 'You're not trying to tell me you believed her?'

Leonie's face was a mixture of hope and fear. 'I, I . . . didn't know what to believe,' she stammered. Rob's expression was one of devastation at her distrust.

'Leo,' he said quietly, sounding deeply hurt. 'Leo, surely you trust me, now, after all this time – after all we've been through?'

'Of course, I trust you. You know that. I didn't take any notice of what she said. I thought it was preposterous, that's why I didn't mention it before. Then . . . today . . . I overheard something Derek said at the studio . . .' Leonie faltered to a halt.

Damn, thought Rob, what the fuck had Derek let drop? 'Derek?

Where does Derek come in to it?' He was playing for time again. His mind was racing. Had Derek seen them in the bedroom? Jesus, if only he hadn't been so drunk. He swore to God he'd become teetotal after this. He was going to have to tell her some of the truth, it was clear, and this was going to take a bluff of monstrous proportions.

'He implied that you fancied her because . . .' here Leonie hesitated and looked hard at him, 'because she was like a younger version of me.'

Rob started to breathe more easily. 'Good grief. Is that all?'

'No,' said Leonie. Rob's heart sank again. 'He said you'd been with her at the party, and – that you'd disappeared together.'

'Oh, my God,' groaned Rob, 'is that what this is all about?' He put his hand under his chin and tipped her face up towards his. Then he gave a wry grin. 'Leo, you know what I'm like – sometimes I can't resist flirting with women. I like them. I think they're a lot nicer than men, on the whole. But you know I don't mean anything by it. I'm just being friendly; it's a bit of fun.'

'I make you feel insecure, don't I,' said Leonie suddenly. Rob looked at her sharply. Did she believe him? He decided honesty was the best policy.

'Yes,' he admitted. 'A bit. Oh, Leo, look at it from my point of view. Here I am living with this stunningly beautiful woman who also happens to be rich and an international star. Yes, I feel insecure. I want to prove myself. I worry about what people think – I try not to, but it gets to me sometimes. Then along comes a pretty little girl who obviously thinks I'm the best thing since Mel Gibson and it makes me feel good. I can't help it, I'm afraid.'

Leonie nodded. His words clearly made sense. 'Now at the party,' Rob added ruefully, 'I'm afraid I was a bit silly. I realize now Amanda was just setting me up . . . I suppose, looking back, she might even have been trying to seduce me . . .' Rob knew he was skating on very thin ice indeed. It could crack beneath him at any moment and the water would be unbearably cold. But he had to take the risk.

There was a long pause. Then Leonie asked, 'So what happened at the party?'

Rob laughed. 'Well, she didn't succeed. I know that much.'

'But she did try?' Leonie persisted.

'Well I suppose that's what she was after. At the time I just thought she was a bit star-struck. It does happen, you know, even to me,' he added playfully. Then he became serious again. 'I have to confess, I got terribly pissed. I was missing you like buggery and terribly worried about Carlo. I know it's no excuse, but I had to drown my sorrows somehow. Really, I can't remember all that much about the evening, or about the bloody girl. I don't know if anyone's said anything but I actually had so much I passed out.'

'You what?'

'God, I had such a head the next day. I was sick as a dog, too.'

'Yes,' Leonie agreed, 'you were looking pretty rough when you turned up here. So where did you spend the night?'

Help, thought Rob, will she never let up?

'Ask Andy. He may remember the details. I crashed out somewhere in the flat. I expect he could be more specific – after all, he had to clear up after me.' He could tell from her face that she was beginning to believe him.

'So you don't fancy her then?'

'No,' he replied, screwing up his face as though the idea revolted him. 'But I fancy you,' he murmured, moving his face close to hers. 'In fact, I fancy you right now.' He brushed his lips against her mouth. She responded. He had won.

It was dark when Lorna pulled up outside Sheila's cottage later that Saturday evening; she'd had some difficulty in finding the way, twice taking the wrong turning. Sheila had sounded so unlike herself. There was something in her voice that had panicked Lorna and she was anxious to see that her friend was all right. She slammed the car door shut and fumbled with the latch of the wooden gate, breaking one of her fingernails as she wrenched it open. Hurrying to the front door, she banged on it loudly. There was silence at first and then the sound of footsteps. Lorna heaved a sigh of relief as the door opened and she saw Sheila standing in the dim light.

'Oh, darling, thank God you're all right.'

She pushed her way into the tiny hall. Sheila didn't say a word, but just stood gazing at her friend. Lorna was shocked by her appearance: she looked hunched and hollow-eyed. It was as though the shock of the news had felled her physically. Then Sheila said brokenly, 'Oh Lorna, I don't know what I'd do without you,' and flung herself into the other woman's arms, sobbing.

Lorna held her there for a while. 'Any chance of a drink?' she said at last.

Sheila pulled herself away. 'I'm so sorry, what am I thinking of? You've driven miles to see me and I haven't even asked you to sit down yet,' she gasped weakly, attempting to dry her eyes on a sodden handkerchief.

'I do hope you have more tissues,' Lorna remarked. 'I suppose I should have brought some with me.'

'I'll be all right now you're here,' said Sheila, but her voice lacked conviction.

'Of course, you will,' said Lorna briskly, moving to the kitchen. Sheila followed her slowly. Lorna opened the fridge and took out a bottle of white wine. 'Glasses?' she said to Sheila enquiringly. Lorna found a corkscrew and opened the bottle, while Sheila fetched two glasses and put them on the well-scrubbed pine table. Then she filled them both up and handed one to Sheila. 'Drink this, you'll need it.' Obediently, Sheila drank.

'You don't want to hear this, but you're going to all the same,' Lorna continued. 'The man is a prize shit. I mean they don't make them like that any more. Most men have pastimes – hobbies. They back horses, watch football, drink real ale – this one fucks up women. Don't look at me like that, you don't imagine you're the first, surely?' She stopped as she saw Sheila's horror-stricken face. 'How long have you worked in the Department? Three years?' Sheila nodded miserably. 'And you were unaware of the activities of the member for South Molding – and I mean member. My dear girl, Gabby Foster could tell you a thing or two, so could Anita what's-her-name, you know, the carrot-top from Agriculture.'

'You don't mean Gabrielle, who works in Finance?'

'I certainly do.'

'But she's not even very pretty,' said Sheila, uncertain whether this was a good thing or not.

'True, but she does have wonderful chestnut hair.'

'How odd.'

'What is?'

'We've all got sort of reddish hair.' Sheila temporarily forgot her misery as she considered this.

'There's nothing odd about that. Men often go for the same type, haven't you noticed? All the evidence you need is in the tabloids. I know you don't buy them, but I'm sure even you've picked up the latest about the beautiful russet-haired Leonie O'Brien and her secret ex-lover, rumoured to be in ministerial circles.'

'But how did you know? I certainly never mentioned it,' asked Sheila amazed.

'Come to that, how did you know? Did he confide in you? Very undiplomatic and unwise if he did.'

'Of course not. We never talked about private matters. Well, hardly at all. He did mention he was having a problem with some girl who was trying to dig up something that had happened ages ago. When I saw the headlines about Leonie O'Brien in the *Globe*, I put two and two together.'

'Did he talk about his wife at all?' asked Lorna curiously.

'He hardly ever mentioned her. But I met her today — '

'You what?'

'Yes, it was frightful. I'm absolutely certain she knew who I was.'

'You're not serious?'

'It was written all over her face. We found ourselves the only two people at the same stall – I couldn't believe it. She caught my eye and somehow we just tuned in on the same wavelength. It was uncanny.' Lorna let out a long low whistle.

'She gave me this,' continued Sheila, picking up the cushion from where she had earlier thrown it on the floor.

Lorna whistled again, this time in admiration. 'She gave you this?'

she asked in astonishment, taking it from her and examining it closely. 'But this is antique; it's very valuable,' she said.

'I know. She paid £250 for it,' said Sheila. Her eyes filled with tears again as she thought of Simon's wife.

'What did she give it to you for? She must be a philanthropic lunatic.'

Sheila started to cry. 'I think it was meant to be my consolation prize,' she sobbed.

'Oh, darling, don't start again. He's just not worth it.'

'I loved him.'

'Balls,' said Lorna. 'You can't love an arsehole like that.'

'Yes, I can,' Sheila sniffed.

'Well in that case you'll be all right,' said Lorna pragmatically. 'There are plenty of them around. You'll soon find a replacement.'

Sheila almost smiled in spite of herself. 'But I don't want a replacement. I want him. I'll never find anyone like him again.'

'I sincerely hope not,' said Lorna in an unsympathetic tone. 'I certainly don't want a rerun of this scene in six months' time.'

Sheila blew her nose loudly and looked at Lorna. 'You're right, you know. He's a bastard.'

'That's better,' said Lorna.

'No, I mean it. I loathe him. We were in bed together only the day before yesterday and now, today, I get given my marching orders by his secretary on the phone. Can you credit it?'

'What on earth were you doing at the fête anyway?' asked Lorna curiously.

'I was perfectly entitled to be there. It was my local fête after all.'

'But you might have known you'd bump into one or the other of them.'

'That was part of the excitement – the risk, the chance that we might be found out at any moment. God, I hate him!'

'Just keep saying that.'

'I hate him – and I want to ruin him,' said Sheila vehemently.

Lorna looked at her seriously for a moment. 'Darling, I hope you won't do anything foolish, anything that you might regret.'

'What have I got to lose?' said Sheila in a challenging tone. There was a pause.

'Sheila, you wouldn't go to the papers, surely? It would be too demeaning, too undignified . . .'

'I'll find a way.' There was a glint of battle in Sheila's eyes as she spoke.

'Don't,' said Lorna soberly. 'Revenge isn't satisfactory, you know. I think people only hurt themselves when they give in to the temptation.'

'Well, at the very least, it might stop some other poor girl getting hurt,' Sheila's tone was savage.

'Oh really,' observed Lorna drily. 'So, what are you going to do?'

'I'm not sure yet, but he isn't going to like it.'

'At the risk of being a bore, he's simply not worth it. Also, you forget how powerful he is. He'll end up getting you instead, and that won't be nice.'

Sheila thought for a moment. 'I could get at him through the girl,' she said eventually.

'What? You mean the daughter? Darling, you're mad – leave well alone. The press would tear you to shreds and you'd certainly lose your job.'

'I've lost it anyway,' said Sheila miserably. She started to cry again. 'How can I stay in my job? I can't bear to see him any more. I shall have to leave . . .'

Lorna rose and went to her side; she took her in her arms. 'Come on, darling, rise above it. Don't let him win, show him that you can cope. That's the best way of getting back at him, he won't be able to take that.'

The following morning Lorna came downstairs to find Sheila already up and dressed and sitting in the kitchen drinking a mug of tea. She looked up as Lorna appeared at the doorway in her dressing gown.

'Sorry I didn't bring you a cup. I didn't like to wake you.' She sounded completely in control, although Lorna noted that she was looking pale and drawn.

'How are you feeling?' Lorna asked.

'Much better, thanks to you,' said Sheila in an overbright voice. 'Here, have some of this. I've just made another pot.'

'How long have you been up?' queried Lorna.

'Not that long. It's quite late you know – it's nearly eleven.'

'Heavens, is that the time?' said Lorna, glancing at the clock on the wall. 'When did we get to bed?'

'Not till two, I'm afraid,' replied Sheila ruefully. 'Sorry for keeping you up, but you were so good to me. Thank you.'

'What are friends for?' said Lorna. 'You'd do the same for me.'

'I already have.' Sheila smiled. 'Don't you remember that ghastly man – whatever was his name – Eddie? Teddy?'

'Terry,' replied Lorna sheepishly. 'What a creep. There, you see,' she exclaimed triumphantly, 'I was desperate about him and now I can hardly remember what he looked like.'

'He was revolting,' said Sheila helpfully.

'Anyway,' said Lorna, ignoring her remark, 'you seem a bit more cheerful this morning.'

Sheila winked and gave her an odd look. 'Oh, I'm doing fine,' she said. 'I admit I feel like a limp rag, and I look appalling, but it's all under control.' Her voice was suddenly cold and unnatural.

'What have you been up to?' asked Lorna suspiciously.

Sheila looked at her with hard bright eyes. 'I've had a most interesting conversation this morning.'

'With whom?'

'I telephoned Rome,' said Sheila blithely. 'The Hotel d'Umberto to be precise. And I spoke to Miss Amanda Willoughby.'

'Who?'

'Simon Shitface's daughter, of course.'

'Oh no! Sheila, you didn't!' Lorna was horrified.

'I most certainly did. She was utterly delightful. We're going to get together shortly – she's on her way to Los Angeles next week and is stopping over in London. I'm meeting her off the plane.'

It was his wrists that she noticed first: strong, tanned and masculine, with a fine downy covering of black hair that contrasted nicely with his gold watch. He wore the sleeves of his pale-blue denim shirt rolled up – yes, it was his wrists that had first attracted her.

Leonie was seated on her brand-new chair, waiting for the lighting to be completed on a scene that she had already rehearsed. It was a night scene in her bedchamber and she had very little to do except pretend to be asleep in the huge carved-oak four-poster, with its banks of snowy white pillows and voluptuous feather quilt. The script required her to be awoken suddenly by a strange noise and to reach for her sword, hidden under the bed. The flamboyant Madame de Rothesay, known to her intimates as Marie la Diablesse – Marie the She-Devil – the villainess/seductress part that Bill had created for Leonie, was a brilliant swordswoman and always kept a weapon close at hand.

Leonie was enjoying herself. She had made it up with Rob in an ecstatic, orgiastic session of love-making which had lasted for much of the night after the row. Rob had been tender and loving with her, more loving than she had ever known him before. At the time she had felt comforted and reassured, but when she returned to the studios and saw Dave and Derek, she could not help remembering their conversation. She became convinced that they were exchanging covert glances, heavy with innuendo, when some bright spark enquired in a friendly fashion about her and Rob's sexual well-being. She had laughed along with the rest of the crew and given some smart answer, but her fears had returned. Amanda had implied that she had bedded Rob; Dave and Derek had remarked on his interest in her; and Derek had seen Amanda and Rob disappear together.

What a fool she had been! She had believed Rob because she had desperately wanted to believe him. But there was too much evidence against him. He must have been to bed with Amanda. Amanda! Her own daughter! The thought sickened her; she was utterly revolted by the idea. Dear God, she had only been away for a few days. What would happen when their work forced them apart for any length of time? What hope did they have?

It was not the first time she had had misgivings. The atmosphere in the apartment had become very tense. She knew that Rob was aware of it too, but suspected that he was putting it down to the pressure of her new role. She had tried hard to forget her doubts, but every time he touched her, stroked her breasts, caressed her neck, or tried to kiss her, she found herself wondering if he had done the same to Amanda. She kept seeing pictures in her head, graphic pictures, that she tried to blot out, to no avail. Mercifully, she did not realize how close some of them were to the truth.

She had become aware of the wrists only gradually, having first noticed an extremely pleasant aroma, a mixture of freshly laundered denim and the faintest tinge of a discreetly expensive aftershave. She glanced at the man standing next to her and that was when she noticed his wrists. She had never met him before, though she guessed that he might be a stand-in brought in at the last minute. He looked to be in his early forties, with deep-set twinkling blue eyes and dark, wavy hair, flecked with silver; he was tall, with a broad muscular chest and – those wrists. What was it about them? They looked strong and gentle at the same time, as though they could defend her with a broad sword one moment, and soothe her to sleep the next. She sat mesmerized by them as he lounged beside her, apparently studying the set. Her eyes were level with his hands, his thumbs hooked into the pocket of his jeans. She let her gaze wander surreptitiously to his crotch and felt a stirring in her loins as she noted the swelling there. What am I doing? she thought to herself with a shock. I'm eyeing another man. I'm fancying another man! But what about Rob.

The bell rang.

'Final rehearsal. First eleven, please.' Leonie rose instantly and crossed to the set. She never dallied, having learnt a long time ago that time was money and every second was precious. She climbed into bed and forgot about everything except the scene in hand.

'All right everyone, settle down. This is a rehearsal,' came Derek's voice.

'And . . . action!' There was complete silence. Leonie was apparently asleep, as the camera panned across her to the window.

'Cue the window,' said Colin softly and someone eased open the window latch. Leonie, alias Madame de Rothesay, instantly opened her eyes to stare at the moonlight that shone through the casement. Very slowly she eased herself across the bed in order to pull her sword from its hiding-place beneath. Then, brandishing the deadly silver blade, she sprang from the bed with a chilling scream.

'Cut,' observed Colin mildly, even though the camera was not turning. 'OK, let's do one.'

'This will be a take everyone,' bellowed Derek. 'Final checks, please.' Hairdressing and make-up rushed in and titivated Leonie for the hundredth time that morning. She stood there impassively while they fussed around her. Then they were joined by wardrobe, who reorganized the frills and flounces of the night-gown. 'Soon as you're ready,' said Derek impatiently. 'Come on everyone, we want to get this one in before lunch.'

Leonie got back into bed. 'OK, this will be a take,' yelled Derek. The bell rang. 'Happy?' Derek asked the lighting cameraman.

'Yup,' came the reply out of the darkness.

'OK then. Turn over.'

'Speed.'

'Mark it.'

'Shot 121, take one.'

The clapperboard was snapped shut followed by a breathless pause before Colin yelled, 'Action!'

Leonie slept, the camera panned. This time a visual cue was given for the window latch. There was a noise at the window. Leonie's eyes snapped open. Stealthily she reached for the sword, leapt out of bed and screamed. 'Cut!' shouted Colin. 'And print.'

'That was OK,' said Colin to Leonie in a faintly surprised voice. He was never a man to fling compliments around. 'Pop back into bed while they're checking the gate, then we'll go in closer on the reaction to the noise.'

'Gate's clear,' said the focus puller.

'Right,' said Colin. 'In for a close-up on the reaction to the intruder at the window. Might as well do it while we're around this way,' he added to Derek.

'Sure thing. Stay where you are, Leonie. This won't take long.'

While she waited, Leonie lay in the bed, letting her mind wander;

all at once she sensed that someone was looking at her. She narrowed her eyes against the lights and peered into the darkness. Yes, she was right. The handsome stranger she had noticed earlier was observing her with a humorous half-smile on his lips. She looked back at him and a sudden overwhelming desire consumed her. She wanted him, she wanted him now, here, in this bed. The idea of his tanned muscular body next to hers, among the frothy, lacy pillows, sinking deeply into the downy feathers, was almost more than she could bear. He was still looking at her and she felt sure he could read her thoughts. She felt herself blushing. She must find out who he was.

'OK. Ready on the set.'

'Shall we go for one?'

'Might as well. Same thing, Leo.'

'Right,' said Leonie, pulling herself together.

'This'll be a take.' The same routine, but this time the camera operator was not happy with the lighting. There was a brief pause while some minor adjustments were made.

'Going again,' said Derek. Leonie did not trust herself to look in the direction of the stranger again. They did another take and everyone was happy. 'That's lunch!' shouted Derek. 'Everyone back on set at five to two, please. Make-up checks at one forty-five.' Leonie picked her way over cables and props to her chair.

'You going to the canteen,' asked Derek, 'or shall I get something sent over to your caravan for you?'

'Oh, Derek, you're an angel. Could you? If someone could bring me a salad, that would be lovely.'

Once she was back in the sanctuary of her caravan on the back lot, she threw off her night-gown and put on a silk kimono. She looked at herself in the dressing-table mirror: she was flushed, she was on fire, she was lusting after that man, and there was nothing she could do about it. If only Rob were here. She needed a fuck, and she needed it right at this moment. Her breasts were heavy, her cunt was throbbing. What on earth was happening to her? She picked up the day's shooting schedule and examined it. In the afternoon she was due to do a fight scene with the intruder whom she had heard at her window. There was hardly any dialogue and it would take ages to shoot, much of it with the stunt double. A tap on the door interrupted her thoughts.

'Come in,' said Leonie, not looking up. The door clicked open and shut again.

'I gather you're hungry,' said a strange male voice. She looked up startled. It was the tall denim-clad stranger. He put down the small covered tray on the dressing-table and looked at her.

'You're very kind,' she replied, staring at him, wide-eyed. Her lips were parted and she was beginning to breathe quickly. He took a couple of steps towards her. She looked down at his loins and ran her tongue over her lips involuntarily.

'I think you're the most beautiful woman I have ever seen,' he said.

As if moved by some irresistible force she found herself walking towards him, never taking her eyes from his face. She closed on him and swiftly and expertly unfastened his belt. Then, in a sudden lithe movement, she knelt down in front of him and slowly undid the fly buttons on his jeans. His cock stirred and she could see a damp patch on his underpants where the lubricating fluids had already oozed out. Slowly and carefully she withdrew his swollen member from the constricting clothes, gently easing the foreskin back and brushing her lips on the head of his penis. He groaned as she flicked her tongue around it and finally drew it into her mouth. Soon, as if he could bear it no more, he pulled her up to him and kissed her savagely on the mouth, mingling their juices. He slid her dressing gown from her shoulders and ran a finger along the curve of her bosom, gently pulling down her camisole top until her breasts were exposed. He gazed at them in admiration for a while and then, lowering his head, ran his tongue tantalizingly round her nipple before taking it in his mouth, making her gasp with pleasure. Moments later he pushed her down on to the day bed, pulling at her lace pants with a practised hands. Within seconds he was inside her and they were fucking violently. Leonie could not remember when she had been so consumed with lust for anyone. They were completely in tune sexually, and when they came together her climax was explosive.

They lay on the bed, panting and exhausted, entangled in each other's arms. 'That was some lunch,' murmured Leonie eventually.

He laughed. 'You're one hell of a fuck,' he said candidly.

'Thank you.' She accepted the compliment gracefully. They eased apart and she sat up and swung her legs over the side of the bed. 'Would you like some of this?' she asked, indicating the tray of food.

'Thanks a lot, but I'd better go now.' He stretched himself and stood up, then reached for his jeans.

Leonie watched him. He had a very nice body. 'What's your name?' she asked, feeling almost shy.

'Larry,' he replied. 'I'll see you later.' He grinned, finished buckling his belt, and left the caravan.

Leonie felt alive and exhilarated. Suddenly she didn't care whether Rob and Amanda had fucked or not. She'd done it with someone else too, and she felt released and exultant. She looked at her reflection in the mirror and decided that some drastic action was need. She was pink and tousled, her hair wild, her face shiny. Grabbing some oil and cotton wool, she removed all her make-up, wolfing down her lunch at the same time. At a quarter to two she put on her costume again and left the trailer with a light step to present herself in make-up. 'Just look at me!' she exclaimed. 'I've been asleep and I look a fright. I've taken off all my slap, so we'll have to start again.'

'That's all right,' replied Betty, the head of make-up, who was a real darling. 'Looks better if you put it on fresh for the afternoon.' At two o'clock on the dot, Leonie was on the set ready to start work and looking radiant.

'Oh, Leonie, have you met Lawrence Trent? He's playing the man who gets into your bedroom,' said Colin's voice.

Leonie turned round to find herself face to face with her most recent conquest. He was dressed in full cavalier rig and looked, if possible, even more handsome in a rough suede and leather slashed jacket with leather trousers tucked into high boots. The jacket was unbuckled at the front to reveal a white linen shirt beneath and a fair expanse of muscular tanned chest. Now sporting a beard and moustache, long curls falling in disarray on his shoulders, he stood and grinned at her. 'Miss O'Brien and I did meet briefly,' he said easily, holding out his hand.

'So we did,' said Leonie, taking it. His grip was firm and sure and Leonie felt herself go weak at the knees. 'It's nice to see you again.'

'OK, quieten down everyone,' Derek shouted. 'Let's take a look at this.'

For the rest of the afternoon Leonie found herself at extremely close quarters with Larry Trent. At one moment he pinned her down on the bed and was lying on top of her, at another she was kneeling astride him on the floor, her sword at his throat. They wrestled and fought, punched and kicked. The short sequence of actual swordplay was expertly arranged by the fight director, an Italian, who had worked with Carlo. It was simple and effective and not too difficult but, after shooting it from every angle several times, Leonie was tired. By the end of the day, when the scene was finally in the can, she was exhausted.

Larry came up to her as everyone was leaving the set. 'Miss O'Brien, it's been wonderful working with you. I've had a fantastic day.'

'Yes,' she said, smiling at him. 'So have I. We must do it again some time.'

12

Bill sat watching Leonie with a mixture of pride and regret. What a fool he had been to louse it all up. Fifteen years ago he had been one of the artistic young lions of California, with the best-looking, classiest young lioness in the Hollywood jungle as his mate. And it hadn't worked out because, in true leonine fashion, it was she who had gone out hunting and brought home the prey. He had felt jealous, usurped, unworthy. He'd made her and she'd surpassed him. Here he sighed and shook his head. There would never be anyone like her again. Inside him was a hunger which would never now be satisfied.

When she had first left, he had felt a gnawing emptiness which he had tried to assuage by gorging himself on every available Hollywood beauty – and there were plenty of young hopefuls who thought they could break into movies through him. He had exploited their delusions ruthlessly, but pleasant though the diet undoubtedly was, it had only taken the edge off his appetite. They were not and never could be substitutes for Leonie. There was something elusive about her: the more he had of her, the more he wanted.

He would never forget the first time. It was after the party where they had met, when he had driven her back to his house at Malibu and they had talked for hours. When she had expressed a desire to go for a walk on the beach in the early dawn – very Scott Fitzgerald she had said – they walked for miles along the sand. He couldn't remember exactly how it had happened, but he could even now recall his astonishment at her glorious body as he gently removed her dress. He had seldom wanted any woman so much; he needed to possess that body more than any other he had seen before. He had laid her down on the sand, almost in reverence, and worshipped her perfect form. But even after he had penetrated her, explored her with his tongue, kissed and sucked every part of her, and filled her with his seed, even then, and during the many times to come that he made love to her, he had never ever possessed her.

They made love often on that beach; it became a ritual with them. And now there she was gazing into another man's eyes, laughing with him, openly wanting him. He watched her with Rob and tried to imagine them on the beach together. Then a cheering thought struck him: they probably hadn't made love on a beach, not in the dawn, not at Malibu, like Scott and Zelda. That was something special to him and Leonie, and he hugged the secret to him happily. Yet he knew he had been a fool: he would never find anyone like her again.

'Something tells me you may have hit on a winning combination, William,' someone said at his elbow. He roused himself from his reverie. The noise around him was deafening. How he had managed to slip away into a dream world he could not imagine.

La Mosca was bursting at the seams. The entire cast, crew and production team were there, even Marvin and his boyfriend, Tommy, who had flown over the day before. It was the end-of-picture party, a lunch for everyone connected with *Swords at Sunset* paid for by Marvin. He had been delighted with the rushes of the picture sent over to California, and especially with the impact of the new pairing of Rob and Leonie. Already there were rumours that he wanted them for another picture, that the whole team might be involved.

They had wrapped only by working overtime the previous evening, but now the film was in the can, finished, ready to splice together. The Americans were thrilled, and Bill knew it was largely due to his inspired idea of replacing Carlo and casting Leonie in the role. To him it had seemed the most natural solution. Only now did he realize that Leonie had been and still was doing her best to keep in the background, to maintain a low profile, to give Rob the limelight. He felt a pang of jealousy that she'd never done that for him. Their marriage could have worked out if only he hadn't got on to that rollercoaster of drink and sex, and if Leonie had been prepared to let her career take a back seat from time to time: then, he thought, things might have been different. But no, he had to admit to himself that women and booze had been his weakness long before he met her. Her success only gave him an excuse to revert to his old bad habits; if he had been stronger they could have been together still.

'Bill?' The voice was impatient now.

'Mmm? Sorry. You were saying?'

'I said, I think you found the winning formula.' It was Marvin speaking. 'They make quite a team, don't they?'

'Yes,' said Bill, smiling wistfully.

'Something potent and volatile happens on screen when those two are together,' observed Marvin.

'Chemistry,' replied Bill. 'Well, I wrote successfully for her in the old days – maybe we can relive our former triumphs.'

'I see no reason why not,' said Marvin smoothly. 'You're one hell of a writer.' Bill was secretly very gratified. He respected Marvin. He had made a handful of excellent movies – not necessarily world-shattering or Oscar-winning, but, well made, well scripted and beautifully shot – and he was a man of good taste, whose judgement Bill respected. 'We might even collect a couple of Oscars one day, if we get it right,' said Marvin, as though he had read his mind. 'What d'you say? Does the idea of further collaboration appeal to you?'

'Do you have a subject in mind?'

'Well, there's an idea I'm playing around with. I'll be ready to talk to you about it soon.'

'Keep me informed.'

'Good. When can we meet? We have to be in LA the day after tomorrow. What are your plans?'

'I had thought of staying on in Rome for a while. I've got a love affair going with this city that started way back in the sixties with Fellini and de Sica.'

Marvin smiled. One of Bill's most likeable characteristics was his sheer enthusiasm for the movies. 'Don't let's forget Visconti,' he added.

'Could I ever?'

'So, how about it?' Marvin wanted to pin Bill down while he had the opportunity. Bill was an important ingredient in the success of his plans, but Marvin knew perfectly well that he was a contrary son of a bitch and that the passion of one day might bore him the next. Already he could see that with Bill's script, clever editing and the right sort of music, he would have a box-office winner. Indeed his first appointment on his return to LA was to be a meeting with a hot young composer, who could turn out a seventeenth-century soundtrack that twentieth-century ears would find irresistible. Marvin's enthusiasm was fired; he realized that this movie would put Leonie back on top and that Leonie and Rob together on screen were hot stuff. He had to exploit the combination. This movie could ease the financial situation for the sci-fi picture. Things were definitely looking up, and with Bill in tow he had an in-built street credibility. The guy was Oscar-winning material, he just needed the right subject and the right star. Marvin knew that with him and Judd producing they would be an unbeatable force, and he wanted to nail him down now for the next picture.

He glanced across at Leonie, whose eyes were sparkling. What had the woman been thinking of? Giving up her screen career for what? Love, he supposed. Well, love was a funny old game. His eyes wandered over to where Tommy was sitting chatting to a good-looking young lighting technician. Tommy had been disappointed that Giovanni, whom he had met on set the day before, was not there, but he would have been wasting his time anyway, thought Marvin. He had heard all about Giovanni and Beryl from Leonie and Rob, who were full of the astonishing news.

'You'll never guess what, Marv! You know Giovanni, Rob's stand-in? Well he's going to be a paid companion to an Englishwoman called Beryl Willoughby. He met her here in Rome. She's a widow.

Isn't it amazing?'

'Paid companion!' scoffed Rob. 'Gigolo, he's a bloody gigolo. She's old enough to be his mother.' Leonie winced slightly as he spoke, but he did not notice the tightening of her expression.

Marvin was genuinely amused. 'Well, good for him, or perhaps I should say good for her.'

'Yes,' agreed Leonie, not looking at Rob, 'it takes courage to go for a relationship like that. But they do seem to get on well and enjoy each other's company. She said that all her married life she was a paid housekeeper. This is her first taste of freedom. It's just for a year's trial – she's quite insistent about that – to give it a fair chance.'

'Giovanni swears it's undying love,' Rob interrupted. 'Romantic fool, isn't he?'

'Well, who knows? It may very well be,' Marvin replied, being something of a romantic fool himself. Otherwise what the hell was he doing with Tommy, who was half his age? Tommy never lost an opportunity to flirt with pretty young men, but Marvin had long ago decided to turn a blind eye to it all. He always hoped that being given a certain amount of freedom would stop Tommy wandering off for good, and so far the theory had worked.

Yes, all in all, things were going pretty well at the moment. If he could just clinch this deal with Bill, he would be on to a winner. There was no doubt in his mind that Bill's rewrites were in a different league from the original script. The original scriptwriters had done a competent-enough job, but the script was lacking in inspiration and Judd had shared his reservations from the start. Well, never mind, it should still make money, Judd had said. Where the hell was Judd anyway? He'd stayed on at the hotel to take what he said was an important call from LA – and as it was first thing in the morning in LA it must be important – but that was an hour ago and he should have been here by now. Darn it! He needed him here now to back him up over this deal. They had to settle the matter before they left for LA.

Marvin was a great believer in doing deals over a meal and this atmosphere of general *bonhomie* was ideal. Although Marvin was good at the soft-soap stuff, Judd could really nail people down. He was about to tackle Bill again and was just considering what approach to take, when Judd suddenly appeared on the stairs. Marvin knew at once, by the look on his face, that something was badly wrong.

His heart sank but he waved cheerfully, gesturing Judd to join them. A few of the people nearest him turned round to see who it was and Leonie called out, 'Oh, there you are! I'm afraid we've started without you . . .' The words died on her lips as she saw his expression. 'Is something the matter?' she asked, concerned. 'Betty's all right, isn't she?'

Betty, Judd's wife, had stayed at home in LA because she didn't like flying. She was also subject to a lot of irritating minor ailments and Leonie felt she couldn't bear anything to mar the light-hearted atmosphere – even one of Betty's famous migraines would spoil things.

Unusually Judd, whose manners were normally excellent, ignored her. He went straight to Marvin's side and Leonie noticed that he was clutching a newspaper. She could not see what it was but a small shiver of anxiety ran through her. At the moment, newspapers meant nothing but trouble, she thought. Judd bent over to whisper something in Marvin's ear. After a moment, Marvin began to look worried. He scraped back his chair and got up to leave.

'Excuse me for a moment, if you don't mind,' he said to his table companions. 'A business problem has just arisen.' He left the table to follow Judd to the exit.

'I hope it's nothing serious,' said Leonie, looking at Rob with a worried frown. It would be too cruel for things to go wrong now, when they had already surmounted so many problems.

'Money,' said Rob. He did not sound concerned, but then he hadn't seen the two men's faces. 'It always is. They needn't fuss, we're going to make them a whole packet of it, aren't we?' And he continued to tuck into his squid.

Outside in the sunshine, the two Americans faced each other. 'Is there a problem?' asked Marvin curtly, knowing full well that there was.

'You bet your sweet ass there is. Take a look at this,' and Judd held out the newspaper for Marvin to examine.

There was a horrified silence as Marvin looked it over.

'Jesus H. Christ!' he said finally. Judd was fairly sure that he had never heard Marvin swear before in the five years that they had worked together.

'I can't believe this. They cannot be serious,' he said, gazing at the headlines in awe. 'They've timed it to coincide with our announcement about the new picture. Can we sue?'

Judd leant against the wall of the restaurant and thrust his hands deep into his pockets before replying. 'I think not,' he said eventually. 'I have an idea that it's the truth – or very near it.'

'You're kidding me.'

'I had a talk with Dave during the shoot yesterday. He hinted broadly at something of this kind.'

'Why would he do that?'

'I asked him how Rob and Leonie were in a work situation.'

'And?'

'He said, oh fine, just fine, except for some sort of a row over a girl Rob had been flirting with.'

Marvin snorted. 'Flirting! This article categorically implies rape.' He read on, the lines of worry deepening on his face. 'She's going to see this. We can't keep it from her.'

'Have you talked with anyone?'

'I checked with an attorney acquaintance of mine who specializes in this kind of thing. That's why I was so long in getting here. He didn't hold out much hope – said Rob was lucky the girl hadn't been to the police.'

'Hell,' said Marvin, 'that's all we need.' He looked at the paper again. 'These British newspapers, aren't they just something else?' he said in amazement.

'But the one hopeful thing he did say was that he thought it unlikely the girl would prosecute Rob now. He seemed to think that she would have been paid a considerable sum for her story by the newspaper group.'

'Well that's something, I suppose,' said Marvin doubtfully. 'What do we do now?'

'Confront him. We have no choice.'

Marvin groaned aloud. 'The new project was just starting to shape up nicely. You don't think that this could be a frame-up?' he asked hopefully.

'It's a possibility, but even if it proves to be so, the damage has already been done.'

Marvin turned reluctantly to go back down into the restaurant. 'There goes the ball game,' he said wryly.

Sheila Mackenzie and Amanda Willoughby eyed each other over the tea table at the Albermarle Hotel. Sheila had chosen the hotel deliberately, with a sense that it lent a dramatic symmetry to the whole venture. Simon had first betrayed Elizabeth with her there and now she would complete the circle and do the same to him. With satisfaction she noted that it was almost exactly six months to the day since he had made her his mistress.

'China or Indian tea?' she asked.

'Indian, thank you.' Amanda was intrigued. This woman had rung her in Rome, out of the blue, to say that she had a proposition to put to her which could possibly be lucrative and which concerned her father, Simon Brentford. She had emphasized that absolute secrecy was of the essence. Otherwise there was no chance of a deal.

'I thought we should have cucumber sandwiches. Something really civilized,' said Sheila, smiling at her guest.

'That would be nice.' Amanda smiled back at her. The woman seemed pleasant enough, but there was a barely disguised tension in her manner that made her wary.

A waiter appeared. 'A pot of Indian and a pot of China tea, cucumber sandwiches and some cream cakes, please.'

'Very good, madam.' He nodded and departed.

'I think we deserve a treat, don't you?' Sheila smiled again. Amanda was still puzzled by their meeting. What could this attractive but apparently ordinary woman have to say to her that could involve money? She must know that she had already sold her story to the newspapers. In fact, her cheque for £30,000 had been handed to her when she arrived at Heathrow that morning. In any case this Sheila

Mackenzie certainly didn't look or act like a journalist.

'I dare say you're wondering what all this is about?' Sheila said quietly, apparently reading Amanda's thoughts. The tea lounge was deserted, but they both spoke in low tones.

'Yes, I am, and I really can't imagine what it could be,' Amanda replied demurely, deciding that her best course of action was to play the innocent young girl.

'First of all, you have to promise me that you will never breathe a word to anyone about our conversation. Otherwise I shall tell you nothing.'

'Of course,' replied Amanda instantly, thinking privately that the other woman was either very trusting or very naïve. 'I wouldn't dream of mentioning anything told to me in confidence.'

'I'm sure you wouldn't, but just to make absolutely certain,' Sheila said, picking up her briefcase from beside her chair, 'I would like you to read this.' She clicked the case open and drew out a document which she handed to Amanda. The younger woman took it and examined it. It was in essence a solicitor's agreement, which had been drawn up under a general heading of Duty of Confidence. It read:

I AMANDA WILLOUGHBY DO HEREBY UNDERTAKE NEVER TO DIVULGE THE SOURCE OF THE INFORMATION WHICH HAS BEEN PASSED TO ME TODAY.

It was dated Friday, 29 June and a space was left at the foot of the page for Amanda's signature and that of a witness. Amanda looked at it and glanced up at her hostess.

'What on earth is this?' she asked disdainfully. She was beginning to feel slightly outmanoeuvred.

'An undertaking, a guarantee, if you like, to protect my own interests. If you are agreeable, I would like you to sign it in the presence of a witness. Once you have done so, I will make certain facts known to you which you will then be able to sell to the newspapers.'

'If you have access to this information, why don't you do it yourself?' Amanda asked immediately.

'Because I want to protect my anonymity,' said Sheila bluntly.

'So what's in it for you then?' said Amanda, her curiosity aroused.

'You'll find out when you sign this agreement.'

Amanda snorted. 'This isn't a legally binding document – you can't force someone to keep a secret, any more than you can trust someone to tell the truth under oath.'

Sheila realized, as a number of people had done before her, that this girl was no fool.

'What about money?' she asked abruptly, trying another tack.

'What about it?' Amanda's voice was level, but there was a gleam in her eye.

'What if I say I will pay you to keep this secret for six months. Would you?'

'What's to stop me telling after three months, or even two weeks?'

'You don't get paid until the sixth month is up. Will you consider it?'

The waiter arrived with a laden tray and Amanda took advantage of the diversion to consider her hostess for a moment. She saw an extremely attractive woman with russet-tinged brown hair, a lovely creamy complexion and amber eyes that looked as though they might on occasion hold a mischievous twinkle, but were now intensely serious. She was wearing a summer suit of the palest pink cotton, a colour that should have clashed with her colouring yet actually complemented it. She exuded energy and this, Amanda decided, was one of the most attractive things about her.

The waiter was very young and obviously nervous. He took a long time to set out the tea things, but when he finally departed, Sheila did not resume their conversation at once. Instead, she began to pour the tea into bone-china cups. 'Do you take milk?' she asked politely.

'Yes, please,' said Amanda. She waited for a moment, but Sheila said nothing. She went on, 'I'm interested in what you have to say. Tell me more.'

'Good. I shall. Sugar?' said Sheila, holding out the bowl.

'Thank you. Two. You said it concerned my father.'

'Yes. Would you care for a cucumber sandwich?'

'In what way does it concern him?' Amanda, becoming irritated, ignored the plate of sandwiches.

'My, you are impatient. These are awfully good,' remarked Sheila, munching one.

'Yes,' said Amanda crossly. 'I'm impatient because I don't have much time.' She took two sandwiches at once and wolfed them down together.

'Fair enough. I want you to sell an article to the newspapers for me. I will supply the details, but you will tell the story.' Sheila smiled at her. 'You know, you'll get fearful indigestion if you eat as quickly as that.'

Amanda ignored this advice and took two more sandwiches. 'How much do I get for doing you this favour?'

'That depends on how much you can persuade the newspaper to part with. As we will be splitting the proceeds, I suggest £50,000.'

Amanda, remembering her own negotiations with the press, looked scornful. 'You'll have to have a bloody good story.'

'Yes,' said Sheila, smiling quietly to herself. 'I have. And I think it will appeal to you too.'

'What's to stop me selling your story and keeping all the money myself?'

'The cheque will be made out in favour of a third party, an agent.'

'But surely as I am the person selling the story, I can simply tell them to make the cheque out to me,' Amanda suggested logically.

This was Simon's daughter all right, thought Sheila wryly. It was a good thing she had thought to prepare herself for a conversation like this. 'But you won't,' she said, smiling sweetly at Amanda. 'I think perhaps I should tell you what I do for a living.'

Amanda's eyes narrowed. She waited. 'I work in a government department,' Sheila continued, 'and I've been able to do some research on your background. I know a good deal more about you than you might imagine. Including that fact that you have a conviction for drug offences.' She smiled at Amanda again. 'Now you and I both know that it was only a childish indiscretion, but you must be aware that the United States immigration authorities don't take kindly to that sort of thing. I have friends in the Home Office. A hint dropped in the right direction and they would make absolutely sure that the American Embassy was informed of your criminal record. Your visa would then be withdrawn and you would be deported as an undesirable alien.' Check and mate thought Sheila to herself.

'OK, fine,' said Amanda, capitulating. 'So, you want me to sell your story now, but I don't get paid for six months. Now you'd better tell me what story you've got that's so valuable.'

'I am Simon Brentford's mistress,' said Sheila simply.

Amanda stared. 'R-e-a-l-l-y. Well, I must say he has good taste.'

'Thank you. I should like you to tell the newspapers all about me.'

'But that won't improve his image. I mean, it could do him a lot of harm, on top of everything else.'

'Yes.'

Light began to dawn in Amanda's eyes. 'You want to ruin him, don't you – why?'

'Revenge.' The word hung in the air for a moment. At last they were talking the same language. 'He's ruined my life,' Sheila went on. 'He's dumped me. I can't continue in my job, because I work in his department and even if I got transferred, I'd still see him around most of the time and that would be intolerable. My home is near his too; I want to sell it and move away. I've got the opportunity to join a friend's business, but I want some capital to invest. I need that £25,000 to start a new life.'

'I see.' Amanda could understand her motivation perfectly. It was so very like her own.

'Also,' said Sheila in a quiet voice, looking at her steadily, 'also, I'm pregnant,'

'God-dammit, man, you've given us a whole load of trouble on this shoot already,' exclaimed Judd. He was quite unlike his normal, charming, boyish self and he was not attempting to hide his anger. They were in the middle of a highly unpleasant interview, in which the two Americans were grilling Rob about his activities, sexual and otherwise, in connection with Amanda Willoughby.

'Look,' said Rob, looking hurt, 'I admit, I got a little frisky —'

'Define frisky,' interrupted Judd tersely.

'Just a minute,' said Rob. He felt stung. 'Just what is this, the third degree or what?'

'Do you have any conception of the damage you have done, not just to your own career, but to our company's credibility?' asked Judd.

'I thought all publicity was good publicity,' observed Rob. 'Or are we all obsessed with the reactions of the Daughters of the Revolution?'

'Young man,' said Marvin gravely. 'We have a scenario here, which we find highly distasteful. It is not to our liking, no, sir. Now you have personally been responsible for the expenditure on this picture considerably exceeding its original budget. We were prepared —'

'It was an accident!' protested Bob.

'That's not how we hear it,' replied Marvin quietly.

'From whom?' demanded Rob angrily.

'That need not concern you —'

'Well, it bloody well does concern me. It's my career that's on the line.'

'And now, unless I miss my guess,' said Marvin indicating the headlines in the newspaper, 'your relationship as well.'

Rob looked black. 'Yes, I doubt very much if it can survive this.' There was a silence as they all contemplated the gloomy future.

'Let me tell you the way I see it,' Marvin said at last. Both Rob and Judd turned to him expectantly They both knew that things were serious, more serious than anyone had really wanted to admit. Marvin was a good twenty years older than either of them and would know best how to deal with this crisis.

It had been after their conversation outside the restaurant that the Americans had called Rob out to join them. Their excuse was an important telephone call to be made regarding the insurance claim for the duelling accident. Rob was needed to present his version in his own words to the lawyer who was acting on their behalf. Leonie had protested. Surely it could wait? They were breaking up a party. Judd, however, was insistent that it had to be done now and that it wouldn't take long. The party would probably end up at their hotel, or Leonie's apartment, and continue on well into the night and Rob would be able to rejoin it later. This was important and had to be attended to immediately. They were expecting a call back from their attorney in the next twenty minutes.

Rob knew from their faces that all was not well, but when Leonie had wanted to go with him, he had insisted that, as leading lady, she should stay with the film unit. They had taken him in silence by cab to their hotel, the Lorenzo de Medici. On arrival they had gone straight to Judd's suite, where drinks had been served. It hadn't been until all three had seated themselves that Judd had produced the newspaper and flung it in challenge at Rob. He could only stare, appalled, at the shrieking headlines, all his worst fears realized. 'Jesus,' was all he had said before burying his head in his hands.

Marvin surveyed him impassively. 'The way I see it,' he repeated, 'is like this: you are between a rock and a hard place. Your only course of action is to publish a denial. It is your word against that of the girl's and you will note that the word rape is in quotes, which would seem to indicate that they think the girl may be either lying, or exaggerating, or that sexual congress may indeed have taken place, but with her compliance. If either of the former is the case, then you are in the clear, at least so far as your conscience is concerned; if the latter, then only you can decide what you tell Leonie. However, regarding the press, if you take my advice, you will lie through your teeth. As I've said, it is your word against hers and she has already caused enough trouble. I believe that you and Leonie together have a cinematic future and I hope we may be able to be a part of that future, but first you must clear your name. The mud will stick for a while, of course, but I think we may be able to counter that by bombarding the world's press with wholesome, homely spreads of you and Leonie. I'll get Mary Beth on to it right away. Then you must make your peace with Leonie. I believe she loves you very deeply and will forgive you in time, but I think you should be prepared for a bumpy ride on all counts.'

Rob breathed a sigh of relief. He had come off lighter than he had expected. 'Very well, I will be advised by you.'

'Good,' said Marvin briskly. 'Now, I propose we draft a statement, here and now, which will be given to the press before the day is over.

With luck it will hit the front page tomorrow and John Q. Public will choose to believe your story rather than that of an hysterical teenager bent on revenge! What do you say Judd?' he asked the younger man.

Judd examined the contents of his whisky glass for a few minutes before replying. 'I reckon if the statement is correctly and carefully worded,' he began, 'if we employ the right kind of emotive terminology, we might just hit this dame's story right outta the ball park.'

'Attaboy!' said Marvin uncharacteristically. 'Get started on it, and I'll give it a go. Between us we'll come up with something that Babe Ruth would have been proud of.' Judd stared at him in amazement. When the hell did he last go to a baseball game, he thought?

'And as for you, young man,' said Marvin, looking at Rob, 'as for you, you will guarantee not to cause us any further embarrassment, that is, if we are to continue our working association.'

'You have my word,' said Rob solemnly, and as they both looked at him he added, 'as an English gentleman.'

'Jeez,' muttered Judd under his breath and knocked back his whisky.

'Mr Sneller, I have some information which may interest you.' Tony Sneller licked his lips and began to perspire freely. The caller was Amanda Willoughby. So far she had provided him with a film star, an MP, an illegitimacy, a toy-boy lover, and a rape. Could there possibly be more? Another scoop and that features job was as good as in the bag.

'I'm sure anything you have to say would interest me, Miss Willoughby. Are you still in London? I thought you were flying out to LA this afternoon.'

'Yes, I've delayed my departure for a couple of days. Something's come up.'

Sneller grabbed a handful of tissues from the box on his desk and mopped the back of his neck. For Amanda Willoughby, bound for Los Angeles to conquer Hollywood, to delay her departure, it must be something good. 'Where are you staying?' he asked eagerly.

'That's my business,' she snapped. 'Now, when can we meet? We need to talk about money.'

Tony Sneller sighed heavily. The girl had been handed a large cheque from the *Globe* at Heathrow that very morning. Now she was already wanting more. Would she never give up?

'Miss Willoughby, as you know I am not empowered to buy material. My editor is the person who decides whether or not a story is worth money.'

'Then I'd better speak to your editor. Where can I reach him?'

'Just a minute. Tell me, are we talking about an exclusive here?' He was trying to think quickly, but he had taken an extended lunch-hour and the vodka had rather over relaxed him.

'I want to speak to your editor. What's his name?'

'Amanda, don't do that. Look, tell me where you are and I'll come round. We'll talk it over.'

Click. The line went dead. Little cow, she'd put the phone down on him. Shit! Now she'd go straight to the *Saturn*, their rival paper and Trevor would not be best pleased. He glanced at the clock on the wall. Thank Christ, it was almost six o'clock. He'd be able to go for a drink soon. Slumped over his desk, he tried to decide on a course of action. Why on earth hadn't she caught her connection to Los Angeles? What a fool he'd been, he should have gone to the airport with the cheque himself. Instead a special driver had been allocated to meet her off the flight and hand it to her. He had a sudden thought: the driver, he might have an idea of where she'd gone.

He was just about to call the Transport Section when his phone rang. He picked it up. 'Tony?' It was Trevor's voice on the other end. 'Get in here, now!'

Tony Sneller did not wait to be told a second time. He'd heard that tone in Trevor's voice before. It meant that someone's head was on the block, or was about to be. Hastily he replaced the receiver, grabbed his jacket from the back of his chair, and quickly opened the side drawer of his desk. No, bugger, that half bottle of vodka was empty. He scurried off in the direction of Trevor's office.

'What the fuck have you been up to now?' Trevor snapped as Tony entered the office.

Tony stood dazed for a moment, trying to collect his thoughts. 'Er,

I'm just finishing off that piece on the poof who married the transvestite he met in the Signals —'

'That bloody girl has just been on to me!' Trevor was plainly livid.

'Girl?' Oh no, thought Tony.

'The Willoughby girl! Little tart! What's she got that's worth that sort of money?' Trevor was glaring at him furiously.

'Money?' he asked faintly, wishing his boss would ask him to sit down, an unlikely event on any occasion.

'£50,000 she says you promised we'd pay her! Fifty fucking thousand pounds! You taking out another mortgage, Sneller? 'Cos I sure as fuck am not paying it.'

Tony Sneller collapsed uninvited into the nearest chair while Trevor Grantley regarded him dispassionately. 'I think you're cracking up, Sneller. It's all been too much for you, these minor scoops of yours recently —'

'Minor!' protested Tony feebly. 'But, Trev, we were the first to get those stories —'

'So we were, old son. But when we're on top, we have to stay there,' said Trevor not unkindly. 'We don't let it go to our fucking heads and start throwing money around like we were in a casino or something. Who do you think you're working for, the fucking Aga Khan?'

Tony Sneller made a huge effort to pull himself together. 'That little cow is lying. I never offered her any money. She hasn't even said what she's got to sell. I suggested we talk it over, but – look, Trev – if she thinks she can get that sort of dosh for it, she must be on to something really hot.'

'What are you trying to say to me, Sneller?' asked Trevor patiently.

'All I'm saying, Trev, is why don't you see the girl? Find out what she has to say for herself . . .' He broke off as he saw his boss's face.

'Ever heard the phrase, "Why keep a dog and bark yourself?" ' said Trevor, regarding him with a deadpan expression.

Tony winced. 'Leave it out, Trev. What I'm saying is that this time I think we may have a really big story here, so she wants to take it to the top, natch. See the girl – she's quite a looker – and don't let the *Saturn* get it.'

'Yeah, you may have something there,' said Trevor, reluctantly. 'OK, I'll give her the once-over. You'd better wheel her in. Where is she?' Sneller took out the damp pad of tissues from his pocket and mopped his brow.

'Well, Trevor, that's what I was about to find out when you called me in.' It didn't sound good and Sneller knew it.

Trevor stared at him in astonishment. 'I don't believe I'm having this conversation,' he said pleasantly. 'I think I'm in an episode of *Lou Grant* and I've turned over two pages of dialogue at once. Are you fucking well trying to tell me you have no idea where the little bint is?'

Tony whimpered quietly. 'She hung up on me, Trev. I was about to ring Transport to find out if they'd seen where she went —'

'Transport employs drivers, not clairvoyant private detectives!' said Trevor explosively. 'How the hell would they know?' The phone rang. Trevor snatched it up.

'Yes!' he thundered, then he cupped the receiver with his hand. 'It's her!' he mouthed to Tony.

Tony allowed himself to breathe again.

'Yes, I've been thinking it over, Miss Willoughby and it's not entirely out of the question. But you must realize that for the sum you mentioned . . . Where are you staying by the way, in case I need to call you back? Yes, yes, I know you don't have much time, but . . . what! Go on,' he said almost holding his breath. 'Yes, yes, fuck me – I mean, good lord, I'm sorry – are you sure?' Here he gave Tony a look that plainly said 'You're never going to believe this.'

'Yup, we'll be round there in . . .', he glanced at his watch, 'twenty minutes.' He slammed down the phone and picked up his jacket. 'Get your skates on,' he said brusquely to Sneller. 'We're off to the Albermarle. Little Miss Willoughby has a story to tell that will make your hair curl.'

13

'Let me get this straight, Miss Willoughby. First, you claim you are Leonie O'Brien's abandoned daughter, then you say your father is Simon Brentford the MP. Next you accuse Rob Fenton, Miss O'Brien's young lover, of raping you. Now you say that your father's mistress, Sheila Mackenzie, has befriended you and confided that she is expecting the Minister's illegitimate child. Is it too much to expect that you are now about to disclose to us that your adoptive mother is an alien?'

Amanda gave Trevor Grantley the benefit of a cold stare. She disliked the man intensely. When she spoke to him on the phone she had decided that he was a toad and this was now confirmed by their meeting. She, Grantley and Sneller were all seated in a secluded corner of the Albermarle lounge, where they had met to discuss Amanda's latest disclosure. She assessed Trevor with distaste. Physically he was not at all what she had expected. He was tall, spare and balding, with an over-generous mouth that had, on occasion, been described as both lecherous and lascivious. His eyes were brown and inscrutable and it was impossible to tell what he was thinking. A keep-fit fanatic and permanently tanned, he did not drink, unlike many of his employees, and at this moment he was sipping a Virgin Mary, a taste he had picked up in the United States. His abstinence probably had as much to do with his success as anything else. He was good at his job and had kept it for a remarkably long time without any really serious challenge; his claim that it was his healthy lifestyle and clear brain that kept him in front of his rivals was not without validity.

The *Globe* boasted a circulation well ahead of its nearest competitors and prided itself on always keeping the people informed, a claim which Trevor Grantley regarded as his sworn duty to protect and promote. Yes, to keep them informed, especially about abandoned daughters who had been raped in what were virtually incestuous circumstances. Every concerned father would want to know about this – possibly even the MP for South Molding.

'Yes,' he continued amiably. 'I can see it all now. "My adoptive mother was an alien, claims abandoned illegitimate daughter of MP tearfully. Following her rape by her film star mother's toyboy lover she was today being comforted by her father's pregnant mistress." ' He chuckled, causing Tony Sneller to wince and squirm uncomfortably in his chair. Trevor was doing his sarcasm bit again. One of these days it would be his undoing.

Amanda was not amused. Her opinion of the two newspaper men was that they represented the slime of the earth. This was her third meeting with Tony Sneller and he had not improved on acquaintance. In some ways Trevor Grantley was even more loathsome, possibly because of his glowing good health which concealed a hidden, inner decadence. Somehow such a constitution and appearance did not tally with his profession of parasite. From his side of the table, Trevor was looking speculatively at Amanda, weighing her up: she was just a slip of a thing, good looking enough and no doubt she had a certain degree of tenacity and cunning, but in the past he'd had dealings with much tougher nuts. He'd certainly be able to crack this one. Why he'd interviewed them all: tricky top soccer stars who had been the victims of kiss-and-tell stories by unscrupulous barmaids; perverts who specialized in child pornography and who had exhibited absolutely no signs of remorse; hardened criminals with half-a-dozen convictions behind them for grievous bodily harm – all first-division tough nuts and hard cases. Oh, he could handle this one little girl all right.

'I dare say it appears to you, Miss Willoughby, that I keep a credulous public happy with an unlimited supply of celebrity trivia, preferably of a sensational nature —'

'Isn't that a contradiction?' Amanda interrupted.

'I'm sorry?' He bent forward, cupping his ear with a hand, as though not able to believe what he'd just heard.

'If it's sensational, can it be trivial as well?'

Trevor laughed immoderately as though at some outrageous private joke. 'Oh dear, oh dear, Miss Willoughby, how little you know about celebrities. Although it would appear you have aspirations yourself in that direction?'

Amanda drew herself up in her chair, an affronted expression on her face. 'I have no wish to become a celebrity, Mr Grantley. I intend to pursue a career as a serious actress. I have no desire to become famous for fame's sake,' she said haughtily.

'Yes,' nodded Trevor sagely. 'yes, they all say that. But I'm afraid it's too late. You've already become famous, or should I say infamous, as we're being pedantic,' and he chuckled mirthlessly again.

'If I have, then it's thanks entirely to you,' she retorted sharply.

'Oh, come, come, Miss Willoughby, you've been paid handsomely for your trouble, and you must admit that you did seek us out.' He sat back smirking, confident that he had won that round.

'Nonsense! I was trailed by your bloodhound!' protested Amanda, the picture of injured innocence.

Tony Sneller, who had been sitting out the interview in silence, looked up from his double vodka, unsure whether this was a compliment or not.

'Ah, yes, our on-the-spot reporter, our "man in Rome". Only doing his job, Miss Willoughby. Nice one Sneller!' and Trevor nodded patronizingly in Tony's direction.

Sneller still couldn't decide whether these remarks were entirely complimentary, but the vodka was going down so smoothly, that he decided to give them the benefit of the doubt.

'Well, thanks, Trev,' he grinned in a slightly inane way. 'Not a bad little story – though I say so myself – but as you so rightly say, Trev, I was just doing my job —'

'Shut up,' said Trevor abruptly, without looking at him. He was beginning to regret having brought Sneller along.

'Anyway,' said Amanda as though the interruption had never occurred, 'the traumatic experiences I have lived through recently could hardly be described as trivial! Although some might call them sensational,' she added heatedly. 'I resent your imputations.'

'Some might indeed,' agreed Trevor. 'Some might even call them implausible, wouldn't you say, Tony?' He deferred affably to Sneller for a moment, giving him a chance to justify his existence.

Tony resurfaced momentarily from a fog of alcohol. 'Oh yes, Trev, implausible. Definitely,' he said vaguely. He wondered how you spelt 'imputation'. It was not a word you used very much on the *Globe*. Or 'implausible', come to that. He had actually tried that one once, but an irate sub-editor had struck it out and substituted 'telling porkies' instead. He had been bitterly disappointed at the time.

'I'm glad you agree with me, Tony. I thought you might,' said Trevor, still sounding ominously affable. 'My point is, Miss Willoughby, or may I call you Amanda?'

'No you may not,' said Amanda.

He raised his eyebrows and continued, undeterred, 'My point is, Miss Willoughby, that we,' here he glanced at Tony Sneller, and revised his remarks, 'that is, that I feel that your most recent revelations are verging on the seriously improbable.'

'Mr Grantley, are you suggesting that I'm lying?'

'Perhaps an, shall we say, over-dramatized version of the truth. Wouldn't you agree, Tony?'

Tony nodded his support, though he was not really listening. He had been trying to attract the attention of a waiter for some time by the use of his own unique brand of semaphore, and had just succeeded in ordering another round of drinks in a manner that would have done credit to an experienced mime artist.

Trevor looked at him sharply. 'Have you been getting any of this down?' he demanded. Sneller examined his notepad with keen interest.

There did seem to be something scrawled in it, in a sort of shorthand. What was that – 'impossible amputations' – what the hell did that mean?

'I was under the impression that we were speaking off the record,' observed Amanda coldly.

'Oh, I'm so sorry, were you?' said Trevor with exaggerated politeness. 'Well, in that case, we haven't heard a thing, have we, Tony? You can scrub all that out,' he added, indicating Sneller's scribbles. Sneller obediently drew several heavy lines through his notes and tore out the pages with relief. Then he screwed them up and stuffed them into an empty glass.

'We seem to have been labouring under some misunderstanding, Miss Willoughby,' Trevor continued pleasantly. 'We thought you were expecting some sort of remuneration for your disclosures, and I must say that I for one am very relieved to learn otherwise.' He was now positively jovial. 'We are, as I am sure you are aware, Miss Willoughby, in the middle of a recession, and we simply don't have the resources.'

'Do you want this story or not?' Amanda snapped, her patience running out. 'Or shall I take it to the *Saturn?*'

Trevor smiled at her in a predatory way. 'Now, Miss Willoughby, let's not be too hasty here. The *Saturn* wouldn't even consider paying for this sort of story, whereas we would be prepared to offer you in excess of £5000.'

Amanda picked up her handbag and rose from her seat. 'I can see I've been wasting my time, gentlemen.' She managed to make the word gentlemen sound like an insult.

Trevor watched her, without emotion and without moving a muscle. 'And the *Saturn* won't believe a word of your story either, Miss Willoughby. Besides, even if we don't have all the facts we now have the necessary headlines to pip them to the post and kill their scoop,' Amanda stopped in her tracks, 'stone dead.'

Amanda stared at him, hatred in her eyes. Then she sat down again. 'All right,' she said in a businesslike manner, 'let's talk about this sensibly. I have a story to tell which is absolutely true. I am prepared to give you the details, and I require in the region of £50,000 by way of payment.'

.

The waiter arrived at the table and started placing the drinks in front of them. 'Is this on you, Sneller?' asked Trevor. 'That's very generous. Could we order some sandwiches, please?' he asked the waiter and in a confidential aside, added, 'Mr Sneller is paying.'

'Yes, of course, sir. What would you like?'

'Smoked salmon, I think. Miss Willoughby?'

'Yes, thank you,' she said tersely.

'Same for you, Tony, I imagine? Yes, three, no, four rounds of smoked salmon, please. With caviar garnish, if you have it.'

Trevor turned to Amanda again. 'How can we confirm the veracity of your story, Miss Willoughby? You do see our problem, don't you?' Veracity. The atmosphere was positively buzzing with good words, thought Sneller. Trev had quite a flamboyant verbal style, he admitted with grudging admiration, and it was criminal that he frowned on such excesses in his employees.

'Miss Mackenzie will be only too happy to confirm it,' said Amanda shortly.

'There's one thing puzzling me about all this, Miss Willoughby.' Amanda did not reply, but waited for him to continue. 'Why hasn't Miss Mackenzie approached us directly?'

'It was my idea. Ms Mackenzie is naturally very distraught. She has had to leave her job, she has been abandoned by her lover, she has no money and — '

'And as if that wasn't enough she's having to cope with morning sickness!' Trevor completed the sentence for her.

Amanda stared at him in disbelief. 'Mr Grantley, we are speaking of a woman's personal tragedy here. This is not a matter to be made light of.' There was outrage in her voice.

'No, of course not, Miss Willoughby, just to make money out of.' There was silence for a while. Sneller felt disappointed. He had been prevented from making a written record and this was all very good stuff. All three sipped their drinks. 'Let me put it this way, Miss Willoughby. I am prepared to pay Miss Mackenzie for her story, told by her, to us. And, as a gesture of goodwill, I am prepared to pay you an introduction fee of, shall we say, £5000?'

.

'Miss Mackenzie will not be prepared to talk to you.'

'Then I fear that this meeting, however socially pleasant, has been a waste of my time and yours, Miss Willoughby.'

'How much would you be prepared to pay Miss Mackenzie for her story?'

'That would be a confidential matter between Miss Mackenzie and myself.'

Amanda decided to ignore the snub. 'All right,' she said slowly, 'I'll speak to Miss Mackenzie and try and arrange a meeting between you both. It may be difficult to persuade her, though, as I know she's not at all keen on talking to the press in person.'

'I'm sure you'll manage, Miss Willoughby. You seem to be a very determined young lady, and, if I may say so, the spitting image of your mother.'

'Oh, so you believe that part of my story at least,' said Amanda wryly.

'The only aspect of your on-going soap opera that I question,' said Trevor, giving her a hard stare, 'is your so-called "rape" by Rob Fenton, and your pathetic little tale about Sheila Mackenzie.'

'She is my father's mistress and she is pregnant!' said Amanda furiously. 'And since when, may I ask, has your newspaper ever concerned itself with the truth?'

'Oh, so you admit that it's all lies, then?' Trevor was quick to pounce.

'Certainly not, but as you've printed everything I've told you so far, you obviously have no qualms about publishing so-called untruths!'

'You may not have noticed, Miss Willoughby, but we mentioned the word rape in quotes, which always means that it's open to interpretation.'

'A little yellow flower,' murmured Tony happily, now well away on his next vodka, 'it grows in the fields in the spring.'

Trevor turned a basilisk-like stare on him. 'I'll deal with you later,' he said ominously.

Amanda picked up her handbag again and pushed back her chair. 'I see,' she said coldly. 'Well, I'll go and talk to Miss Mackenzie and try to persuade her to give you something you don't need to publish in quotes.'

'Excellent,' said Trevor, smiling benignly. 'Aren't you staying for your sandwiches?'

'No, thanks,' she replied. 'Give them to your bloodhound here; he'll need something to mop up all that vodka.'

'It didn't work.'

'What do you mean?'

'They didn't bite.'

'I don't believe you.'

Amanda was getting tired of being called a liar, especially by someone whom she thought was on her side. She sighed heavily. 'Look, Sheila, I can't help what you think. The fact of the matter is that they want the story from your own lips or you can forget all about any money.'

'How much are they prepared to pay?' asked Sheila sharply.

'They wouldn't tell me. You would have to negotiate that yourself. They were willing to pay me the incredibly generous sum of £5000 for making them aware of the story.'

'Big deal.'

'Precisely what I thought.' There was a pause. 'What are you going to do?' said Amanda.

'I don't know yet. I'm thinking about it.'

'Ring me back then, will you, when you've thought?'

'OK.' Sheila replaced the receiver and sat for some time, lost in thought. Damn! She either had to come out into the open and do the scorned and vengeful mistress routine, which would certainly make her look cheap and money-grabbing, or she had to keep a discreet and dignified silence when the news leaked out – as it now inevitably would – and win the admiration of the world, but stay poor. No, she wanted that money, she deserved it, and anyway she didn't feel like being dignified or discreet. She wanted to humiliate Simon publicly. She wanted to see him cringe and crawl and she didn't really give a damn what the world thought. Since Charles Pendlebury's phone call on his behalf, she hadn't heard a single word from him – not a call, not a line, no message at all – and no attempt had been made to get in touch with her at work or through a friend. Nothing. One word from him, and she would have understood, would have forgiven. But it was as though the last six months had never happened.

What she would have done without Lorna, she could not imagine. Lorna had been on the phone every day, had driven over to see her several times, even offering her a bed in her flat if she didn't want to be alone. Sheila was touched and grateful, but declined the invitation to stay. She felt that she had to see this thing through on her own. She was like a lion that crawls into its den after a bloody battle and hides away from its fellows in self-imposed solitary confinement, licking its wounds until they are healed. When she mentioned this idea to Lorna, Sheila had said, 'I find it comforting to think that I'm reacting in an animal-like way. There's something very basic about it.'

'Yes, I suppose so,' said Lorna doubtfully. 'Do you think then, when you're better, that you're going to climb the nearest tree and wait for the big-game hunter who wounded you to come along? And when he does, spring down from your branch and maul him to death?'

'Yes,' said Sheila, smiling slightly. 'Something like that.'

Lorna looked worried. 'I'm not sure, you know, that this revenge business is such a good idea. After all, if he is the hunter, he's the one who carries the big gun.'

'Don't worry,' said Sheila calmly. 'He won't know what's hit him, I promise you.'

Sheila was quite sure that Lorna considered her to be slightly unbalanced – at least for the moment – but Sheila herself had never felt more sane. It was perfectly simple: she loathed Simon, She wanted to destroy him, to tear him to shreds. She knew that once she had loved him, but she could not remember why. How could she love someone who had given her so much pain? 'Heaven has no rage like love to hatred turned. Nor hell a fury like a woman scorned'. Congreve certainly knew a thing or two. Maybe he had suffered too. She still felt pain, terrible pain, there was no doubt of that, and she knew it would not go away until it had been dealt with, amputated, exorcized. She was not sure of the exact term for the operation needed to cure her, but she was certain that it involved the destruction of the other person and that it had to be carried out soon. Amanda had initially seemed the perfect tool: hell-bent on revenge herself, she had jumped at the chance of another stab at her parents and Sheila had liked her too, sensing that she had guts. She would be prepared to do the dirty work from which Sheila herself had initially shrunk, and deal with the hyaenas of Fleet Street on her behalf. This setback to her plans was an irritating nuisance; she had not anticipated it at all. Then an idea occurred to her. She picked up the phone and dialled the Albermarle Hotel where, on her ironic recommendation, Amanda was staying.

'Miss Willoughby's room, please.' There was a pause as her call was transferred, then Amanda's wary voice, 'Yes, who's speaking?'

'I think we should go for it,' Sheila said decisively, without preamble.

'How do you mean?' Amanda could hardly conceal the eagerness in her voice.

'You want to be an actress, don't you?'

'It's all I care about in the whole world!'

'Well, this may surprise you,' said Sheila, 'but I'm pretty good myself. That is to say, I was considered hot stuff at Cambridge. Believe it or not I was in the Footlights revue. And I played the Duchess of Malfi with the Mummers.'

Amanda was impressed in spite of herself. She knew that both these famous university societies had launched the careers of many highly respected and successful actors.

'Anyway,' Sheila continued, 'the idea is that we combine our talents – mine slightly more experienced and practised, yours raw and untutored – and put on a show.'

'Who for?' Amanda was puzzled.

'The press boys. It'll be good, believe me. They might expect a performance from you – actress's daughter and all that – but they certainly won't suspect me. We can fool them totally. Together we're an unbeatable force.'

Amanda was intrigued. 'What are we going to do?'

'You're going to ring them again. Tell them that I'm willing to talk. You can say that I'm in London, staying with a friend. I don't want their dirty feet all over my lovely cottage and Lorna's dying to get me into her flat. She wants to look after me, bless her.'

'So what are you going to do?' Amanda sounded breathless with anticipation.

'Give them what they want: a distraught woman in a state of collapse, face stained with tears, eyes swollen with crying. She's trying to be brave and face them, but she keeps on breaking down. Shaking. Trembling. Wringing her hands. Dear God, I've had plenty of practice recently!' Sheila's laugh was hollow.

'I'm sorry,' said Amanda. 'It's been bloody for you, hasn't it?'

'Yes,' said Sheila shortly. There was a pause, then she went on in different tone, 'Do you think bandages around the wrists would be going too far?'

Amanda laughed delightedly. 'Probably. What a pity. But otherwise it sounds brilliant. What do I have to say?'

'Play along. Believe every word. Every tear. Support me, comfort me. Try to persuade me to go back to bed. Bring me tea, drinks. I shall refuse all food, of course.'

'Of course. What are you going to tell them?'

'Everything. At a price. We'll screw them for all we can get and split the proceeds. It'll be your first public performance.'

'Not really,' said Amanda, laughing again. 'I gave a few previews to Sneller in Rome and I must say I was very convincing. But it was the truth, after all, though there were a few omissions,' she confessed.

'And they printed it, of course?'

'Oh yes. It made very good copy, and they can never resist that? Didn't you read about it?' Amanda's voice was slightly hurt.

'I skimmed through some of the headlines. You see, at first I didn't realize there was any connection with Simon. Anyway, I can't bear those sort of papers. They revolt me.'

'Yet you're prepared to take money from them?'

'That's different. Besides, Amanda, at the moment I don't give a damn about morality and ethics. I want to be able to live again, and the only way I can do that is to get this man out of my system. It sounds crazy, I know, but I need to hurt him as much as he hurt me. Then I can forget about him. Now are you on for this?'

'Absolutely. Just tell me where and when.'

'I'm going to ring Lorna tonight. You call your two press boys now, and we'll all meet at your hotel tomorrow afternoon. I'll make sure I get to you first, so we have plenty of time to rehearse!'

'What about the money?'

'I shall be asking £30,000. But remember, they think they're doing the deal with me. I think you should try and up yours to £10,000. That'll be £20,000 each, then.'

'What if they won't pay up?'

'Then I simply shan't talk. I shall plead poverty in any case. Now, what do you think?'

'Sounds good to me,' said Amanda. 'What else do I need to know?'

'That I've given up my job, which is true. That I'm pregnant, which is true. That you and Lorna are both trying to get me through the ordeal. That you feel sympathetic to me because your father has treated us both so badly – and that you want your little half-brother or -sister to have a better start in life than you did. All of this is true, except perhaps the last. You see, we shall hardly have to act at all. We just expose our real feelings. I am beginning to have a feeling I might find the whole experience very therapeutic.'

'What does Lorna think of all this?'

'She won't approve, so I'm not going to tell her. She's an absolute darling, but she doesn't understand that I have to do this my way. I shall simply tell her I'm meeting you for a drink; she already knows we have a lot in common.'

'I think you're incredible.'

'We're actually very similar, you know. By the way, what are these newspaper boys like?'

'The usual scum,' said Amanda gloomily.

Sheila laughed. 'Oh, good. Then that'll make it all the more fun.'

MISTRESS OF MP IN LOVE-CHILD STORM IS PREGNANT, CLAIMS ABANDONED DAUGHTER.

An exclusive interview by
TREVOR GRANTLEY and TONY SNELLER

AMANDA WILLOUGHBY, THE LOVE-CHILD WHOM SIMON BRENTFORD, MINISTER IN THE DEPARTMENT OF THE ENVIRONMENT, ABANDONED NINETEEN YEARS AGO, AFTER A TORRID LOVE AFFAIR WITH BUSTY ACTRESS, LEONIE O'BRIEN, REVEALED TODAY THAT THE MP'S MISTRESS, SHEILA MACKENZIE, WAS THE ONLY PERSON TO WHOM SHE WAS ABLE TO TURN TO FOR COMFORT AFTER BECOMING RAPED BY LEONIE'S TOY-BOY LOVER, ROB FENTON. AND DISCARDED SHEILA IS EXPECTING THE MP'S LOVE-CHILD, SHE REVEALED IN AN EXCLUSIVE INTERVIEW WITH THE *Globe* TODAY. AMANDA TALKED TEARFULLY OF HER MEETING WITH ATTRACTIVE, CURVACEOUS SHEILA, 29, WHO HAS BEEN SEEN CONSTANTLY BY THE MINISTER'S SIDE IN RECENT MONTHS. THE MP'S PETITE BLONDE WIFE, ELIZABETH WAS NOT AVAILABLE FOR COMMENT LAST NIGHT. TURN TO THE CENTRE PAGES FOR AMANDA'S AND SHEILA'S FULL STORY, ONLY IN THE *Globe*.

Sheila Mackenzie viewed the result of their handiwork with grim satisfaction. All the pain of rejection slipped away, the torment of the past weeks suddenly gone. Was it really that simple? Was revenge so incredibly sweet? It certainly felt so. The hurt and the agony had completely vanished. Well, almost. There was still one thing left to do: she had to get rid of this thing inside her, the embryo that was burning a hole in her womb. She only wished she could rip it out physically herself.

One morning she had woken up, clawing at her stomach, after a dream that she had given birth to a monster. Then she knew that she must act. Later that day she had purchased a douche; remembering stories she had read of the pre-pill days, she had filled it from a basin full of hot water and soapflakes. Then she had inserted the tube inside her vagina, in an attempt to penetrate the uterus. She knew that it would hurt a lot, but even so she was not prepared for the agony that it caused. The whole business was so excruciatingly painful that Sheila, determined as she was, had to abandon it after the third attempt.

What she did not abandon was her need to seek a termination of her pregnancy. On the day following Simon's exposure and disgrace in the *Globe*, she set off alone for an address in Ealing, a district of West London, where a doctor had arranged a place in a nursing home for her. At the appointed time of 9.45 a.m., she arrived by taxi and walked into a waiting-room already packed with girls and women of all shapes, sizes and nationalities. Some were very young indeed; others were in their forties, but looked considerably older, worn out by years of child bearing and subservience to men, able to take no more. Most, she realized, were from Catholic countries and many were Muslims, but all without exception were victims of a society which cared not a jot for their personal misery. At least these women here had found the courage to free themselves from male domination and the tyranny of their bodies. As she looked around, Sheila felt a hatred of the entire male sex that almost consumed her; she felt that her brain was going to burst and pressed her fists to her mouth to stop herself from screaming out loud.

Suddenly her name was called, and she was directed through a door and along a bleak, echoing corridor to the second door on the left. She found herself in a small room that contained only a stretcher on wheels, a sink, and a trolley furnished with metal canisters and various surgical instruments. Here she undressed and donned a freshly starched hospital-theatre gown. A nurse put all her things into a large polythene sack, writing Sheila's name on a piece of sticky tape which she attached to the bag. Sheila lay down on the stretcher, and her arm was swabbed with cotton wool saturated with some alcoholic substance. Then she was given an injection. In a very short space of time she felt woozy and was only dimly aware of being wheeled through into another, brightly lit, room. She was conscious of figures hovering above her; her legs, which seemed to have gone numb, were hoisted up into stirrups set far apart. She felt a sucking sensation in her womb, and then a voice saying, 'All over, off you go.' She remembered nothing more.

Sheila awoke in a dormitory full of narrow beds, still clad in the theatre gown and draped in a blanket. A nurse offered her a cup of tea, which Sheila accepted gratefully. When it arrived, she was told to get dressed and go home as soon as she had drunk it. As she left the nursing home, Sheila smiled at the other women, similarly released from their bondage, and they smiled back in return. She experienced at that moment a sense of fellowship and camaraderie that she was to remember all her life. She also thought of Lorna and of her support in her hour of need, of the patient and long-suffering Elizabeth, of the other women that Simon Brentford had casually used and discarded. As her taxi bore her away, she felt free and happy and at peace with herself. She was empty, clean and whole again, and released. She felt as if she had won a victory for the whole of womankind. Her spirit was triumphant.

Elizabeth sat expressionless, watching her husband from across the room. They had adjourned to the study to discuss the newspapers' revelations about Simon's affair with Sheila Mackenzie. And her pregnancy. To her surprise, Elizabeth felt a sense of relief. At least now she knew. That was something. Unfortunately, so did the rest of the country, of the world for that matter. Well, she thought philosophically, it would save her the trouble of writing to her cousins in New Zealand, or to her friends in Canada to tell them of her impending divorce from Simon. For divorce there would certainly have to be. So long as the pretence had been kept up, she could cope, she, too, could pretend. But now the truth was out, there was no point in pretending any longer.

She regarded him objectively. He looked appalling, haggard and hollow-eyed, and there was very little of his arrogant good looks apparent at that moment. He appeared almost wizened and there was a petty, embittered, downward twist to his mouth which did not suit him. His looks would return, of course, once all this was over. Oh, yes, in six months' time, he would be handsome once again, but older, though. The strain of the last few weeks' events would have taken their toll, would have etched themselves into his face, and there would be a hard expression in his eyes that would remain.

'Don't leave me, Liz, I beg you,' he said quietly, not looking at her as he spoke. The remark hung in the air for a moment.

'Give me one good reason why I should stay?' she said eventually, her voice harsh.

'I'll give you three,' he replied. Could the wretched man never forget he was a politician, even for a moment?

'Go on, then, give me three.'

'The boys. You'd never desert them — '

'I don't intend to desert them,' she interrupted sharply. 'Naturally, I'll take them with me.'

'My lawyer might have something to say about that,' he retorted, 'but we'll let that pass. Your marriage vows: "For better, for worse". I don't believe you would renege on them.'

'Then you have overestimated my tolerance level,' she observed coldly. 'I don't think that the recent events come under the heading of "worse". I think they deserve a category all of their own.'

Simon ignored this. Elizabeth was behaving in a way he'd never seen before. He'd never heard her sound brittle or bitchy. It amused him in other women, but not in Elizabeth. He put it down to the extraordinary pressure she was under and decided to overlook it, to humour her.

'And, thirdly, you're the bravest woman I've ever known. You're at your best in the hour of battle – I've never known you shirk a conflict. We've got the biggest fight of our lives on now and together we can win, Liz, we can come through.'

'You'd do well in the War Cabinet,' she remarked drily. 'But I fear you are confusing our personalities. Yes, I'm good in adversity, but I don't seek it as you do – oh, yes, you do,' she insisted, as he was about to protest, 'You like living on a knife edge, on the eve of battle, but like most commanders, you rely absolutely on an able aide-de-camp, in your case Charles, and a doughty batman – me. Well, I've been in the field too long. As you observed the other day, I don't deserve this. No, I don't. I think I'm worthy of something better and so are the boys.' She turned away to cover the break in her voice, then she cleared her throat to continue. Simon didn't interrupt her. He always allowed an opponent on the opposition benches to have his say, before rising to his feet to demolish the argument with a verbal lucidity that was his chief talent.

'I admit I volunteered, that I wasn't conscripted,' she said, continuing the motif. Simon smiled, in spite of himself. She was employing one of his favourite tactics, that of picking up on the opponent's analogy, but reducing it to a simplistic level, making it seem absurd. 'But I was young then, and able-bodied. I've fought too many campaigns – oh, you don't even being to know about them' Her voice was starting to rise as she saw the lack of comprehension in his eyes. He had no idea. 'Well, I'm tired of fighting, I think I've earned my discharge.'

Simon started to laugh, a soft derisory laugh. He clapped his hands in mock applause. 'Bravo, Liz. You've been wasted all these years, you'd have done well in politics. Let's see, which department would have suited you best — '

Elizabeth suddenly turned and went for him. All the years of waiting and wondering, of silently coping, of putting up with his cruelty, his neglect and his biting sarcasms, unleashed themselves as she flung herself on him. His chair toppled over backwards as he recoiled from the ferocity of her assault and they fell to the floor together. She started to hit him on the head, on the chest, on the face and shoulders, biting and clawing at him like an animal. Quite unprepared for her onslaught, he twisted wildly to free himself from her so that he could defend himself. He tried to grab her arms, but she continued to scratch and kick him, fighting with a vicious single-mindedness that was totally unnerving to Simon. Eventually his weight and strength began to tell, but he was only able to pin her down on the floor by lying firmly on top of her.

She glared up at him. 'Well, now you're in a position you're accustomed to, what are you going to do about it – make me pregnant as well?' she hissed.

'I wouldn't mind, you look bloody fanciable at the moment,' he said, and meant it.

She spat in his face. 'You unspeakable bastard! You'll never touch me again! I'm leaving you. Do you understand, I'm leaving you!'

There was a long silence. Finally he said coldly, 'That's desertion.'

It was Elizabeth's turn to laugh. 'So what are you going to do about it. Have me court-martialled?' He released her and got heavily to his feet. As he stood looking down at her, she made no attempt to get up, but continued to laugh quietly to herself.

'I'm going to fight on . . . alone,' he said finally.

Elizabeth gave another snort of contemptuous laughter as she started to get up off the floor. 'Alone? You? Not for long, my dear. I'm sure you'll find another Leonie O'Brien look-alike – oh, don't think I haven't noticed – another clone to share your bed, and prop you up. You're going to need propping up, you know. What do you imagine is going to happen to your wonderful career now?'

They were both on their feet now, facing each other. 'I shall survive,' he said between gritted teeth. 'I'll show them that I can survive, in spite of all you – bloody – women.' He spat out the words.

'Yes, I do believe that's how you really think of us,' she said pensively. 'That frightful mother of yours has a lot to answer for. Yes, she is frightful and you know it!' she added as she saw his look of incredulity, 'I've loathed her for years.' For once Simon was lost for words. He was genuinely hurt by this last betrayal. Elizabeth took advantage of the moment. 'So, shall we assume that hostilities are at an end? Shall we call a truce and work out a peace formula?' she asked sarcastically. Simon bowed his head in defeat; he knew it was pointless to argue any further.

'Very well,' he agreed. 'What do you suggest?'

'I propose that the boys and I move out to live with my sister. So far as the world is concerned, we shall be on holiday. If anyone asks, you can tell them that I need to escape the unwanted attentions of the press, and recover from the trauma of recent events. I will, however, be standing by you.' He raised his head in amazement. 'Oh, yes,' she said bitterly, 'I intend that my character shall remain unblemished. It will appear that I am the loyal and devoted wife doing her unpleasant but necessary duty. Then, in six months' time, I shall divorce you. If the divorce goes through quickly enough, and I'm sure you'll be too much of a gentleman to contest it, you might just have enough time to do the decent thing and make an honest woman of Sheila whatever-her-name-is before she makes you a proud father for the fourth time. And then you can all live happily ever after. But not in this house. You will sell the place, and we shall divide the proceeds equally. I shall be quite fair. I don't require any other alimony or settlement, as I have money of my own after all. My father will be only too happy to pay the boys' school fees and doubtless see them through university as well. You may see Kit and Jamie from time to time, if you wish. Whether they will want to see you, however, is debatable. Doubtless our respective solicitors will work out something to our own satisfaction and their mutual financial advantage. And now, if you'll excuse me, I'm going to pack.'

With these words, she turned on her heel and left the room, without so much as a backward glance at her stunned husband. That afternoon, after she had finished her packing, she sat down and wrote a note to Charles Pendlebury. Then at 4.30 p.m., she drove away from the house, her Volvo estate laden with suitcases. She stopped briefly in the village by the post-box. The letter would catch the five o'clock post. The message inside was brief. It said, 'Wait for me. Elizabeth.'

Mist swirled through the alpine valley, hiding the green flower-filled meadows, the chalets with their carved wooded shutters, the patient-eyed cows grazing by the roadside. With nothing to look at outside, Beryl stole a glance at the person beside her. Giovanni – he was here in the coach with her, driving through Austria, surrounded by middle-aged music lovers from Ashebourn. It hardly seemed credible.

She gazed happily at his handsome profile, at the thick dark lashes veiling those merry brown eyes. He was wearing a new and expensive leather jacket which she had bought him before they left Rome, smart cord trousers and a soft cashmere sweater in palest yellow. Their shopping expedition to kit him out for the rest of the tour had cost more than she had expected, but she did not grudge him a penny. She thought he looked beautiful.

As if sensing himself observed, Giovanni turned to look at her. He grinned at the expression on her face. 'Carina,' he said softly, putting a brown hand over hers, 'you are happy, yes?'

'Of course,' said Beryl, smiling at him. 'What about you?'

'Oh yes,' said Giovanni happily. 'Very nice people, very nice hotels, very nice music and a beautiful lady beside me. How can I not be happy?'

'Good,' said Beryl. 'I want you to enjoy yourself.'

So far things had been perfect, she thought. Their stay in Vienna had been a dream, Giovanni as loving and attentive a companion as she could have possibly hoped for. She had wondered what the other members of the tour would make of her explanation that Giovanni was a music student and a friend of her daughter's who had taken the opportunity of joining them for the Austrian section of the trip because Mozart was one of his major interests. However his inclusion in the party had passed with little comment, indeed people had taken to him surprisingly well – especially one or two of the single women, whom she had seen eyeing him with covetous appreciation. Tactfully, Giovanni had treated her more like a fond nephew than a lover when they were in public together, but at night – Beryl shivered with pleasure as she remembered – at night he had taught her more about the enjoyment of sex in a week than she had learned from Arnold in twenty years of marriage.

Yes, he was rather extravagant, and very young in some ways, but that was half the fun of being with him. He made her feel young too, and frivolous. Now they were on their way to Salzburg together, where they would leave the tour and go back to Italy. Giovanni wanted to say goodbye to his family in Naples, then they would return to England together to put her affairs in order before setting out on their travels. It was sweet of him to want her to meet his family. Somehow it gave her confidence that his affection for her was not entirely mercenary. She only hoped it would remain that way.

Meanwhile – she shook her head to banish any momentary doubts about what she had done – meanwhile, she was happier than she had ever been in her life. Whatever happened next, she had already experienced the sort of pleasures that she had always thought reserved for younger, prettier, more interesting women than her staid suburban self.

Giovanni noticed her sudden movement and squeezed her hand, an anxious expression on his face. 'Carina, is something wrong. You are worried?'

'No,' said Beryl, 'I'm not worried at all. I think everything is absolutely fine, Giovanni dear.'

'I think I loathe you more than you would believe possible. Dear God, I'm living with a prize bastard.' Leonie picked up a photograph in a heavy silver frame and hurled it across the room at him. It was a picture of the two of them, in happier times. Rob ducked and it crashed to the floor beside him, the glass splintering into shining shards on the marble floor. 'You low-down, fucking, lazy prick.' she screamed. 'What the hell did I ever see in you? You're nothing but a piece of shit!' She picked up a heavy alabaster ashtray from the coffee table and flung it at his head. It missed him by inches, smashing to the ground just beside him.

'For God's sake, Leo!' Rob's face was white. 'You could have bloody killed me!'

'What d'you think I wanted to do?' she hissed. 'You deserve to die.'

He backed away, watching her apprehensively as she cast around for another weapon. The copy of the *Globe* with Amanda's story in it was open on the floor beside her. The room was littered with debris from the party that had gone on in the apartment when everyone moved on from La Mosca. Rob cursed his stupidity for bringing the paper back from his meeting with Judd and Marvin. She would have had to know sooner of later, of course, but he had hoped to break it to her tactfully, preferably in bed, to show her the story when he had had a chance to soften her up. But some drunken moron had snatched the *Globe* from him as he came into the apartment, saying, 'Oh, look, Leonie, you're on the front cover again. What is it this time?' Then the shit had hit the fan.

There were broken glasses everywhere. Most of them had been aimed at him by Leonie. Now she had a champagne bottle in her hand and was advancing on him with a menacing expression. He held out his hands to ward her off. 'Leo, please, I can explain.'

'What's the matter?' she sneered. 'Can't you take it? I thought you liked a bit of rough and tumble, particularly tumble.' She spat out the words sarcastically and surveyed him for a moment. 'Do you know, I really used to think you were good looking!' she said, a look of disgust on her face. 'but you're not, in fact I find you bloody repulsive. I don't think I ever want to see you again, starting right this minute.' To his

relief she dropped the bottle and stormed off towards the hall. He
followed her, at a safe distance.

She opened a cupboard and pulled out a suitcase. Then she slung it
down the corridor towards him. 'I want you out of here, now. I mean it.
Out. Go on, get going, you little turd. I can't bear to look at you any
more.' She pulled out another suitcase and threw it on top of the first.
Then she strode off in the direction of the bedroom. As she passed he
flinched, instinctively. 'Oh, don't worry,' she sneered. 'I'm not going to
hit you. I don't want to touch you ever again. I wouldn't demean myself.
You're not worth it. You're filthy, disgusting – go on, get out!' The
bedroom door slammed behind her with an almighty crash.

Rob went into the drawing-room and poured a large Scotch into
one of the few unbroken glasses, breathing a huge sigh of relief as he did
so. Then he lowered himself thankfully into an armchair and waited.
There was no point in trying to speak to her now. He heard thuds,
bangs and smashing sounds from the bedroom. The noises gradually
subsided. He finished his drink and poured himself another. It was half
an hour later before he made a move.

'Leo, will you speak to me now?' Rob stood in the doorway of the
bedroom, watching Leonie. She was half-sitting, half-lying on the bed,
propped up with pillows, staring blankly at the far window. She did not
react to his words. 'Please, Leo, I want to speak to you,' he repeated.

'There's nothing to say,' said Leonie in an empty voice.

Rob sagged against the door-frame. He knew this would be a tough
one. 'We can't give up now – not after everything we've shared. Please,
don't let them win. I love you so much.'

Leonie turned sad eyes to him. 'Yes,' she said finally, 'I really
thought you did. I was wrong.'

'No,' said Rob, 'I do love you – more than anything in the world.'

Leonie surveyed him coldly. 'But not enough to resist a quick fuck
while I'm away for a couple of days. What sort of love is that? I thought
our love was based on mutual trust.' She glared at him. Rob said
nothing. 'Why do we live together?' she asked aggressively. 'I mean
why bother? Why not live separately and each have a wonderful time
fucking anyone and everyone any time we choose, and possibly each

other when we feel like it? What's the bloody point?' she asked savagely, punching the pillow to emphasize her words.

'You're right,' said Rob in a quiet, resigned voice. 'There's no
point. Either we've made a commitment to each other or we haven't. I
thought I'd made one to you and I broke it – I failed you. No – worse
than that – I failed myself,' he added. He looked up at her. 'It's no good,
is it?' he asked. 'You don't want to know, do you?'

Leonie was silent for a moment, then she said slowly, 'I shall never
be able to trust you. I won't dare go away again. What sort of life is
that?' She looked at him sorrowfully. 'You were my mate, my partner,
somebody I could rely on absolutely . . . and now, it's all gone.' She
looked away again, her expression desolate.

Rob moved closer. 'Please don't say that. It's not all gone – it's not!
Darling, please believe me, I was drunk – I didn't know what I was
doing.'

'You lied to me.' She shook her head mournfully.

'Because I didn't want to lose you. Don't you understand? I never
meant this to happen, it didn't mean anything; it was you I wanted, Leo,
not her. Can't you forgive me, please?'

'I can't forgive you. I can never forgive you. With my own
daughter. Why it's practically incest.' Her voice shook with disgust.

'But I had no idea who she was,' said Rob desperately. 'How could
I have known? She certainly wasn't going to tell me. She wanted to hurt
you – through me – and that's just what she's succeeded in doing, hasn't
she?'

'Of course she has,' said Leonie in a hard voice. 'But you, you
betrayed me. You went to bed with someone else. What's the matter,
aren't I enough for you any more? And why did it have to be her? What
was so special about her?'

'Oh, Leo, she's your own daughter, of course she's attractive.
Don't you remember how men reacted to you when you were — ' He
stopped suddenly. He could have bitten his tongue off, 'I'm sorry, I
didn't mean — '

'Young,' said Leonie bitterly, finishing the sentence for him. 'Yes,
you did! That's precisely what you meant. She's young. Not an old bag

like me, right? Well, for your information, you are not the only man around who seems to find me attractive. I have no shortage of admirers, young and old! And, unlike you, I find the older ones extremely attractive!'

'Like who?' said Rob suspiciously. He did not like the sound of this at all.

'Never mind, it doesn't matter.'

'Of course it does. Come on, don't tell me you've been screwing someone else. I can't believe it.'

Leonie smiled for the first time for several hours. 'I see. It's all right for you to be unfaithful to me, but not the other way around, is that it? Well tough.'

'What do you mean? Leo, what are you trying to tell me?' She did not reply, but looked away, an enigmatic expression on her face 'Leo! You *haven't* been unfaithful, have you?'

There was no answer. She smiled again – a pleased, reminiscent smile.

Rob could not believe that she meant what she seemed to be implying. When he had suggested that she might have been unfaithful to him, he had meant it as a quick, below-the-belt jibe. He had wanted to get her off balance, to take her mind off Amanda. It had never occurred to him as a realistic possibility. After all, why should she want anyone else? He was young, handsome, talented, everything a woman could desire. He was practically doing her a favour, for Christ's sake! A woman's magazine had referred to him as a possible successor to Mel Gibson, the world's number-one sex symbol! What more could she possibly want? She was forty-three. He was twenty-five. She should be so lucky! And now it looked as if she had actually fucked somebody else. He simply could not credit it.

'Who was it?' he said in a low voice.

'Rob, it's really none of your business.'

'Who was it?' he persisted, his pride outraged.

'It's unimportant. I don't know him. I'd never seen him before – or since.'

'You mean, he was just a casual fuck, is that it? That's terrific, I must say.'

Leonie rounded on him, eyes flashing. 'Well, what do you call that bloody girl, then? If that wasn't a casual fuck, what was it? A major affair? The great love of your life? Well, you can't have it both ways. You went to bed with Amanda. You lied to me. You told me you lied to me because it was unimportant, but — '

'It was totally unimportant,' Rob cut in.

'Not to me, it wasn't. You betrayed me . . . with my own daughter. If I turned to someone else for a bit of comfort, can you blame me?'

'But you didn't know, then,' said Rob in an exasperated voice.

'I suspected,' said Leonie. 'I suspected all along.'

Rob knew he was on a hiding to nothing. There was only one way to try and salvage the situation now. 'Leo, darling,' he said coaxingly. 'All right, I admit, I deserved it. I couldn't blame you if you did go off with another man. I've behaved like an absolute shit, I admit it. But I was drunk, we'd had a row, I thought it was you — '

'I was away, if you remember,' she corrected him coldly.

'Exactly. I was miserable and lonely, because you were away and because of Carlo's accident and what you said to me. I felt I'd let you down, so I got blind drunk and somehow it got into my head that she was you, you when you were . . .'

'Young,' she finished the sentence for him.

'Younger,' he amended.

There was a pause as they both eyed each other. Rob detected a slight softening in Leonie's manner. He pressed his advantage, saying quietly, 'Who was this man? Where did you meet him? How did it happen?'

'You don't want to hear it.'

He looked at her with a strange expression on his face. 'Yes, I do. I must know. Come on, it's important to me. I might have lost you. I want to know what happened.'

Leonie hesitated. Rob had caused her so much pain, and now she had the chance to hurt him in return, but she was not sure that she wanted to do it. She looked at him, his face tense and drawn. Yes, he should know. He deserved to think that he could have lost her . . . he still might, though she could feel the fury and the disgust draining away, leaving her tired and passionless. She started speaking in a low voice. 'I really don't know how it happened. It was the last thing in the world I was expecting, or wanting. I was really enjoying filming, I mean, really enjoying the work. I felt completely alive again – I had missed it, you know.' She glanced up at him briefly, then continued, 'And then came the ghastly day at the studio when I overheard Derek and Dave talking about the party and I couldn't believe it.' She shook her head thoughtfully. 'But then I remembered what Amanda had suggested to me. At the time, I dismissed it as a final thrust – just another way of hurting me – and I didn't believe her for a second. But after our row, when you'd managed to make me believe my fears were ridiculous – by lying to me,' here she glanced at him again, ' – then to overhear those two talking, well, I couldn't get it out of my mind. It festered away in there, it began to eat away at my love for you, to erode what we'd built together. Then one day on the set – you weren't there that day – I was doing the bedroom scene . . .' Her voice began to falter as she remembered the hot tide of lust that had flooded through her at the sight of those wrists.

'Oh, so you mean you didn't have any knickers on?' said Rob sarcastically.

'Of course I had knickers on. I was wearing a nightdress – sort of.'

'How very appropriate.'

'Well, I was in bed.'

'Convenient, wouldn't you say?'

She went on, ignoring him, 'And I suddenly became aware of this man looking at me. I'd never seen him before, I'd no idea who he was. Then he came to my caravan at lunchtime, and . . .'

'And?' Rob spoke at last, his voice a mere thread of sound.

'Well, it just happened,' Leonie finished lamely. She had no desire to go into details. It didn't seem fair.

She looked at Rob; he was staring at her in amazement. 'You mean,' he said slowly, 'it was as simple as that?'

'I suppose so,' said Leonie dreamily, remembering again.

'No preamble. No chat-up line?'

'No.'

'Just pure animal lust?'

'I suppose so.' Leonie smiled slightly. 'No, it wasn't only that, it was his wrists.'

'His *wrists*?' Rob's voice was incredulous.

'Yes, they were so strong and caring and reassuring, and I was feeling so insecure, so unhappy.'

'You're breaking my heart,' he said.

'Rob, don't be a fool. I felt better afterwards, can't you understand? I wasn't sure that you'd been unfaithful, but it seemed likely – and I needed something to make me feel better.'

'Fine,' said Rob, 'so you felt better. Where's that supposed to leave me?'

'I don't know,' said Leonie bleakly, 'I really don't know.'

Rob's face suddenly crumpled; tears began to trickle down his cheeks and he started to sob like a hurt small boy. Leonie could not help herself. She took him in her arms and held him close, letting him nuzzle at her breasts as though for comfort.

'Don't, Rob, don't,' she said, stroking his hair as though he were a child that needed comforting. 'I can't bear this.'

Rob's sobs died away. He raised his head and looked at her. 'Leo, do you remember we always said we'd prove to everyone – no matter what happened – that nothing would part us. We'd prove them all wrong, all the killjoys, the dreambreakers, do you remember?'

'Yes, I remember.'

'Don't let them win. Don't you see, if our relationship can survive this, then we really do have something special.'

'Rob, darling, I'm not going to get any younger and you're going to stay young for ages yet. There will be other drunken nights and other temptations, probably quite a few. I can't go through this hell every time,' said Leonie sadly.

Rob took both her hands in his. 'Leo, you always said that love meant you cared more for the person you love than for yourself. You did say that, didn't you?'

'Yes,' she said ruefully. His memory was too good. An actor's memory.

'That the happiness of the person you loved meant more to you than your own?'

'Yes,' she agreed.

'Well, if we stay together, you will make me the happiest person in the world. And I believe I can make you happy.'

'I know you mean it, Rob,' she said sadly, 'the trouble is, I'm not sure if I love you any more.'

He was still gazing at her in disbelief when the telephone rang. Leonie sat down and picked up the receiver from its stand on the bedside table.

'Yes? Nigel! How are you? Yes, I know, it's ghastly isn't it?' Her voice was perfectly steady. 'Who? Oh tell them to get lost! Absolutely. No, I have no desire to speak to any bloody newspaper. I see, well,' she sounded doubtful, 'if you think it best.' She cupped the mouthpiece with her hand and said, 'He wants me to make a statement to the press. He'll fax it to all the newspaper groups. What do you think?' Rob nodded resignedly. She returned to Nigel on the telephone. 'Yes, Rob agrees with me. Well, what do you think? Yes . . . yes . . . OK . . . something along the lines of, "Miss O'Brien denies absolutely that there is any rift between herself and Mr Fenton. In fact they have never been happier and are looking forward to their next joint venture." ' She looked at Rob. 'What . . . yes . . . you too. Oh, and Rob sends his love.'

She put down the receiver. 'Well?'

'If only it were true,' he said wistfully. There was silence for a while as they both sat quietly trying to come to terms with what had happened to them.

'What do you want to do?' he asked finally.

'I don't know,' she said. 'I just don't know.'

'Leo, we'd be fools not to take the opportunity to make another movie together.' His eyes were pleading. The opportunity of a lifetime was slipping away – and, after all, there was no other woman like her.

She gave him a direct look. 'Rob, there is no way we could work together unless we were 100 per cent committed to each other.'

'I know. Come on, Leo, let's give it another go. We can still do so much for each other.'

An odd choice of words, thought Leonie briefly, but perhaps he was right. And she was so very tired. Too tired to start all over again.

He was speaking again, his voice sincere. 'Look, Leo, darling, let's face it out now, together. I believe we can come through; I think we can learn to trust each other again. I want to try. I want it to work. If you don't want that, why did you make that statement?'

The truth. She had to admit the truth. 'Because I want it to work too.'

His smile of relief was dazzling. 'Shall we try, then?'

'Yes,' said Leonie, 'let's try.'

Amanda sat back and luxuriated in the comfort of the British Airways Boeing 747's first-class cabin. The comfortable, well-spaced seats, the glass of champagne in her hand, the delicious canapés served on Wedgwood china, the free drinks, the innumerable little extras, the attentive cabin staff – all these were in marked contrast to the cramped discomfort of the charter flight on which she had first travelled out to Rome only a few weeks ago.

She smiled to herself as she thought over all that had happened since then, and of how she had achieved everything she had set out to do. She had revenged herself on her parents for rejecting her, that was for certain: she doubted very much if Leonie and Rob would ever be able fully to repair their relationship after her revelations, and Simon's marriage was finished, she felt sure of that. So was his career. She felt sorry for Elizabeth – she had liked her at their brief meeting – but she was convinced that she would be better off without Simon. Then there was the mistress: she had been an unexpected bonus. Yes, Sheila Mackenzie had been a gift from the gods. Not even Amanda would have been able to anticipate that particular twist to her plot. She could hardly believe her luck.

Yes, luck was with her for sure, and – she glanced down at the little diamond frog with emerald eyes that glistened on her lapel – now she was going to trust to it one more time. Mamie King had promised her undying gratitude if she returned the Duchess of Windsor's brooch. Soon she would find out how much that gratitude was really worth. But she had another string to her bow as well. She smiled again as she remembered how Julius T. King's piggy little eyes had lit up when Harmony had introduced her to him so reluctantly at the van der Velt's villa. Yes, with both the Kings on her side, a screen test would be the very least she could expect.

There was just one slight niggle at the back of her mind: her name. She had no desire to be Amanda Willoughby any more, and she certainly could not be Amanda O'Brien, while Amanda Brentford was equally out of the question. No, she must have an entirely new name with which to start her new life. Perhaps even Amanda should go. She had never liked it very much and she hated having it shortened to Mandy. Not Amanda, then, but something with a ring to it. Amanda . . . Alexandra . . . Miranda. Miranda . . . that was a good name, it had the right sound and it was not too unlike her own. It came from that Shakespeare play they had done at school. What was it? *The Tempest*, that was the one. She could even remember some of it. 'O brave new world,' Miranda had said. How appropriate to her own circumstances. Miranda Tempest – how about that for a name? She liked it. Yes, she liked it very much indeed.

So, on the whole, things had gone very well for her. And with all the money she had accumulated from Simon and those pigs on the *Globe* she certainly had enough money to hit LA in style. Amanda sipped her champagne and gazed out of the cabin window at the rays of the dazzling sun, gleaming on the clouds below. She was going to make it. She was young, beautiful, well-heeled and already notorious. Miranda Tempest was on her way to conquer Hollywood.